MIDDLEARTH
TRADEMARKED

BEN CASH

ULLEN & ANWIN LLC

To those who helped me believe I could finish this quest,
this book is for you.

To Wes Cash, for coming up with the idea for what would eventually become the front cover of my book. To Julie Cash, for constantly encouraging me and wanting to read this book in every possible version. To Robert Hill & Jessie Harris, for encouraging me to undertake the quest to begin the writing of this book. To Daniel Jellicorse, for believing my dream of finishing this book was possible. To Niki Harris, for encouraging me along the way and believing in me. To Ryan Medlin, for providing constant inspiration for humor and characters. To Isaac Buck, for listening to me and tolerating me pining about this book at your house while I drank from your supply. To Jessie Jellicorse, for believing in me, encouraging me, and helping guide me in my quest to find a cover designer. To Parker Colbath, for enjoying reading an early version of my book perhaps more than anyone else will. To all of the Knights, including those not previously named, for being with me through thick and thin. And to my lovely bride, Lindsey Cash, for constantly loving, constantly believing, and constantly inspiring me to be me.

Thank you.

CONTENTS

A WORK OF SATIRE

Middlearth Trademarked is an epic satire fantasy parody coming of age romance novel. The events described below are not verified to be accurate or true, and are likely in no way related to this book.

In 1976, an enterprising man named Saul Zaentz bought the movie rights to two very important and famous books from J.R.R. Tolkien. With those rights, he started a company called Middle Earth Enterprises, and now that company owns the trademark rights for every character, place and thing in LOTR (this is not verified to be true). I discovered all of this one day when I read an article about a restaurant being forced to change its name after receiving a 'cease and desist' letter from a corporation named Middle Earth Enterprises (I believe the name of the restaurant was the 'Hungry Hobbit' or something to that effect).

The reader can find out more about all of this if they wish, by simple research. I will say nothing further about it here.

When in college at Baylor University, I took a course called 'Oxford Christians', because I saw that my favorite book (LOTR) was one of the required readings in the syllabus. Each week before class, the professor gave a quiz made up entirely of questions you'd get wrong if you'd only seen the movies. His teaching assistant had to come up with the quiz questions, because the professor refused to watch any of them. This was an intentional decision because the professor didn't want to sully the visions and pictures of the story from his own imagination. His dedication to the story in its purest form was and is a continual source of inspiration to me.

Now, my dear reader, I feel that you know all of the irrelevant details you need before reading my book. I do hope you enjoy your time in Middlearth.

CRITICSM

"They eviscerated the book by making it an action movie for young people aged 15 to 25... And it seems that 'The Hobbit' will be the same kind of film..."

— CHRISTOPHER TOLKIEN

"Tolkien has become a monster, devoured by his own popularity and absorbed into the absurdity of our time..."

— CHRISTOPHER TOLKIEN

"The chasm between the beauty and seriousness of the work, and what it has become, has overwhelmed me. The commercialization has reduced the aesthetic and philosophical impact of the creation to nothing. There is only one solution for me: to turn my head away."

— CHRISTOPHER TOLKIEN

Middlearth Trademarked

CHAPTER 1

THE UNEXPECTED PARTY

YOUNG FROBO DAGGINS, GRANDSON OF THE MOST FAMOUS OF all hobbicks, reclined with his friends in his cozy hobbick hole in the very heart of the Chire. It had been *eleventy-one* years since his dear old grandad had carried that *Insidious Ring* to Morbor and destroyed it with the help of the most unlikely person imaginable, Grollum. Frobo was accompanied that evening by his gardener Sham, who had taken up the same occupation as his grandfather (gardener of the most famous hobbick who ever lived). He was also accompanied by Happy Brandybeer (descendant of their companion Old Mister Brandy*deer*) and last of all (and probably least of all), he was accompanied by Martin Shaken-Notstird, hobbick of the Chire (no relation to any well-known persons).

Frobo had recently come of age at his thirty-third birthday not one month ago. He was a smart young hobbick, with ruddy flush cheeks that were either plump, or thin and drawn depending on the season and if the Chire's brew of *Gold Hobbick Ale* was particularly good that year. His hair was long, dark, and brown, with as many curly locks as straight ones, and his green eyes always saw more than they let on (or at least they would have said so if they had the ability to speak). In all ways, he aspired to maintain himself as the visage of his alleged grandfather, the most famous hobbick who ever lived, or at least the film's portrayal of him, as Frobo had never actually seen his grandfather in real life. Thus, he always dressed himself in the various draperies, vests, frocks, and trousers that any good hobbick might see being sported in the films. And it needn't be stated here that those clothes were woven and stitched in a complete array of vibrant colors that would be sure to pop on a film's reel, if a filmmaker ever requested his appearance in one.

Frobo was reading the evening edition of the Chire's newfound newspaper, *The Morning Muffin*. He scanned the front page for stories of interest. The top was embossed with the pressing story of the day in the Chire: *Miss Margo's Committee for Festivious Events Plans TROLL Sized Party for ELEVENTY-FIRST FILM CELEBRATION.*

Frobo read on. *The day that the Chire has been waiting for has finally (almost) arrived, writes corresponding correspondent Pepper Porklegs. I, Pepper was able to catch up with Miss Margo Proudfoot from the Committee to Plan Festivious Events, to discuss the very exciting evening she has planned for all of us! "Of course, we're thrilled about the festivious event we have planned," Miss Margo commented. "It's an evening we've been anticipating for quite some time, Pepper." When asked by this correspondent what Miss Margo had planned for the evening the infamously allusive hobbick had only this to say, "Eleventy-one years is a long time. I can only hope my little party still explodes into your memories and imaginations the way the film portrayal of the most famous event in the history of the Chire does." Miss Margo refused to elaborate further on her plans for what is sure to be a magnificent evening. But she did remind me that hobbicks planning to attend the festivities should be sure to arrive early and on time, with their invitations in hand. One might deduce the climax of the party by recalling Miss Margo's previous parties..."*

The story continued but Frobo was well versed in the

history of Miss Margo's parties and needed no reminder of them. While the films were of particular interest to him, he had always felt as if they'd been slightly off in their retelling of his grandfather's old book. He was sure he'd read it at least once all the way through, even if that reading had taken place over twenty years ago, before the first film had ever been made.

He flipped through the paper, searching for another story, *ROGUE SWEETS CART SMASHES INTO BALFO BRICK-HEAD'S GARDEN... LADY ELLAMIR MISSING FROM GRONDOR... FISHERHOBBICKS GROUP TO PROTEST BRANDYBEER RIVER MAGICK TRANSFORMATION... BELOVED TRAVELLING ACTING TROUPE: 'THE RUGGED DWARFS' EXTEND TOUR TO BREETOWN.* Frobo tossed the paper away as he was accustomed to after reading the major headlines of the day. It was the same sort of news that was always provided by *The Morning Muffin*, the newspaper whose procrastinating staff had never risen early enough to produce an edition before afternoon tea.

"*Elventy*-one years..." said Happy. "Elventy-one years since that *Insidious Ring* was destroyed."

"*Elfenty*-one," corrected Sham, taking a sip of his fifth beer that evening.

"You're both daft, it's *eleventy-one*." said Martin. "It's no wonder you're still Frobo's gardener, Sham, as dense as you are. After all these years your family couldn't manage to climb the ladder of society one rung."

Sham erupted in laughter with the rest of them. "Oh, right you are, Mister Shaken-Notstird, right you are, sir!" shouted Sham. "As my dear old gaffer used to say..."

"If I have to hear one more sentence of your dear old gaffer's great gardening wisdom I'm going to sleep," said Martin.

Happy and Frobo burst into laughter.

Sham looked like his pipeweed had just been stolen. His

golden straw-colored wispy hair tousled back and forth as he sat up in his chair in alarm. His already wide eyes beamed like glowing lanterns in shock at the notion that someone had grown tired of anything his *dear old gaffer* used to say; but his two most pressing attributes, his constantly apologetic disposition, and broad opened mouthed smile, quickly extinguished any fire of offense that might have been perceived by Frobo and the others. One couldn't look at Sham without noticing his bulging blue eyes and bright red nose. Hobbicks often complained that those two stark features groped for their attention when speaking with Sham. In almost the same manner his friends competed for landing the best verbal jab at his expense. And although Frobo tried his hardest to abstain from joining in with this, he rarely achieved in doing so.

"Oh, forgive him, Sham," laughed Frobo. "It's just the beer talking. The Filmmaker knows all Hobbicks have had enough of it."

"The Filmmaker, Middlearth Enterprises, guffaw..." spat Sham. "The whole lot of em' can kiss my potatoes."

Frobo, Martin, and Happy pondered the double meaning of Sham's crude remark as the stout, rosy cheeked Hobbick continued.

"Sometimes I wonder if I can take it anymore, Mr. Frobo," he said.

"Take what, Sham?" sighed Frobo, feigning polite ignorance. They'd had this conversation hundreds of times, and Frobo knew exactly what was coming next.

"You know, Mr. Frobo, the trademark laws!"

"Here he goes again," drawled Martin as he drained his glass. Martin was, without a doubt, the surliest hobbick Frobo had ever met. He was Frobo's elder by seven years, but sometimes Frobo thought he was younger even than Sham. He was never seen wearing anything save his dull gray trousers, white shirt, and brown vest, and he wore them so often Frobo was starting to assume he might possess an entire closet full of them. His hair was lighter than Frobo's. It curled up in little brown wisps, flecked with grey like tiny spinning clouds. Already, the grey was starting to reveal the effects that age and incessant smoking can have on a hobbick.

But Martin's greying curls were in fact the only feature that would betray the proximity of his expiration to the casual observer. His body was drawn and thin, fit and tight like one of the planks at the Brandybeer River bridge. His demeanor, attitude, and speech were often decried by the elderly citizens of the Chire as *"uncouth, unfavorable, and sometimes even unproper."* Of course, the use of the word *"unproper"* in that context, was entirely improper, but the use of the correct word would have felt to the citizens of the Chire a little too *uneffective.* Martin was infamous for the impolite manner in which he expressed his wit.

Nonetheless, the knowledge of Martin and his unpolite wit hadn't deterred Sham from opening his mouth, and his sarcastic yet gentle commentary of "Here he goes again..." wasn't going to stop Sham from making his point.

"Doesn't it ever bother you?" asked Sham. "It's like the filmmaker knew something when he left the Scouring of the Chire out of the films."

"The scouring of the what?" asked Happy. Happy was perhaps, the kindest of the four of them, though Sham would've taken offense to the notion, had it ever been expressed. His hair was as bright red as one of the carrots of Sham's garden, like the dying fire of Frobo's black stove, when he opened it to check and see if he needed to add more wood to it. His eyes were dark, dark brown. If he was not the kindest, Happy was most certainly the most unassuming of the four hobbicks. He kept his thoughts and opinions to himself for the most part. One rarely saw more of his mouth than the curve of his smiling lips, which for the majority of the time, remained closed. Indeed, sometimes it seemed to Frobo that he hardly spoke or made a sound, save for a good laugh and a hearty song, or in this case, a curious question. His friendship and fierce loyalty to Martin had always puzzled the inhabitants of the Chire, as the two friends were complete opposites in every way. But Happy seemed to be the one person whom Martin's cheek and surly disposition spared.

"Grandalf™ the Grey!" shouted Sham in response. "Have you even read *The Story of the Most Famous Hobbick Who Ever Lived*, Happy? It's the last chapter! The best part of the whole book where the hobbicks rise up against Sauluman™ and the evil men who've taken over the Chire."

"Was that the part where he comes home and his hole is up for sale?" asked Happy.

"No, that's the end of The Hobbick, erm... The Hobbick™," said Martin.

"Son of Ashelob!" shouted Sham. He slammed himself against the back of his chair so hard that Frobo worried it might shatter. It wouldn't have been the first time Sham's weight had broken one of his chairs. "You're all hopeless! The lot of you," he resigned.

"But what do you expect us to do?" asked Frobo. "Hobbicks made a deal with the filmmaker and Middlearth Enterprises fair and square. They got the rights to make the films, as well as the trademark rights to all of our names and likenesses for financial profit. And we got a lifetime supply of beer (through the *Magick Transforming* of the Brandybeer River), as well as the theatre with the projector in the party tree, with the complete extended edition films playing every night, on rotation. We made a deal Sham."

"I know that, Mr. Frobo, I do," said Sham, whose glowing cheeks were now a fiery bright red blush. "It's just that, and pardon me for saying so, sir, sometimes I wonder if we didn't get the wool pulled over our eyes in that deal."

"And what exactly are you suggesting?" said Frobo.

"Nothing, Mr. Frobo, nothing!" said Sham anxiously. Happy and Martin's relaxed waists suddenly tensed. They sat up in their chairs and collectively held their breath. This sort of thing simply wasn't suggested, especially not in the company of one Frobo Daggins.

"Because Sham, if you're suggesting what I think you're suggesting, that my father Froyo made us a bad deal, then I suggest you stop suggesting that!" shouted Frobo.

"I didn't mean it, Mr. Frobo, really I didn't! Please, please forgive me!" cried Sham. With the quickness of a cat that had been crouching on his haunches, Sham threw himself out of Frobo's chair and began to grovel on the floor before him.

Frobo's father, Froyo, son of the most famous hobbick who ever lived, had been a very odd hobbick indeed. And the legitimacy of his claim as *the heir* had always been suspect amongst hobbicks. According to Froyo, the most famous hobbick who ever lived had originally been married to his mother Leglock, daughter of none other than old Lotto and Lobsteria Sackville-Daggins. The most famous hobbick's first and only marriage had happened ten years after his coming of age when he received that *Insidious Ring* from his uncle, and twelve years before he left the Chire on his quest to destroy it at the age of fifty-five. According to Leglock, the marriage was the one part of the most famous hobbick's life that he wished to remain secret, in order to spare his son Froyo from unrealistic expectations being placed on the poor lad, of course. After all, there was only one *Insidious Ring* that could be destroyed and the most famous hobbick who ever lived had already done it. By writing his first marriage and only son out of his story, he had spared his son Froyo from a life of humiliation.

Froyo Daggins had burst onto the scene when Sham's grandfather had followed the most famous hobbick who ever lived and Grandalf into the West to seek the undying lands. Of course, the Chire had been suspicious at first, for the account of the Sackville-Dagginses in the tale of the most famous hobbick who ever lived had been anything but favorable.

But Froyo had seized Daggend from the Gramgee's nonetheless, demoting them once again to the gardeners of Bragshot Crow, and soon thereafter, Froyo had been elected mayor of the Chire, though some still claimed that election had been rigged.

Frobo of course, knew all about the rumors and doubts surrounding his father. If he was honest with himself, he had doubts of his own. Would the most famous hobbick who ever lived really marry a Sackville-Daggins? It was a question that had kept him from sleep on many a night, one he had no answer for, but that he detested others for asking.

When Middlearth Enterprises had come to purchase the rights to make the films from the hobbicks, as well as all of their names for trademarks, his father Froyo had negotiated the deal. And shortly thereafter, the hobbick (as they were now forced to call themselves) Frobo had known for only ten years had mysteriously disappeared.

Of course, a search party had been formed for poor Froyo, but nobody in the Chire had ever discovered what happened to him. Some thought he'd taken additional compensation for the deal and gone back to Sackville (Frobo's birthplace) to assume a new identity. There he could spend his new monies freely and without suspicion. But Sackville was a grubby place, and the hobbicks who lived there subsided by selling their dirt to the inhabitants of the Chire for placing hills over the new holes they built.

Others suspected Froyo had drownded in the Brandybeer River, just as the most famous hobbick who ever lived's parents had, though none could claim to have seen him do it. The general theory still of those who assumed Froyo had drownded was that he had gone to dip a glass in his new beer river and slipped in. "It's irony, it is!" they said, with only a slight under-standing of what the word *irony* really meant.

Frobo didn't have the faintest notion as to his father's fate, though he suspected that whatever happened had been quite tragic. His disappearance had left Frobo as heir to Daggend before he was ready for such a task. But that was of no matter now. Wherever his father was, Frobo wished him well and thus he raised his glass to the wooden ceiling of his hobbick hole in toast. Sham lifted himself from the floor and wiped the quickly cried tears from his eyes that Frobo was quite sure were ingen-uine. Martin and Happy then raised their glasses, and at last, so did Sham.

"To my father Froyo," he said. "To Froyo and the Chire," said Frobo.

"To Froyo and the Chire," they repeated, draining their glasses, only to have Sham then refill them all from the large pitcher like an eager bartender.

"And to that old grey wizard who accompanied my grandfa-ther on his journeys across Middlearth!" said Frobo. "To Grandalf!"

Halfway through their second glass Sham spewed beer from his mouth and nose. The hobbicks gasped in disgust.

"What in Middlearth?" exclaimed Frobo.

"Mr. Frobo, the trademark!" said Sham, his usually smiling face now stricken with terror. "You forgot the trademark!"

Frobo's heart stopped. He'd forgotten. For one slimy second, he'd forgotten it. The trademark. And in that moment, Frobo's somewhat dull gardener, whose family had been unable to climb the ladder of success for generations, had been smarter than him. Horns were blowing outside. The filmmaker's goons would be on their way.

They could hear a voice outside speaking over a megaphone. "Hobbicks of the Chire, please make your way to the party tree.

Hobbicks of the Chire, please make your way to the party tree. This is not a test."

Frobo made his way with Sham, Happy, and Martin out onto the broad green lawn that coincidentally happened to be Daggend's backyard, where other hobbicks were cursing and grumbling under their breath. Most of the Chire was there already, rewatching the extended edition of the fifth film for what might've been the thousandth time.

"By the filmmaker's beard, what is it now," grumbled Balcones Boffin. "This thing's still got three hours left!"

Most of the hobbicks grumbled and murmured in agreement.

As the few remaining hobbicks of the Chire who hadn't been watching the films filed onto the lawn, two of the men of Middlearth Enterprises (privately referred to by the hobbicks as the filmmaker's goons) appeared at the far end of the field from the large house where they lived. The dark of night was the only time when the Hobbicks could watch the films, and they gathered out on the large party lawn en masse. The lawn was naturally bowl shaped, so the hobbicks could lay back and gaze up at large white sheets that had been stitched together and erected at the rim of the bowl for the films to project onto. Frobo couldn't help but be reminded of the grand birthday celebration that had taken place eleven-one years ago in exactly the same spot. On that evening the second most famous hobbick who ever lived had disappeared in a flash before his guest's eyes, never to be seen by another hobbick in the Chire again. But this allusive knowledge did little to console him.

Frobo whispered to Happy, "I just don't understand how they heard me say it."

Happy shook his head in agreement.

Although he was trying to maintain the appearance of strength, as he always did, Frobo was shaking on the inside. He couldn't believe he'd been so foolish. And now what would happen to him? What would happen to the Chire? There were nasty stories about hobbicks who violated the trademark agreement. Some were taken down to the Lockholes. Others were completely kicked out of the Chire and cast out to Sackville or Drywater.

Frobo could stand it no longer. He wouldn't let another hobbick be punished for him. He had to take responsibility. He was a Daggins for goodness' sake, and it was about time he started acting like one.

"It was me!" he shouted at the top of his lungs. A sudden hush fell over the crowd. "I did it. I was the one who broke the trademark agreement! Take me away. No one else need suffer."

Gasps emanated from the crowd of hobbicks that were splayed out across the green field. They reminded Frobo of a garden of bulging red tomatoes, but though they were all round and rosy-cheeked, a vast majority of them were also full of opinions and instructions for young hobbicks like himself (though Frobo assumed that the most of these opinions and instructions were rooted in jealousy for his position). Suddenly, those red round hobbicks that had been docile film-watchers a moment before sprang up in alert. Every eye of the lawn was fixed upon Frobo.

"You broke the agreement?" asked one of the goons. "How?"

"I said the name," Frobo paused, "*Grandalf*... without saying ™ afterwards." Gasps erupted from the crowd like a river through a breaking dam.

"What do you mean? Did you print it or make any money off of it?" asked the goon.

"Not a penny!" said Frobo, as defiantly as he'd ever spoken in his entire life.

"How many times do we have to tell you little creatures?" said the goon. "You can call yourselves or your little town whatever you like! You just can't sell it on merchandise or in print. Don't you even know what you agreed to?"

"Pardon me for saying so, Mr. Jackson's goon," said a wizened old hobbick, "but us hobbicks aren't ones to go back on our word, and we'll keep it whether you make us or not."

"But we don't care what you call yourselves."

"David, it's not worth it," another goon beside him said. "Trust me, I've tried. They don't understand. Let them call themselves 'hobbicks' all they want."

The goon named David sighed, "Fine. Listen, the reason we called you here is *not* because one of you broke our trademark law."

The hobbicks shuddered in unison. The same old wizened hobbick who had spoken up before stomped his bare feet in anger and growled in defiance. Frobo scratched his head. Did the old fellow want him to get in trouble?

"So, you're not taking him away to the Lockholes?" shouted Fatty Bulger the Third.

"Disappointed by that are you, Fatty?" asked Frobo.

Fatty's father had been one of the first to start the rumors about Froyo's relation to the most famous hobbick who ever lived as being a complete sham. As such, Fatty was considered by Frobo to be the equivalent of his own arch enemy. Fatty was the most annoying type of hobbick to Frobo, even more annoying than Sham could be. But despite his name, he had never quite *grown into* his grandfather's shoes, or his trousers. The only *fat* part of Fatty was his bulging cheeks and double chin. The rest of him was built like the strong haunches of an ox. He towered over most hobbicks by a few inches, and therefore much of the Chire gave ear to the rumors he spread about the lies of Frobo's heritage.

"You're no more a Daggins than I'm the son of an elf, Frobo!" shouted Fatty. "And I think they should lock you away forever!"

At this, the whole lawn (including Frobo and his friends) erupted into a great brawl. It was a ridiculous reaction to Fatty's statement, but as open insults were extremely rare in the Chire, one never knew what they might bring about. Most of the hobbicks didn't have a side in the disagreement, but they were all thrown into a general state of confusion but the suddenness of it all. Frobo struggled through the Hobbicks as they threw food, dumped beer, pulled hair and bit each other's feet. His aim was to reach Fatty who'd been standing twenty hobbicks away when he'd made the comment. When he did reach him, Frobo would give him a piece of his mind, and perhaps his fist.

A large red-haired hobbick to Frobo's right (named Ronald) dove at Frobo, tackling him and sending him on backwards. That's when Frobo realized what was happening. The hobbicks weren't fighting, but were doing what they called *film-fighting*. Ronald's tackle hadn't been forceful at all. It had felt more like the hobbick was landing next to him while gently coaxing him to fall over. He wasn't trying to hurt Frobo. Of course, Frobo should've known. As he fell, he saw a hobbick to his right over-react to a punch that never made contact with his face. He feigned that it had been a knockout and fell to the ground in a heap. In the heat of the moment, Frobo had thought the hobbick brawl was real, but he should've known better. His real fight with Fatty would have to wait until the act was over.

It wasn't long until the clamor died down as most of the hobbicks were too drunk and lethargic to make the film fight last. David interrupted the crowd with shouting, "Enough! Enough, you worthless little hobbicks! We haven't called you here because you violated your trademark agreement. We called you here because it was reported that a suspicious person was seen nearby. Now, this person is extremely dangerous. And if he is seen, should be reported to us immediately."

More gasping echoed through the crowd. A fearful dread suddenly settled over the crowd of hobbicks. Mothers grasped their young and pulled them close to their bosoms. A few younglings pulled their blankets up over their faces. The elders tried to appear resolute, but Frobo noticed even the stoutest amongst them shifting in their boots. It was quite unsettling.

"What does this 'extremely dangerous' person look like?" asked Martin.

The goon shifted uncomfortably, "Err, tall pointy blue hat, grey robes, and he carries a big walking stick."

Frobo pondered the description. Something about it seemed... familiar to him. But what could it be?

"Sounds a lot like Grandalf™ if you ask me!" cried Sham.

Of course, it did! It was an exact description of the old wizard from the book when he had first arrived in the Chire!

"Grandalf™'s staff was broken by the Lord of the Nazgool!" shouted a hobbick from the crowd.

"For the last time," said the goon named David, "You don't have to say ™ every time you say Grandalf™. Only when you're printing something or selling merchandise!"

"You old weed-smoking Bracegriddle!" shouted Sham in retort, completely ignoring David the goon's helpful clarification. "Have you ever read the story of the most famous hobbick who ever lived? The breaking of Grandalf™'s staff was only a film adaptation. The real Grandalf™ still has a staff!"

"Well, didn't he also sail into the West with the most famous hobbick who ever lived?" shouted back the Bracegriddle.

"An excellent point," said David the goon, chiming back in. "This individual is obviously an imposter of the real Grandalf™ and therefore could be attempting to profit from his name. Of course, I don't have to remind you that only the filmmaker and Middlearth Enterprises are allowed to make any sort of money off of Grandalf™'s name."

"Pardon me, Goon of Middlearth Enterprises?" said Fatty Bulger the Third.

The goon sighed, "If I've asked you once, I've asked you a thousand times not to call me that."

"Oh sorry, right you have, my apologies Mister Goon, sir." Fatty covered his mouth. "Son of Ashelob, I did it again!"

"What is it, Fatty the hobbick?" asked David the goon.

"Well Mister Goon sir," Fatty covered his mouth in shock again after stopping himself too late.

"Oh, get on with it, Fatty!" shouted the Bracegriddle.

"Well Mister Goon sir, I was just wondering why earlier, when you said Grandalf™, why you said the ™ part after it, after you told us we didn't have to."

"The bloke's trying to trap us so he can take us off to the Lockholes or excommunicate us to Breetown, that's why!" shouted a hobbick from the crowd.

Another commotion broke out and cries of "Son of a Fillippa Boyens," could be heard all through the *gross*.

When at last calm resumed, David the goon cried out, "I am not trying to trap you! I just got confused is all. The filmmaker knows I've been here too long. All I wanted to say was, if any of you sees this Grandalf™..."

"Did it again," interrupted Fatty.

David the goon rolled his eyes and continued as quick as he could before another interruption, "impersonator, report him to us immediately! Now all of you, get out of my sight!"

"But we were here first," shouted another of the hobbicks. "You're the one who has to leave if you want to stop looking at us!"

"Somebody, start the film again!" shouted the old Brace-griddle.

David and the other goons, too tired to interrupt now that the films were resuming, left the gathering to return to their large house.

The majority of the hobbicks then returned to their accustomed places on the lawn to watch the final three hours of the second installment of the second trilogy by the acclaimed filmmaker who had bought the rights to their names. Frobo, Sham, Happy, and Martin began the walk back to Daggend.

"Mister Frobo..." said Sham, "why would someone be impersonating old Grandalf™?"

"You know as well as I do, Sham," said Frobo.

"I reckon it's just like that old goon of the filmmaker's said," piped in Happy. "Just some bloke trying to make a dime off Grandalf™'s good name."

The trudge back up the dark green hill to Frobo's front door was not a long one, yet Sham could still be heard huffing and puffing during the climb. They crested the hill and saw long shadows from the film's blue light stretching out on the grass before them. They then descended the hill, and their shadows disappeared as they landed on the short path back to Daggend. Frobo's home was not ten feet away, but now there were no lights shining from inside it as there were when they left. In the darkness, they could only hear the creaking sound of Frobo's green door swinging on its hinges.

"Hullo," said Martin, "who left the door open?" Wary of any number of possible dangers (though Frobo assumed this precaution likely unnecessary) the hobbicks crept on tipping toes through the swinging door of the now pitch black hobbick hole.

"Wind must've blown out the candles," said Happy. "But it wasn't me. I didn't leave it open."

"Who was the last one out?" asked Frobo.

"Son of Ashelob, Sham Gramgee, how many times do we have to tell you to close the door!" shouted Martin.

"It was not Sham Gramgee who left the door open."

Frobo and the others turned to Sham, whose flaming red cheeks had suddenly turned a ghostly shade of white.

"My goodness Sham! You look like you're about to faint! And why the devil are you referring to yourself in the third person now? You sound ridiculous and I won't tolerate that kind of talk! Not in my house," Frobo said.

"Mister Frobo, please sir! That wasn't me that spoke just now," said Sham.

Frobo struggled to comprehend the entirety of what this could mean. But the cold feeling creeping up the back of his spine and the pale vision of Sham's white face in the darkness explained to him what words could not. He peered throughout the dark house with his sharp hobbick eyes and wished for the life of him that he had the vision of an elf. He thought he could perceive a still smoking candle through the light from the film in front of the window of his study. But in the living room before him, all he could see were dark lurking shadows.

"Well, if it wasn't you speaking Sham, then who was it?" said Martin.

"It was me," bellowed a deep voice from the dark. The hobbicks froze. In the pure light of day, they would've been able to perceive that each one of their faces were all as pale as Sham's.

"Someone, light a candle!" said Happy. Frobo retrieved the smoking candle from the windowsill in the study to their right and struck a match from his pocket to light it. Holding it out before them, he was still unable to see who was speaking in the darkness before them.

"Me who?" Happy asked timidly.

"What is this, a knock-knock joke?" said the voice.

"Me who?" the four hobbicks asked, this time in unison. Though their voices were trembling, they repeated the question as any hobbick would have until it was properly answered.

"Alright," said the deep voice. "Me Grandalf."

"Me Grandalf™," corrected Happy.

"Who is me Grandalf™?" asked the voice from the dark.

"Who is me Grandalf™?" spluttered Sham. "Well, he's only the most famous wizard from the greatest story ever told whose name was trademarked by the filmmaker and Middlearth Enterprises!"

"I know who Grandalf is," said the voice, "but I have never heard of Grandalf™."

"Well, let me explain it to you, sir, you see..." Sham began, but he was quickly cut short by Happy.

"Sham, I think this might be the *impsy whatsy*..." said Happy.

Sham stared back at Happy and cocked his head. Happy was trying to help Sham understand, but the urgency stated by the whites of his eyes and the implications of his raised eyebrows had no effect on him.

"You know Sham," said Happy, "the *impsy whatsy* that the goonsy just warned us about..."

Sham shook his head, mouthing the word *"what?"*

Frobo and Martin stared into the darkness, waiting for any shift that might indicate that this person was going to attack them in which case they would run or call for help.

"The *impsy whatsy* pretending like he might be Grandalf-sy™sy!" shouted Martin.

From the darkness before them, the small crackle of a striking match was heard. The trickling flame revealed two glowing eyes, peering out at them. The match lit a long-barreled pipe that hung from the mouth of someone with a very long white beard. At last, Frobo was finished with the mystery. If for no other reason than to reveal the identity of the smoker to Sham so he would stop asking questions about him, he marched over to his large chandelier and lit it with his candlestick.

Light filled the room, and at last Sham understood who the "impsy whatsy" was. Sitting near the back of the room, wearing a dirty grey robe, pointy blue hat and holding a large walking stick that looked very much like a wizard's staff, was someone who looked quite similar to Sir Ian McCallen. Frobo's attention was immediately drawn to the forefinger of his right hand, upon which a golden ring with a bright red stone was adorned. Of this ring's significance (if it had any at all) Frobo was wholly unaware.

"We have much to discuss my young Hobbicks," the old man said.

Frobo gulped.

CHAPTER 2

THE SHADOW OF THE MAST

FROBO AND THE OTHER HOBBICKS STARED IN UTTER SHOCK AT the old man. Clearly, this was the imposter the goons had warned them about, as the real Grandalf had left Middlearth forever eleventy-one years ago. But why was he here? With his get-up and facial recognition, he could've been anywhere in the Chire, turning profits reading fortunes or signing film posters. Frobo was too afraid to sit. This man had broken into his home.

"I should call the goons on you!" Frobo said. "You're the imposter we were just warned of! And you're trespassing!" But despite Frobo's exclamation and fear of the imposter, curiosity kept him from running out his door that instant and alerting the goons of the intruder. And so, it kept each of the hobbicks. For in their hearts, they all stole a hidden hope that perhaps this old man was no imposter at all.

"I have trespassed many times in my life," the old man said. "But I have never been accused of doing so here, in Daggend. Before you go and write me off as this imposter, I implore you to listen to what I have to say. Now take your seats."

The hobbicks reluctantly complied, sitting around the wizard where they could listen attentively. Frobo scolded himself for being so brash initially. It wouldn't have been polite to call the goons without first hearing what the imposter had to say. Where had his manners got off to?

"When I realized I had to return to Middlearth," the old man said, "I decided there was no place better to begin my quest than Daggend. Of course, it was not an easy decision, for hobbicks are a very strange folk, indeed. But the more I considered it, the more I realized the quest that lay before us could be accomplished by no other race. 'As soft as butter they can be,' I told myself. 'Yet when provoked, and under the right circumstances, they can be as tough as the underbelly of a dragon.'"

"Pardon me for asking, Mister *Impsy Whatsy*, but isn't that the weakest part of a dragon?" asked Sham.

"Well... yes, it is. But it's still a sight harder than butter," responded the old man.

"What if the butter was frozen, sir?" asked Martin, shooting his hand up into the air like a soaring firework before it explodes. "Which one would be stronger then?"

"Oh Martin, would you shut up?" said Happy. "It's a metaphor, it's not to be taken literally."

"It's not a metaphor," retorted Martin. "It's an analogy! But you're missing my point. I'm talking about a stick of butter that's rock hard, frozen solid. Like it had been up in the peaks of the Musty Mountains for years under the snow."

"Enough!" shouted the old man. "I did not sail back to Middlearth to analyze foolish comparisons about hobbicks and sticks of butter, frozen or not! I should have compared you to the dragon's dung to avoid the confusion!"

"But what if the dung was frozen," commented Martin.

The old man breathed a long sigh. "A thousand leagues at sea for this. But what did you expect? Should've known better than to think..."

"Excuse me sir, I would hate to listen to you talk to yourself all night..." said Frobo. Listening to the old man talk to himself (even for only a brief moment) felt to Frobo and the others like wading through a bramble of thorns. Talking to oneself had become taboo since the hobbicks had seen the portrayal of Grollum in the films. Now the activity was absolutely dreadful to them. Many times, Frobo had seen mothers cover the eyes and ears of the younger hobbicks while they watched the portrayal of the creature Grollum out on the lawn. It was Frobo's least favorite part of the films.

The old man stopped fortunately, and looked up at Frobo, cocking his head at the sudden request.

"If you don't mind me asking, who in Middlearth are you, really?" Frobo asked.

Sham grabbed his beer, preparing himself for the lengthy repose of the old man's origins and intentions that he wanted to hear, but that might need just a little alcoholic assistance to endure.

"Isn't that obvious?" asked the old man. He leaned back and puffed at his pipe. Small white rings of smoke drifted up over the heads of the four hobbicks and around the wide sitting room. Then, almost magically, the still in-tact smoke rings flitted over to the open window where Frobo had taken up the candlestick upon entering Daggend, and exited through it.

"No," said the four Hobbicks at once.

"Well, I'm Grandalf of course," said the old man.

The shock felt by each of the hobbicks at this statement was ill-concealed. Frobo, who had been leaning forward intently listening to the old man, instantly threw himself back in his chair. Happy's customarily cheerful face frowned and turned a pale shade of grey. The pipe that Martin had just managed to light fell right out of his mouth onto Daggend's floor. Sham's beer seemed to go down the wrong pipe and he started to cough quite loudly. And though the coughing didn't stop, Frobo, Martin and Happy were much too concerned with the man calling himself Grandalf to pay Sham any attention.

Martin was the first to speak up. "If you're the real Grandalf™, then what's nine plus seventeen?"

He asked the question as if he had just told a riddle. Then Martin sat back in his seat like a coiling snake, ready to strike a wrong answer like it was a prancing field mouse.

"Twenty-six!" answered Grandalf, just as unconcerned with Sham's continued coughing as the hobbicks were. A smile beamed beneath the whiskers of his white mustache and long beard.

"Don't worry about me, I'll get it down!" Sham shouted through coughs and gasps of breath.

"You're wrong, it's twenty-four," said Martin, still not paying Sham the slightest bit of attention.

"No, it's not," said Happy. "Nine plus seventeen is twenty-six! He is the real Grandalf™."

Sham spluttered and choked behind them. He really was quite annoying sometimes. Didn't he realize they were trying to have a conversation?

Frobo interrupted the two hobbicks, completely ignoring Sham. "Wait, how does that make him the real Grandalf™? The real Grandalf™ wasn't exactly known for his abilities with basic addition."

"By the filmmaker, Frobo!" exclaimed Martin, throwing both hands in the air. "Of course, he wasn't known for that. That's why I asked him a question that the real Grandalf™ wouldn't have known the answer to."

Frobo shook his head at Martin's logic. Surely, his guile would've stumped even the brightest of reasoners.

Martin winked at him, revealing his yellow smoke-stained teeth in a wide grin, "a little reverse psychology!"

"Forget him," said Frobo, throwing up his hands. "If you're the real Grandalf™, then why is your cloak grey? We all know the real Grandalf™ has a white cloak." Frobo wagged his finger at the long grey cloak that hung down to the man's knees where he wore long brown boots.

"A fair question," said the old man, his smile widening as he eyed Frobo. "With a simple, yet obvious answer. It's been eleventy-one years since I was given these robes. They were white then. Now, suffice it to say that say they are soiled."

"Disgusting!" said Martin, looking at Grandalf like he was some of Sham's refuse.

"Well, you're not exactly one to talk about dirty clothes, are you?" Frobo asked him. "You've been wearing the same dark gray outfit for the last three months. Every time you sit in that chair it smells like smoke for a week."

"Just because I don't change into a different colorful garment every four hours doesn't mean I don't keep myself clean," said Martin, the yellow-toothed smile now concealed behind pursed pouting lips. He furrowed his brows at Frobo so low that his grey eyes were barely visible.

"If you're the real Grandalf™, then what's the Elfish word for friend?" asked Happy.

"Mellon," said the old man.

"That just proves he's seen the films," said Martin. "Besides, that was such a ridiculous scene. Who uses tropical fruit for their secret passwords anyways?"

"There is only one proof I will give for my identity," said the old man. "And it is in fact, the very reason I have come here." With one hand, he reached and pulled the golden ring with the red stone from his forefinger and held it before them. The bright red stone shimmered in the light and each of the hobbick's gazes were drawn to the ring like young children being shown a magic trick (save Sham who had still not managed to stop coughing). So bright and so beautiful was this ring that it seemed that all the lights in Daggend dimmed in comparison to its shine.

Then he said, "This is the Ring of Fire, one of the three Elfen Rings of Power, and I, Grandalf, am it's keeper."

Frobo, Martin and Happy gawked in awe at the thing, mouths wide open like it was a beautiful hobbick lass. Each of them were wholly captivated by it, except for Sham who was still very distractingly coughing on his beer.

"If you're the real Grandalf™, do a bit of magic," said Martin, "just so long as it doesn't involve turning any of us into a toad."

The so-called wizard stood to his feet. Frobo, Happy and Martin all stood back. Sham had fallen out of his chair and was bent over on the floor. His face was a florid shade a red. Amazingly, in the middle of his fit of coughing he reached for his mug of beer once more to try his luck at another swallow, but with no success. The beer spewed from his mouth in all directions so that the hobbicks and the so-called wizard were sprayed by it.

In a commanding voice, the so-called wizard exclaimed, "Choako Stoapo," thrusting the glowing end of his staff right into Sham's midsection. Frobo was unable to tell if what happened immediately after was by magic or the sheer force of the blow from the glowing staff, but Sham stopped choking, flew backwards into one of Frobo's bookshelves and proceeded to throw up all over the floor. The beer flowed from Sham's mouth like he was a cask that had just been upturned, a golden river as strong as the Brandybeer itself. They had obviously done a very poor job at monitoring Sham's consumption that evening.

"Oh, thank you for that, Mister Grandalf™ sir. Thank you very much," Sham said, hopping up from in front of the bookcase after his face had regained its color. He then wasted no time, for though he had just vomited all over his master's floor, he did not plan to be rude about it, and he smartly went to Frobo's pantry to fetch a mop. Sham spent the next fifteen minutes repeatedly thanking the wizard and apologizing to all of them for throwing up, as he flitted the mop back and forth across the floor. The stench blessedly did not linger as long as Sham's repetitious *"thank you's!"* and *"oh I am so sorry's!"* and soon the place smelled as fresh and hole-like as ever.

When Sham at last finished his mopping and started sipping another mug of beer, Grandalf said, "Not to be too forward, as I did break into this place, but I have no idea who the lot of you are. However, since you now know who I am, perhaps you may introduce yourselves to me."

"Yes, of course," began Martin. "My name is Martin Shaken-Nottstird."

"Martin Shaken-Nottstird," repeated Grandalf. "You sound like something a spy would order at a tavern's bar."

"Thank you, sir," said Martin crossing his arms in satisfaction.

"I, sir, am Happy Brandybeer. Pleased to make your acquaintance."

"Brandybeer, Brandybeer... I've never heard of the name."

"Well sir, I'm the descendant of none other than my grandfather, Mister Brandy*deer*, ahem ™ of course. But with the trademark and all, we err, just changed the name to Brandybeer."

"You changed the what?" asked Grandalf.

"The name sir, Brandy*deer*™. You know... the animal that runs about with horns and eats the lettuce from your garden. You see sir, after the release of the films, this fellow came to the Chire, Mister Grandalf™," but Happy was interrupted by the annoyed wizard.

"If I hear those two letters after my good name one more time, I will turn you all into toads! Now continue! But spare me all this ™ ork mischief." The wizard settled back down in his chair as Happy continued.

"Right sir. Well, after the release of the films, this fellow came to the, well, he came here. sir, offering all sorts of things to us hobbicks, hobbick™s mind you, sir, though we dropped the ™ when saying 'hobbicks' long ago from laziness."

"What in the name of Grandalf is wrong with you little people?" the wizard asked.

"Now there you go again, referring to yourself in the third person," chimed in Martin. "It's bad luck talking to yourself, Mister Grandalf™, and bad things'll come of it!"

"Please," interrupted Frobo, "just let him finish... Mister Grand... Mister Grand... Mister Grand-arrlf!" Frobo coughed and spluttered the last syllable of Grandalf's name out. It was shockingly difficult to say without changing it or adding the ™ to the end of it. "Sorry, sir, just let him finish. It'll all make sense, we promise."

The wizard settled back down, bristling his eyebrows and crossing his arms. He seemed intent to let Happy finish the story in complete silence. Happy stood to his feet, eager to tell his story, and as he spoke, he paced about the room, occasionally running his hand through his bright red hair, as if he thought doing so would keep it in place. Each time, the red locks bounced back into their hanging curls, just as the pads of his hairy feet seemed to bounce him around the room in delight that someone was listening to him.

"As I was saying, one day this fellow comes about telling us hobbicks how valuable all our names were, see: hobbicks™, The Chire™, but mainly all of our ancestors' names, all of it, see." Frobo, Martin, and Sham all drew close in anticipation. Of course, they knew this story, but hobbicks thoroughly loved to recount even the most obscure and random chapters of their history as a people. It was a very rare chance indeed that allowed them the opportunity to tell someone who'd never heard them. Happy continued, "So this fellow tells us all that he works for a filmmaker and a company called Middlearth Enterprises. You see this bloke and his goons had somehow found the story of the most famous hobbick who ever lived about destroying that *Insidious Ring* and had made something called a 'film' about it. Umm, let's see how do I explain? It's like a moving, talking picture with..."

"I know what a film is, young hobbick," Grandalf groaned, standing up suddenly to his feet. "Now please wrap up this story before it puts me to sleep," he said, and began to pace around the room whilst puffing his pipe. His tall head was just barely shorter than Daggend's ceiling.

"Oh, thank you sir," said Happy, considering the idea of someone falling asleep during his story the highest of compliments. After all, sleep is one of the things all hobbicks love most, behind only food, ale, smoke, good friends and occasionally gardening.

"So, this goon tells us all that this bloke the filmmaker is willing to give us anything we want, with one condition. And of course, us hobbicks had a mayor at the time, and so we let him do the negotiating on our behalf. And after a time, sir, the mayor, Mister Froyo, comes out and tells us all what he's agreed to with the goon. Us hobbicks gave up the rights to all our names, and we had to say ™ after everything having to do with the films, because he owned it now, see?"

"He owned it?" asked Grandalf.

"Yes sir, he owned it sir. But us hobbick folk, being a smart and sensible lot, decided we'd had enough of the whole ™ bit one day, and started calling ourselves by different names."

"That's when all the name changing started," cut in Martin. "The Brandywhine River™ became the Brandybeer River. The last name *Brandydeer* became..."

"Well coincidentally it was also changed to Brandybeer..." said Happy. "I know I know, it's confusing," he said, nodding in acknowledgement as this particular name change was rarely understood by outsiders when visiting the Chire. "The bottom line was, those who lived around the Brandywhine River and the Brandy*deer* family both fancied the name Brandybeer. My family was given first choice for the name and we would've kept it all for ourselves, but since the river was changed into beer by magic, we thought it made more sense to name the river Brandybeer as well."

"Anything that wasn't changed, had to have a ™ after it," Sham said, then stood up to go refill his empty mug.

"I see," said the wizard. "And what did you... hobbicks get in return?"

There was a brief pause as Martin, Happy and Frobo all grinned in anticipation at the answer to Grandalf's question.

"Well," he asked, "what was it? What did you get in return?"

A moment later, Sham returned with two pints of beer. "A drink, Mister Grandalf™ sir?" he asked.

"Don't mind if I do," said the wizard, taking both pints from Sham's hands (who had obviously meant to drink the second glass himself). Sham turned around looking sour for a moment, but Frobo had no shortage of glasses, and he went back to the kitchen to fetch another for himself.

"Now what did this filmmaker give you in return?" asked Grandalf.

"You're drinking it," said Happy proudly. "A lifetime supply of it! Turned the Brandybeer River into an endless river of beer, he did, and..."

The wizard, who'd since resumed his seat after his brief pace around the room when the story began, threw his legs forward spewed the beer from his mouth all over the freshly mopped floor.

Seeing the mess, Sham sighed and said, "I'll get the mop."

"You traded the monetary rights to your names for a life-time supply of beer?" The wizard was exasperated. "What in the name of Aragron?"

"Aragron™ sir!" corrected Martin. "At least while you're in the Chire."

"Dragons and Nazgool!" shouted Grandalf. "By Old Toby

himself, what in the South Furthing is wrong with you people? I'm gone for eleventy-one years, and the whole Chire goes mad. Who is this Froyo fellow anyways who made this ridiculous bargain? I'd like to give him a piece of my mind."

Frobo felt a great desire to lash out at the wizard, to scream and yell that he himself was Froyo's heir, but instead he sat silently, with crossed arms, wondering bitterly if this Grandalf impersonator might be as right as the rain itself.

"And who might you be," Grandalf asked, motioning to Sham. "You must be the Gramgee's butler, though I daresay you do remind me of one of them."

"Thank you, sir," responded Sham, confused by Grandalf's comment. "But I'm not the Gramgee's butler, I am a Gramgee, sir. I'm the grandson of that very Gramgee who was the gardener of Daggend and accompanied the most famous hobbick who ever lived on his magnificent quest."

"Ahh yes, I thought I saw the resemblance, in looks and in mind," said Grandalf. "But that doesn't make any sense either. The most famous hobbick who ever lived left Daggend, along with all his possessions to the Gramgee's before he sailed into the West with me. Who owns it now?"

"I do," said Frobo with an air of timidity in his voice.

"And who might you be, my good hobbick?" asked Grandalf.

"I'm Frobo Daggins, sir. Frobo, son of Froyo, son of the most famous hobbick who ever lived and Lockleg Sackville-Daggins."

Frobo expected the wizard to contradict him, to tell him why that was a lie, but instead the old man burst into laughter. "Oh yes, of course you are! And I'm the son of Galadriyell and Sauluman! Hahaha, to think that the most famous hobbick ever would've married the daughter of old Lobsteria and Lotto, two of the most dreadful hobbicks the Chire has ever known!"

Sham, Happy and Martin remained silent, each wondering what Frobo would do. They'd never heard someone speak this openly about Frobo's heritage before, and especially not in such a disparaging way. Not even Fatty Bulger the Third would've laughed at the idea that he was the *heir*. Frobo simply sat in his chair, painfully aware of how red his face was becoming at the embarrassment of it all. This was not how he'd imagined meeting the greatest wizard in the history of Middlearth.

Grandalf continued, "But surely you must know, even *you* Frobo must know that it's utter lunacy to think that *the* most famous hobbick who ever lived would've married a Sackville-Daggins! When exactly was this supposed to have happened?"

"Sometime during the twenty years between his thirty-third birthday and your return to the Chire for his fiftieth," said Frobo. "It was seventeen years. Growing up, I was told there was probably a nasty separation, which made him feel guilty, which is why he sold Daggend to the Sackville-Dagginses before he left the Chire to go on his quest."

"Well, I can't say I know for certain it didn't happen," said Grandalf. "And although I find the whole story entirely unlikely, I can't rule out its possibility completely." Grandalf seemed to be inspecting Frobo now, and far behind the depths of the wizard's grey eyes, Frobo imagined spinning wheels of thought, the very machinations of a purpose for him. It made Frobo feel uncomfortable.

"There is something about you..." Grandalf said. "Perhaps an elfish air, I'm not entirely sure. But by the most famoust's uncle himself, you do remind me of him. Maybe that old fox did have a trick or two up his sleeve he wasn't telling me! And while your father, this *Froyo* fellow seems to have been quite the Sackville-Daggins; of you, young Frobo, I must say, I am wholly unsure."

"Begging your pardon, Mister Grandalf™ sir," interrupted Sham.

"Yes, Sham?" said Grandalf.

"Well Mister Grandalf™ sir, if you don't mind, sir, I'd like to ask you a question, sir."

The other hobbicks groaned.

"You could've asked the question five times by now if you weren't being so polite," muttered Martin, rolling his eyes.

"Spit it out, my young hobbick," said Grandalf.

"Oh, right you are sir, my apologies sir!" spluttered Sham. Happy rested his head in his hands. "Well, let's see, I'm just wondering how I should say this..." Sham continued. He sat down in one of Frobo's armchairs, crossed his legs, and began to stroke his chin with his forefinger and thumb contemplatively. The other hobbicks with Grandalf sat in anticipation, waiting for the question.

Long drawn-out awkward seconds passed as they all awaited Sham's question. This was one of his more annoying habits, to ask permission to ask a question, when of course, by asking permission, he had already asked one. He finally seemed to have conjured up his own preferred diction and spoke up, "Thank you, Mister Grandalf™ sir, but I believe I'll wait."

"Thank you for what?" asked the wizard. "By the great sea, what kind of question is that?"

"Well, Mister Grandalf™ sir," Sham explained, "I was trying to think of a question, but couldn't get one, sir. Leastways, I couldn't get one to come to the front of my head sir, where the talking part is, but I thought I'd go ahead and ask your permission, so that when I did think of a question, I'd be able to ask it."

All Frobo could do in response was shake his head, while Happy threw his hands in the air and exclaimed, "How many times do we have to ask you not to do that Sham?"

"If you want to ask a question, just ask it," said Martin. "Otherwise, stuff your yapper with potatoes and spare us all the misery!"

"Oh alright, alright, I'm sorry!" said Sham. "It's just not every day that a hobbick meets a famous wizard."

"Here Sham, let me show you how it's done," said Happy, "Mister Grandalf™, what in Middlearth are you doing here? I thought you had sailed off into the West and were gone forever."

"Oh, right you are mister Happy sir, right you are sir. My apologies, Mister Grandalf™ sir, please let me know if there's any way I can make it up to you, sir!"

"For starters," said the wizard, "you can take young Martin's advice, keep your yapper stuffed with potatoes, and let me answer the question."

Finally, comprehension that he should stop speaking seemed to dawn on Sham. He sucked in a great breath and held it for some time, his face slowly becoming more and more red.

"Now, to your question. Believe it or not, I didn't sail all the way back to Middlearth and the confounded Chire just to exchange pleasantries and perform anti-choking spells on a somewhat... sickeningly apologetic Hobbick. I came back here for a purpose, and that purpose is, unfinished business... loose threads at the end of a very long rope. Now, let me ask you all a question. It's been eleventy-one years, but which of you knows why the most famous hobbick who ever lived went on his quest?"

"Well, everyone knows that don't they?" said Frobo. "He went to destroy that *Insidious Ring*."

The other hobbicks (including Sham, who was still holding his breath) nodded in agreement.

"Exactly," said Grandalf. "He went to destroy that *Insidious Ring*, the one ring that could rule all other rings of power, including this one." He motioned to the red stoned ring on his forefinger. It was simply adorned with no ornate markings other than the bright red ruby at its center. "This is the elfen ring of fire, with which I can strike courage into the hearts of men, and even some young hobbicks from time to time. Now, which of you knows how many other rings of power there are?"

Frobo shuffled his feet, and Martin and Happy tried to appear as if they hadn't heard the question. Sham however looked as if he were about to burst with the answer. His hand had shot up into the air like a giddy tween and he bounced up and down on his armchair.

Grandalf sighed before finally saying, "Yes, Sham?"

A great gasp of breath escaped Sham's mouth and he struggled to put his next few sentences together through repeated gasping. "Thank you, Mister," he paused to breath out. "Grandalf™, sir," he sucked in deeply. "You see," he huffed, "sir, there are," he puffed, "nine for..." but the poor hobbick was unable to speak the words he knew by heart through his belabored breathing.

"Enough!" shouted the wizard.

> *"Three for the elf lords who seldom die,*
> *Seven for the dwarfs who prefer to live in stone,*
> *Nine for men, who will surely cry,*
> *About the one on the hand with the dark skin tones..."*

"Did you change that? It sounds different than I remember," said Frobo, shaking his head at the recital of the infamous poem. He squinted around the room at Grandalf and the others, but they all ignored this remark, eager for Grandalf to continue his story.

"That *one*, as you know, that *Insidious Ring* has been destroyed. The three are accounted for. One was given to me, the other two were worn by Galadriyell and Felrond."

"Galadriyell™ and Felrond™," corrected Sham. The wince in his face betrayed his expectation that such a correction might only lead to a sharp rebuke in turn, but he couldn't stop himself. "Sorry sir, I just don't want to get dragged out onto the

Party Lawn and interrupt the film again. You never do know when those goons are listening."

Grandalf's bristling eyebrows ill-concealed his utter disgust with Sham's correction, but the wizard continued, perhaps even more eager to be finished with this chapter of dialogue than the readers. "Of the seven given to the dwarfs, four were consumed by dragons, and three remained that were recovered by the Dark Lord. And of course, you know of the nine that were given to men."

Frobo looked to his right and left. Ahh yes... Martin and Happy were just as confused as he was by all this. Martin's customary raised eyebrow that signified he was cocked and ready to reply with some comment of cheeky wit had been replaced by dim furrowed brows and an open mouth. Happy in turn, was doing what he always did when confused by something (nodding so profusely and aggressively that it seemed his head might fall off). What was wrong with them? How did they have such little understanding of the history of Middlearth? But this was all very sudden and beyond their brief knowledge of ring lore they had obtained from the films. Sham might've been able to help them but alas, the poor lad was still breathing deeply in an attempt to regain his wind after holding his breath for so long, and he hadn't paid attention to a word Grandalf had said since then.

"I see," groaned the wizard, rolling his eyes in frustration and clear comprehension of the hobbicks understanding of the discussion. "Nine rings were gifted to the nine wraiths. These were the creatures dressed in black who pursued Frobo's grandfather from the Chire and were eventually destroyed. One was slain by your ancestor," he said pointing to Happy, who pointed to himself as if Grandalf had mistaken his identity. Happy had seen the films many times and was quite sure that his curly haired grandfather had never slain anything.

"Question, Mister Grandalf™," said Martin, "are these

wraith creatures you're talking about the ones who rode around on horses, or the ones who flew around on those black dragons?"

The wizard held his head in his hands and muttered to himself in a barely audible voice, "Why did you send me back to this?"

This made the hobbicks all shift uncomfortably. Frobo whispered to Martin in a voice that he could barely hear himself, "The old buzzard has really lost his marbles, hasn't he?"

"No, I have not Frobo Daggins!" exclaimed the wizard, "I am afraid it is the Chire that has lost its marbles, and not I that have lost mine! But to answer your question Martin, the creatures are one and the same. The nine wraiths first rode horses, and then mounted the flying black beasts, once their horses were destroyed at the Fords of Bruidia." Suddenly, Martin's eyes exploded open. He gazed at Grandalf like the wizard was a lost treasure he had just dug up, for he had never before understood that plot point when watching the films.

"My point," said the wizard, "is that although that *Insidious Ring* was destroyed, the others were not. The three given to the elfs were intended to pass into the west. The three that remained of the dwarfen rings and the nine given to men were all recovered by the Dark Lord and kept by him, for all we know in his tower of dark power."

Suddenly a great unease came upon Frobo. Was this how his grandfather had felt when Grandalf had first visited him so long ago?

"As you know, I sailed into the West many years ago to find the undying lands with Frobo's grandfather, *his* uncle, Galadriyell, and Felrond." Sham attempted to interrupt to add in the "™," but Grandalf held up his hand, a warning for Sham to keep silent. Sham frowned and pined in worry that the goons might break down the door at any second. He was so worried that he even got up to peek out every window to make sure the goons weren't listening from just outside. But he did not interrupt.

"The elfs, the ring bearers, and the last remaining rings of power, or so we thought, were leaving Middlearth forever. We sailed for years and years, but when we should've reached our destination, when our boat should've touched the white shores, they were not to be found. There were no white shores for us. Our path was closed, and we ended up in a most horrible land called *America*, a dreadful place of metal and wheels. Of course, Felrond assumed we had missed the turn, but I knew there was something else at play, something more sinister. For a lone ship had begun following us just as soon as I had thought we should have been arriving at the undying lands.

"So, we turned around and sailed back to Middlearth, but the lone ship kept its distance from us, and we did not encounter it on our return. Then we set out for the undying lands again, thinking that perhaps we had somehow missed a turn along the journey. But all the while the shadow of the pursuing ship in the distance grew in the back of my mind. We sailed back into the West, and missed the undying lands, again and again and again.

"When I'd finally had enough, I set our anchor myself and waited until the wretched ship caught up to us. 'The ship is the reason we can't reach the shores,' I told the others. 'Let us confront them now lest we sail in vain for another hundred years.' But had I known young hobbicks, who it was on that ship, and what their purpose was, perhaps I would've continued the search in an effort to outrun our pursuers. For when the ship did catch up to us, I learned the truth: the person aboard was none other than the maker of your precious films."

Sham cocked his head and Frobo felt the hairs of his arm stand up with chills. Happy and Martin were so quiet, that Frobo was wholly unsure if either of them were breathing. This was far more interesting to them than the histories of their own

people they'd heard recounted time and time again. The darkness outside Frobo's windows suddenly became even darker, for
the evening's film had just ended and the light of the projector
went out. The voices of the weary hobbicks returning to their
various neighborhood holes were heard in the road outside
Frobo's doors. He quickly rose from his chair and proceeded to
shut each and every one of his beloved drapes. The last thing he
wanted was for some roving eye to spot him conversing with
someone who looked an awful lot like a Grandalf impersonator.
Politely, the wizard had waited for him, and upon the comple-
tion of his endeavor, Frobo returned to his chair.

"But what would a decent, hobbick loving bloke like the
filmmaker want with you, Mister Grandalf™?" asked Sham.

"His purpose became clear very soon," responded Grandalf,
his deep rumbling voice echoing with the gravest tones Frobo
had yet heard the wizard use. "I could see the lust in his eyes
the moment he spotted the ring upon my finger. I remember
he danced around the issue for a few hours, but eventually he
told us." Grandalf paused, apparently in deep thought, recol-
lecting his encounter with the filmmaker. "It was a sunny day,
and the wind was in the east when he boarded our ship. The
light blue waters of the sea where we set anchor were calm and
clear, but the evening was growing nigh. We welcomed him
aboard with as much courtesy as we could muster, but from
the time he boarded our vessel, there were only three things
that could hold that stout little man's gaze. No matter where
he walked, and no matter to whom he spoke, his eyes were
fixed on the three magical elfen rings. And at last, when he
revealed to us his purpose, the sun was nigh setting, and
standing there in the shadow of the mast, he refused to halt
pursuit until we surrendered the three elfen rings of power to
him."

"Did you do it?! Did you hand them over?" cried Sham
eagerly from the edge of his chair.

"What in the name of the Chire do you think *this* is?!" shouted Grandalf, flashing the elfen ring of fire before them.

"Well, I think..." pondered Sham with a most sincere expression, "I think, although I could be wrong, that that is a ring, Mister Grandalf™ sir."

"Good heavens," Grandalf exclaimed, snorting in incredulity and running his fingers up over his brow through his long strands of white hair.

"Mister Grandalf™, sir," interrupted Martin. Rising from his own armchair he stepped over to Sham's chair and stood next to him. "Sham here somehow is even thicker in the head than he is in the gut." Martin then threw a sharp elbow into Sham's midsection. The elbow bounced back, and Sham chuckled. "See what I mean sir?" Martin said, returning to his seat.

"As round as a barrel, and as thick as the hide of an Olifont," said Grandalf. "This, my dear Sham, is the elfen ring of fire. And I did NOT surrender it to your precious filmmaker. No one knew what would happen to the powers of the other rings if that *Insidious Ring* could be destroyed. Some thought their powers would be lost. Others thought they would mostly fade. I can tell you that the power of the ring of fire has faded, but not nearly as greatly as I assumed it would have. Many of its powers still remain, and I must assume, so have the powers of the other rings."

"But what became of the other rings after that *Insidious Ring* was destroyed?" asked Frobo.

"That is the very question I began pondering as soon as the filmmaker asked us for the elfen rings of power. If he wanted the three, I had to also assume that he desired to obtain the dwarfen rings, and the nine given to men. A shadow fell over my heart when he said it, and that shadow has not left. For Middlearth is in peril once again."

A baleful dread fell upon Frobo. He had grown up his whole life in peace, especially since moving into Daggend. He'd been brought up to believe his grandfather had taken care of any evil left in Middlearth eleventy-one years ago, and that knowledge had always been a comfort to him. But now, with the return of Grandalf, and this talk of magic rings and peril... well he would just as soon rather spend the rest of his life in the Chire, enjoying the simple comforts and pleasures that it brought him. He shifted in his chair and shook his fear and dread away. It was more than likely that Grandalf was overblowing this entire issue, making a mountain out of a hobbick hill. He assured himself that he had nothing to truly worry about.

"But I don't understand," said Happy. "What would a good-hearted bloke like the filmmaker want with the elfen rings of power?"

"I have my suspicions, though I can't prove them," said Grandalf.

"Then, why even bring them up?" asked Martin. "I have my suspicions as well, but you don't see me over here bragging about them, like I know more than the rest of my friends, do you?"

"Then you'd best keep them to yourself!" snapped the Wizard. "But to me, the answer is quite clear. Your precious filmmaker has simply run out of material. You see, he has no true creativity within himself, all he can do is attempt to mimic in vain mockeries. First, he made the films of the story of the most famous hobbick who ever lived, a profitable yet poor interpretation of the original story. Then, he made *The Hobbick* films, once again turning a penny with a near abomination of the original. But now he has no more stories to ruin. He has run out of material. He hopes that the rings of power will give him something he has never possessed: the creativity to write his own story."

"Blimey!" spluttered Sham. "That's the smartest thing I've ever heard. Of course, that's why he wants the rings!"

"He is not the only one..." said Grandalf.

"What do you mean?" asked Frobo.

"Leaving Middlearth was very hard on your alleged grandfather, Frobo. We have no idea of the toll that losing that *Insidious Ring* forever at the dark mountain had on him. If we could've taken him straight to the West... but alas, hope for his healing and restoration is over. He never even made it back to shore."

Frobo's head shot up and his eyes burst open. "What are you talking about?" he shouted. A terrible fear, far worse than before enveloped him and dread overcame him.

"The loss of that *Insidious Ring* was too great of a pain for your grandfather, the most famous of all hobbicks to endure. When the filmmaker boarded our ship and began to speak of the elfen rings of power, your grandfather's strength of will failed. When no one was looking, he flung himself overboard and began trying to swim back to Middlearth."

"But why?" shouted Frobo, "Why didn't you stop him? Why didn't you make him stay?"

"Stop him? Make him? Why, I do not think I could have *made* him do anything, not without breaking his mind. Your grandfather made a choice, Frobo, and we let him. For none of us wished to become like the dark lord, ruling and controlling all others. Being separate from that *Insidious Ring* was torture to your grandfather, and I can only guess that having the three elfen rings discussed so openly pushed him over the edge. He cannot reclaim it now that it has been destroyed, for it is truly gone forever. But his intention was clear to me. Return to Morbor, to the foundations of the dark tower, and search to find the other rings of power."

"Gasp!" shouted Sham.

"Sham, you idiot, you don't say 'gasp,' you just do it! How many times do I have to explain..." Martin began his rebuke, but he was cut short by Frobo.

"Did he make it?" asked Frobo. "Do you think he could've swum all the way back to Middlearth?"

"We were over a thousand leagues away when he jumped. Your alleged grandfather drowned, Frobo, just like his parents." Grandalf wiped a tear from his eye. "He should've stayed in the boat! If only he would've known that we were coming back here anyways. I would've let him leave us."

A mix of shock and grief overwhelmed Frobo. He of course had known that he would never be able to meet his famous grandfather in life, but this ending... it was just too sad.

"You mustn't blame yourself, Grandalf," said Happy, rising from his chair to reassure the crying wizard. He placed his hand on the old man's shoulder and offering his handkerchief. "It wasn't your fault."

"Thank you, lad," said Grandalf, taking the handkerchief to wipe his eyes. "I keep telling myself that. There was little hope left for the most famous hobbick who ever lived if we couldn't reach the West. The memory of that *Insidious Ring* had simply become unbearable for him. But he is in a better place now."

"Where?" shouted Frobo. "The bottom of the sea!"

"I meant to say his *spirit* is in a better place now," said Grandalf. "Believe me, Frobo, the loss of your grandfather is one of the hardest I've ever had to endure, but his spirit and memory live still."

"So where does this leave us?" asked Happy.

"It leaves us in the Chire, of course..." said Sham, feeling as if he'd finally said something smart.

"We must..." began Grandalf.

"Decide what to do with the time that is given to us!" recited Sham in his best impression of the wizard.

"Will you hold that ridiculous tongue of yours for five seconds!" shouted Grandalf. Sham immediately moved his thumb and forefinger to his mouth, pinched the end of his tongue, and began to count.

Grandalf groaned but endeavored to otherwise ignore

Sham's behavior. "What we have to do is destroy the remaining rings of power before they fall into the wrong hands."

"We have to find them all, and take them to the fiery mountain, don't we?" said Martin.

"Don't be a fool," said Grandalf. "That was only for that *Insidious Ring*. The rest are destroyed more easily. A simple hammer, sword, or axe should do the trick."

"Well, that's simple enough," said Martin. "Shall we start now?" Martin rose from his chair and began rummaging about in Frobo's kitchen. In a matter of seconds, he had procured for himself a large hammer. He was standing to the left of Grandalf, slightly behind his chair and just out of the wizard's line of vision. Grandalf placed his ringed hand on the small chair side table next to him. As soon as his hand relaxed, Martin raised the hammer over his head and swung the hammer down with all of his might onto Grandalf's fingers!

The wizard cried out in pain, snatching his hand away and holding it close to him. The elfen ring of power had not shattered but had cracked over Grandalf's finger. Completely shocked and with their mouths agape, the hobbicks watched as Grandalf's finger rapidly began swelling around the fractured ring. "What in the name of the West do you think you're doing!" the wizard shouted. His face paled with glares of death at Martin, as the pain surged through his hand. He looked ready to whip out his staff at any moment and smote Martin where he stood.

"Trying to destroy your ring, obviously," shrugged Martin. He looked at Frobo, Happy and Sham as if seeking reassurance that he had done the right thing. "If you wouldn't have moved, I could've gotten it!"

Frobo's and Happy's jaws dropped to the floor. What was Martin thinking? Even Sham would've known better.

Grandalf held up his hand and groaned in pain. "If you think you could hold still better, then next time, we'll put the ring on *your* finger before destroying it!" Grandalf began muttering to himself again, holding his increasingly swelling finger as Frobo and the other hobbicks watched anxiously.

"Cursed hobbicks, confounded creatures. I wasn't prepared for this... I wasn't prepared for this... my task was over... why did you send me back here?" The wizard's face twisted and contorted with anger and the pain of his finger. It reminded Frobo of the old knotty tree stump in the middle of Hobbickton square, that the children frequently painted faces on and dressed in various hats and scarfs. *Sir Knots* was the stump's affectionate nickname. And the wizard's face, wringing in agony and frustration, was a spitting image of *Sir Knots*.

As the wizard muttered to himself, the Hobbicks were reminded, as they always were when someone spoke to themselves of the creature Grollum. They couldn't help but cringe and imagine his gruesome, raspy, repugnant voice crawling into their ears in those horrid scenes of the films. Terrified of such mutterings, Sham began to suck his thumb.

But Grandalf's unbearable soliloquy continued. "At least I still have it... at least the nincompoop didn't destroy it... *ahhhhh!*" he cried out in pain again. For while speaking about his *precious* but damaged ring, he had tried to lift his hand to inspect it more closely, and a spasm of pain had taken him.

Frobo slowly started to feel nauseous at the wizard's talk, for the parallels to the creature Grollum were all too noticeable. He grabbed his stomach, hoping the extra pressure would mitigate the rising pain. As he shifted back and forth, unable to stay still, he caught a glimpse of something different in Grandalf's ring.

"Grandalf™," Frobo said, "I just noticed something." He pointed to Grandalf's now purple finger. "The stone on your ring. It seems to be flickering."

"What?" screamed the wizard, as he jerked his throbbing hand before his face. Barely visible under the swelling skin, he could clearly see the light of the red stone, but it was now flickering, as if some power within was fading. Grandalf's eyebrows bristled and twisted above his eyes so terribly that Frobo thought he might end Martin right then. "You imbecile!" Grandalf shouted.

"I'm the imbecile? You said we needed to destroy the rings, and I said we should get on with it," started Martin. He shook his head and tried to toss the hammer up and catch it in a neat trick, as if he dealt with hammers frequently. But it was far too heavy for him, and the hammer fell right through his hands on its way to thudding against Frobo's floor. Martin continued as if this had been intentional and dusted off his hands as if wiping them clean of the whole affair. "I don't know much about you wizards, Mister Grandalf™, but us hobbicks aren't ones to waste time when there's a job to be done. Especially when that job is a warm dinner that needs tucking away after a hard day's work. And the way I see it is, one ring of power down is a nice day's work, so how about you thank me for doing your job for you, and let us get on with that supper?"

Grandalf cried out in frustration, clenching his fists, but then quickly released the ringed hand from the clench after the spasm of pain shot up his arm. He then rose from his chair, standing up to his full stature.

"This," cried Grandalf, leaning over Martin and peering into his eyes while pointing to the flickering ring on his swelling finger, "is the best chance we have at defeating the enemy! Who knows who has the other rings of power by now? But we are going to need *this* one to have a chance of recovering them! It's the best weapon we have, you fool hardy hobbick!"

Just then, three solitary knocks sounded from Frobo's door. A hush fell over the room.

Frobo shot up from his chair and tip toed his way to his round green door, the very same door that Grandalf himself had knocked upon so many times before and had once even burned the first letter of his name into. Frobo leaned forward, fingers barely pressing against the grains of the wood, and held his ear close to the door. To his astonishment, he heard absolutely nothing outside. How odd? Had the three knocks been nothing more than the tapping of one of their feet? He turned to look at Sham who had been known to be guilty of this before when... he heard something. It was the faintest sound, but yes, it was something. Something was breathing just outside his door; he was quite sure of it. And therefore, with that knowledge he delayed no longer before yelling at the top of his lungs, "Who is it?!"

"One of The Filmmaker's goons!" said the voice from outside before correcting itself, "I mean, Trademark Enforcement Squad of Middlearth Enterprises. It's been reported that the Grandalf™ impersonator was seen in this area and we're searching all the hobbick holes. Open up."

"Just a moment!" Frobo yelled, running back into the living room to develop a plan.

Sham gasped, "What are we going to do?"

"Wait a minute," whispered Happy. "Wait a minute, wait a minute, wait a minute..." He was so nervous that he began pacing about the room. The way his bright red hair bounced with every anxious move, it reminded Frobo of a small fire playing in a field.

"Could you use your ring to become invisible?" Happy asked Grandalf.

"Perhaps I could have," said Grandalf holding up his throbbing ringed hand, "if some fool hadn't damaged it five minutes ago!"

The goon knocked again, "Open up, or we're breaking the door down!"

"Just a minute," said Frobo, "I'm... getting dressed... just got out of the bath!"

"Frobo, what are you talking about?" said Sham. Standing up

confused and scratching his head, he said, "You haven't bathed in days!"

"Sham, it's to keep the goons distracted! But how in the Chire do you know the last time Frobo bathed?" said Happy.

"Well," said Sham, looking furtively from side to side. He then puffed up his chest to appear a little taller and said, "I'm no peeping Tom, it's the smell!" He then started sniffing the air as if this would somehow strengthen his argument. "I've got a very sensitive nose."

Frobo reckoned he did *smell* at that moment, for he had begun to sweat in his ragged search for a place in his home to hide the oversized wizard. He was quite sure he looked as if he needed a bath too (though he had in fact taken one that morning), for his hair was a disheveled mess after the film fight in the lawn and this frantic panic-stricken rush through Daggend. Neither the pipeweed cabinets, the old treasure holes, the bread cellar, nor even the dinner table were big enough for Grandalf to hide in, who was becoming increasingly more frustrated each time Frobo tried to cram him into the various small spaces.

More pounding echoed through the hallway. "You've got thirty seconds till we tear this door down, Mister Frobo!" said the goon. "I don't care if you are the son of Froyo Daggins!"

"Give us a moment," cried Sham. "We were taking a bath and are getting dressed!"

"Sham, what's wrong with you?" said Frobo. "Now all of the Chire's going to think...!"

"What? The bath was your idea!" said Sham.

"I've got it!" said Martin. He had the same crazed look in his eye he'd had the time he'd gotten them all to break into Maggie Buttermoor's milk vats and they drank 'till they vomited. The stunt had gotten them all sent up to Sackville for two weeks of hard labor while they *thought about the kind of hobbicks they wanted to be*. And now, with that same crazed look in his eye, Martin held Grandalf's staff in his hands, wielding it like it was a pitch-fork. He pointed the bright glowing end of it directly at Grandalf.

"What now?" groaned the wary Wizard.

"I'll use this wand to make you disappear!" said Martin.

"Wait!" said Grandalf, shaking with fear, "That's not a wand, it's a staff! And you don't know how to use it!"

"It's magical, isn't it?" said Martin. "How hard could it be?"

"Alright, Mister Frobo! Time's up!" the goon shouted from outside. A loud boom resounded from the door a moment later. Frobo was quite sure it wouldn't hold for long for it was far too old to be able to maintain any sort of real structural integrity.

"Look," said Grandalf holding up his hands to Martin but speaking to all of them, "I'll just explain that I'm an imposter who was passing through, but please don't!" It was too late. Frobo's door was already hanging on its last unbroken hinge. Just before the ancient thing broke, Martin shouted the only spell he'd ever heard with the staff pointed straight at Grandalf, "Abbra Kedarbbra!" In the same moment, Happy darted from the bathroom with a bucket of soapy water.

The door broke at last, falling flat on Frobo's entry rug, and the goons rushed in as Happy flung the bucket of water on Frobo and Sham. But in the same instant, a blinding flash of light filled the whole room, stunning the goons the moment they stepped over Frobo's threshold.

"What in the name of the filmmaker is going on here?" shouted David the goon.

"Sorry, sir!" said Frobo, dazed from the light and the douse of soapy water that had just been dropped on his head. He tried to wipe the suds from his eyes. "Just a late-night bath and a few too many ales."

"You know us little folk and our ales, sir," belched Sham. "Can't drink 'em fast enough."

"And what is *that?*" asked another goon, pointing behind the four hobbicks.

Frobo wondered what he could be pointing to. Hopefully, Martin's spell had worked and Grandalf was invisible, but when had anything Martin tried ever worked? Fortunately, Frobo knew just what to say.

"That, sir, is a beer dispensary. It pulls beer straight from the Brandybeer River, and it was installed by my good gardener here, with whom I have a perfectly platonic relationship... what I'm trying to say is, we don't make a habit of taking baths together, I mean, we *never* bathe together," but Frobo was cut off.

"No," said the goon, "I'm talking about *that!*"

Frobo winced, holding his breath and bracing for the inevitable, as he turned about. Of course, Martin's 'magic' had been nothing more than a cheap parlor trick: lights, smoke and mirrors. The real Grandalf was still standing right behind them. It was just that, for some strange reason the wizard was standing as still as a stone. That would've been strange enough if not for the fixed look on his face of anger, shock and... could Frobo call it madness? The wizard's right arm stretched out towards the place where Martin had struck him with the spell.

"You four have got some explaining to do," said David the goon.

"Well, you see sir..." began Sham, shifting his weight and holding out both hands as if he was a king addressing his subjects. "It all started when you were banging on the door. We were wondering how best to distract you and make you believe we weren't up to anything suspicious see..."

"Shhhhhhhhhhhut it, Sham," shushed Martin.

"Oh, come off it, Martin," said Sham. "The jig's up and run it's course. You see, we've been..."

"*Sculpting* sir!" interrupted Martin again. The other hobbicks turned to look at him in shock. In fact, Martin looked quite shocked himself that he had just spoken thus.

"Sculpting?" asked David.

"Yes sir," replied Martin. "Sculpting. We've been sculpting this life-sized wax statue of none other than the greatest, most famous wizard who ever lived, Mister Goon: Grandalf™." Frobo couldn't believe what he was hearing. And yet, as he continued to stare at the perfectly still Grandalf, or what had been Grandalf... what in Middlearth had Martin done?

"And what were you four going to do with this wax statue?" asked David. He was standing in the center of the room, admiring the wax statue's likeness, closely inspecting it perhaps for any flaws or oddities. The other goons had all fanned out and were rummaging through Frobo's house, checking to see if they could verify that this statue was in fact all that the hobbicks had been hiding.

"Donate it!" exclaimed Happy. "We were going to donate it to the Old Moth House, weren't we?"

"Of course, we were," added Martin. "Wouldn't dream of trying to turn a personal profit from Middlearth Enterprises property. No sir, we wouldn't."

"Of course not," said David. "So, all the rumors about the old Grandalf™ impersonator weren't true at all. It was just your statue people were seeing?"

"Of course, it was," said Martin, chuckling nervously.

"Well then," David the goon breathed a sigh of relief. "I'm glad we can finally put this issue to bed. Goons, I mean, men, take the wax statue and let's go. The boss will be happy to have another piece of memorabilia to make money off of."

"Wait a minute," said one of the goons. "Boss, are we sure this thing is wax? It's a perfect replica..."

At this, one of the goons walked up to the wax statue, struck a match and held it underneath one of Grandalf's hands.

As the wax hand began melting, Frobo though he heard a faint muffled groaning near the statue.

"What was that?" said David.

"Oh, that was me, sir," said Sham, feigning that he'd made the noise. "Upset stomach, I mean... hungry. I'm just hungry, that's all."

"That didn't sound like a stomach growl to me," said David, eyeing Sham suspiciously. "Forget it. Grab this thing and let's get it to the Moth House."

As the goons lifted Grandalf from the mid-section and left Daggend, Frobo thought he heard another groan come from the wax statue of Grandalf.

"Middlearth Enterprises thanks you for your generous contribution to our collection," said David. If only Frobo could have closed the door behind him. Instead, he stood in the empty round threshold, watching as they loaded Grandalf up into their cart, and wheeled him away.

Sham was the first to speak up behind him, "Goblins and Olifonts, how did you do that?"

"Never mind how he did it," said Frobo, "*What* did you do?"

"I turned that old storm crow into wax, didn't I?" said Martin.

"And why did you do that!" yelled Frobo. He crossed his arms as he often did when trying to stay calm, but he doubted there would be any comfort for the fear that had taken his heart.

"Didn't have a choice, did I?" asked Martin. "What do you think those goons would've done if they'd seen Grandalf™ when they came in?"

"I thought you were going to make him disappear?" said Happy.

"How would I do that?" asked Martin, rolling his eyes. He scoffed as if the mere suggestion was the most ridiculous thing he'd ever heard. Then, he turned his back to them and walked from the living room into Frobo's dining room. Taking a seat at the long table, he grasped a mug of beer and drunk as if it was a hard-earned treat.

Frobo was flabbergasted. He marched into the dining room in pursuit of Martin. He meant to give the hobbick a piece of his mind about this issue and wasn't going to let Martin get away with what he'd done. But Martin was just sitting at the table, leaning back and slouching in an utter state of relaxation while he sipped his beer. Frobo then spoke up sharply, "Well perhaps you could have made him disappear the same way you turned him into wax!"

He then took his own seat at the table across from Martin and drank a swig from his own mug. He was joined by Happy. The warm beer touched his mouth and soothed his anxiety for the moment. If it wasn't one of the finest he'd ever had, he wasn't Frobo Daggins. Yes... he was Frobo Daggins, heir of the most famous hobbick who ever lived. But despite the wonderful taste of the beer, an uneasy dread was slowly overcoming him. His stomach was churning and aching with discomfort. He brushed his forehead and felt beads of sweat upon it. He was the heir of the most famous hobbick who ever lived, but his grandfather had never been put into a situation like this. How on earth were they going to get Grandalf back?

"I don't see why you're all so upset about it," said Martin. "Besides, I'm not even sure that is the real Grandalf™."

"Hmm..." Happy mused, looking up and tapping his forefinger to his nose. "Based on the fact that you used his staff to turn him into a large candlestick, I'm going to guess he was the real thing."

Martin squinted at Happy, considering this for a moment. "True," he said. Then he shrugged and held up his hands, "but how was I supposed to know that before I used it?" Upon asking the hypothetical question he resumed the drinking of his beer. Martin had transformed the poor wizard into a statue of wax, but at least he wasn't going to lose any sleep over what he had done.

"I don't believe this," said Frobo, regaining some sense after swallowing another swig of the delicious beer. It tasted like Frobo imagined pure sunshine would taste, liquid gold with hints of berries and barley. "You just turned the greatest wizard in history into a sculpture of wax. You just turned the greatest wizard in history into a *sculpture of wax!*"

"He's gonna kill you when he wakes up, Martin," said Happy. "I mean, when you turn him back into himself."

"You must be quite mad!" said Martin, pounding the table with his mug as he slammed it down and pointed his long finger at Happy's face, "I'm not turning him back! He'd kill me!"

"We're not going to let the goons of Middlearth Enterprises keep the greatest wizard in history in the Old Moth House, Martin! What's wrong you?" asked Frobo.

"Oh alright, alright," said Martin. "I was afraid you might see it this way." He rose from his chair and paced to one of Frobo's windows, resting his arms on the sill and peering out into the darkness. Frobo had no idea what the hobbick was looking at for the moon was black that night, and there was naught to see outside.

"Besides," said Frobo, remembering the details of their conversation with Grandalf, "we need him to help us destroy the rings of power. I don't think there's anyone in Middlearth who knows more about them than he does." What had they gotten themselves into? Destroy the rings of power? Was he crazy? He couldn't destroy any rings of power, he was Frobo Daggins, and he was living his best life in Daggend. "But..." he thought to himself, "perhaps this is how *he* felt. Perhaps this is how the most famous hobbick who ever lived had felt." If he really was his heir, which he was, then he was born for such a quest.

"Come to think of it," said Happy, continuing their conversation, "that wizard still has one of the rings of power on that finger of his."

"Which I was trying to destroy!" added Martin, opening his eyes wide and pointing his finger at all of them in his defense. "I still can't help feeling like you all, (including Grandalf™) should be thanking me for that."

"Next time we get a ring of power, we'll put it on your finger before beating it to dust with a hammer," said Happy.

"Brandybeer... oh sorry, Mister Grandalf™ sir, I didn't see your beard..."

Frobo, Happy and Martin turned about towards the living room where the noise had come from. There was Sham, lying on the floor, fast asleep in a dream. He'd never made it into the kitchen.

"Apologizing in his sleep now too, is he?" said Martin. "Well, that's it for me gents. Frobo, dibs on sleeping in the bread cellar. It's too late to go all the way back to Cricket's Hollow and I sleep better on your stone floor than I do on my own bed."

"I s'pose I'll stay the night too," said Happy, massaging his hands across the pockets on his waist coat. "We can get a quick start on our rescue plan in the morning."

"Yes, Mister Grandalf™ sir, I've always known you think my grandfather was the real hero of the greatest story ever told." Sham was still sleep talking. "It goes without saying really... and we all know the filmmaker thinks he is... between you and me, I've always thought the Dagginses role in the whole story was somewhat overstated."

"I can't decide if he's more dense awake or asleep," said Martin. "And that's saying something."

"Forgive the poor chap," laughed Frobo. "I'll see you all in the morning." And without another word, he retired to his room, collapsed on his bed, and instantly fell into an uneasy slumber. He dreamt of a shaggy dark brown dog that was running and creeping throughout all the lands of Middlearth. He was a nice enough looking mutt, with clean well kempt fur and unusually large paws. But there was something very unsettling about the creature's large dark brown eyes. They had an ill-favoured look.

CHAPTER 3

THE FOURTH CONSPIRATOR

THE FOLLOWING MORNING THE HOBBICKS DID NOT AWAKEN early, at least not according to the standards of men. Frobo rose around eleven to find Happy curled up on his armchair like a cat. Martin was still asleep on the brick floor of his bread cellar, sprawled out so that each of his arms and legs were pointing like the four directions of a windvane. Sham should've been asleep on the large armchair next to Happy, but he was nowhere to be seen. Frobo sniffed the air. The aroma of sizzling meat, bacon he guessed, was wafting through the hall from his kitchen and he could hear the crackling pops of grease on a frying pan. Few things excited Frobo as much as breakfast, so he rushed through the hallway as quick as he could without breaking into a full-blown trot. He discovered Sham in the kitchen, fastidiously attending to three separate pans and frying an entire buffet of herbs, eggs and bacon. He had seemingly been up for hours, for the lines and creases of sleep that are so frequently evident on hobbick's faces were nowhere to be found on his.

"Sham, you're a marvel! How can I thank you?" asked Frobo, stepping into the kitchen. Although he was not normally the touching type, Frobo patted Sham quickly on the shoulder, feeling he owed it to him for the wonderful meal he was about to eat.

"Oh, don't you worry Mister Frobo," said Sham, tossing his golden hair out of his shining blue eyes. There was a large bead of sweat across his forehead that he wiped off with the upper arm of his rolled-up shirt. His hands were obviously indisposed at the moment, covered with mits that held two of the sizzling pans. "It's my third time making it, and I'll make it a fourth time if I have to. Kept thinking you'd all wake up, I did. And then I'd have to eat the whole thing me-self to keep it from going to waste, see. Twice! Now this is the third time making four breakfasts, and I feel sicker than I would've if I'd eaten a rotten Olifont, I do, Mister Frobo sir."

"What?" asked Frobo. He reacted by stepping back from Sham and the breakfast. Hobbicks were accustomed to multiple breakfasts of course, but Sham had eaten enough for the whole neighborhood. "Why would you make all *four* the second time? Why not just make three if you'd already eaten four by yourself?"

"Well, that's a silly question, Mister Frobo!" said Sham, shaking his head as if Frobo had just asked him why roosters crow or why dogs bark when they see strangers. "I didn't want you three to feel bad, did I? A good host knows to never let hobbicks eat alone, my old gaffer taught me that yes he did sir, and I mean to live by it."

Frobo thought Sham's logic, whether good mannered or not, made about as much sense as an elf falling in love with a dwarf, a plot point of the films he'd personally never bought into.

Martin and Happy awoke before Sham finished making the third breakfast, sparing Sham the need to eat all of their breakfasts again. When they'd all sat down at the table to eat, Sham placed a steaming hot plate before each of them. The breakfast was fried to perfection as always when Sham was in the kitchen.

The bacon especially was to Frobo's exact specifications, not too crispy, but not too juicy either. The bacon and the potatoes were the chief focus of his plate, while Happy aimed to put a dent in the eggs. Martin's plate was an even mix of bacon, eggs, and potatoes, and he found nothing to complain about or criticize in the meal. They each took their breakfast with tea, of course, and the hot steaming liquid did Frobo's senses well after his indulgent drinking the night before. After each of the hobbicks had eaten their fill to the great expense of Frobo's pantry, they all sat around his table and began to smoke their pipes. Simultaneously, they began to discuss the rescue plan. Their main debate was if they should try to save the old wizard at all, or if they should simply try to remove the ring from his hand, before continuing their quest for the remaining rings alone.

Frobo reminded them they would have no idea where to look for the rest of the rings without Grandalf, and Martin brought up the fact that they would have a much harder time getting anything accomplished once the filmmaker's goons knew they were a target. Sham still wasn't sure why they had to destroy the other rings of power in the first place.

"Is it the worst thing in the world if the filmmaker uses the rings to create more films?" Sham continued asking. "Personally, I like them, from the sense that they give a different perspective than the books, is all..."

"Yes, yes," responded Martin with a wink to Frobo, "we know you do."

After hours and hours of the repetitive discussion, the four hobbicks came up with the resemblance of a plan to rescue the poor old wizard and try to turn him back into his old self.

That evening, as most of the Chire gathered around the party tree to continue their viewing of the next film, the four hobbicks planned to sneak away to the Old Moth House. The darkness of night had stolen over the lawn for perfect film

viewing conditions, and the outdated previews were just beginning to end. There was not a light to be seen, save that of the
film, when suddenly, the projector shut off, and utter darkness
fell.

Through the darkness, the hobbicks heard the sound of a
creaking wheel, spinning across the lawn to the very front of it
where the films were projected onto the white sheets. The
projector flashed on again, its light flooding the lawn. In front
of the projector sheet, the filmmaker's goons stood beside a
cart at the grassy knoll. Something like this was unheard of in
the Chire. Everyone on the lawn paused with baited breath at
the scene occurring before them. The films were sacred, and
the secret fear that was rarely discussed by the hobbicks was of
the big goons taking the films away. David the goon stood tall
before them, ready to explain himself. But before the words
could leave his mouth, Fatty Bulger the Third threw a rotten
onion that struck David the goon's cheek.

For the second night in a row, chaos broke out. The film
viewing hobbicks that were scattered throughout the lawn
suddenly began pelting the wagon and the goons with rotten
vegetables of various degrees. David and the other goons ran for
cover behind the wagon and ducked down to avoid the
onslaught.

"Goblins and Olifonts!" said Sham. "It's like they were
expecting a bad show... but they've seen the films a thousand
times and always love them, don't they?" They were all standing
near the outer rim at the back of the viewing area and had just
been ready to sneak away to the Moth House when the
projector had shut off, and curiosity had gotten the better of
them. Now they were far too interested to leave.

"Well, I can't say I blame them after hearing about Young
Brickhead's town hall forum," said Martin.

"What are you talking about?" Happy asked. "Nobody told
me about any town hall forum."

"Oh, you missed out then. The whole entire thing was dedicated to laying out all of the film's plot holes. Turns out they're full of them," Martin said.

"It's just the waste that bothers me," said Sham. "I'm no Gramgee if I won't be wading through that stock of vegetables when this is all over. I'll wager there's a few taters in that lot that haven't gone all bad yet."

Frobo didn't know whether to laugh or wretch at the thought of Sham rummaging through the pile of rotting vegetables. He could picture the young lad pushing his trusty wheelbarrow across the lawn later that evening, stopping and pausing to inspect each and every squashed tomato's ripeness. He probably wouldn't stop muttering his dear old gaffer's proverbs to himself once during the whole affair.

"Enough!" David the goon cried at the top of his voice from behind the wagon. The vegetable pelting finally ceased, but whether it was from tired arms or the goons commanding voice, Frobo did not know.

"What in Middlearth Enterprises is going on here?" David shouted, raising his head at last from behind the wagon.

"We're throwing 'em cause you goons are trying to stop the show!" cried Fatty to a roar of approval from the other hobbicks. Then he pulled his arm back, as if ready to release another volley. "That's a violation of our agreement!"

"I am doing no such thing!" cried David the goon. He locked eyes with Fatty Bulger the Third, recognizing him as the main instigator of this disturbance. David's words, along with his piercing gaze, compelled Fatty to lower his arm. The crowd of angry hobbicks calmed themselves as he did so.

"I am here to make an announcement," David said.

"Booo!" the reached back into their jackets for more rotten vegetables, but David threw his hands defensively up into the air.

"It's a *brief* announcement!" David shouted.

Cheers arose from the crowd.

"We should get going," said Frobo. "This is the perfect opportunity to slip away."

"No, let's stay for a moment," Martin said to the others, tapping Frobo on the arm. "I want to hear this."

"I am here to announce that a few of you have done something truly remarkable," said David the goon.

Murmurs of approval echoed through the crowd of hobbicks.

"Several of you hobbicks, who were previously considered... oh what's the word?" He snapped his fingers in the air as if doing so would conjure the word that escaped him. *"Unoriginal..."* he said at last.

"Get on with it, goon! We haven't got all night to listen to you yap!" shouted a stout hobbick near Fatty Bulger the Third. Roaring laughter emanated through the crowd, and Sham threw a jesting elbow into Frobo's ribs. He was grinning as all hobbicks did when one of the big people "got their due through and through," as hobbicks liked to say to each other.

"Well," continued David the goon with as condescending of an air as he could conjure, "maybe unoriginal *is* an accurate descriptor."

"The only *descriptor* I need for you, is that you've got the ears of an Olifont with the teeth of a warg!" yelled the same hobbick back to David.

The hobbicks erupted in laughter once more.

"Not to mention the breath of one!" added Fatty the Third.

Hobbicks were now keeling over with laughter all over the lawn. This was better than the film. Only orks and trolls got their comeuppance in the films, but a few of the hobbicks (Fatty Bulger the Third and his friends included), remembered what happened to the big people who stuck around in the Chire in the real story of the most famous hobbick who ever lived.

"Silence!" shouted David the goon, his face like that of an angry mother goose who's lost control of her chicks. Despite his puffed-up chest and clenched jaw, the hobbicks continued to roll around the lawn with laughter. When at last they grew tired of their joke, David continued. This time he got to the point.

"This," David said, pointing to the wagon, "was created by some of you." David motioned to the goons who had pulled the wagon up to the front of the lawn. One man yanked a linen sheet from the wagon revealing nothing other than...

"Grandalf!" shouted Sham. In an instant, the entire lawn turned its attention from the wax statue in the cart that had been rolled in front of the screen. Each and every one of the hobbick's heads craned around to look at where Frobo, Martin, Happy and Sham were standing at the far back of the lawn atop the crest of the hill where they'd been about to slip away and out of sight into the trees. "I meant to say, Grandalf™!" shouted Sham. This satisfied them.

David sighed in frustration but continued. "This is a statue depicting none other than a likeness of your precious Grandalf™, I mean... *Grandalll*... guffaw! It depicts the famous wizard you're about to watch in the film!"

"How intriguing..." Frobo thought to himself, marveling at David's inability to pronounce Grandalf's name if he didn't say those two small letters (™) afterwards. He himself had encountered the very same difficulty yesterday.

"We know who Grandalf™ is, you big oaf!" shouted Fatty the Third's cousin Rory. The roars of approval again sang out from the hobbicks.

David didn't want to give them time to start rolling in laughter on the lawn again. And he especially didn't want them to laugh anymore at his expense. Before the hobbicks could grow too rowdy, he shouted out above their laughter saying, "This statue, although crafted in good spirits and donated generously to Middlearth Enterprises is a horrid likeness of the real Grandalf™, as you will see when you watch the films. I will leave it here for the duration of the evening, while the film plays. But at the end, this wax statue will be incinerated."

"Just like that *Insidious Ring!*" shouted a hobbick from the crowd amidst a cacophony of gasps.

"Exactly!" shouted David. "This statue is simply not a good enough likeness. Middlearth Enterprises will not and does not tolerate imperfection. After the burning of the statue, you will all have three days to produce a real quality likeness of Grandalf™, or else!"

Unable to contain himself at the suddenness of the announcement, Frobo shouted, "But what's wrong with it? Why burn it? Just last night one of your goons said it was nearly perfect!"

David looked at Frobo with a penetrating gaze. "It's true. This is a remarkable edifice. But this order comes from the very top. And as I said before, Middlearth Enterprises does not tolerate imperfection. We will take not less than an *exact* likeness."

"Or else what?" shouted Fatty the third.

"I don't know," said David. "I'll think of something really nasty, though!"

"Get off the lawn and start the show again!" shouted Fatty's friend to roars of approval.

"Son of Ashelob," said Martin under his breath. "Well, I s'pose that's the end of you know who..."

"Martin!" said Happy, slapping him across his forehead, "What's wrong with you? We're not giving up on the poor old crow that easily."

"Happy, he's only in front of the whole of the Chire!" said Martin. "Pardon me if I don't wanna be taken to the Lockholes for attempted robbery of Middlearth Enterprises!"

"I wonder who David was talking about," said Frobo. "He said the order came from the very top. Whose he referring to?"

"If I had to guess," said Sham. "I'd say it was someone whose very high sir. Someone whose so high they're up above all of this, at the very, very top of it all."

"Yes... but who?" Frobo repeated rhetorically. "I suppose it doesn't matter. And there's no backing out of this now Martin. We need Grandal... I mean, the wizard." Frobo winced again at his inability to spit out Grandalf's full name without using the trademark letters afterwards. It was like he had a case of the stutters!

"Let's just stick to the plan," Frobo continued. "What I wouldn't give for my dear old Grandad's *Insidious Ring* right about now, but we'll just have to steal him outright and proper, like good, decent Chirefolk."

"Alright then," said Martin. "But we're going to have to come up with a new plan. And quick! Because the film's already starting."

Their new plan was not overly complex. It involved a large woven piece of fabric, a shovel, a major distraction, and a very risky balancing act. Frobo circled around the dense tree line that surrounded the far end of the lawn behind the film-watchers. He would be the distraction when the time came. The wax statue of Grandalf was standing directly to the left of the film's linen screen.

Sham, whose role was the gardener, took his shovel and began to slowly meander over in the direction of Grandalf. If anyone asked him what he was doing, he would say his job was to bury the hot wax once the goons were finished burning it.

Martin and Happy had the difficult job. Once Sham was finished digging the hole behind Grandalf, Frobo would distract the crowd by emerging from the trees and shouting out something to draw the hobbicks attention. Though he had no idea what he would shout, Frobo assured his three companions of his improvisation skills and he was quite confident he'd be able to come up with something. When this happened, Happy would climb atop Martin's shoulders and stand directly in front of the Grandalf sculpture.

They'd gone back to Daggend to retrieve the necessary props for their disguise. Happy would don a large woven cloak-like fabric thrown over the top of them. There was also a fake beard, hat and mustache. They even practiced mimicking Grandalf's frozen pose. Martin and Happy would then remain perfectly still while Sham knocked over and buried the real Grandalf sculpture behind them.

With the plan in motion, Frobo gained his position at the back of the lawn of hobbicks and began to creep around the trees to the far right of the large lawn, just beyond the tree line. The film was playing.

"Yes, I know I'm an elf," said the gentile voice from the film. Frobo looked up to see the image of the undeniably beautiful elf maiden projected onto the curtain. The dialogue continued, "And if I'm being honest, I'm probably one of the most beautiful elfs to ever walk this Middlearth, but for some reason, I find myself..."

"Unable to resist me?" The gruff voice from whence came this line was abrupt and had always seemed out of place to Frobo. Something, and he wasn't sure what it was, just didn't seem right about this whole part of the films. Yet every male hobbick in the yard had started whooping and yipping as soon as the ruddy dwarf had said 'unable to resist me?' The dwarf in the film continued, "Unable to resist me? A dwarf who's less than two thirds as tall as you?"

"Yes," the elf maiden responded, "even though it be an abomination to my people, I cannot resist the instincts of the filmmaker..."

Shouts of "yippee," and "huzza" echoed throughout the lawn.

"Which is why," the elf continued, "I'm about to do something you'll *never* forget!" The female elf pressed her lips through the iron bars onto the dwarf's lips. The male hobbicks cheered and whistled to this, while the females had an entirely different reaction. Some frowned and shook their heads, while others rolled their eyes at their counterparts. Frobo saw elbows fly from several matriarchs into the ribs of their hobbick husbands who less than apologetically responded, "But it's my favorite part of the films!"

Frobo laughed to himself from the trees. He could see Happy and Martin meandering as close to Grandalf as they dared. Sham was already digging his hole with the shovel. Once Frobo saw Sham place the shovel over his right shoulder, he would create the distraction that would cause every hobbick on the lawn to turn their backs to the films for enough time to make the swap.

Now that the most popular scene of that particular film was over (the kissing scene), Frobo would have his best chance at creating his distraction. He just had to figure out what it was going to be. But at that very moment, Frobo saw something that quite distracted him.

Not twenty paces away from him, just beyond the tree line, a small group of dark figures were gathered. They all wore black clothing, and tones of their skin ranged in color from pale ashen grey to leafy green to dark black sable. When they opened their mouths, yellow fangs reflected in the light of the film.

"Orks!" Frobo breathed the word in a barely audible tone, shuddering and slinking to the ground behind a bush. His heartrate increased tenfold at the sight of them. He had never seen an ork before. But these orks were sitting on wooden chairs that seemed to have been built in place. To Frobo's utter dismay, they were leaning back and were watching the film! One of them was even eating from a bucket of the Southchire popped corn, the newest sensation of the Chire since they'd acquired the films.

Frobo then perceived a hearty yet inaudible laughter from the bouncing chest and wide open mouth of one of the orks. They all smiled and held their stomachs, doubled over and clapping each other on the shoulders, but not a sound was heard from them. The large white ork in the film had just killed one of his scouts, and the film watching orks found this funny!

Frobo was terrified beyond his imagination. How long had these orks been watching the films with them from just beyond the trees? So shocked was he, that he lost his wits. He forgot about Grandalf, the rings of power, and the grand plan to save the old wizard. Even so, fate was with Frobo, because a better distraction than the one he created would've been nigh impossible.

"Orks!" he screamed from the top of his lungs. He sprung from his hiding place behind the bushes and sprinted from the trees to the party lawn, throwing his hands in the air. He only had to hope he could outrun the orks across the field to the dip in the lawn where the hobbicks were watching. "Orks!" he continued to shout as he ran. "In the trees! Fire! Foes! To arms! To arms!"

Every hobbick in the lawn was soon up in arms, wielding the first thing they could find, (which happened to be the leftover rotten vegetables) and began hurling them at the forest as Frobo ran from the trees. And although they tried to throw them beyond him, the forest was much too far for the arms of the inebriated hobbicks. As he ran towards them, it seemed the rotten food seemed to rise into the air like a flock of crows that he'd scared up. They soared and flew into the air in sudden ascent, but then, unlike the birds, the rotting food fell upon Frobo. A potato pelted his stomach, a cabbage broke upon his face, and he was knocked to the ground by a flying melon. Each time he tried to rise again, it seemed that more of the rotting food was hurled at him. When he finally reached the party lawn, he was crawling like a wretched vagabond, gasping for breath, reeking of the filthy vegetables.

"Where are they, Mister Frobo?" shouted an eager young hobbick.

"Lemme at 'em, Mister Frobo!" shouted Fatty Bulger the Third.

"What were they up to, young laddy?" said an elder hobbick. "Back up, back up, give him some air!"

Frobo wiped a rotten cabbage from his hair and pulled an onion from the left leg of his trousers. He would be quite bruised tomorrow. "I said the orks were in the trees! Not that I was one of them!" he shouted.

They all drew back as Fatty's friend ran up to the encircling hobbicks. "I've just been at the tree line," he said. "And I didn't see a thing. No orks, no tracks, no sign of them. If I was a thinking hobbick, I'd say I think Mister Frobo's aim was to play a nasty joke on us all, yes I would."

This revelatory idea took a few seconds to reverberate through the crowd.

"It's not true," said Frobo. "I saw them! Five of them just beyond the tree line! They were, they were watching the film, just like us sitting and laughing and eating the Southchire Popped Corn."

They all murmured to each other. This was just too farfetched for their simple minds to comprehend.

"Aha! Mad Daggins is off his rocker now, ain't he?" shouted Fatty to the raucous laughter of the hobbicks. "I've been telling you he was all Sackville and no Daggins, but this story tops any of the foolishness that he might've gotten from his ancestors."

"You must fancy yourself quite the tale teller, don't you Mister Frobo?"

"He thought he'd take us all for a crop of cracked corn, didn't he?" The clamor of other such jeers resounded from the surrounding hobbicks, as they shot dirty looks at Frobo, who recoiled at every single one. His social status as the heir of the most famous hobbick who ever lived was the foundation of his identity, and now he was going to be nothing more than the laughingstock of the whole of the Chire.

"Let's start the film up again!" shouted Balfo Brickhead. "I'm as sore as a stubbed toe at Frobo, but we shouldn't let it spoil the entire evening." The circle of hobbicks that had first pelted him with rotten food and subsequently formed around him retreated to their customary places on the lawn as the film resumed. But Frobo was livid inside. He was confident he'd seen the orks. He knew he had. He'd seen the orks when he was hiding in the trees. The question was only this: why had he been there in the first place?

But of course; the *distraction!* He'd forgotten all about their rescue plan. Frobo looked up to the place where the statue had been standing next to the screen of sheets to see... yes, it had worked! Happy was squirming atop the shoulders of Martin. With the grey sheet thrown atop of him and the sheepskin they'd converted into a beard, they might just pass as the Grandalf statue.

Behind Happy and Martin, Frobo could see Sham cautiously piling more and more dirt atop the real wax statue. The plan had worked, even though this wasn't how they'd planned it.

Frobo kept his eye on Happy and Martin. Sham had almost covered Grandalf. He was just finishing the last few shovels of dirt when it happened. Frobo saw Martin's leg take one step backward and the pair began to topple over.

One of the hobbicks yelled, "Hey! What's going on with the Grandalf™ statue?" It was over. Happy fell from Martin's shoulders and instantly, the goons rushed in on them. Frobo ran straight into the tussle, but it was too late.

Their plan had failed. By the filmmaker, this was a disaster! Frobo's reputation would be the least of his worries if he got thrown into the Lockholes for attempted robbery of

Middlearth Enterprises merchandise. If he thought the pelting of rotten fruit and vegetables when running away from the orks had been bad, he was in for a rude awakening.

When the dust settled, the big goons had Sham, Martin, and the Grandalf statue all tied up, arrested, and thrown into the back of one of their big wagons. Quite curiously, Happy was nowhere to be seen as he'd somehow escaped.

"Now wait just one moment!" shouted Fatty Bulger the Third to the crowd. Everyone stopped what they were doing to listen.

"These two conspirators tried to steal the Grandalf™ statue," he said, pointing to Sham and Martin. "But they aren't smart enough to pull a stunt like that alone. I think they had a *third* conspirator! My good hobbicks, we've once again been *Dagginsed!* Frobo created the distraction about the orks, so they could steal the statue when our backs were turned. Seize him!"

Hobbicks were (except in rare cases) a peaceful, forgiving folk who enjoyed a laugh as much as a puff of *Middle-Aged Toby* after a pint. Their greatest insecurity was their small statured-ness as a people, which made them very distrusting of the "Big Folk." Their second greatest fear was of being tricked, bamboo-zled, hoodwinked, or as they privately referred to it, *Dagginsed*. These two fears played upon the minds of the hobbicks. Though at one time they would have detested the idea of the big folks tying up Sham and Martin, they were too enraged at that moment with the idea of Frobo trying to trick them. Deep in their hearts, though they dare not admit it, the hobbicks of the Chire had grown too afraid of the big folk tying *them* up. And so, Fatty shouted for the goons to sieze Frobo.

The term 'Dagginsed' had been coined for the second most famous hobbick who'd ever lived. His disappearing act with the inherently mistrustable Grandalf had been egregious enough, but at least the odd chap with his mischief had been out of the Chire. But lo and behold, as soon as the first of his possessions were put up for sale, that old bamboozler clicked his heels right up Bragshot Crow to stop the sale of his hole, only then to disappear before their eyes again almost sixty-one years later. They'd had enough. They'd been *Dagginsed* one too many times. The mere fact that Frobo was a Daggins only made matters worse.

The big men rushed Frobo, not even caring to take the time to verify if Frobo was part of the conspiracy. They bound his hands, and hoisted him into the back of their wagon alongside Sham and Martin. Then the food pelting started again. Frobo could barely see from all of it being thrown, but he could hear Sham mourning the loss of it next to him, as he was tied up and placed in the wagon.

"It's just the waste of it!" Sham cried, as he muttered the words between the barrage of rotten food. "And I won't even be able to come back tonight to inspect it all! Because we'll be in the Lockholes!"

"It's not a waste Sham, it's rotten!" said Martin who was ducking as low as he could in the wagon to avoid the array. "That's why they're being thrown in the first place."

"Well, if this much food had been in my house, I would've eaten it before it went bad!" retorted Sham.

"We don't doubt it Sham," said Frobo, assuring his young gardener. "We don't doubt it for a second."

The cart was rolling away now to the boos and jeers of the hobbick crowd. Frobo now knew that he was officially finished in the Chire. Even if they somehow escaped this mess, his reputation as the heir of the most famous hobbick ever would be forever in doubt. And he would always henceforth be known as the Sackville-Daggins who claimed that orks were watching the films from beyond the tree line so he could steal a wax statue. A ridiculous thing to have one's reputation be shattered by, but, as unbelievable as the scene had been even to himself, he *had* seen it.

When the wagon reached the Lockholes, Frobo remembered their missing friend. "Where's Happy?" he whispered, as the men came to unload them from the back of the wagon.

"He was right on top of me," he whispered to Frobo. "But somehow he got away."

Frobo had to remember they had still hope. Happy would rescue them.

"Is that all of them?" asked the goon at the gate to the driver.

"It's all we could get our hands on," said the driver goon. "One of them slipped out of reach."

"The boss won't like that," said the goon at the gate.

"No, he won't. I heard he was on his way. The statue has him interested. Wanted to inspect the wax once it melted."

"What for?"

"Beats me, I don't make the rules, and I ain't told the grand plan. I just follow orders, same as you."

Frobo, Sham, and Martin were led by the two goons into the darkness of the Lockholes. It was not a very big cave, but it was large enough of a space to hold prisoners, and it was confining enough to frighten even the coziest hole loving hobbicks. The Lockholes were a nasty little place. They'd been used to confine hobbicks in the past, and unlike the decent hobbick holes, the walls were exposed and raw with dirt, grubs, worms, and other things that squirmed and crawled beneath the earth. The cells were closed by wooden stakes that had been bound together and drove into the earth by men. Frobo was immediately concerned for his frock coat and breaches. He wouldn't be able to sit down anywhere in this place without getting them soiled.

A single torch protruding from the dirt wall lit the hole. Besides them and the men that escorted them inside, the Lockholes were empty. The goons carried the wax statue behind them. They deposited the hobbicks into a single, locked cell and placed the statue upright just outside the wooden door.

Then they exited the Lockholes to go and smoke outside. Frobo soon heard the vibrations of trotting hoofs and another set of rolling wheels on the Chire dirt. Another wagon had come.

"Who do you think that is?" asked Sham.

Several hushed moments were followed by the soft padding footsteps of whoever had ridden up to the Lockholes in the wagon. Perhaps it was Happy, impersonating someone of great importance there to save them. But as the iron outer door to the Lockholes swung upon its creaking hinge, the hobbicks realized they did not recognize the person who appeared in the doorway.

He was an old stout fellow, with a bald crown of a head that protruded over the rim of his short white hair. His beard was also white, and his skin was dark olive, a tone seen in the Chire only on the rarest occasions. His other facial features were all dwarfed by his very broad nose. He wore a stained cloak, and his swollen belly bulged beyond the rope he had tied around his waist in a vain attempt to restrain his girth. The man, whoever he was, strode up to the wax statue and began to chuckle, but then his beady black eyes twitched and shifted from hobbick to hobbick. Inspecting them, yet ignoring their confused stares, he turned back toward the statue.

"So Grandalf, you have returned just as I suspected you would. And in just the nick of time. You always do turn up right before the storm, don't you? Of course, you tell your hosts that you come to save them from the storm, but in fact you are nothing but a meddling wizard who brings the storm with him! But what has happened to you now? It looks like all that time at sea has you caught off guard." The man then turned to the three hobbicks, "You little folk are not exactly known for your guarded tongues, are you?"

"Begging your pardon, sir," interrupted Sham, "but I take

exception to that statement. I keep my tongue guarded just like me Marm taught me. I'm a real *gentlehobbick* sir."

"Sham, what are you talking about?" chided Martin. "This not the time for pleasantries!" The fearful tone in Martin's voice would've made an impression to silence any other hobbick. But Sham continued as if this discussion was taking place over afternoon tea.

"Well, let's just say if we were down at the old spit swapper bluffs, I wouldn't exactly be the type to kiss like an any old ill-mannered hobbick would. I'd be a real *gentlehobbick*, just like me Marm taught me and keep me tongue guarded behind my teeth, sir."

"If you ever make it to the spit swapper bluffs, be sure to tell that to the unfortunate hobbick lass that's with you," cackled Martin.

Sham looked back at him as if he didn't understand the reason for his laughter.

"Enough!" shouted the cloaked man. "Forgive me for not speaking more plainly, for I should've remembered you people are not known for your quickness of wit."

"Forgiven, sir," said Sham, who bowed with a slight curtsy as if he'd just received a compliment from a house guest.

The man laughed. Yet his maniacal mirth was of the sort that only brought unease to those who heard it. This person had spoken as if he knew Grandalf, but who in Middlearth did *know* him? Everyone from his dear old Grandad's story had left Middlearth by now, hadn't they? And everyone in the present was too young to remember him (unless they were elfs, and this person was obviously not an elf).

"Tell me, my little folk," the man continued. "For I know that you did not carve this statue out of wax yourselves. How did it come to you? Where did you get it?"

"Well," Sham began, "we just found him in Mister Frobo's living room, didn't we?"

"Sham, no!" shouted Martin, and he jumped to cover Sham's mouth his hand.

"Let him speak!" shouted the old man whose voice was so potent, so intoxicating, and so powerful, that suddenly it didn't seem that Frobo or Martin had the strength to stop Sham from continuing. Martin's knees buckled and his arm fell to his side from Sham's mouth. Frobo felt like he was in a daze. That voice was so persuasive, that Frobo wanted (against his better judgement) to hear Sham tell the story of how they found Grandalf too. He shook his head, regaining his wits against the persuasive voice. What was this devilry?

"Continue, my young hobbick. Tell us how you found this statue."

"Well, you see sir, as I was saying, we came in from drinking one night not that long ago… let me think just a minute, how many days ago was it? It wasn't three days ago, because that was me old Marm's dinner party, but it also couldn't have been two nights ago because that was the night I was still hungry after eating all of my dinner, and had to go trade the pup for some of his leftovers, so it couldn't have been then either, sir!"

The old man was growing tired of Sham's account of his last few evenings. Frobo breathed a short sigh of relief. He should've known that letting Sham talk was almost just as good as shutting him up. If he just didn't give away that this statue was the real Grandalf!

"I don't care when you found the statue, you nitwitted bushel footed creature! I want to know *how* you found it!" shouted the old man.

"But that's just it, sir," said Sham, not noticing the personal insults from the stranger. "We didn't find the statue. He found us! Walked right into Daggend, didn't he?"

Frobo's heart sank. They were finished. Sham could do much more harm talking than he could with his mouth shut.

However, this only made the old man's mustache bristle

with anger. "Do you take me for a fool, young master hobbick? Do you take me for a block headed nincompoop whose wits run no farther than your head stands above the grass you smoke! How dare you insult my intelligence! To think that I would believe a cock and bull story about a statue prancing and dancing around the Chire speaking to all the young hobbicks of the land and inspiring them to rise up in rebellion! You must take me for a *fool!*" He raised his voice to such a height that 'fool' echoed through the Lockholes.

"Not at all, sir. It's just that..." Sham tried to continue to no avail.

"SILENCE!" The great voice shouted so loudly that Frobo thought he could feel the walls of the Lockholes quivering. "I am not a man that I will be lied to, and I am not a hobbick that I will be made a fool of."

"Who is he, Frobo?" whispered Martin in a barely audible voice.

"I haven't the slightest idea," said Frobo.

It would've been impossible for the man to hear them speaking, for not even Sham had heard them, and he was only two feet away from them.

But nevertheless, in response to Martin's question, the old man turned and looked straight at them saying, "You wish to know who I am, my young hobbicks?"

Frobo said nothing, and neither did Sham, to the surprise and shock of all.

"If you wish to know who I am, I will tell you who I am," he shouted. "I! Am! SAUL-U-MAN-™!"

Martin screamed and staggered back further into the cell. Frobo merely stood stunned, immobile, and silent. But the old man, Sauluman, stood before them and laughed, somehow reminding Frobo of a coiling serpent.

"Sauluman™ the wise?" Sham asked through his shock.

"One and the same," Sauluman said.

"Sauluman™ the powerful?" Sham continued.

"Yes, yes, it's me, it's me." Sauluman said.

"Sauluman™ the White?" asked Sham, but this time skeptically.

"Sauluman™ of many colors!" shouted the wizard as he swept off his tattered stained cloak to reveal a shimmering robe that reflected an array of dazzling light.

"I thought Sauluman™ fell from the top of the tower of Isengrad™, right after Grandalf™ broke his staff?" said Martin. "Of course, that wasn't revealed until the release of the director's extended cut of the films. A detail that I'm sure was overlooked by the casual viewer."

An evil laugh rumbled from Sauluman. "Indeed, a detail of the films that I personally ensured was added to them. But I'm afraid you are incorrect, my young hobbick. Anymore guesses?"

"I know how you... I mean, how Sauluman™ died," said Sham.

"Yes, yes, please do tell," jeered Sauluman.

"He was murdered," said Sham. "He was murdered by Grema Snakelips, on the same ground we stand right now. In the Chire itself. He was trying to rule it he was, but he was stopped, he was. Him and all his goons were stopped by my old granddad and by the other three most famous hobbicks who ever lived."

"Bravo, young chap, bravo!" laughed Sauluman. "Another detail I was sure to have left out of the films! But I see that my designs have not entirely succeeded, for there is still at least one hobbick left in the Chire who does remember the story written by the most famous hobbick who ever lived."

Sham grinned at Frobo, feeling proud of himself as if his immense and very selective knowledge of the Chire's history would somehow be able to help them escape the Lockholes.

"You are only incorrect on one account!" snapped Sauluman.

His piercing voice startled the hobbicks, and especially

Sham. For he was very used to being wrong, just about things other than the history of that *Insidious Ring*.

"The only thing you were wrong about was that they *didn't* stop me. If they had, how would I be standing here before you now? No, no, no, my dear hobbicks, I am still very much alive and in charge."

"But how?" asked Frobo. "I remember the old story too. You were murdered. Here in the Chire. How is it that you've come back?"

"It's a nice little puzzle, isn't it?" drawled Sauluman, whose devious eyes shifted and cut to each of them like sharp knives as he spoke. "One that I could let you spend your whole lives trying to put together... if I wasn't going to kill you in the morning. But..."

"But?" asked Martin.

"Oh, son of Ashelob, I'll tell you. No!" he spun around to face them, his beady black eyes winnowing their gaze at the hobbicks as if they were freshly picked grain. "I'll make you guess how I did it!" he said, and once again those maniacal eyes opened wide as if the idea of making them guess possessed and now controlled his mind like an evil demon.

"Oh goodie, I love a good guessing game!" said Sham, rubbing his hands together in anticipation, excited to have something to pass the time.

"Good!" shouted Sauluman, "it'll be so much fun!"

"Is it just me," whispered Martin, "or does this fellow seem a little *Dagginsed?*"

Frobo drew back, feigning injury at the usage of the phrase. "Well, if by *Dagginsed* you mean a wealthy respectable individual who... oh son of Ashelob. Yes, fine. He does seem a little off the cock, doesn't he?"

"If this is the real Sauluman™," Martin continued whispering, "then we need to get Grandalf changed back as soon as possible."

"I hope the two of you are whispering about how I was able to come back from the dead!" interrupted Sauluman.

"Yeah," said Sham. "Help me out you two! I'll never get it by myself."

"What's in it for us if we do guess?" asked Frobo. "Will you set us free if we get it right?"

"No," laughed Sauluman. "Not possible, unfortunately."

Sham quickly slapped the back of Frobo's bare hand like he might've if Frobo was a young tween trying to steal carrots from his garden.

"Ouch!" cried Frobo, drawing back his hand. "What was that for?"

"It's not polite to bargain in the Chire, Frobo," chided Sham. "Not after what your dear old dad did when he bargained the rights to our names away, bless his soul. You should know that as well as any hobbick, and shame on you for not!"

"Sham, he's going to kill us in the morning!" shouted Martin.

"And Frobo's impoliteness is only going to make him want to kill us even more! In an even more excruciatingly painful way," reasoned Sham. "Besides Mister Frobo, you wouldn't want your last known conversation to be one where you were dreadfully impolite. Just imagine the stories they'd tell about you. Think about the reputation of your family name for once!"

"Sham, I'm trying to save our lives!" shouted Frobo.

But Sham stood in the corner, raising his chin so high they could see all the way up to the top of his nose, and said, "Some hobbicks just never did learn their manners, and for that Mister Sauluman, ahem, Sauluman™, I am sincerely sorry."

"I don't care about the manners of your ridiculous country!" said Sauluman. "I just want you to guess how I did it!"

"Oh yes sir, yes you do!" said Sham. "But you see, sir, I just won't stand for impoliteness. I don't take cheek if you understand me sir, and I don't tolerate elders taking cheek neither, and that means..."

But at last, and none too soon something that often occurs when people talk too much happened. Sham was cut off by a voice outside.

"Sharky!" shouted the voice. "Sharky, it's the filmmaker. He wants to talk."

Sauluman then proceeded to waddle out of the Lockholes. But before he left, he turned and yanked the red stoned ring from the finger of the Grandalf statue, bringing it close to his face and inspecting it. Sauluman cackled in laughter as he stared at the ring. "At last, I have beaten you, old fool. I have beaten you just as I should have eleventy-one years ago. Then I was robbed by chance. But my plans have prevailed. And yours have utterly failed." His evil laughter rose to such a deafening, terrifying pitch that Frobo could hardly stand to listen to it.

"Pardon me, Mister Sauluman, sir," Sham spoke up, "but I'm not entirely sure he can hear you. What with him being wax and all."

"It matters not my young fool!" jeered Sauluman. And with that he stormed out of the Lockholes wearing Grandalf's ring on his finger, and slammed the outer door shut behind him.

"Now he's got the ring, and he's meeting with the filmmaker!" said Sham.

"It's like the poor old wizard's plan was doomed from the start," said Martin, shaking his head. "I mean, I did like the old chap; he just got mixed up with the wrong folks is what he did. That's where he went wrong, the poor old buzzard."

"You're the one who turned him into wax in the first place," said Frobo. "Now you're blaming him for that?"

But Martin shook his head again in disagreement, holding his two forefingers to a gray lock as if he was a lecturing philosopher, "Now, now, Mister Frobo, mind your manners like Sham was telling you earlier!" Sham cocked his head, now listening, and tried to look important, in total unwavering agreement with whatever it was that Martin had just said.

Martin continued, "Don't forget Frobo, this Grandalf™ fellow came to *us* for help. But does he knock on the door first? No sir. He breaks in in the middle of the night like a burglar and waits for us in the dark, he does! And he does so, right after we heard that he's a fugitive! So, we sit around like a bunch of blockheaded fools listening to his story, all the while him giving us cheek, interrupting us with bits like, 'what in the name of the Chire is wrong with you?' and, 'all this ™ business sounds like ork mischief.' But I sat there, Mister Frobo, and as soon as he told me what our mission was, I did it see, and I made to destroy his powerful ring. And then what does he go and do but scold me for it and then get himself turned into wax five minutes later!"

"Of course. I suppose I should be thanking you for losing my ring!" said a familiar grumpy voice from outside their cell.

The Hobbicks all turned to see Grandalf, in the flesh, standing outside their cell. He was breathing, living, and *moving*. Most importantly and incredibly, he was no longer wax. Standing next to him, holding a staff that was more than twice his height, was their good friend Happy Brandybeer.

CHAPTER 4

THE DESOLATION OF SMOG

"QUICK!" SAID GRANDALF. "HAND THAT OVER BEFORE someone gets hurt." The wizard snatched his staff from Happy's hands before the hobbick could surrender it. "And conceal yourself the same way you did before!" Happy's bereft hands were left fumbling with something that he slipped quickly into his pocket.

"The manners of that old man," remarked Martin, gawking and pointing at Grandalf. The wizard ran to the door of the Lockholes and stooped to press his ear to the keyhole. Offense was written on Martin's face like the title of a book, incensed as he often became when he perceived some injustice. "Can you believe him? His life was just saved by Happy and..."

"We don't have time for please and thank you, young troublemaker!" shouted Grandalf from the door. "Now keep quiet and... wait! Someone's coming!" he whispered. Grandalf then ran back to his previous position in front of their cell. "Now be just as ignorant as you were a moment ago!"

They once again heard footsteps outside approaching. Grandalf snapped into the same pose he'd been frozen in as the wax statue, but this time with staff in hand. Frobo looked for Happy, but he was gone. What in Middlearth?

The door to the Lockholes swung open and Sauluman strode over the dirty threshold, gliding like a cresting wave of white foam. Grandalf stood perfectly still in front of him.

"Well," said Sauluman, a jeering grin forming around his yellow teeth. "What were you able to come up with?"

"Come up with?" asked Sham.

"Yes, yes, my dear dull hobbicks!" said Sauluman, with bristling brows. He was speaking so quickly that with every word he spewed saliva onto Frobo's forehead. "Surely you aren't daft enough to have forgotten that you were trying to find out how I managed to come back from the dead!" Sauluman now stood with his back to Grandalf, so that he was between the bars to the cell and the old wizard.

"By my potatoes!" shouted Sham, whose eyes opened even wider than usual. His right hand closed over his gaping mouth, utterly alarmed at his own forgetfulness. "Why Mister Sauluman, I knew there was something you wanted us to do when you left. I just got so distracted when..."

"Distracted?" screamed Sauluman. Frobo couldn't wipe Sauluman's saliva off his cheeks and forehead fast enough. "You are sitting in a dark cell under the earth! What could possibly distract you?"

"Oh n-n-no sir," stammered Sham, his big blue eyes looking as sad as a guilty cur's. "My apologies, but it was their fault, not mine, honest sir! And please, don't mistake my meaning sir, it's not that I didn't find your riddle intriguing!"

"Oh yes, you found it so intriguing that you forgot about it entirely," said Sauluman.

"It was their fault, sir! I promise!" babbled Sham. "If he hadn't..."

Frobo stopped Sham by throwing a sharp elbow into his ribs. The fool was about to give away their only hope of escape, all so he could make the person trying to kill them think he was a good mannered hobbick.

"Am I the only person in the world who finds it extraordinary that I returned from the dead?" He screamed these words at the top of his lungs and fell to his knees in manic desperation. Frobo had now wiped so much of Sauluman's spit from his face that the sleeve of his shirt was growing damp. Sauluman may have come back from the dead, but the crazed look on his face made him appear as nothing more than a phantom. Frobo had never thought phantoms could spit like this. "Am I the only one who thinks so!" Sauluman cried once more.

"I'm afraid..." said a deep, bumbling voice from behind Sauluman, "that returning from the dead isn't as impressive as it used to be. Not after I did it, at least."

Sauluman's face turned a ghastly shade of white, and his eyes grew large like white saucers. "Guards!" he shouted at the top of his lungs.

As the door burst open and the guards rushed in, a bursting shaft of light erupted from Grandalf's staff and flooded the Lockholes, stunning all inside, and knocking Frobo on his back. He heard the door to his cell unlock, then he felt himself being drug from the cell. He couldn't see who was dragging him out but to his left, Grandalf was pulling Martin and Sham from the cell.

"Can you run, Frobo?" whispered a friendly, familiar voice beside him. It was Happy speaking, but the hobbick... was he invisible?

"Yes!" said Frobo, realizing that he must be in shock for such a thought to cross his mind. The light was so bright, he could hardly see anything.

"To the wagon, young Hobbicks," shouted Grandalf, as Martin and Sham rose to run with Frobo. "To the wagon now!"

Frobo turned as he ran from the Lockholes to see Grandalf stoop down above Sauluman. Taking the red ring back from

Sauluman's finger, Grandalf burst through the door of the Lock-holes to the outside world, shafts of light still streaming from his staff. In an instant, the wizard leapt up on the wagon, striking the goon who sat atop the driver's perch with the end of his staff. "Get up here now! Get in the back!" Grandalf shouted to the hobbicks. They pulled themselves cautiously up onto the wagon Grandalf had chosen, an entirely different one than the wagon they'd taken to the Lockholes.

Sham was still lifting his girth over the wagon's back gate when Grandalf snapped the reins, urging the horses forward at a much greater pace than they were accustomed to. Frobo and Martin grabbed Sham's arms and hoisted him all the way into the back of the uncovered wagon. The horses charge jolted all three of them, and they fell hard onto the wagon floor. Frobo sat back up just in time to see Sauluman running from the entrance to the Lockholes with a face of frenzied fury. "Call them!" he bellowed. "Call them! Call them now!"

As the wagon rolled behind a grove of trees, the goon at which Sauluman had so rudely screamed produced a horn from his tunic. Its blast was a screeching, scrawling noise the likes of which Frobo had only heard in the films. It was the call of the black riders. Frobo shuddered. Had Sauluman brought them back from the dead too?

"What was that, Grandalf?" shouted Happy from beside him. Frobo drew back as he saw the hobbick appear out of thin air!

"I don't know," Grandalf said. He looked back as the wagon rumbled and tumbled along the road. "But you can be certain we're being pursued. See if there's anything in this wagon that could help us. If they pursue us on horseback, we'll soon be caught."

Nothing could aid Frobo as he tried to feel beneath him in the darkness of the wagon. It bounced along the road, and any light from the moon or the stars was blocked by the trees overhead. Every nook, pit, tree root, and gopher hole that the wagon wheels sped across bounced him back up into the air. Frobo hated every moment his feet weren't firmly planted on the ground, and thus, this entire event was torture to him. He'd far rather walk ten miles all day to his birthplace in Sackville then ride in a wagon to get there in a matter of hours. And that was in a wagon being driven at a decent pace. Grandalf, on the other hand was driving their wagon so fast, it felt to Frobo as if it would break apart at any moment.

The wagon rolled over a hole in the road that bounced Frobo up into the air. He soared above the side walls of the wagon but somehow landed inside of it. He crashed to his side upon colliding with the wagon floor. Part of Frobo wished he had landed on the side of the road or off in a grove of bushes so he could be off this dreadful wheeling cart. He sighed and started to lift himself from the wagon floor, but there was something odd about that.

He'd smelled a familiar scent ever since he'd climbed into the back of the wagon. And there it was again, only stronger as he lay on the floor. For some reason, it reminded him of last year's film celebration. Yes... it was the smell of the exploding black powder! Frobo felt with his hands. Instead of a wooden wagon floor, he felt the smooth ridges of fine craftsman ship. It felt like many layers of thickened parchment that had been molded together. Then the wagon rolled out into the starlight, and he finally saw what he'd been sitting on.

Frobo grasped the oblong object with a stick tail, pointed end and combustible core, holding it up to his face. He wasn't the only one to come upon such an item, for the other three hobbicks each raised identical objects into the air. The wagon floor was covered with them.

"Fireworks!" shouted Martin, as a conniving grin spread across his face.

"We can shoot them at the black riders!" shouted Happy.

Frobo, Martin, and Happy all began to prepare their fireworks in case any black riders did arrive out of thin air.

"But these fireworks are to be used for the eleventy-first festival," cried Sham. He was cradling at least fifteen of the fireworks in his arms that he'd gathered in haste to keep them away from the others. "They're Dalish Firebreathers. They've been on back-order for two years, and the *Committee for Festivious Events* has been planning the show for as long as I've been a member!"

"I don't care what kind of fireworks they are," shouted Grandalf, glancing back over his shoulder from the wagon driver's perch, "as long as they will light! And it looks like you might need to start shooting them soon."

Frobo looked back. He peered through the evening dark at the woody winding road behind them. Two riders on horseback had just appeared from beyond a bend in the road and were fast approaching the wagon. Their horses were as black as the night, and they wielded torches in their hands. Cloaked and hooded just as the black riders who'd once pursued the most famous hobbick who ever lived had been, they closed in on the wagon with amazing speed. Frobo couldn't be sure, staring back into the dark, but to his naked eye, the riders seemed slightly translucent.

"They've returned," shouted Martin. "The black riders have returned from the dead! And look! Another one is coming from the woods." He pointed to a third rider galloping in the darkness, plumes of dust rising from the ground in his wake.

"Don't be ridiculous," shouted Grandalf. "These are not the same wraiths who pursued your ancestors. But nonetheless, they must be stopped before they catch us. Use the fireworks, my young hobbicks!"

The wagon swerved at a sharp bend in the road ahead causing each of the hobbicks to lose their balance. Frobo's head banged against the wagon's wooden sidewall. The air of the humid summer wind stuck to Frobo like a spider's web. He wiped beads of sweat from his forehead where he'd hit the wagon. Fortunately, hobbicks were made of the sternest stuff on the earth, so he'd wake up the following morning with no more than a small lump.

"How do we light them?" asked Happy, holding the huge firework like it was a garden rake.

"Use the staff Happy. But only you!" Grandalf said, casting a stern glance at Martin from the corner of his eye.

"Alright then," said Frobo to Happy. He did not attempt to fully stand up again. Instead, he gained his balance by kneeling and bracing his waist across the wagon's back gate as they bounced and thrashed along the road. Frobo held up the Dalish Firebreather before the staff.

"No!" Sham said, throwing himself between Frobo and Happy. In doing so, he dropped every firework in his hands.

"I won't let you ruin the eleventy-first anniversary festival. Poor Miss Margo Proudfoot would be too upset!"

"Sham, these men are going to kill us if they catch us," shouted Frobo. "They'll set every firework in this wagon off at once and blow us all to smithereens."

"What in Middearth is going on back there?" shouted Grandalf. "They're right on top of us!"

The three riders were not more than twenty feet behind the wagon. With every turn and bend of the road, the light of their torches drew closer and closer. Frobo saw another light out of the corner of his eye through the trees to his right, a fast-moving fire that sprinted through the trees as quick as their wagon along the road. But nay, he pressed his eyes and discerned it was the torches of three more riders.

"Frobo look!" Happy was pointing to the opposite side of the road where three more torches were riding through the trees. Three to the right, three to the left, and three behind; nine black riders.

"It's now or never," shouted Grandalf. "Light the fireworks!"

"Sham, we have to!" shouted Happy.

A deep understanding of what he must do slowly dawned in the slow, all too well-mannered mind of Sham Gramgee. "Yes," he said. "Save the fireworks." Immediately the fool began throwing the fireworks over the side of the wagon, each time saying, "by Miss Margo's apron, don't go a-breaking on me when you fall, and help me find you after this is over!"

Frobo was too shocked at Sham's actions to stop him, but Martin seized the staff from Happy and swung its blunt end at poor Sham's head. Then the hobbick fell to the wagon floor, quite unconscious. No more permanent damage could be done to Sham's brain, but he would hopefully remain knocked out for the time being.

"Hope that makes us even, Mister Grandalf sir," shouted Martin up to the wizard who was doing all he could to spur on the horses.

"Get that staff out of your hand, stop congratulating yourself, and start being useful!" Grandalf snapped back. Martin immediately surrendered Grandalf's staff to Happy and took up one of the Dalish Firebreathers. Frobo had his ready first, as Happy moved the crown of the staff to the fuse. The staff's tip glowed blueish white, lit by whatever magic was inside of it, and after a shaky moment, the small fuse of Frobo's firework crackled with shooting yellow sparks.

"Point it away! Point it away!" shouted Happy, jumping up and down like the bottom of his feet were on fire and he was trying to put them out.

Frobo pointed the firework in the middle of the three riders that were behind them, holding it like he would a baby in his bosom, as the crackling fuse burned away. "Wait," he shouted. "What's going to happen when this thing goes off?"

"It's going to take you with it, if you don't let go," shouted

Grandalf, turning back for a brief moment from the horses and the road ahead.

Frobo held the firework, which was as thick as the flue of his stove, and waited, trying desperately to keep it pointed at the galloping riders as he watched the fuse burn away.

Then the firework went off. An explosion of fire erupted in the wagon, and the red flames that the Dalish Firebreathers were so famous for burst from the rocket. So ferocious was that blast and so amazing was it, that it indeed appeared like a dragon had just taken flight from their wagon, hunting the woods of the Chire for any who dared show their face. The rocket spun in an orbiting circle as it hummed towards the pursuing riders, but Frobo did not see any more than that. He was thrown backwards by its recoil to the front of the wagon.

"Atta hobbick, Frobo," shouted Happy, "right in the chest, you got him!"

Frobo looked up. His shirt and vest were covered in soot and gunpowder, but by some miracle, the firework had hit one of the riders, though not the one he'd been aiming at. The firework exploded into even more flames the moment it hit the rider, sounding a louder boom than when they'd set it off and shooting more rockets of gold and red in all directions.

The rider fell from his horse and began running like a madman through the forest, waving his arms and trying to beat out the fire in a furious frenzy. He'd soon set the whole Chire ablaze if he wasn't careful. Frobo saw him leap into a small brook beside the road as the wagon took another sharp turn and his view was cut off by the trees.

Grandalf sped the wagon onward. Frobo had no clear notion of how far they'd driven, or when they'd be free of these riders. What was the old wizard's plan? He gulped. *It had better not involve any eagles,* he told himself. *"Or I'm going to be sick."* Frobo was afraid of heights. They were as unnatural to him as boats were to most hobbick-folk, and he was not in the slightest bit prepared for soaring through the air in the clutch of their talons.

Martin held up his own firework, aiming as best he could for the rider behind them who was veering to the left. The rider had ridden up dangerously close beside them, and was no more than ten feet away.

"Son of Ashelob, shoot!" shouted Grandalf from the wagon's perch, desperately driving the horses before him.

Happy lit the fuse of the firework, which Martin was holding over his right shoulder. The fuse crackled and popped and burned down until the firework boomed. Light illuminated the wagon and the forest road as another flaming dragon spun and soared into the air, but missed the rider entirely.

Frobo snatched up another firework. The galloping hooves of the rider's horse sounded in his ears like the raging torrents that used to flood Sackville and wash the dirt away from his hobbick hole. He held the firework on his shoulder just as Martin had, no longer cradling it like he'd done with the last one. Just as he did, the rider raised his arm to throw his torch. The fuse of the firework crackled in Frobo's ear as he tried to aim it, every jolt of the wagon undoing his efforts to study the thing. He aimed for the rider's head, but the wagon bounced, again throwing off his aim. The thing would explode any second. With the fuse still crackling, he redirected his aim for the midsection, but he was jerked off target by a sharp turn in the road. Finally, he aimed for the rider's horse, and BOOM!

Frobo collapsed into the wagon as the dragon shaped firework shot out and exploded upon impact, hitting the rider's leg and showering him with sparks and flames. To say that Frobo's ears were ringing would have been a gross understatement. They were a continual resounding internal explosion of echoing chaos, repeating the loud eruption of the firework again and again in his mind. Despite the ringing dizziness, he groped on the floor of the wagon for another firework.

"Almost there, my young hobbicks," shouted Grandalf from the front of the wagon.

"Son of Ashelob!" shouted Frobo to Martin. "That's loud!"

Martin nodded in agreement as he held up the next firework, aiming at the closest rider in sight. The tree line broke to their left allowing three of the riders to join the other that still followed directly behind them. Frobo craned his head towards the front of the wagon, looking beyond Grandalf. The road ahead cut straight through a small gorge then hooked to the right. He turned back again to the riders. They'd taken down two of the nine with the fireworks, but seven were still in hot pursuit.

Martin's firework blasted from his shoulder and exploded on the ground in front of the four pursuing riders. Three of them sped around the explosion, but one horse reared up and threw its rider into the flashing flames that were shooting up from the ground. Six riders remained.

"Frobo, look!" shouted Grandalf.

Frobo glanced to the wagon's starboard side just in time to see a rider reach it. Frobo hadn't seen him because the cursed creature had dropped its torch. And now he had one foot over the wagon's sidewall.

"Take the reins Frobo," shouted Grandalf, leaping suddenly to the back of the wagon. The rider hoisted his other foot over the side of the wagon, and his horse fell back. Frobo stared at the man in black with fear and awe. He was in their wagon, standing like a sentinel, tall and menacing. His black cloak and hood billowed and blew like a midnight flag flying in the wind. Unlike the films, Frobo could see the entire man beneath the hood and cloak. He was not invisible, but he was also not visible. His skin, hair, mouth, nose, and eyes were all there, but Frobo could see *through* him too. Grandalf did not pause to observe the man as Frobo did but began wrestling the rider at once.

Through muffled grunts and groans from the wizard as he struggled with the black rider Frobo discerned the following directions.

"The reins, Frobo! Drive the wagon!"

Frobo swayed and staggered, struggling to ascend and take the seat atop the wagon's perch while Martin and Happy exploded firework after firework into the pursuing riders. The perch, a flat board mounted high on manmade springs, was almost as tall as Frobo himself. He'd never be able to pull himself up.

Uncontrolled and unguided, the horses rumbled on to their own devices, veering from the beaten path. The wagon suddenly encountered such a strong bump that Frobo was bounced up high into the air. He soared like a hand knit kite and tumbled over the top of the perch, landing on his back where a long-legged man would've rested his feet when driving the thing. From there, he lifted himself up, slid his backside onto the perch, and gained the seat, though his short hobbick feet were not nearly long enough to reach the footrest. All he could do was lean back against the short back of the bench with his bare feet swinging in the wind.

Then, taking the mysterious leather cords that were attached to the galloping horses' mouths in both hands, he exclaimed, "Go horses! Go!" Somehow, with those cords he was supposed to be able to command the large beasts and make them do his bidding.

"What in Middlearth are you doing up there?" Grandalf said as he threw a right-handed punch at the rider's jaw.

"I'm trying my best, thank you very much!" replied Frobo.

"They're slowing down Fro..." Grandalf was cut off by a retaliating punch in the mouth from the rider. "Snap the reins," shouted Grandalf.

Frobo felt so uncomfortable he could have tossed up his entire dinner right then and there. It wasn't just the fact that he was trying to control these horses, and that his feet weren't firmly planted. If there was one thing he'd always hated in his life, it was being pressured to do something, especially when other people were depending on him to do that thing, and when he himself knew that he had no idea how to do it. In the deepest corner of his mind, and in a way that perhaps even he wasn't fully aware of yet, he'd always been doubtful of his acclaimed relation to the most famous hobbick who ever lived. Frobo hated, dreaded, and *detested* feeling like people were depending on him. Wasn't that the essence of his grandfather's quest? A world depending on the most unlikely person imaginable to come through for them and save them?

"Frobo, snap the reins!" this time it was Martin shouting at him.

"Where does he get off screaming at me like that? Especially in such close quarters," Frobo thought. *"Doesn't he know that I'm... that I'm..."* but Frobo couldn't make himself say it. For at that moment, not even in his mind could he claim to be the grandson of the most famous hobbick who'd ever walked upon the soils of Middlearth. And there he was, sitting up on the commanding chair of the wagon, pursued by black riders. He felt absolutely useless. He was going to feel like a complete fool when they were caught.

"Frobo, the horses! Snap the reins!" It was Grandalf again. The translucent rider had the wizard pinned on his back. The rockets that Happy and Martin were firing at the pursuing riders were now almost point blank, and the riders they'd previously hit had caught back up to them.

"It's now or never," Frobo said to himself, and taking the reins in both hands, feeling the leather cords sit between his fingers and thumbs, Frobo did exactly what they'd told him to do. He snapped. With all his might, he snapped his thumbs from his middle to his index fingers. And he did it repeatedly, again and again. But still the horses did not speed up. "Son of Ashelob!" he cried, still diligently snapping his fingers.

"Frobo, what are you doing?" screamed Happy.

Now he was furious. And he was done snapping for them. With all his might, he threw the reins down in terrible frustration. The horses whinnied as if to complain about the fact that the reins had cracked against their backs like whips. But Frobo didn't care. The ridiculous animals had made a fool out of him. But just as he was to turn about and tell Happy to "come up to the front and do it himself," the horses sped up to a much faster pace, even quicker than when Grandalf was driving them.

Frobo now understood. Snapping the reins wasn't actually *snapping*. What they'd meant by *snapping* was actually *hitting* the horses with the reins. He couldn't believe how inaccurately they'd described what he'd managed to do, but he decided to keep their mistake to himself for the time being.

He *snapped* the reins again. The horses pounded their hooves against the cloddy road as fast as they could. Frobo looked back. They'd put a little distance between themselves and the pursuing riders, but not much. The riders were quicker on their single horses than the wagon was and the only thing keeping them at bay was the fireworks, which were flying out of the back of it at an alarming rate. But how could they truly escape?

"Frobo," uttered Grandalf, still struggling beneath the rider. "The bridge! Look out!"

The mention of the "bridge" was enough to help Grandalf give the slip to the rider who'd pinned him. With a quick swipe of his leg, Grandalf knocked the rider off balance, punched him once more for good measure, and tossed him over the side of the wagon.

Frobo had yet to turn and see any bridge. He was still snapping the reins as the horses sped on, staring back at Grandalf with a big grin on his face.

"Frobo! The bridge!" shouted Grandalf again, this time pointing ahead.

Frobo finally turned, sensing it was important to do so, to see the long bridge that crossed the Brandybeer River before him. The bridge was wide enough for the wagon to cross, but that would only work if Frobo directed the horses on the right course, not into the river as they were headed now. He panicked again. He was no better at directing horses than he was at *snapping* reins, and he had seconds, no moments, before they reached the bridge. With all his might, he yanked the reins hard right in the direction of the bridge.

So sharp was the turn, that the wagon quite nearly toppled over, as it swung about across the face of the pursuing riders. The sudden change in direction (though a great accomplishment by Frobo) was all the riders needed to close the final gap between them and the wagon. Happy and Martin tumbled to the wagon floor. Grandalf would've fallen over the side if he hadn't already been laying down.

The black riders were mere inches from the wagon now as Frobo turned the wagon back hard left on the tracks in line to cross over the bridge.

The clodding earth beneath the horse's hooves turned to a clapping wood. The horses and the wagon mounted the arched bridge that crossed over the broad river. He'd done it! Frobo Daggins had snapped the reins, outrun the black riders, and even steered the wagon onto the Brandybeer River Bridge.

"Frobo you did it!" shouted Martin. Joy and elation swept through Frobo like fire. Victory pulsed in his veins. The thrill of escape was his. "You did it. The riders aren't even trying to cross!"

Frobo couldn't help but reflect as the wagon reached the crest of the bridge. There was something strange about that last detail. *"The riders aren't even trying to cross the bridge..."* But that made no sense. They had been nearly upon them. They'd practically caught up when he turned the wagon. Why weren't they still following? He was so perplexed by the complete conundrum of it all, that he quite forgot about driving the exhausted horses, who rolled to a stop atop the bridge. Grandalf, Happy, and Martin seemed just as puzzled as him, because they were all staring back in confusion at the riders who remained on the Chire side of the river.

There was something familiar about the scene, but yes, he'd seen it before. Or at least he'd seen riders afraid to cross water in the films. Because they were afraid that if they crossed, they'd be engulfed by a stampede of white foaming water horses! Grandalf would make them come. But, if that was his plan, why was he sitting at the back of the wagon, scratching his head like an old fool and looking just as confused as Frobo?

"By old Mister Bombagrill himself," said a groggy Sham who'd just awoken. "You're going to blow up all of Miss Margo's fireworks at once!"

Frobo, Grandalf, Happy, and Martin now saw what they'd overlooked. A single torch, dropped into the wagon by one of the riders, had lit the fuses of the fireworks, and every Dalish Firebreather in the wagon was a moment from exploding.

"JUMP!" they all shouted at the same moment. And then they leapt from the wagon only a moment too soon before the incredible explosion.

Frobo felt the heat of the blast of flames propel him as he shot out of his wagon seat. He flew in midair, swinging his arms like a flailing bird, and fell down into the flowing, sweeping, bubbling Brandybeer River, the home of overweight ducks, beer bellied beavers, and totally inebriated fish. Frobo let a little sip of beer flow into his mouth which tasted unusually foul. *Don't be like Sham and drink the beer straight from the river you idiot,* he thought to himself.

Sham had once been sick for weeks after drinking straight out of the river. He'd claimed he'd been told by one of the goons that it was safe, so long as you bought some of the now rare *Kingsweed* from the goons and ate it immediately afterwards. Sham had bought and eaten the *Kingsweed* but had still become deathly ill. Frobo had always suspected that whatever Sham had purchased was not actually *Kingsweed*.

Opening his eyes in the golden haze below the surface, Frobo thought he could make out a few of his companions. There was Grandalf, twice as large as the rest of them, swimming away towards the far bank. Two hobbicks were clearly following him, while a third golden haired hobbick had just opened his large mouth in delight as if drowning in a river of beer had always been his lifelong ambition.

The fool! Frobo swam through the golden, carbonated river to the blockheaded hobbick. Now that Sham had inhaled the beer and begun to choke, he seemed to come to his senses. He began struggling wildly, thrashing about as if he'd never swam before. But of course, Sham didn't know how to swim. For that matter, neither did Frobo. Hobbicks were infamous for their fear of water. In fact, his own great grandparents had died of drownding. So had his grandfather... Frobo had always avoided the water, boats, or anything related to them, as any good hobbick should, but now he was going to die just like his ancestors.

And yet, he had somehow made it through the beer to Sham quite easily... what if he just kept doing that until he got to shore? He only had to remember what he'd just been doing. Frobo grabbed onto Sham's hair with one hand, kicked with his legs and tried with all his might to pull the beer back towards him. It worked! He was moving towards the opposite shore, although he had a long way to go.

He glanced back over his right shoulder. Sham's eyes were staring into the river of beer like a dead fish. Frobo yanked and jerked Sham's long curly locks as hard as he could, but all this did was pull Frobo deeper and deeper into the beer. He could hear his own heartbeat now. He'd gone without breath for too long.

Baddum... Frobo's heart pounded. Sham had drug him all the way to the bottom of the river now. He had to... *baddum...* he had to get to the surface... *baddum...* he released Sham and... *baddumm... baddumm...* Frobo's last memory before the river went dark was the taste of old beer flowing into his mouth, nose and lungs, and furry paw-like hands closing in over his mouth and eyes.

CHAPTER 5

QUESTIONS THAT NEED
ANSWERING

FROBO OPENED HIS EYES THE FOLLOWING DAY TO A CLEAR blue sunlit sky. The light of a blinding sun flooded his eyes, and he immediately snapped them shut. The sun was far too bright for them. His head was pounding and felt as if it had been split open. He reached up for his temple for what was sure to be source of the throbbing pain. He was certain that upon doing so, he would find a huge monstrous sized protrusion from the place where he had been hit. But the bruise he felt was no larger than a lump, roughly the size of an acorn, and that was if he was being generous.

For some strange reason he was lying flat on his back, but whatever he was lying on (though he was not about to open his eyes again to find out), was most certainly not a bed. Unwilling to look around him, he touched the hard surface beneath him with his other hand but quickly shot it back. His finger had just procured a splinter, and the painful prick caused Frobo to reason with still closed eyes, that he was lying on hard wood. What idiot had laid him on a wooden board out in the middle of the sun? They at least should've put him in the shade so he could cool down. If Sham had done it, he'd have words with him. The young hobbick was so insufferably ludicrous sometimes.

Frobo bit the thorn with his foremost teeth, securing the splinter between them, and pulled his finger away. He smelled his own fresh blood oozing out and felt its warmth running down his finger, but the splinter was removed. He spit it to the side and began to suck the blood from his new wound. It was a miracle he didn't have splinters stuck into every inch of his back. His body ached and the sun was terribly bright even through his closed eyelids. As he lay there on his back, he wracked his brains, but for the life of him, he could not fathom why he felt as dreadfully worn down as he did.

There was also an unpleasant odor: the musty mixture of muddy clay, and... what was that other aroma? It smelled like Sham's armpits after he'd been working in Frobo's garden all day and came barging in for afternoon tea. Only whatever this scent was, it was far stronger, wilder, and if possible, fouler. Few things Frobo knew of smelled as foul as Sham could after a hard day's work.

Clop, clop, clop, clop...

Frodo slowly peeped open his eyes again despite his head's urging pleas to spare it from the light. He saw that he was lying on his back on a wooden plank, and next to him, fast asleep, was Sham. So, that explained the smell. As he sat up and glanced about, he saw that he was in a farmer's field in which the crops were moving past him. But the reason for that became clear as his senses returned to him. He was being dragged, along with Sham, by the two horses that had been pulling their wagon, and he was lying on what Frobo assumed was all that remained of said wagon.

"Mister Grandalf™, he's awake!" The merry joyful hobbick voice was full of glee. Happy ran up from behind him, jumping up and down beside the broad plank.

"Which one?" asked Grandalf. "And for the last time, *enough.* Stop saying my name with those ridiculous letters after it. You're fugitives now, official enemies of Middlearth Enterprises. You need no longer acquiesce to their demands."

"It's Mister Frobo. He's the one that's woken, Mister Grand...arf!"

"Call me by name, or don't call me at all, Master Martin," the wizard snapped. "It's like the whole lot of you are possessed by that hideous trademark just like the old king of Brohan was possessed by Sauluman. Say my name correctly! Or I'll drive the spirit out of you just like I drove it from him."

"Grand...*aaaaaalllffff!*" Martin screamed as if he was about to explode, then held his mouth shut with all of his might to keep from saying "™," afterwards. At last, the fit passed him, and a look of relief dawned upon his face.

"Feel better?" asked the wizard, a grin cracking out of the side of his mouth.

"Yes, loads!" said Martin. "Thank you, Grandalf. Thank you, I'm free!"

The makeshift wagon (if it could be called one) rolled to a stop, and Frobo saw Grandalf's face appear over his head. The large round brim of his hat cut off the afternoon sky. From this angle Frobo could stare right into the wizard's silver eyes and discern the many crooks that formed the shape of his long nose. In fact, he could even see up that nose, right into the large, cavernous nostrils with abundant bushels of white hair. The mere sight of it made him dizzy and faint.

"What's wrong with me?" asked Frobo. "I feel so... tired."

"Isn't it obvious?" asked Grandalf. "You almost drowned on beer. You have a hangover, and a deadly one at that."

Grandalf, Happy and Martin were all huddled over Frobo's side of the plank. Sham lay to his right, still fast asleep. Grandalf at least provided a momentary respite of shade from the bright sun, but every time the wizard moved, its unrelenting heat enveloped him again.

"Where are we? Which one of you saved me?" asked Frobo, glimpsing up at them from his plank through squinting eyes.

"What are you talking about?" asked Happy.

"Which one of you dove back into the river?" asked Frobo. "I saw a hand grabbing me, right before everything went black. It was a strange looking hand though..."

"Frobo, we barely made it out of the river ourselves," said Grandalf. "It's rather difficult swimming in beer. But not long after making it out, we did find you and Sham on the banks. You were both just lying there unconscious, but you were breathing. I don't have the slightest idea of who could've saved you. I'd venture to guess you probably saved yourself and that this strange hand is some figment of your imagination."

"I don't understand," said Frobo, still lying on his back next to the still dozing Sham.

"You aren't the only one among us who still has unanswered questions, Frobo," said Grandalf. "Especially after finding out that Sauluman is still alive. That decrepit cock-headed snake whisperer. Back in the Chire... back in the very place he was supposedly killed eleven-one years ago. But how can he have come back?"

"Umm, Mister Grandalf," interrupted Martin. "I'm afraid you're doing *it* again sir..."

"Doing *what* again?" snapped Grandalf, a dark gray thunderstorm brewing in his silver eyes.

"Talking to yourself sir," said Martin, standing with hands crossed behind his back and addressing Grandalf like the wizard was some defiant pupil whom Martin had chosen to be patient with. "It wasn't polite when we were back in Daggend, and it's not polite now either."

"Perhaps Master Shaken-Nottstird, I am talking to myself, because there is no one around me capable of carrying on a conversation! But..." Grandalf continued before Martin could retort, "I do have more questions, questions that need answering. And they can only be answered by one of you young hobbicks."

Frobo felt immediately uncomfortable. Was Grandalf going to ask him about the snapping? Had he seen him? The whole Chire would be laughing at him if they ever returned. But he didn't care. He just didn't care what anyone thought anymore. He was done caring.

"Alright fine, yes it's true!" Frobo said. "I didn't realize what 'snapping the reins' meant when I was driving the wagon. I thought it meant you snapped your fingers while holding the reins. And I realize that only a complete idiot would've thought this, so I hope you're happy now that you've made a complete fool out of the last descendant of the most famous hobbick who's ever lived!"

Happy, Martin, and Grandalf all gazed at Frobo with dropped jaws for a horrible awkward moment. Frobo breathed a sigh of relief. It was good to get that off his chest. He could only hope now that since he had shared his secret with them, they would show him appreciation for saving their lives.

Happy and Martin burst into sudden and swift laughter. Grandalf tried to contain himself but failed to hold in his muffled fit of chuckles.

"Well, Frobo," the wizard said, "while I do appreciate your candor, the question I wanted to ask was not about your confusion over the meaning of the phrase, 'snap the reins.'" Grandalf, Happy and Martin all burst into laughter again. Frobo's face grew red hot with embarrassment.

"Snap the reins!" Happy exclaimed, snapping his fingers as he mimicked Frobo the wagon driver.

"Go horseys go! Neigh!" shouted Martin as he stood perfectly still snapping his fingers violently.

"Oh, that's not bad, young hobbick, not bad at all!"

chuckled the old wizard. A smile broke on Grandalf's face, the likes of which Frobo had never seen upon it. And though he should've been able to laugh with them, he was utterly unable to do so.

"I'd say that's quite enough!" snapped Frobo, hoping with every fiber of his being that the joke had run its course. "You've had your fun now, what was the real question you were going to ask Grandar... Grandall... Grand*aaaalf!*" Frobo held his own mouth shut just as Happy had until the queer power of the trademark passed. He too, to his own personal shock and relief, could say Grandalf's name without the annoying little "™" after it. It was simply amazing what being a fugitive had done for him.

"Yes, quite right Frobo, quite right," said Grandalf, "I wanted to ask, what do you think is the best way to set off a firework? Lighting the fuse with a match or snapping your fingers next to it?"

Grandalf, Martin, and Happy all broke out in laughter again. Happy was so overcome by the hysterics that he fell into the long grass beside the road. His long red hair played against the green grass like the bursting flames of a tinderbox. Frobo was furious. He stood to his feet. He'd been foolish enough to tell them what he'd done (a mistake he would not soon make again) and although he did have to listen to this, he didn't have to listen to it lying on the thorny remains of their wagon.

"Oh Frobo, you must forgive me," cried Grandalf through tears of laughter. "That's not what I wanted to ask, but I simply couldn't resist."

The other hobbicks were carrying on and on in ecstatic giggles and cackles.

"Well," shouted Frobo sharply. "What was it? What was it you *did* want to ask me?"

But the laughter was not quite finished yet. How immature

of them all. A laugh or two at his expense was one thing, but this was simply ridiculous.

"The question," said Grandalf, as he continued to wipe the tears from his eyes, "was not even for you, Frobo. It was for Happy."

Almost as quickly as he had fallen to the ground, the rolling laughter of their red headed companion ceased, and his grin faded. Martin helped him up from his bed of grass and he rose to his feet. His white nose was bristling and writhing as if it was trying to curl in upon itself from extreme discomfort. But perhaps it was trying to distract them all from seeing the dark shade of red now inflaming his cheeks. Frobo and Martin seemed to have missed the reason for this entirely. What was Grandalf going to ask?

"How did you do it?" the wizard said.

"Err, what exactly?" said Happy, subtly shuffling away from the wizard as he spoke. They had resumed their march through the field, and now Frobo was walking ahead of the horses with Grandalf, Happy and Martin. Sham was still being drug behind on the wagon remains, fast asleep.

"The escape from the guards on the party field... sneaking past them to break us out of the Lockholes, all of it. How did you do it?" Grandalf said.

"Well, I suppose I was a bit lucky," said Happy. "My grandfather always used to say that nobody achieved anything without a good deal of luck involved."

"No, he didn't," replied Grandalf.

"I'm quite sure I heard him say that," said Happy.

"I'm quite sure I never did," said Grandalf. "But even so, explain how you were so *lucky*. I'm anxious to hear the story."

"Well, you see Mister Gr... Grandalf," stammered Happy, forcing himself to quickly continue before adding the trademark after Grandalf's name. "Most folks don't know this, but hobbicks can go unseen by most if they choose. And that's what I did. It was just a simple bit of luck really. Nothing that would ever make it into one of the great stories. I was just at the right place at the right time."

"Ahh yes..." mused Grandalf, as he eyed Happy. "Right place at the right time... I'm sure you were. But it appears Frobo and Martin, that there is more to this hobbick than meets the eye."

"*More to this hobbick than meets the eye...*" repeated Frobo. "I've heard that phrase before!"

"Yes, you have..." replied Grandalf. "I've said it before. It even made its way into your precious films."

"*Mythrill!*" shouted Sham from the same wooden plank Frobo had risen from.

"Quite right, Sham," said Grandalf. Frobo was kicking himself for not remembering before Sham. The confounding hobbick was always on top of the trivia game.

"So, what you're saying," Sham continued, "Is that Happy made it past the guards with a special coat of *Mythrill*, given to him by his ancestor, and that he's been hiding from us all these years! It's value is likely more than the whole Chire itself!" Sham hoisted himself up onto the sliding plank as if all grogginess and fatigue had vacated his body. He stood perched on his haunches like a fat cat scanning a field for an unsuspecting mouse. He held that pose for a brief moment, then sprang from his perch and rushed at Happy, grasping the hobbick's shirt and ripping it open.

"Son of Ashelob!" shouted Happy. "What in Middlearth do you think you're doing?"

Sham had ripped Happy's shirt right down the middle, but no secret garment of armor was revealed, save for Happy's hairy hobbick chest.

"Well, that can't be right!" said Sham.

"I'm afraid Sham, that you should've looked in his pockets,

if you wanted to discover a clue to his secret," said Grandalf. "Although I don't pretend to know any of the details myself. Go ahead Happy, tell us all how you really did it. Show us your *ring*."

Frobo, Sham and Martin gasped. Happy's reddening face suddenly made his fiery hair look tame in comparison, betraying the truth in Grandalf's words.

"What ring?" said Happy ducking even farther behind the horse in an effort to hide his red face from them all.

"You know what ring," said Grandalf. "And you had better start explaining yourself quickly. Wizards are not known for their patience. Go ahead and take it out of your pocket. Show it to them. I should like to see it myself."

"But I'm afraid I don't know what you're talking about," said Happy, recomposing himself and pointing his nose in the air.

"Enough!" shouted Grandalf. "You have kept this ring secret for too long and it is time to reveal the truth. In the name of the West, show it to us now!"

Happy gulped, and with trembling hand, reached into his right trouser pocket and brought forth a ring. Frobo didn't think it was much to look at, this mysterious ring. And he didn't understand what all the fuss about it was. It was silver in color and adorned with a single white stone. It didn't look like any of the rings of power he'd ever heard of.

"Tell us how this ring came to you," said Grandalf, eyeing it suspiciously. "For I recognize it, but from whence it came, I cannot tell."

"I..." began Happy slowly, as his eyes shifted to each of them. "I inherited it."

"From whom?" asked Frobo.

"From my grandfather," said Happy.

"Which one?" said Sham. "We all know you've got two of those, don't we, Mister Grandalf?"

"From grandfather Brandy... well you know what our last name used to be," said Happy.

"And how did he acquire such a ring?" asked Grandalf.

"Do you remember the flotsham and jetsham of Isengrad, Mister Grandalf?" asked Happy.

"Of course, I do," said Grandalf. "Your grandfather was there."

"Well, twenty years ago when old gramps was about to pass, he decided he'd rather kick the bucket down in Grondor with his best friend."

Frobo cocked an eyebrow, waiting to see if Happy was about to speak the name of Tooken, for that name was no longer used in the Chire, as it was taboo.

Happy looked up and met Frobo's eyes. An unspoken under-standing passed between them, and Happy continued. "Of course, *that* family had all migrated to that section of the world, and Gramps heard that his best friend was also near his last days. So, one night he pulls me aside. I was a young lad mind you, not even ten years from my tweens yet, but he says to me, 'Young Happy, you are my favorite grandchild out of my many descendants, and I think one day, you may just be the best hobbick in all of the Chire.'"

Frobo couldn't help but turn up his nose at this. He was of course, good friends with Happy, but Happy's grandfather had crossed a line if he didn't think Frobo would also one day be the finest hobbick in the Chire.

Happy continued, oblivious to Frobo's offense at the private compliment Happy's grandfather had paid to him more than ten years ago, "'Now laddy,' he says to me, 'I'm going to tell you something that I've never revealed to anyone. Not even your grandmother knew about it. Do you remember the part of the films where old uncle Pip finds the black stone in the waters of Isengrad?' 'The Seeing Stone?' I asks him. 'Yes, the Seeing Stone,' he says to me. 'When old uncle Pip found that stone in the water, I looked down and saw something shining myself. There was something else shining in the water that day, and while everyone was looking at your old uncle, I slipped off my pony and picked up *this*.' Then, from behind his back my Gramps pulled out this ring," said Happy, showing it to them again. "'What is it?' I asked him, and he says to me, 'It's a *ring*, my lad. It's a magic ring. I reckon it belonged to that Sauluman, but don't worry! It's not evil like that *Insidious Ring* that was destroyed in the films. It's quite simple really... you put it on and you,' *pop!* Just like that he disappeared right before my eyes, then he took off the ring and revealed himself again. 'There, you see,' he said. 'And it's yours now my boy, for I'm afraid that where I'm going, I won't have much use for the thing.'

'But how do you know it's not evil,' I asked him, afraid from the films. 'Look,' he says to me, 'and places the ring in my hand as freely as if he'd been passing me some pipeweed. 'If it was evil, I wouldn't be able to hand it over at all, would I?' he asked. And he was right. I took the thing and have had it ever since then. No nagging thoughts or obsession with it most of the time, not anymore than with any of my other possessions. The thing's quite harmless," said Happy, shoving the ring quickly back into his pocket.

"And so, you've had it all these years?" asked Grandalf.

"Yep, ever since old Gramps gave it to me that night," said Happy.

"Wow," Sham mused, holding his forefinger up and tapping his nose as he often did when he was in deep thought. "Another ring of power. Strange, considering we're going on a quest to destroy all of the rings of power. But something's telling me *this* specific ring of power isn't all that important."

"Is that so, Sham?" asked Grandalf. "What is telling you that?"

"Oh, just a hunch," said Sham.

"Well tell your hunch to go back where it came from and stop blabbing its uninformed opinions," Grandalf said.

Sham drew back from the wizard and hung his head. As much as he could annoy Frobo from time to time, these were the moments when he couldn't help feeling sorry for Sham. "Begging your pardon, Mister Grandalf sir," said Sham, pulling out his handkerchief to stifle a sniffle, "but that's no way to talk in the Chire."

"Enough with your manners! I've been a fool until now," shouted the wizard.

"Sorry, did he just say that *he's* been a fool?" asked Martin. "That's not like him. He's usually accusing other people of that."

"Yes, I have been a fool!" said Grandalf. "And I've been surrounded by too many other fools, particularly short stout hairy footed fools to notice it. I was there. It was the day that Sauluman imprisoned me on top of his tower. The day I noticed that his cloak was no longer white, but many colors. The same day I saw *that* ring on his finger."

"So, it is Sauluman's ring?" asked Frobo.

"Yes, I'm afraid it is," said Grandalf. "And I should've known. Sauluman was the master of ring lore. He had studied the rings of power more than any of the wise. And then, when he turned evil, he set up a tower and a little kingdom for himself, as much in the image of Morbor as he could muster. He is nothing more than an imitator, and he mimicked his master in the closest way he could. His master had created that *Insidious Ring* to rule all others, and I suspect Sauluman has done the same. He created this ring to rule the other rings of power in case our plan to destroy that *Insidious Ring* succeeded.

"Alas, he created it before he knew it had been recovered. And just like his master, he poured the force of his life into his ring. On the day I broke his staff, it must have slipped from his finger into the water at Isengrad. And when he was murdered in the Chire, his life force must have survived. It appears, he's been waiting all this time to return, for that very ring of yours Happy, has enabled his spirit to endure. And when he returned to form, after eleventy-one years, he started looking in the exact place he suspected his ring would be... the Chire. It was here, right under his nose, and now, once again it has slipped from his grasp."

"Son of Ashelob!" said Happy, gazing at the silver ring in the palm of his hand. "So, what you're telling me is, *this* is now the ring of power? And we're right back where we started eleventy-one years ago?"

"Begging your pardon," said Frobo, "But if that is the ring of power, I think it would only be fitting, when considering all things: historical context, tradition, respect for the past, not to mention the story of the greatest hobbick ever..." Frobo paused, trying to come up with the right words. "What I'm trying to say is that I can't help but think that it would be fitting for a *Daggins* to be the bearer of the new ring of power," said Frobo.

Happy drew back and his hand grasped something in his pocket, eyeing Frobo with deep suspicion, who now felt the need to defend himself.

"I'm not saying I *want* the thing!" said Frobo, instantly feeling the weight of all their suspicious eyes upon him. "We've all seen how much it tortured my poor grandfather. Only a fool would desire such a thing. I just think we've got to be smart about this is all. Let someone with ancestral experience bear the ring. And, I'm sure Sham agrees with me," Frobo added, kicking Sham in the shin.

"Oh yes, of course sir!" said Sham. Upon feeling Frobo's kick, he mentally rejoined their conversation, and he hadn't the faintest idea of what he was agreeing to. He shot up from his normal walking slump into perfect posture and a wide, open-mouthed smile. "Whatever Mister Frobo says, that's what I say.

Go along with it blindly if I must. That's what keeps bread on the table, and beer in the barrels..."

"And there you have it," said Frobo, clasping his hands together in earnest as if Sham had just convinced them all. "Now, if you please Happy, you're clearly out of your depth in this matter so if you don't mind..."

"Are you mad, Frobo?" asked Happy. "I'm not handing anything over! My grandfather gave me this ring, and I'm keeping it, no matter if your name be Daggins or Stridder."

This completely flummoxed Frobo and rendered him speechless for almost five full seconds before he managed to spat out, "how dare you!" For his whole life, ever since he'd heard the story of his grandfather, Frobo had wanted to do something important. He'd wanted his own *Insidious Ring* to destroy. He'd wanted to be a hero. And here was his chance lying right in front of him, but Happy was being too foolhardy and stubborn to see it! "How dare you refuse to give the ring to me! I'm a Daggins! Make him, Grandalf. It's what's right, make him hand it over!"

"I will certainly..." said Grandalf, "do no such thing."

Happy breathed a sigh of relief.

Frobo blanched in shock, not believing what his ears were hearing.

"The Daggins have no claim to the rings of power, Frobo, and your lust for this ring only proves to me that Happy's grandfather was wrong in his assumption that it wasn't evil. Your *supposed* ancestor was given that *Insidious Ring* by his uncle, just as Happy was given this ring by his grandfather. And for that reason, we must assume that he was *meant* to have it. If anything, I would think that your obsessive desire to possess this ring disqualifies you," said Grandalf.

Frobo drew away. He could feel them all looking at him, judging him, thinking him the traitor of their fellowship. But they didn't understand. He didn't want the ring for power or glory, he wanted it so he could be important. And he wanted it so he could redeem the Daggins name after everything his father had put it through.

"I agree with you, Mister Grandalf sir," said Sham. "You see, poor Mister Frobo means well, but he just isn't qualified, is he? We all know what happened to his grandfather in the films. Poor bloke told me own gramps to go home, he did, but my dear old grandgaffer, he stayed with him all the way until the end. And I just want you to know that if you need a replacement ring bearer, you know, if Mister Happy gets tired, or needs a rest, that I'll be happy to oblige, Mister Grandalf sir."

Frobo recoiled as if he'd just been slapped in the face. "How dare you Sham. You're my employee!"

"Oh, would you two give it a rest already," drawled Martin, picking a long yellow blade of straw like grass and chewing the end like it was a pipe. "Frobo, you don't have employees anymore. We've left the Chire and we're on a dangerous quest. You're just as penniless as Sham is."

"Quite right you are," said Grandalf. The wizard then plucked his own long blade of grass and began to chew it just as Martin had. "As surprising as it is to say that to *you*. You hobbicks never do cease to amaze me. But Happy, you'd best keep that ring of yours out of sight. While I don't doubt that it's quite less potent than that *Insidious Ring*, that doesn't mean a little ambition from some good meaning hobbicks couldn't get in the way of our mission."

This last word from Grandalf quite ended the discussion of the ring and the five of them walked through the last golden fields on the eastern side of the Brandybeer River. The sky was bright overhead and Frobo could see trees and a road cutting through a woody cluster of trees at the end of the field.

"Where are we going?" he asked.

"To Breetown of course," said Grandalf, "just as your ancestors did when they went on their quest. We need provisions and more horses for our journey. Let us hope we get there before the riders do."

"Those riders," said Happy. "Who, or what are they, Mister Grandalf?"

"Yes..." said the wizard, "that is quite the next question after the riddle of your ring. Although, I must admit that I'm not sure of the answer."

"Well, isn't that perfect?" spouted Sham, plucking his own blade to chew from the ground. Martin had started a trend. "What good is having a wizard around if he can't even answer your questions?" Sham kicked a dirt pile in front of him and shrugged his shoulders.

"Will you keep that ignorant mouth of yours shut!" snapped Grandalf. "And spit that blade of grass out of your mouth!"

"But I like it," said Sham. "It makes me feel big and important."

But Grandalf was so annoyed by Sham placing that stupid blade of grass into his mouth, that the wizard proceeded to chase the short legged hobbick around and around the horses. It reminded Frobo of a hobbick ma'arm chasing a cat that had just stolen her child's vittles. Frobo thought the whole thing was ridiculous. He didn't understand what could be making the wizard so upset. Sham however was giggling and laughing from the chase, sprinting and ducking like a squirrel that was trying to escape the jaws of a wolf. At last, Grandalf relented, composed himself and continued to walk along the road, the blade of grass still hanging from Sham's mouth.

"Mister Grandalf," said Happy, "if you don't mind me saying so, you seem a little different than I remember from the stories of the most famous hobbick who ever lived. It's like... you're more easily angered now, quick to a temper, slow to laughter."

"Yes..." Grandalf sighed. "And perhaps if any of you had been sailing the seas for the last eleven-one years, unable to reach your home in the west, you'd feel the same as I do. But back to the question of the riders. I do not *know* the answer Sham. I am a wizard, not the wheel of time itself. But I can guess.

"Sauluman, although he has not recovered the ring that *he* forged, has recovered the nine rings of men. He has given them to nine servants and named them his own black riders. Of course, those rings lost most of their power when that *Insidious Ring* was destroyed, which makes their new bearers only partially invisible."

"Then they beat us?" asked Frobo. "They found the rings before we did?"

"So, it appears," said Grandalf.

"Then why are we leaving?" asked Frobo. "If our mission is to destroy the rings, and the rings are in the hands of the riders behind us, we're headed in the wrong direction."

"Well, Frobo," said Grandalf, "if you want to take on the nine riders all by yourself, with no weapons, one against nine, then go right ahead and turn back. I, on the other hand, am going to get some help first. And before that, I'm going to get some food and drink, two things I know Hobbicks like yourself to be quite fond of."

The Hobbicks then marched on in silence behind Grandalf. Frobo soon forgot his frustration at not being allowed to bear the new master ring as his stomach began to growl and his feet began to ache.

Ever since Frobo had woken from the wagon plank, they had been walking through wide open fields of partially harvested barley. Now at last, they came upon on a large grove of trees that had been looming in the distance and had seemed to Frobo unreachable for the last hour. Frobo hadn't realized it before, but the moment they reached those tall green trees with broad branches, he would officially be out of the Chire, and in the wild country on the outskirts of Breetown.

They decided to take the road through the grove (despite

Grandalf's fear of the black riders seeing them), for taking the horses through the brambles and trees would've been impossible. As they walked, it sounded like a light breeze playing in the trees was singing a sort of song. The wind had a faint humming rhythm to it like a babbling brook that sprung up after a long winter. And yet, the melody was rough and unpleasant. It reminded Frobo of old drunken gruff hobbicks singing bar songs (the ones whose voices were so bad, they only should've sung even when they were alone in the bath).

But they were not having a bath, they were walking on the road to Breetown, and the gruff yet rhythmic voice was growing clearer and clearer behind them.

"Grandalf," said Happy. "Is that singing?"

"We're being followed! Get off the road!" said Grandalf.

Shuffling as quickly as they could, Grandalf helped them pull the two horses out of sight. They parked behind a small thicket not ten yards off the road and waited.

Frobo discerned the words of the song before spotting the singer, who appeared around the corner. The man wore a dark weather-beaten cloak with a deep hood pulled over his head. Frobo noted the leather boots that stepped out from beneath the long cloak with every stride, a long-barreled pipe that the man was smoking, and perhaps most curious of all, was the fact that he was carrying a saddle on his shoulder. If not for that, and if not for the singing, Frobo might have assumed he was another black rider.

And about that singing... Frobo did not take pleasure in casting aspersions on any hobbick, elf, man, or wizard. But when asked to describe the song he heard many years later, he was well known to say that it was without a doubt, the worst song that he'd ever heard. The man sang it thus:

> *Most people who see me, call me a ranger*
> *And to those who do, that's travelling danger.*

Riding, walking, strolling through the woods,
Don't call me Strider, the name's Roban Hoods.
That's who I am, a forgotten lost ranger,
And to most who see me, that's travelling danger.
My uncle's a King, and my aunt is a Queen,
But those are two folks, whom I've never seen.
Because I was born, in a field of gold corn,
And ever since then, I've been lost and forlorn.
My Mum was a wolf, and my father a fox,
And because they were dogs, I've never worn socks.
Bare paws in the winter, bare paws in the summer,
But bare paws with no boots, make me look even dumber.
Nothing to see here, just a dark ranger,
And to most who see me, I'll always be a stranger.
Stay away from this stranger, because he's a danger,
He's Roban Hoods, the Dangerous Ranger..."

Roban Hoods, the "Dangerous Ranger" strode past them down the road with his saddle slung over his shoulder. He walked right by the spot where they'd taken the horses off road to hide in the trees, and if he noticed their tracks, he made no sign of it.

"Do you think he wrote that himself?" whispered Sham.

"I have no doubt of it," replied Grandalf.

"It's beautiful, isn't it?" asked Sham.

They stared at Sham as they always did when he said something idiotic.

"It's about as beautiful as a painting..." began Martin. "A painting of old Ashelob's arse."

Sham looked offended. "Now don't go disrespecting that poor man's song! He didn't know we was listening, did he?"

"Whether he knew we were listening or not is irrelevant," said Martin.

Sham continued to feign offense at their disrespect as the

gruff man, "Roban Hoods" passed on ahead of them. Evidently, he was also going to Breetown, and they kept far enough behind him so that he didn't notice he was being followed. For all they knew, he could be one of the black riders whose horse had been lost, but Grandalf's better judgement had suspected this was not the case. Still, they couldn't be too careful, out in the wild as they were.

CHAPTER 6

THE DIFFERENCE IN THE SIGN

THEY REACHED THE GATES OF BREETOWN JUST BEFORE nightfall and were admitted with their horses and the wagon remains into the town. Grandalf kept the brim of his large hat pulled over his face during the inspection and went through the gates separate from the hobbicks. News traveled fast between the Chire and Breetown. It was better not to take any chances of someone dressed like a film wizard being seen with four hobbicks after their dramatic departure.

Once inside the gate, Frobo couldn't stop the queasy uncomfortable feelings of insecurity from overtaking him. Sure, he'd seen the big folk who hung around the Chire, the filmmaker's goons namely, but he'd never been so outnumbered by them, as was the case in Breetown. Tall long-legged men walked the streets, driving their tall horses, shouting at each other to stay in their own lanes.

Breetown felt like a misguided place of mud and metal, far too developed and industrial for Frobo's tastes. Through every block, every street, every nook and cranny of the place, Frobo could not spy a single solitary tree, nor did he see a blade of grass. The trees had clearly all been cut down to build the walls, houses, bars, shops, and inns that littered the streets of the town. The tall buildings on all sides of him were like mountains compared to the open fields and meadows of the Chire. But Frobo and his companions were stuck in the valley between the mountains, walking the muddy road that cut through the towering dark buildings. The light from the many windows seemed like torches of fire held by the hosts of the armies of Morbor that watched him struggle in this valley, laughing down at him, as he desperately tried to breath and gain his footing.

"So, where are we headed?" asked Martin. The unconcerned tambor in his voice quite interrupted Frobo's morbid imagination.

"Where else, but the best bar and inn east of the Brandybeer River?" Grandalf said. They rounded a corner and Grandalf pointed to a sign protruding from a large building, "The Prancing..." but Grandalf paused. He had just seen something he had not quite expected. Frobo looked up to the sign with the image of the golden pony brandished on it. The pony that had become nearly immortalized by film legend had drastically shrunk in stature from the one in Frobo's imagination.

"The Prancing *Shetland* Pony™," muttered the wizard. "Well, if this isn't foreboding, I don't know what is. Come along Hobbicks, come along. We can only hope that just because the name has changed, the quality of the beer has remained blessed by my enchantments. But I'll be as angry as a troll if all this orkish, filmish, trademark mischief has made its way into Breetown too. What I wouldn't give for a taste of the beloved Middlearth I left eleventy-one years ago..."

Beneath the swinging sign of The Prancing *Shetland* Pony with the emblazoned prancing miniature horse was another sign that had been temporarily placed in a slot. The text of the sign read, *"Beloved Acting Troupe: The Rugged Dwarfs at the Shetland Pony this Month Only!!!"*

If that wasn't lucky! Frobo had read the headline for their

tour extension to Breetown in the *Morning Muffin* just two days ago. Of course, he'd heard of the *Rugged Dwarfs* before reading about them in the *Muffin*. Their fame spread throughout all Middlearth. But Frobo had never expected to see them live before, as he had never left (before now), nor planned to leave the Chire, and knew little of their act.

Grandalf stood at the door shaking his head. "Would you look at that?" he said. "The door frame's been lowered." He struck the top post of the door frame with his staff, then threw it down on the street in frustration. The top of the door frame was at least a foot lower than the top of Grandalf's head. "I'm not sure I want to grace this nonsensical establishment with my company anymore."

"Now what exactly do you have against the little folk of this world, Grandalf?" said Sham.

"This is a town of men," snapped Grandalf, stooping to pick up his staff. "Men live here. And the last time I checked, you halflings would still be able to fit through the door if it was a foot taller." Grandalf held his fingers to his forehead and ran them up through his hair as if a great burden was being put upon him. Something about looking at that lowered door seemed to make the wizard sick to his stomach. The hobbicks however, didn't mind it at all.

"Well, it isn't a foot taller," said Martin. "And personally, all this signage and decor has piqued my interest in the place. I'm going in whether you can fit through the door or not, Grandalf. And I suspect, if you'll *lower* that towering ego of yours, you'll be able to fit beneath it quite easily."

Martin then reached for the latch, swung open the door and strode through with pride. Sham followed after him, as did Martin and Frobo. Once through, Frobo peeked back over his shoulder. Though he was muttering curses in ancient languages under his breath, the tall wizard did manage to stoop his head and duck beneath the door frame.

Once inside, they found the *Shetland* was in fact built to the proportions of men, just as they would've anticipated. The place was lively with guests, and the roar of their chattering reminded Frobo of a cluster of squawking chickens just before their feed was to be put out. The ambience of the bar was dark and dim, the preferred lighting for beer drinkers. The bar was long and well crafted, hewn of some of the same dark wood that the rest of the town was built with. Frobo did notice that the bartop was just deep enough for a so inclined hobbick or two to dance and sing upon, if the mood took him. The place was so crowded that there was hardly an open stool in it. Frobo crossed his fingers that they'd be able to gain a table to view the show.

At the very far end of the bar, in the very center of the wide, open room, all the chairs at the various tables faced something that Frobo had no recollection of ever seeing in the films. A stage stood no higher from the floor than the head of a hobbick. Drawn across it was a bright crimson curtain with golden embroidered tassels. The whole thing seemed so very out of place to Frobo. There was nothing like this in the Chire. But the ornateness of it all fascinated him.

The only thing between them and the delights of the fine tavern was the tall front desk at the entrance to the place. Grandalf did not waste time observing the novelties of their surroundings. Instead, he cut right in front of the hobbicks and strode up to this desk, brushing the hobbicks aside. Having regained his pride, he leaned against the desk and said to the thick warm air of the inn, "Where is the keeper of this house?"

An extremely portly man with a balding head and short nose waddled out from around the corner. He had an unkempt frisky mustache that was the same paltry color as Grandalf's cloak. From his perspective looking up at the man, Frobo couldn't tell where the hair of his mustache stopped, and the hair of his nose began. It all joined together at the nostrils, like two waterfalls of hair pouring into a flowing river. And the same grey shoots of hair even sprouted from the man's ears, shooting out from them like tiny tufts of mis-planted grass. His eyebrows were black and bushy, curling up in volute ends that were too symmetrical to be natural. The sides of his head were adorned with the thin greasy curls of any man who'd worked one too many shifts in a sweaty tavern. They hung and bounced like the springs of a small hob-in-a-box. The man wore an old brown shirt that stretched over his massive chest and resembled something Frobo might have worn to bed as a nightgown. It was an undershirt at best, with dull stretched out buttons whose threads had been shoddily sewn back on whenever they popped off after a heavy meal.

"Barlimur Butterburbur at your service." The man's voice sounded like the rumblings of a groaning dog. "And what can I do you gentlemen and gentlehobbicks for this fine evening?"

"Barlimur Butterburbur?" repeated Grandalf incredulously.

"Yes sir, Barlimur Butterburbur, that's me name, sir," said the innkeeper.

"Barlimur Butterburbur," began Grandalf, before he was cut off by the man.

"If you say it too much, you'll wear it out sir, hope you don't mind if I say so," said Butterburbur.

"Would you let me finish my confounded sentence! You're worse than these hobbicks. Before I was interrupted," continued Grandalf, "I wanted to ask why the Ashelob you changed the name of this fine establishment, and why you lowered the front door post. What's all this *Shetland* nonsense?"

"Well, if you wanted to ask, then you should've just gone right ahead and done it, shouldn't you? It's not like I need to be reminded of my own name three times, is it?" The innkeeper chuckled, winking at the hobbicks who snickered in turn.

"Excuse us for him, sir," interrupted Sham, bowing before

the innkeeper. "He's not the most... polite chap to begin with. Doesn't like anyone thinking they're smarter than he is, see?"

"Ahh yes," said Butterburbur in reply to Sham. Looking back to Grandalf with a pointed stare, he said to the wizard, "But to answer your question sir..."

"Finally!" snapped Grandalf, throwing his hands into the air.

"We changed the name a long time ago. Soon as I bought the place. The original *Pony* was trademarked after the films, but of course you know that. It was trademarked by Middlearth Enterprises. They came in claiming they deserved all the profits from the place and that they'd sue if we kept selling. The poor owner didn't have a choice, did he? Not with the Middlearth Enterprises goons bearing down on him. He sold the place for a nickel, and I bought it. Then I changed the name, right and proper as soon as I could so those goons couldn't make no more claims. As far as changing it to The Prancing *Shetland* Pony, and lowering the front door post, I just figured that short was the new tall after the release of the latest films. Especially when it comes to these dwarfs, see; the women are going crazy for them! Absolutely crazy I tell you! You wouldn't believe it. And not just normal women, not just humans, I mean. It's elf women too who've caught the fever."

"What are you talking about?" asked Grandalf.

"Look around the place," said Butterburbur. "The place is chalk full of 'em. Elf women, human women, it don't matter. They're all taken with the *Rugged Dwarfs*. And you can't blame them, can you? Look at this," he said, gesturing to a poster behind him of what did indeed look like a rugged dwarf. Flush red lips puckered through a beard that was one of the most well looked after Frobo had ever seen. It was so fresh and fetching that it didn't even cover the dwarf's red cheeks, that burned like a dark setting sun. It was trimmed so short that the dwarf's jawline was also visible, a ruggedly cut work of art that appeared as if it had been chiseled out of stone. Falling at his back was his thick long braided drawn back hair. Frobo looked closely at the picture, for he thought his eyes had betrayed him, but nay, he could not spot a single tangle!

His hair shone like the molasses did when Sham poured it into Frobo's vat. The gleaming green eyes of the dwarf were like bushels of freshly plucked grapes, smiling out at him, tempting the women of Middlearth to come and observe the show. The painting had obviously been touched up. Frobo had never seen a dwarf in person that didn't have bushels of hair protruding from their ears, nose, chest, and sometimes even their eyes. He double checked just to make sure, but saw naught but the perfectly curled and manicured, thick but smooth eyelashes spiraling out perfectly from the dwarf's eyelids.

"Still looks like a dwarf to me," said Grandalf. "Even if he has been *improved* by the painting..."

"Well, that's Ringo, that is," said Butterburbur. "You folk haven't been around much, have you? Ringo now, he's the star of the whole act. The ladies go absolutely bonkers for him, they do. Just wait, you'll see once the show starts tonight. That is one dashingly *rugged* dwarf that is."

Grandalf's eyes rolled. "We'd like a room, if you have one big enough for the five of us..."

"Yes sir, absolutely I do sir," said Butterburbur.

"And we'll take five seats for this... *show*," said Grandalf.

"Yes sir, absolutely, find any seats you like, but keep in mind it can get a little rowdy when the women get excited," said Butterburbur. "If you smaller laddies keep your heads up and find yourselves some beards, tonight might be the finest night of your lives..."

"I don't think any of them have to worry about finding beards tonight," chuckled Grandalf, stroking his own thick beard like it was a lucky charm.

"Oh, I wouldn't go getting any ideas now, sir," said Barliburbur. "They won't have naught for you, no matter how impressive your beard is. It's all about *short* now, short and stout."

Grandalf groaned as he walked away from the innkeeper's desk. Frobo could hear him muttering to himself again. It wasn't every day that the old wizard was talked to that way and Frobo couldn't help but grin at Grandalf's grumpy, quick-tempered frustrations. "You all can go up to the room if you like, but I'm going to have a drink!" the wizard announced.

Sham decided to go up and inspect the room and make sure everything was "up to snuff," but the rest of them went straight into the inn's common area to get some well-earned drink and provender. They didn't have any baggage to leave in their room anyways.

Now that he was inside the tavern, Frobo could see the various mounts and big game that hung about on the walls of the place. Large stags with long pointy horns were on every surface, with the occasional wolf or long tusked boar sprinkled in among the rows of the mounts. He had never seen such large creatures before, save in the films. He couldn't help feeling like they were gazing down at him, waiting for him to turn his back so they could stomp on him or strike him.

Just as the innkeeper had warned, the place was packed with women. Naturally, there were also a fair number of males in the room, as there always were in the Prancing *Shetland* Pony, but for the past month, the men had been continually outnumbered by the women. The tavern was full of females, and a raucous bunch of them they were, too. Frobo had never seen anything like it. Women and elf-women whooping, hollering, and drinking copious amounts of beer. Just as Frobo and the others entered the large room, a chant erupted from the women:

"RUGGED DWARFS! RUGGED DWARFS!" They shouted and whooped, banging their fists on their tables as they did so, overpowering every male voice in the place.

Happy found a table for the four hobbicks. It was out of the way in the back and stood on a raised platform – the perfect hobbick-sized table with an optimal view of the show. They were fortunate, for it was one of the few of its kind in the whole tavern. It had steps leading up to it so that they could easily access it and still see from the perspective of a taller man. Frobo wondered where that old wizard had got off to, for he had disappeared as soon as they had entered the tavern. It was no matter. He would probably be too embarrassed to sit with them anyways.

It wasn't long before steaming hot plates and cold pitchers of beer were brought round to their table. It was a merry feast for the hobbicks who would now go on to attest for the rest of their lives that the Prancing *Shetland* Pony was indeed the finest establishment east of the Brandybeer River. When Sham returned from inspecting their room, he devoured a side of pork all on his own. The bellies of the hobbicks were full and their mouths were wet with the taste of fine beer that must indeed have been blessed by that old wizard. This beer, they could all agree, was far better than the stuff they drank in the Chire that ran from the Brandybeer, which was difficult to admit, because hobbicks had great difficulty admitting that anything was better in other places than it was in the Chire.

After their glasses had been filled and emptied, filled and emptied, and filled and emptied once more, Frobo went to the bar to have their pitcher refilled... again. They were drinking the stuff too quickly for the wait staff to keep up. He waded through the sea of patrons cautiously and carefully, feeling like he was a small child sneaking through a neighbor's corn field, desperate not to break a single stalk.

To his right, a woman with thick eyebrows that connected above her nose like a long, burned slice of bacon, slammed an empty mug onto her table. The mug shattered into a hundred pieces, and Frobo wiped some of its broken flecks from his hair.

"We want the show!" the woman cried to the approving roars from her companions.

To his left, a table of dark-haired elf women were cackling with laughter. Frobo followed their eyes to the object of their fascination and hilarity to see a table of long bearded dwarfs in the middle of a beer chugging contest. The first one to finish slammed his mug on the table and revealed a gap toothed grin to the table of elf women.

As fascinating as all of these women were with their alarming and rowdy behavior, Frobo thought it best and prudent to keep his distance from them and not draw attention to himself. His good hobbick sense couldn't help feeling that somehow all of this just wasn't proper. Upon reaching the bar, he realized that it stood well above his head.

"Of all the rubbish," he muttered to himself, but then he saw it, a tiny ladder to a barstool peeking at him from not ten paces away. Frobo made his way to the small ladder that was fashioned as part of the bar and had clearly been placed there for someone like him: an out of luck hobbick who desired a barstool at the fine establishment. He ascended the ladder and hoisted himself onto the stool that was adjacent it. Then he waited patiently, swinging his legs as they dangled in the air until the barman noticed him.

"What'll it be, Master Hobbick?" the barkeep asked.

"One pitcher of the *Hoppy Hobbick*," said Frobo. "No wait!" he said. He began browsing the hand carved menu of beer selections mounted on the back wall behind the barman. Each beer had its own small illustration skillfully etched next to its name. One image in particular caught his eye, a large black dragon spewing fire at a lakeside town. "How's the *Erebporter?*" Frobo asked.

"Do you like bitter beers?" asked the bartender.

"Not especially, no," said Frobo.

"Well, the *Erebporter* is so fiery bitter, it'll burn the hair off your chest. Seeing as you probably don't have none anyways, I'll fill you up with it."

Frobo twinged at the thought and told the bartender to stick with the *Hoppy Hobbick*. Martin was very particular about his beers and Frobo didn't want to have to make a second trip back her and be forced to climb that ladder again.

"But that's impossible, Wondell," said a familiar voice next to Frobo. He looked to his left and noticed the person next to him at the bar was none other than Grandalf. The wizard was so deeply engaged in conversation with a thin male elf that he had yet to notice Frobo's presence. The elf looked to Frobo like something out of a painting. He was like a sculpture of perfection, with high cheekbones, glowing skin, and golden hair that flowed in unfettered locks from his head like a lion's mane. The only thing about the elf that did not seem perfect were his eyes. They were the saddest and also the bluest, most depressed eyes Frobo had ever seen. Each one was like an entire ocean, glowing like deep blue crystals that had been crafted by the heart of the sea itself.

"It's not impossible Grandalf, it's true." He drawled his words out like a whining child. "I've been a bachelor for five hundred years... my whole life... and with looks like these, the ladies used to gather around me like hungry pigs around their evening slop. Elf maidens were pledging their undying love to me. I had loaves of heart shaped lembras bread sitting at my door every morning. I could've married any elf maiden in Middlearth. Any one of them could've been mine, Grandalf! Mine! My beautiful perfect elf wife! And then, nineteen years ago, the films arrived, and with them, I'm afraid, my bachelorism was finalized." The elf drained the last drops of beer from his large mug and banged it down on the bartop.

"But Wondell," protested Grandalf, "don't take this to mean I'm personally interested, but you're more beautiful than most of the elf maidens in here. Surely they can see that!"

Wondell released a long, loud belch, "Elf women don't want a beautiful face anymore, Grandalf. Not since the films, they don't. Not since the filmmaker made that beautiful maiden kiss that disgusting creature." The elf hissed causing his perfectly symmetrical face to form an ugly grimace as he said the word *"creature."* It seemed to Frobo that Wondell had a bit of an anger management problem. And although Frobo was slightly frightened by the sudden outburst, he leaned in, fascinated by what he was hearing.

"Hold yourself together, Wondell," said Grandalf. "I'm sure it isn't as bad as you say. Just because elf maidens aren't clamoring at your door like they used to, I don't believe you can't find a good number of elf maidens in all of Middlearth who'd be willing to marry you."

"Oh Grandalf..." drawled Wondell. "You poor naive old fool. If only the elf maidens of Middlearth thought like you..." and at that the male elf with the incredibly picturesque face burst into song,

The elf maidens of this Middlearth
Used to knock upon my door,
They used to want to give my children birth,
But that's not the case anymore!
Oh sure! I've been the judge of beauty contests,
Of elf maidens most men would die for,
Blue eyes, golden hair, white teeth, perfect breasts,
And to them I'm now just an eyesore!
But if I'd known then, what I know now,
As quick as I could I'd go recite my vows!
But Alas! Alas! is all I can say!
I don't have a lass, even though I'm not gay!
Alas! Alas! I don't sink in the snow!
There's no hair on my chest! And my skin always glows!

Apparently unable to contain himself, Wondell's song had thrown him into a state of inspiration. Upon the recitation (or creation) of his chorus, "*Alas! Alas! Is all I can say!*", Wondell had been unable to remain in his seat. The elf began to dance and prance around the tavern and across the bartop with every rhyme and lyric of his song. But this only served to cause an uproar, for he was the exact opposite of the show the ladies of the Prancing *Shetland* Pony had paid good wages to enjoy that evening. Beers flew and sausages soared at his face. Boos and jeers rained from the crowd. But despite all that, Wondell continued his song, driven on by inspiration and courage at the knowledge of the inherent limberness of his race. There was not a sausage, beer, or loaf of bread thrown at him that the elf couldn't dodge without missing a note.

> *These are the things ladies used to love,*
> *About the wonderful Wondell, who sings like a dove.*
> *But then one day those wretched films arrived...*
> *With the foulest ideas that have ever been contrived!!!*
> *The most backwards thing I have ever beheld,*
> *Occurred inside that scene!*
> *An elf kissed a dwarf perhaps falling in love,*
> *And I still think it was obscene!*
> *Ever since then, my life's been over,*
> *Ever since then, I've been nothing but sad,*
> *Cause ever since then, all the elf women want,*
> *Is a short little man, with a beard and big nads.*
> *Ever since then, my life's been over,*
> *Ever since then, I've been simply depressed,*
> *With my clear skin and my manicured eyebrows*
> *Elf women today are no longer impressed...*
> *Ever since then, my life's been over,*
> *Ever since then, I've been nothing but sad,*
> *Cause ever since, all the elf women want,*

Is a half sized degenerate beer chugging dwarf!
Ever since then my life's been over
Ever since then I've been simply depressed,
Cause ever since then all the elf maidens want,
Is a dwarf with a beard who comes up to her chest!

At last, to Frobo's amazement, Wondell's song ended, mainly due to the cries, protests, and boos from the throng of elf women around the room. The jeers and taunts had come from the very same elf maiden's who'd once been gathered outside Wondell's door, eager to bear his children (at least if his story was true). But their feelings had clearly changed about the poor elf, whose eyes still looked as sad and as blue as ever.

"You see Grandalf," said Wondell, returning to his barstool next to the wizard. "Elf women today aren't like they used to be. It's been like this... well, it's been like this since that last set of three films arrived. And since the Rugged Dwarfs started gallivanting across the countryside like they were royalty!" Wondell's last comment was directed more at the crowd of eager elf women than it was to Grandalf. "I've tried Grandalf, I've tried everything," he babbled as he reached for his pint-sized glass again, draining it with one large chug. The glass was instantly refilled by the bartender.

"Well, Wondell, as much as I hate to say it, it's not like you didn't have your chances," said Grandalf, shaking his head and taking a sip of his beer. "I mean, you said it yourself in your song, you could've had any elf maiden you wanted. Maybe next time you won't be so picky..."

"Maybe next time I won't be so picky?" the quiet restraint in Wondell's voice seethed from between his bared teeth.

"Well yes," said Grandalf as if it was a matter of fact.

"Maybe next time I won't be so *picky!*" shouted Wondell as the room quieted. "What do you think I've been kicking myself about for the last nineteen years you crazy old buzzard? There isn't going to be a next time!"

The whole of the inn stared at Wondell and Grandalf for a moment before the dull roar of the place started up again. Frobo couldn't believe someone could have such little self-awareness, not to mention that he had spoken to Grandalf the great wizard in such a manner! Grandalf's reaction was far from what it would've been had one of the hobbicks spoken to him that way.

"Alright chap, alright," said Grandalf, patting poor Wondell on the back and massaging his shoulder. "I didn't mean it like that. Now pull yourself together. Look, the show's about to start."

Had Grandalf possessed the full measure of his faculties of thought, as opposed to his current state of partial inebriation, he might've known that the last thing this show was going to do was help Wondell feel better about his plight. But Grandalf, much like Frobo, was in a new world. The old Middlearth he used to know had changed so much in the eleventy-one years he'd been away. It had left him behind like the sea leaves the rocks on the shore. And if his brief time in the Chire, along with the spectacle he'd beheld so far that evening with Wondell hadn't convinced him of this, Grandalf was in for a rude awakening as to just how much Middlearth had changed.

A short little man suddenly peeked from behind the stage's red curtain, shifting his beady little eyes across the tavern. Cheers erupted from the women in the audience as he strutted out from behind the curtain. He wore a green coat and a black top hat. His face was all smiles with rosy, red cheeks and he had a curly mustache. The applause he received was like none Frobo had ever heard before. These people... nay, these women were downright enthusiastic about these Rugged Dwarfs.

"Ladies and..." the jolly short man began, "well, I must say, I can see that I am mainly speaking to ladies!"

The laughter and roars of approval quite drowned out poor Wondell screaming at the top of his lungs, "It's not just ladies here, thank you very much!" The wizard did his very best to console the poor elf, putting his arm around him and pulling him back into his barstool.

"Another beer for him, barkeep," Grandalf said, motioning to Wondell's mug.

"Ladies," the red-faced man continued, "it is with great pleasure and my utmost joy that I introduce to you, for the first time in Breetown and exclusively at the Prancing *Shetland* Pony, sponsored by the films themselves, the Rugged Dwarfs!"

The lights dimmed and a hush fell over the entirety of the crowd save Wondell who moaned like a frightened dog. Frobo sat on the edge of the barstool he'd adopted. He'd completely forgotten he was supposed to be bringing the pitcher of *Hoppy Hobbick* back to their table because of the intrigue of this curious show. He took a big drink from the pitcher as the lights now glowed on the stage, where the red curtains with golden tassels were drawn back.

Somewhere in the inn, perhaps from behind the stage, a pianist began to pound the keys of a piano, echoing a delicate melody throughout the whole inn. It was followed by a rhythmic beat that reminded Frobo of a marching army, one that was marching to a rhythm.

Then the source of the marching appeared as four dwarfs, arm in arm, danced their way onto the stage in a sort of sideways jig. Their muscular bare legs, exposed below their matching bronze kilts from the middle thigh down to their boots, crossed and shimmied in the rhythm of the dance, every pounding foot colliding with the stage in the unison only perfect coordination can achieve. Each dwarf donned a belt with a large shining silver buckle above their kilts. They also wore low cut skintight white shirts with sleeves rolled up to reveal their glistening bulging arm muscles. Frobo recognized the dwarf he'd seen in the poster, Ringo. Amazingly, he looked every bit the part of his image in the advertisement, but the other three dwarfs didn't seem to quite match him in appearance or his level of personal grooming. He was by far the superior dwarf of the four, with the strongest muscles, the darkest hair, the reddest cheeks, the greenest eyes, and the most cut jawline. If Frobo's eyes did not deceive him, Ringo the dwarf also appeared to be just a few inches taller than the other three.

The cheers from the women of the Shetland Pony drowned out the rhythmic tapping of their boots but the eager crowd soon resumed their hush, anxious not to miss a single step. The dwarf's dance was perfect and on beat, and at the end of the first sequence, as suddenly as they had appeared on stage, the dancing dwarfs all at once burst into song.

> *We are dwarfs! We are dwarfs!*
> *We are rugged handsome dwarfs!*
> *And we're here to show you ladies*
> *Just how much you need a dwarf!*
> *Come look down, cause when you do,*
> *You'll see us smiling up at you!*
> *Here to sweep you off your feet*
> *Here to complete your honey-dos!*
> *We can wash! We can clean!*
> *We'll do the best chores that you've seen!*
> *And as you're resting on your couch,*
> *We'll cook a wonderful cuisine!*

Roaring screams, cheers, and whistles erupted from the crowd at this line. "I just don't get it Grandalf!" whined Wondell. "What do they see in them?"

The dwarfs then danced another quick tapping jig, stepping between each other's shimmying feet like a weaver's loom. Then as the sequence concluded, the three dwarfs kneeled looking up at Ringo in their center. Ringo strode forward as the rhythm of the tapping was replaced with soft humming. When the crowd quieted he began his solo.

> *Everywhere I travel, I see women far and wide,*
> *Who need more than elfs or men have been able to provide!*
> *You need someone who's special and can be there when you're blue*
> *And you're tired of that someone weighing slightly less than you!*
> *That's where I come in!*

The pianist pounded the keys.

> *I'm here to rescue you!*

Screams of "Ringo!" and "Oh Ringo!", preceded several women collapsing in a swoon.

> *From life's terrible barbecue!*
> *Where these men have entangled you!*
> *And locked you up iiiiiiiiinnnnnnnn!*

Ringo then ripped off his white shirt with a single tug of his strong arm revealing a muscular bare chest the likes of which Frobo had never imagined a dwarf could possess. As he strode back and forth across the stage to deafening catcalls and wailings, Frobo assured himself that it had to have been shaved just moments before the dwarfs took the stage. In fact, that was probably why it had taken the dwarfs so long to appear. They were all shaving their chests and backs. Only a male elf could have been that naturally hairless.

"The maiden who catches my shirt earns herself the right to bring it up on stage," yelled Ringo the dwarf. "To me! And she'll get to share a dance with the most Rugged Dwarf east of the Brandybeer River!"

The expected eruption ensued. Frobo glanced over to see Wondell in tears with his head resting on the bar. Grandalf could only stare in apparent shock at the scene, still as a stone, with an open gaping mouth.

"Now now, ladies!" Ringo continued as the women struggled for position. "Be nice! But after all, this is your chance to dance with *me* on stage!" Ringo then balled his shirt into a wad and turned his back to the crowd.

"One! Two! Three!" he shouted, then tossed the shirt over his shoulder. As the shirt flew, a few flecks of salty water landed on Frobo's forehead. He reached his hand up to his face, wiping away the salty liquid. Had some of Ringo's sweat flown off the shirt and landed on his face?

A struggle ensued as women rushed in on the area where the shirt had landed. Clearly, they were unperturbed by the sweatiness of Ringo's shirt. Screams, shouts, and a hair pulling name calling catfight brawl ensued. Frobo stood up in his barstool to watch the incredible scene. He'd never seen women fight before!

"Alright then, alright!" shouted Ringo from the stage. "As much as I'd like for this to continue, I think I see a winner. Come on up here lassie! That's right, you in the green dress."

Frobo stood up in his stool trying to spot the woman who'd caught the shirt. He could see one woman standing apart from a crowd of others who crossed their arms and hung their heads. As she crested the stairs to the stage, Frobo first beheld her disheveled golden hair that was neither brown nor blonde. She then threw her head back and behind the golden locks was revealed the face of what looked to Frobo like that of a blessed angel. As Ringo had mentioned, she did in fact wear a green dress. It fell to her feet and flowed like a sparkling emerald pool behind her. Her cheeks were pink, and her eyes were bright green like those of an elf who had seen the light in the west. But though her beauty was nigh equal one, she was no elf, that

Frobo could see. A thin belt of gold was tied around her narrow waist, drawing the green fabric tight below the effigy of her bust, before hooking around her otherwise bare exposed shoulders. Frobo's breath left him, and his face felt flush. He had never seen such a beauty before.

Upon ascending the stairs, she ran her fingers through her golden hair, frantically rearranging it into what she thought was a presentable fashion. Frobo did not understand why she did so, for he found her effortlessly beautiful.

"Step right up, my lady!" said Ringo. The dwarf now appeared short again, for the top of his head stood only as high as the exposed shoulders of the golden-haired lady. He grinned from ear to ear as she walked towards him, and his greedy eyes gleamed in the light like one who beheld a chest of treasure he had just unearthed. "Try not to swoon," he said, chuckling to the crowd. "I know the effect I can have on a beautiful woman like you."

The crowd seemed to laugh and sigh simultaneously, for every woman in it envied this lucky maiden. Frobo gazed at the angelic woman on the stage. Of course, Frobo knew better than to fancy any sort of relationship with her. He wouldn't think of himself with her any more than he'd think of himself with the setting sun. There was something that was just too high and lofty about her. Frobo dared not sully that with his own longings. He would admire, but not desire.

Perhaps, the same could not be said for Ringo the Dwarf. "Well, well, well! Aren't you a pretty one?" he chuckled, rising up on his toes as she approached. "I'm sure you're excited to be on stage with me! Why don't you introduce yourself to all of these jealous ladies out in the crowd?" Ringo stood next to the gorgeous woman, the top of his head barely reaching her shoulder, and placed his arm around her waist.

The woman giggled and swayed nervously at Ringo's touch, laughing like Ringo possessed the golden touch of a king.

"Hello, Breetown," she began, waving at the crowd of ladies. Suddenly she was the only woman in the whole place who was smiling. "Umm, sorry... I'm supposed to introduce myself. My name's Ella, and I'm so happy I decided to be here tonight!" Ella was giggling so much from nervousness that she could barely speak. Frobo couldn't imagine why a woman as beautiful as her would've been nervous around any male, much less one that barely reached her shoulder.

"Well then," said Ringo. "Ella! Perhaps you'd like a kiss for returning my shirt before our dance?"

"Oh!" giggled Ella, blushing suddenly like a red dawn as women throughout the room groaned. "Well, yes of course... if that's a possibility!"

Ringo then trip-dipped Ella in a sudden sweeping movement. She fell into his arms so quickly that any who blinked would have missed it.

As the females gathered in that assembly all swooned, Frobo found himself feeling absolutely disgusted at the turn of events. He thought deep down that he should be happy for Ringo, and that the little folk of all *short* races had to stick together. But there was something... that didn't feel quite right about the little man with the freshly shaved body holding that woman who was beautiful beyond description. As he glanced away from the onstage scene in temporary nausea, Frobo espied someone he hadn't yet seen in the room, a tall figured man, with a dirty dark cloak rise from a dark corner to retire to his bed. There was something familiar about his stride.

Was that the very same man that had been singing on the road to Breetown? What had he called himself... *Roban Hoods*. The man had long dark brown hair that was flecked with sun turned streaks of blonde. It hung about his face like the leaves of a willow tree. His dark beard was trimmed and well kept on his dirty grimy face, as he clearly hadn't washed up before coming down to the tavern to have a drink. Indeed, the sight of him made Frobo wonder how clean he looked himself. The man did carry a sword at his side, a detail he hadn't noticed when first seeing him in the forest, and also a long looping rope hung from his belt.

Very few Middlearthers carried swords anywhere but upon their horses these days, since the threat of orks no longer existed. With the destruction of that *Insidious Ring,* the films had revealed that evil had been defeated forever, rendering all swords, knives, bows, and axes as little more than fitting decorations for those trying to stand out or surprise. This had always been the case in the Chire, but Frobo had heard that the other parts of the world had become just as civilized. To confirm his suspicion, he glanced about the place to check for swords in hilts or other weapons strapped to waists... however, almost all of those waists were beneath the tables at which they sat, and he was plumb out of luck.

But glancing about the room, Frobo did see something out of the corner of his eye. In a high window, far above the entrance to the inn, he could barely make out a dark black figure peering into the inn with beady yellow cat-like eyes. Was someone watching all of this from the roof?

The distraction was interrupted by the clear sound of a glass bottle shattering on stage and an abrupt crash. Ringo dropped the woman Ella and held his hand up to his forehead, which gushed red blood. Screams echoed across the crowd before Frobo heard a distressed voice not far away from him shout up to the stage, "How dare you!"

Frobo winced in pity for the poor elf. The voice was Wondell's. He was so drunk he'd started a fight with the most popular dwarf in all of Middlearth.

"How dare you defile a woman so high above your stature! You impotent belligerent disgusting dwarf!" Wondell rose from his barstool in defiance as Grandalf tried for a second to restrain him, but then quickly held himself back, feigning disassociation. The elf's face was angry, with dark furrowed brows and a dreadful grimness. His cheeks were red either from the flames of anger inside of him or the excessive quantity of drinks he'd consumed. He was a tall elf, and though he looked as lithe and brittle as the reed of a flute, Frobo thought he was terrible to behold, a fell force of wrath.

The observing women didn't know how to react. They were glad the elf's outburst had interrupted all the attention Ella was receiving, but felt nothing but disdain for Wondell. The latter mixed with their love for Ringo (whom Wondell had just injured) proved the stronger. A punching, biting, hair pulling mob of women rushed at Wondell. The elf had little hope of escape.

Ringo was being tended to on stage by several of his adoring fans who'd quickly rolled Ella away from him. She had been lying on the stage where Ringo dropped her, and those loving, caring women had nearly rolled her off it. Thankfully, she had come to, and stopped them from doing so.

Frobo, along with Grandalf, put as much distance between himself and Wondell as possible. Wondell was lifted above the heads of the angry women like a slain carcass. Yet though he was drunk, he was an elf nonetheless. Somehow, he managed to remove himself from the grasps of the topmost hands by standing up and running across them.

Ringo, whose bleeding head had been more than amply bandaged and whose lips and cheeks were red with a mixture of his own dried blood and the lipstick of his attendees, rose from the stage and began striding towards the skirmish. Wondell skipped from hand to hand to hand, until at last one clever woman moved from his path and he crashed to the floor in a heap. He'd almost made it to the door, but looking up from the ground, he found the exit blocked by Ringo's three dwarf companions.

"Turn and face me, cowardly elf!" shouted Ringo to the crawling Wondell.

Wondell stood to his feet. Scratches and bruises from the attacking women riddled his otherwise perfect face.

"In all the towns, in all the villages, in all the countries across all of Middlearth," began Ringo, "I have never been so disrespected as I have been tonight. How dare you attempt to injure the face of Ringo the Rugged!"

The onlooking women cheered in excitement.

Wondell laughed, and then began crying, "You don't understand. They used to love *ME* like they love you. You're nothing more than a cock-eyed warthog prancing in a zoo for maidens to point to and laugh at!"

"I! Demand! An apology!" shouted Ringo.

"Fight him, Ringo!" a woman in a green dress shouted next to Frobo. He looked up to see her golden-brown hair hanging about her bare shoulders. Bless him, but she was not just any woman. Frobo realized he was standing next to *Ella*.

Frobo nearly fainted with nervous energy. Her perfume was like the exotic oil of a budding flower, overtaking Frobo's senses as he breathed in the intoxicating aroma. She was so close to him, so close that he could have touched the bright green dress that was stretched around her waist if he had a mind to... *"Pull yourself together Daggins, you're acting like a child!"* he scolded himself, before returning his attention to Ringo and Wondell.

The women broke out in unified cheers at Ella's encouragement for a fight. Ringo, to the surprise of Frobo, seemed to be trying to calm them down, as if he'd be perfectly content with an apology from Wondell.

But that would simply not be tolerated by the angry mob, and upon this realization, with an uncomfortable look on his face, the dwarf started to stretch out his arms. Frobo couldn't imagine what the dwarf had to be nervous about, if he was in fact nervous. When he looked at Wondell and he looked at

Ringo... Frobo was closer to Ringo now and he could see the prickling back and chest hairs that were returning in tiny sprouts after what couldn't have been more than an hour's time since the dwarf had shaved them. But the body from which they grew was strong like burnished bronze, as broad and burly as a black maned lion. On the other hand, Wondell resembled a more majestic creature... perhaps a horse? His thin tall body and handsome face had been alive for four centuries, and yet he looked as young as an eager stag in its first rut.

There was no question, in Frobo's mind at least, as to who the winner of the fight would be. Ringo would annihilate poor Wondell, which is what made the dwarf's nervous disposition so baffling. He was sitting on a barstool in the middle of the circle the women had formed, and his right foot tapped the wooden floor incessantly. And he was breathing so deeply one might think he'd just ran here from Drywater! But the pallor of his face was the most betraying feature of his fear. His characteristically ruddy cheeks were as white as a wedding gown.

Wondell, cockeyed and bruised, struggled to stand tall in his corner (partially from the beating he'd taken, but mostly from his extreme state of drunkenness). But suddenly Grandalf appeared behind him, standing tall and rubbing the elf's shoulders, whispering advice into the elf's ear as to where he might gain an advantage over his foe.

Ringo stood up from his proffered stool at the opposite end of the circle that had formed around them, speaking to his fellow *Rugged Dwarfs*. From the front desk of the Prancing *Shetland* Pony a bell rang, signaling for the fight to begin.

Ringo cautiously stepped forward, crouching on his haunches. He held up both of his fists, rotating them like the vanes of the old Chire windmill in broad slow deliberate strokes. Wondell also approached. His hands formed fists too, but he held them at his sides. The whites of his blue eyes were set ablaze with red fire (from crying, anger, or intoxication

Frobo could not tell). The two circled each other for a cautious time as the crowd jeered, until Ringo made the first move. He charged the elf, roaring suddenly like a bear, and dove for him in a head down bull rush.

Despite Wondell's drunken state, he was far too quick for the blundering thuds of Ringo's charge. Wondell feinted to the left (like any experienced hog hunter would have) and dodged the charge while simultaneously grabbing Ringo's belt and hurling him with his own momentum into the onlooking crowd. The ladies parted and Ringo crashed into one of the *Shetland Pony's* large oaken tables.

Wondell laughed at the confused dwarf, "Dashed to bits, I see! Take that my Rugged Dwarf!"

Ringo arose from the splinters of the broken table with a bright red face that twinged and pulsed with the fire of humiliation. The crashing fall had amazingly managed to dislodge the dwarf's long thick ponytail and now his hair hung in all directions like a frizzy unkempt mess. A large vein appeared on the dwarf's forehead. "Now you've done it, you dimwitted imbecile. You've ruined my hair!"

As Wondell burst into laughter at Ringo, the dwarf charged him again, but this time he threw himself sideways at Wondell as the elf tried to dodge. Frobo was shocked at the leap. The slow, rumbling, drudging trot had hidden the heights to which the dwarf could fly when he had to. Ringo's outstretched arms caught Wondell across the chest, toppling him to the floor like a falling tree. At once, Ringo sprang upon the elf, but his first punch connected with the wooden planks of the floor. Wondell slithered beneath the dwarf's legs like a sidewinding snake, and delivered a sweeping, crushing kick to the side of Ringo's head.

This was the elf's first mistake. For the crushing was all done to Wondell's foot! The elf cried aloud in pain and began hopping around like a one-legged buffoon. Ringo, whose head appeared to be harder than stone, laughed and shook his long mane of hair back behind his shoulders. Striding up to Wondell, now as confident as he'd been on stage, Ringo swung his right arm at Wondell's perfect face. The elf dodged.

Ringo swung again, and the elf dipped his head back, with Ringo's fist not inches from Wondell's face. Another swing, another dodge, but this one was too close to the surrounding crowd. The ladies pushed Wondell right at Ringo. Wondell, showing his truly incredible athleticism, hurdled Ringo with a front flip, and delivered a swift punch to the dwarf's kidney.

This time, both Ringo and Wondell cried out in pain. Wondell cringed and held his hand as if he'd just punched a wall and Ringo collapsed to his knees. But Ringo recovered first, approaching Wondell from behind. He grabbed the elf by the shirt and the belt, lifted him over his head and tossed him over the surrounding crowd into the very same oak table he'd broken just before.

The ladies gushed in congratulatory applause, but Grandalf winced at the crash. Frobo fully expected the elf to stay down, his thin frame and handsome face would surely not be able to withstand a blow like the one it had just suffered.

But from the dust of the broken table the elf stood up before their eyes holding one of the table's thick wooden legs in his hand like a club. He approached the dwarf with a grim expression. Ringo stood firm like a boulder, crouching in anticipation but steadfast and unmoving. Wondell rushed at him like a storm and struck down at the dwarf with the thick wooden post again and again.

The ladies began to boo. Ringo fell back to the floor amid his efforts to defend himself, but he was outmatched. The dwarf was doing all he could to block the blows, but the fury of Wondell would not be deterred. Wondell struck too quickly and too forcefully and Frobo saw that the dwarf's resistance to the strikes had failed him.

Beneath Wondell, Frobo could see the bloodied and bruised

arms and frightened face of a dwarf who had no strength left to resist his enemy. Wondell stood over him and raised the post back for one final blow, then swung the post down like a miner swinging a pickaxe. The women gasped as Wondell brought the post down to connect with the dwarf's head. He'd beaten the dwarf, and this would be the final finishing blow. But then, just when they'd all assumed he was finished, Ringo's hand shot up from his side, and *caught* the swinging post just before it collided with his head! The women erupted in cheerful glee. Wondell looked down in shock at Ringo, a wild expression on his face. With both hands, Ringo twisted the post, spinning it like a top sending Wondell, now an extension of its other end, hurling into the ground in a crashing cartwheel.

Ringo arose, spreading his arms to the crowd's adoration and pumped his fist in celebration. Clearly, he thought the fight was won. Until from behind him, Wondell smashed a chair over his head.

Long indeed may that fight have continued, if at that moment the Breetown magistrate, along with the entirety of his sheeriffs, had not entered the inn. They'd been summoned by poor Barlimur Butterburbur, who hadn't in the least enjoyed his precious *Shetland* Pony being turned into a boxing ring. The sheeriffs rushed at Ringo and Wondell, tackling them both and binding their hands with rope.

"Not Ringo too!" protested Butterburbur, waving his hands and running at the sheeriffs like Ringo was his own child. "He's the star of the show! If you arrest him, where do you think all these ladies will go?"

The magistrate swaggered into the middle of the circle, looking down at both Wondell and Ringo like they were rotting carcasses on the side of his road. He was obviously the magistrate, his costume and garb revealed that. His long green dark coat with golden trappings and brown buttons hung down past the rim of his boots. And beneath it, he wore a white frilly shirt. A broad rimmed black hat donned his head, a ridiculous choice since it was night time and they were inside. Frobo had seen this type of garb before. It was the exact same thing worn by the goon bosses of Middlearth Enterprises.

"Disturbers of the peace will be treated all the same!" the magistrate exclaimed, stroking his shiny black mustache. Perhaps he was just as eager as his men to arrest Ringo, because the dwarf had enchanted away the affections of so many beautiful women. A bitter sneer of contempt was revealed in the magistrate's curled upper lip, looking down at Ringo as his sheeriffs bound his arms. "Justice must prevail Butterburur, no matter the cost."

As the sheeriffs led away Wondell, the poor elf cried out to the wizard, "Help me, *Grandalf!* Don't let them take me!"

A hush fell over the crowd as all eyes turned to the wizard. Frobo's heart leapt into his throat.

CHAPTER 7

MIRACULUM EX MACHINA

"DID YOU SAY GRANDALF?" ASKED THE MAGISTRATE, HIS EYES flaring like glowing embers upon the utterance of the name. "Surely not Grandalf™? The famous or should I say, infamous wizard?" The magistrate strode up to Grandalf, eyeing him like he was trying to discover if he was a priceless relic or a cheap counterfeit.

"Reports reached me this very evening that a Grandalf™ impersonator had escaped from the Chire, was headed for Breetown, and that I should be on the lookout for suspicious characters. And now this disturber of the peace elf calls you Grandalf. What do you have to say for yourself old man?"

"Preposterous!" Grandalf exclaimed, the moment the magistrate stopped speaking. "Can't you see the poor fellow's drunk? Stay around him a little longer and he might call you the Queen of Grondor."

"Interesting," replied the suspicious magistrate. "The Grandalf™ impersonator was accompanied by four hobbicks, but as I don't see any of those little folk with you, I must assume that you are not the Grandalf™ impersonator. But!" he added, "We'll be keeping an eye on you."

Frobo tried his best to remain as inconspicuous as possible as the men led Ringo and Wondell away. What fools they'd been! Surely, they should've known that Sauluman would warn the Breetown-folk of their coming.

Grandalf retook his seat at the bar, now alone as the hubbub of the ladies resumed and the magistrate left with his sheeriffs and prisoners. Butterburbur shuffled all the way from his reception desk back around behind the bar to speak to Grandalf. There was a nervous look on the portly man's face as he approached, looking from side to side to see if anyone was watching or listening.

"You didn't tell me you were a Grandalf™ impersonator!" accused Butterburbur.

"Well, naturally I didn't tell you that, because I'm not one," Grandalf replied.

Frobo approached the two, then once more climbed the ladder at the stool next to Grandalf, inserting himself presumptively into their conversation.

"But what about the hobbicks you came in with?" shouted Butterburbur. "What about him?" he said, pointing to Frobo. "Am I really supposed to believe that this is all a coincidence?"

"Well, you asked if I was a Grandalf™ impersonator, my good innkeeper, to which I truthfully replied that I was not. However, both you and your precious magistrate failed to ask me if I was *the* Grandalf, Grandalf™, or whatever in Middlearth it is you people call me these days."

Butterburbur jumped back open mouthed at this so that his backside toppled over some mugs that were propped up on the backbar. But he was too flabbergasted by Grandalf's statement to mount a retort. Grandalf continued, leaning over the bar and piercing the barkeeper's eyes with his gaze.

"But if you want your beer to be as blessed with good taste as it was under the previous owner of this inn, you will keep your mouth shut about that. If you don't, you can rest assured that I'll lay a curse upon it so terrible, that five thousand imported barrels will not be able to overcome it!"

The innkeeper's mouth shut so suddenly at this statement, that his face seemed to swell up like he'd just been stung by a bee. It was all he could do when he looked at Grandalf to nod in vociferous agreement.

"Well, now that that's settled," said Grandalf, "I think I'll have some of that beer. Complimentary!"

"Bl...bl...blimey! What'll it be sir?" stuttered Butterburbur.

"A *White Wizard!* And it had better be troll sized!" shouted Grandalf.

"And one more for his half-sized companion!" shouted Frobo, although he was not sure Butterburbur heard him.

Grandalf leaned back in his seat at the bar like a conqueror, smiling and satisfied with crossed arms. The women, who were sadly realizing the show was over, began to file out of the inn. Now all that was left was the hobbicks, the three remaining *Rugged Dwarfs*, Roban Hoods, who apparently hadn't made it up to his room before the fight, and a few stragglers who'd come to see the show. Frobo looked for the beautiful lady, Ella, but did not see her. She must have already retired to her room.

"The *Rugged Dwarfs*..." muttered Grandalf. "What a ridiculous gobble of hogwash mischief! I've never seen women, beautiful elf women mind you, behave themselves in such a fashion as I saw tonight. Absolutely ridiculous!"

"I know what you mean," said Frobo, as Grandalf eyed him over the mug of beer. "It's like that Ella who was up on the stage. Of course, I thought her beautiful, but she was much too far above my status. She was too high in a way... beautiful like the sunrise over a mountain peak. She's not someone to be touched or even imagined in the same way a hobbick would love another hobbick."

"Yes..." said Grandalf. "I quite agree... I say, Frobo my lad, if you keep talking like that, I may start to think that you may just be the heir of the greatest hobbick who ever lived. A Sackville-Daggins would never say what you just said."

"I'm not sure what to believe anymore, Grandalf..." said Frobo.

The other three hobbicks were laughing merrily at their table behind them. It was their first time out of the Chire, their first time away from home. And just like their ancestors, they had a purpose. Frobo had been told his whole life who his ancestor was, but if he was honest with himself, he'd never believed it. Envy of Sham, who had no responsibilities now that they were out of the Chire, and especially of Happy, stole over his heart. *Happy...* Happy had the new ring. If only he could be the ring bearer, then no one would be able to deny his claim as the true heir of the most famous hobbick who ever lived. But he couldn't. Not yet at least.

"Three beers for the road, Butterburbur, and make it quick," said a gruff voice to Frobo's left at the bar.

"For the road?" said Butterburbur with a confused voice. "But you've only just arrived! And Ringo's been taken to the jail. Surely you aren't leaving without him!"

The other three members of the *Rugged Dwarfs* were standing at the bar. They had packs strapped across their backs and long travelling coats had been pulled over the tight white shirts they'd been wearing for the performance. Each one of them bore a walking stick in his hand.

"We're sorry, Butterburbur," said the foremost of them. "We know about the contract, but we can't take it anymore. For five years now we've been doing this act! And everywhere we go, Ringo is the only one of us who seems to get any... *action*... if you take my meaning. And well tonight, with the sheeriffs taking him and all, well I'll just say we've been looking for a chance like this for a long time, Butterburbur."

"But what about the show?" cried Butterburbur. "Who will dance on stage with Ringo?"

"I don't know!" said the dwarf. "But it won't be us no more, and that's that. It's not easy, you know! Standing up there, strutting around like fools, while we watch him embrace the most beautiful maidens in every town and village in Middlearth. All the time, us three being glared at by the men of that town. We've had it, I tell you! We're finished Butterburbur. Tell that conceited, high headed, chest shaving buffoon when he gets out tomorrow that we're finished!"

The three dwarfs took their beers, much to the chagrin of Butterburbur, and left the Inn of the Prancing *Shetland* Pony that very evening. "But what'll I do now, Grandalf?" asked Butterburbur. "Who will bring in the women like the *Rugged Dwarfs* promised to?"

Martin, who had overheard their conversation from the hobbick's table spoke up, "Pardon me for saying so, Mister Innkeeper Buttersir, but what about the three of us?"

Butterburbur gave no response and simply hung his head in discouragement.

"I know I wouldn't mind holding a lass like that Ella between my arms!" cracked Sham as a long belch erupted from his mouth.

"You wouldn't mind it if she was missing half her front teeth either, would you, Sham?" chimed in Happy as all three of them burst into laughter. Sham nodded playfully, acknowledging the truth of the remark.

"I don't believe I caught the names of you two gentle… men?" A familiar voice had spoken from behind Grandalf and Frobo. It was a far more palatable voice to hear when it was speaking instead of singing.

Frobo turned his head and saw the exact person he'd expected, with the dark frizzy locks flecked with sun turned streaks of blonde. He smiled at the two of them as if they were old friends, as one smiles when he is aware of something you are not. Frobo couldn't imagine what this knowledge might be.

"The name's Hoods. Roban Hoods. And you are?"

"Gra-" began Grandalf before catching himself, "Glandalf is my name sir, grad to meet you, ahem... pardon me, glad to meet you."

"Glandalf, the pleasure is all mine. And your name, sir?" he added, turning to Frobo.

"Floooo...." began Frobo who spied Grandalf trying to dissuade him from speaking this name out of the corner of his eye. But it was too late! "Flobo Blaggins at your service, Mister Hoods," he introduced himself so emphatically that there was no taking it back.

Grandalf threw up his hands and rolled back his eyes behind Roban.

"Flobo?" remarked Roban with a laugh. "Flobo Blaggins and Glandalf, grad to meet me? Well, aren't you two just the pair? I'll be in touch Mister... Glandalf. I have a feeling our paths may meet again." The tall man walked away from the bar and ascended the staircase up to the inn's rooms.

"Flobo Blaggins," Grandalf whispered at Frobo in utter vexation. "I say my dear lad, could you be any more obvious?"

"Could I be more obvious?" shouted Frobo incredulously. "I was following your lead *Glandalf, grad to meet you!*"

"Glandalf was creative," explained the wizard. "It was original. But when you copied it, it ruined both our disguises! Now every bloke in Breetown is going to be looking for Flobo Blaggins and Glandalf, thanks to you."

Frobo could only roll his eyes, drain his glass, and take the stairs to their sleeping quarters. He was tired of that know-it-all wizard telling him what to do. Once his head hit the pillow of his soft bed in the Prancing *Shetland* Pony, he fell fast asleep.

He awoke the following morning to the kicks and squirms of a hobbick that was sleeping so close to him, Frobo could feel his sour breath on his cheek. He peeked beneath his eyelids to see the bright morning sun shining at him through the window.

The large bed on which he'd slept was also occupied by his three hobbick companions: Happy, Martin and Sham, the one who'd been breathing on him. Each of them were snoring loud enough to awaken a pack of orks a mile away. The room's other bed (the one where Grandalf should have been sleeping) was not occupied at all.

As the sun continued to rise, the light flooded the two small windows which faced the beds. The window on Frobo's side of the room was considerably larger than the one on Grandalf's side, an architectural oddity that hobbicks like Frobo were unusually prone to both notice and love. Hobbicks were obsessed with the simple things of the world, and their architecture reflected that. Two misshapen, uneven windows in an inn brought an odd comfort to Frobo that morning and made him feel as if he wasn't quite as far away from home as he truly was. But when he looked out that larger window and realized just how far he was from the good green ground, he quickly remembered he was in Breetown.

Frobo rolled off the bed to escape Sham's breath when Grandalf walked in. In his left hand was his staff, and in his right hand he held his long barreled smoking pipe.

"Up, up, my young Hobbicks! There is much to do this day," said Grandalf.

"Don't you ever sleep, Mister Grandalf sir?" asked Sham, rolling over and pulling the sheets back over his face.

"I had no need for sleep last night, Master Gramgee," said Grandalf, "but for thought. I have been planning our next move."

"Now, now Grandalf, don't even pretend like you didn't take a few hours last night," said Martin. "I saw you come in myself around half past midnight and collapse upon that very bed." Frobo was astounded as ever at Martin. Nothing seemed to get past the hobbick.

"I did no such thing!" replied the wizard.

"Did too," said Martin.

"Did not! And there will be no more talk of it. Why don't you four put yourselves to use instead of wasting the day like a bunch of worn-out horse bridles. I'll see you in the lobby!" Without another word, the wizard stormed out of the room.

When the hobbicks descended the stairs half an hour later, Grandalf was sitting at the bar, hitting his pipe at such a rate that the smoke looked like a rain cloud above him. The wizard's impatience was obvious. "What in the name of Grandalf took you so long?" he shouted.

"What difference does it make?" said Martin. "We're here, aren't we? Besides, this is supposed to be like my vacation. And I don't appreciate being rushed and spoken to like a child on my vacation."

"Martin!" chided Frobo.

"What?" said Martin. "I saw the old crow going to roost last night, and he can't convince me otherwise!"

"Young Master Martin, let me inform you that you are no longer on any sort of vacation. You are far from home, you are a fugitive, and if you don't start learning to hold that tongue of yours, I will hand you over to the black riders myself! Do I make myself clear?"

Martin nodded.

"He didn't mean it, sir, honest he didn't!" Sham added.

"Well then," said Grandalf. "Good. If the four of you are finished acting like lunatics, I will tell you what the plan is."

"Finished, sir!" said Sham. "Oh, I can assure you, sir, we are completely finished acting that way, absolutely, sir! Wouldn't dream of it, sir, no sir, I would not. You won't see me acting like a lunatic no more sir, no you won't. Not even if me old grandgaffer needed me to I wouldn't..."

"And yet, you are acting like one right now!" shouted the wizard. "And since it appears that waiting for you all to stop acting like lunatics is something that will never happen, I won't wait to tell you the plan. Come if you wish or wait here for the black riders to find you!" With that final warning, he strode from the lobby in a walk so fast that all four hobbicks were forced to run to keep up with him.

"Well," said Frobo between gasps of breath as he struggled to keep up with Grandalf's long strides. "What is this plan?"

"To go and wake Wondell, of course. I'm sure they'll be releasing him this morning," said Grandalf. "We'll get him out of this rag-tag town's jail. He will be of great value to us on our mission."

"Our mission?" said Sham. "What mission?"

Martin started to speak up but was interrupted by Grandalf, "Don't tell him! Let him figure it out on his own. If you answer him now and continue to spoon feed him information his entire life, he'll never learn to think for himself, and we'll be answering ridiculous questions like this all the way to Morbor!"

"Well, I do declare!" said Sham. "I have never seen a more withholding ungrateful lot of companions! Come now, Mister Frobo, please tell me what it is!"

"Sorry Sham, I just can't. He's right," said Frobo, jogging a little faster to keep up with the fast pace of the long-legged wizard.

"But I know what it is, honest sir, I do. I just... can't remember it!" said Sham.

"Well, if you know what it is, then he shouldn't have to tell you," said Martin.

Sham continued like this as the four of them jogged all the way over through the cobbled streets past the bleak shoddy shops, stables and mills to the magistrate's station.

The Magistrate's Station was not a difficult building to find as it was on the main street, and a completely independent structure, although it was similar in style to those surrounding it. A large sign sat high over the door post with black lettering that read *Magistrate Carrabud's Office: Enforcing Trademark (and other) Laws since TTA 1402.*

"How foreboding..." muttered Grandalf, as they rounded the corner and read the sign. "I can't seem to escape these ridiculous legislations, nor those who wish to enforce them. Sauluman's arm must've grown long indeed."

"It ain't grown that long sir," said Sham. "Least ways, it ain't grown no longer than his other arm has. Not the last time I saw it at least."

Grandalf's eyes closed as he tried to recover from his annoyance at Sham's literal understanding of the tongues of men. But for the moment, he seemed resigned. He was far too tired of correcting the poor hobbick.

The wizard composed himself, turning to the four hobbicks, and kneeling down to meet them at eye level. The five of them had hidden behind a covey of barrels at the mouth of a dark alley opposite the street from the magistrate's station.

"Here is the plan, I'm going to go into the station and get Wondell. You four, stay here and keep a lookout for the *you-know-whats* and if you see them closing in, sound the alarm!"

"*You-know-whats?*" said Sham. "You may *know-what*, but I'm sure as the Chire, I don't."

Martin smacked the back of Sham's head.

"Ouch!" said Sham. "What was that for?"

"The *'you-don't-know-whats'*, obviously," Martin said. "He's talking about the new black riders. The ones who chased us out of the Chire when we were in Miss Margo's firework wagon, and almost blew us all to Morbor."

"Yes Martin, and thank you for saving me from having to explain *everything* to him. Now that you all understand, I am going," said Grandalf.

"Wait!" interjected Frobo, grasping the hem of Grandalf's cloak. "Let me come with you. You might need help if things go wrong. You might need... a *burglar*. What if the magistrate's goons don't want to set Wondell free? If that's the case, it would be better if I could see the inside of the station beforehand."

Frobo wasn't sure what made him say this, but he desperately didn't want to be left behind to keep watch. He wanted to be useful. He wanted to be a hero like his grandfather. It was bad enough that he didn't have the new ring, but maybe if he could do enough to separate himself, they'd see that he really did deserve it.

"But the magistrate is looking for a Grandalf impersonator who's accompanied by hobbicks," said Grandalf, eyeing Frobo curiously.

"Accompanied by four hobbicks," said Frobo. "Not one hobbick."

"Yes... that's a fair point." It was as if the wizard's investigating eyes were boring holes into Frobo. They were searching, roving, prying, and digging for the motivation behind Frobo's insistence to be included. But at last, the painful eyeing stopped, and Grandalf said, "Alright. You may accompany me, *Burglar*. The rest of you, keep watch!"

Grandalf began the walk from the alleyway across the road to the station. Frobo followed, now suddenly overwhelmed with feelings of inadequacy. Had he really just asked Grandalf to be included in this? A burglar? He didn't want to be a burglar! What in the Chire had he been saying? He'd never burgled anything in his life, not even a biscuit from his old marm's cupboard! If he was lucky, he wouldn't have to start today. As they climbed the steps and mounted the rotting porch of the station, Grandalf said to him, "If you want to be a successful burglar, you'll keep your mouth shut and follow my lead. Look sharp Frobo! I don't think these men have our, or Wondell's best interests in mind."

Grandalf struck the iron door knocker thrice for good manners, then threw open the double doors to the rude awakening of a couple of the magistrate's sheeriffs. They'd been dozing with their feet up at their desks.

"Who is in charge of this establishment?" Grandalf shouted at the men. One fell from his chair completely and the other was now busy trying to adjust his sheeriff's hat and badge as he stood to his feet. The magistrate whom Grandalf had spoken with the night before was nowhere to be seen.

"Magistrate Carrabud is in charge, sir!" said the sheeriff who had slipped from his seat. The man wore a green coat with a white shirt and white pants, the same uniform as the sheeriff's they'd seen the previous night. He had light eyes and flowing blonde hair that he kept brushing out of his face as he tried to stand still at attention before them. "But he isn't here right now, he's home eating his breakfast cakes."

"And who is in charge when he's gone?" Grandalf said.

"We are, sir!" said the other sheeriff, a young man with a mustache and beard that were as thin as a piece of parchment. Neither of the sheeriffs could've been older than twenty.

"*You* are in charge!" shouted Grandalf incredulously. "This is a disgrace! Don't you realize I could've walked in here and out with your prisoners and you sleeping buffoons would've been none the wiser?"

"We're frightfully sorry about that, sir! Truly we are," said the blonde haired sheeriff. "And we won't let it happen again sir! Mister... who are we speaking with, sir?"

"Mister Grand..." the wizard paused for a moment, gathering his thoughts before proclaiming, "Grand Marshall Halesthame, head of the North Regional Magistrate's Commission, here on official business for the King of Grondor."

The two young men suddenly looked as if they were about to soil their trousers. Frobo couldn't believe it. The old storm-crow had nearly let his actual name loose but had switched at the last moment to 'Grand Marshall.'

"Grand Marshall Halesthame!" exclaimed the sheeriff with

the parchment thin mustache. He then rendered Grandalf a textbook salute. "And may I ask, who is this with you?"

"Who is this with you... *sir*," corrected Grandalf.

"Yes sir, of course sir! Who is that with you, sir?" bumbled the sheeriff.

Frobo waited for an anxious moment, expecting Grandalf to continue his tale spinning story about who exactly he was. All eyes turned to Frobo and awkward silence pervaded the room.

"Well, go ahead and introduce yourself!" urged Grandalf. "What are you waiting for?"

"I am..." Frobo began, then paused to gather his thoughts. He had to think! *Think!* Something quick; come up with something... "Fro...fro... frozen to the bone with chill. Would you happen to have a cup o' tea?"

"I can certainly brew you one!" said the blonde sheeriff.

"And will you be telling them who they are pouring this cup of tea for?" said Grandalf.

"Of course, I will..." Think! Come up with something! Anything! "Of course, I will... not be!" exclaimed Frobo to the shock of all in the room. "And you'll be lucky if I don't report you for sharing yours, Grand Marshall. Revealing your identity when on a secret mission from the king! I could demote you for this." Though Frobo had never acted before in his life, the thrill of the mysterious character he was playing started to coarse through his veins. It was brilliant. He was tired of taking orders from Grandalf, and now he would make Grandalf take orders from him.

"Well... I thought it important to share our identities with these men if we want them to do what we ask," said Grandalf.

"Quiet, Halesthame!" exclaimed Frobo. The men jumped at the order, and Grandalf looked incredulous. "You've let that wagging tongue of yours play enough for a lifetime today!" Now he was gaining confidence. Why couldn't he be this way in his real life? The feeling of power was incredible!

"Yes... of course," said Grandalf, sighing in deference to him. But Frobo caught the old crow rolling his eyes. How dare that old buzzard do such a thing in front of the two sheeriffs. Grandalf, not assuming Frobo had noticed, addressed the two sheeriffs. "Now, you will take us to your..."

Frobo slammed his foot down on the wooden floor of the station and made fists out of his little hands. "I gave you an order Halesthame!" he shouted at the top of his lungs. His face burned red in fury, the same color as a bright tomato. He wasn't about to take cheek from a subordinate, not in front of two strangers when he was on a secret mission from the king himself. He had put his foot down, and when he put his foot down to give orders, he expected to be shown respect. "When I give you an order Halesthame, what do I expect?" he asked.

Grandalf and the two sheeriffs were speechless and stunned. They had never seen a hobbick act this way before. Grandalf's mouth swung open like a door with no latch.

Grandalf didn't understand what Frobo was looking for. He didn't understand what Frobo wanted him to say. Well, Frobo would have to make him understand, wouldn't he? "When I give you an order, you say 'sir, yes sir'!" shouted Frobo. "Do I make myself clear?" He really had their attention now.

Grandalf sighed and hung his head.

"Do I make myself clear, Halesthame?" repeated Frobo.

"Sir... yes sir," replied Grandalf in a most resigned tone.

"Excellent," said Frobo. "Now, you will take us to the prisoners. The ones you arrested last night in The Prancing *Shetland* Pony. And where is that cup of tea?" The last sentence shot from his lips like a boulder shoots from a catapult. There was so much force behind his words, so much power that they caused an instant reaction.

The sheeriffs sprang into form and the blonde one who had offered to brew the cup of tea scrambled into the next room. The other sheeriff grabbed a heavy set of black iron keys and said, "This way, sir." He then unlocked a door at the far end of the room and led Frobo and Grandalf down a spiral stone staircase. The prisoner's cells were apparently underground in the basement.

The first prisoner Frobo saw was the surly dwarf, Ringo. He wore naught but his green kilt, as he had surrendered his shirt to that beautiful woman the night before. Frobo did note that the shaven hairs of his chest had sprouted to shocking lengths overnight. He was standing, as tall as his stout legs would allow, leaning against the iron bars of his cell. The dwarf's rugged and handsome face had turned grim overnight and his formerly ruddy cheeks were as pale as grey ash.

In the cell across from him lay Wondell, and the sound of his light snoring echoed and bounced off the stone walls of the chamber. The elf was fast asleep on a ratty mat that was strewn across the bare ground of his cell.

"That elf's been snoring all night," said Ringo. "I haven't slept a wink."

"I would've guessed the exact opposite," said Grandalf.

"Hah," snorted Ringo. "Me sleep in a place like this? You must think me a *dwarbarian*." A loud piglike snore interrupted them from Wondell's cell.

Grandalf cleared his throat, "Wake up, Wondell," he said.

Wondell snored louder.

"Wondell, wake up!" the wizard cried. Frobo saw the faintest blue light shoot from the wizard's staff and land upon the dozing elf. Wondell sprang to his feet in an instant, suddenly wide awake.

A smile of relief dawned on the elf's face upon seeing them. "Granda..."

"Grand Marshall Halesthame!" interrupted Grandalf quickly. "Yes, of course it's me. You thought you could continue to evade me, did you Wondell? Thought you could give the old Grand Marshall the slip, did you? Thought the old decrepit has been wouldn't be able to catch up to you? Well, this time you ended up on the wrong side of the law!" From where Frobo was standing, he spied the wizard wink at Wondell.

"I don't understand," said Wondell. "Isn't that you? Grandal-" but he was cut off again.

"Grand Marshall Halesthame is here to take you back to the King of Grondor!" shouted Grandalf, winking his right eye so rapidly that Frobo thought it might fall out. But somehow, Wondell seemed completely oblivious to the message Grandalf was trying to get across.

"I don't understand..." he said. "Grandalf? That isn't you?"

"Enough!" shouted the wizard in frustration. "How dare you call me that!"

The sheeriff who'd brought them down to the cell was now eyeing them suspiciously. "Grandalf..." he said to himself. "Someone was talking about him only yesterday... warning us to be watchful."

"That sounds like a very illuminating story my young sheer-iff, but unfortunately it must be interrupted!" said Grandalf. "Now open this cell immediately and release the prisoner into my custody."

"But you're not Grandalf..." the sheeriff continued to himself, "because Grandalf was travelling with four hobbicks. So, this can't be Grandalf, because this is Grand... Marshall Halesthame. Unless..." the man paused, glancing over at Frobo as his slow mind began to understand. "Unless the other three hobbicks are somewhere else..."

"Don't be ridiculous!" said Grandalf as Frobo cowered behind him, trying to become invisible. "If you don't stop this nonsense, I will be forced to report you for insubordination! Isn't that right Frobo... I mean, Frozen Bone, Son of Ashelob, why couldn't you come up with a fake name?"

The sheeriff was about to cry out to his companion upstairs when Grandalf swung the butt end of his staff up against the poor man's jaw. The wizard then spun and swung his staff again, hitting it against the side of his skull. The sheeriff fell to the ground like a lump of salt.

"The keys, Frobo," said Grandalf.

Frobo reached down and lifted the keys from the Sheeriff's coat pocket, feverishly tossing them to Grandalf.

"I still don't understand..." said Wondell frantically. "Grandalf, is that you, or isn't it?"

"Of course, it's me, oblivious fool!" shouted Grandalf. "I come back to Middlearth and I find myself surrounded by morons. Since when have you not been able to take a hint, Wondell? You're worse than the hobbicks!"

"I'm sorry Grandalf, really I am, but you must excuse me," said the elf, wringing his hands together. "I did just awaken moments before from a very pleasant dream, and I hadn't taken any tea yet." Grandalf rifled through the keys, inserting each of them into the keyhole of the iron door's lock trying to find one that fit.

"What in Middlearth are all of these for anyways?" Grandalf asked. "There are four cells in this whole jail, but at least twenty keys on this ring!"

Frobo twiddled his thumbs, unconcerned with the keys now that he was no longer under the pressure to act or burgle. But at last, Grandalf placed the correct key into the chamber's keyhole and the cell door sprang open.

"Be swift!" cried Grandalf. "It won't be long until the other sheeriff comes down here and sees that we're imposters!" The three of them rushed to the stair, but as they reached it, Frobo halted.

"Wait just a moment!" For some strange reason, an overwhelming force had come over the hobbick, compelling him to turn around. It was a very heroic feeling, something that only the most noble of hobbicks, those who were worthy of possessing a magical ring would have felt.

It was a refusal, nay it was a resolve. Nerry, it was an absolute determination to do the right thing. And in this splendid attitude of self-appointed heroism, Frobo realized he could not allow them to leave the dwarf Ringo in his cell. No one was coming for the wretched dwarf. His traveling band had left him, and the sheeriff's all hated him because of their jealousy. But they couldn't keep him as their prisoner forever, could they? If only Frobo could be more decisive in times like this!

"What is it, Frobo? Speak up and speak quickly. We have no time to waste!" shouted Grandalf.

"It's Ringo," said Frobo. "We can't leave him here."

"Ha! Mercy from a hobbick," the dwarf exclaimed. "Well, I can't say I expected it."

"Surely you speak in jest, Frobo," said Wondell. "You want to help *him*?"

"Save your help for someone who needs it," replied Ringo. "I'm just grateful you'll be leaving me here in peace, elf. Help from your kind is the last thing I need!"

"There, you see. He doesn't need us, let us fly," said Wondell.

"He doesn't know it, but he does need us," said Frobo. "His band of Rugged Dwarfs left late last night. They abandoned him."

Ringo's face twinged at these words, but he masked his feelings quickly, looking away and feigning apathy.

"If his own people can't stand to be with him, why should we help him?" said Wondell. "Come Grandalf, let us leave this place!"

Grandalf hesitated, weighing their options whilst bearing a look of annoyance that seemed to have become perpetual on his wrinkled face.

The wizard cringed and spoke at last, "I'm sorry Frobo, but we just have to..."

Frobo snatched the keys from the wizard's hand and rushed

to Ringo's cell. He refused to leave the dwarf behind. He jammed the first key into the keyhole, and by fate or fortune, the door sprang open.

"Swiftly!" shouted Grandalf. Frobo, Ringo, Wondell, and Grandalf ascended the stone staircase and stood at the closed door that led to the Magistrate's main office. Grandalf pressed his ear to the door.

"Do you hear anything?" asked Ringo.

"Maybe he could, if you would stop yelling at him!" rasped Wondell.

"Be silent," Grandalf said. "I can't hear myself think, much less hear anything outside this door!"

"He started it," said Ringo.

"I didn't start it, you started it!" retorted Wondell.

Before the two of them could continue, Grandalf flung open the door. To the great surprise of Frobo and the others, it revealed no one other than Happy, Martin, and Sham! They were all out of breath and had just slammed shut the front doors of the magistrate's station.

"What in the name of the West are you doing here?" shouted Grandalf. "You're supposed to be keeping watch!"

"We were keeping watch, sir!" said Sham, still struggling to catch his breath. Happy and Martin nodded in agreement, but something was clearly wrong because the two of them bore looks of terror on their pale faces. Sham however, besides his struggle to gain his breath, looked calm and relatively unconcerned.

"Correction," Sham continued. "We are keeping watch, but we came to ask what we were supposed to do if someone was coming."

"Never mind that now. We've got the prisoners and can escape," said Grandalf.

"Right sir, yes you are, sir," said Sham, "but you said we were supposed to keep watch in case the magistrate or the black riders showed up."

"Yes, and you are clearly doing a terrible job of that," said Grandalf.

"On the contrary, sir!" said Sham. "That's why we're here. We came to tell you that they *did* show up! The riders, the magistrate and every sheeriff in Breetown!"

"What?" shouted Grandalf, rushing to the front window that looked out to the street. He pulled a dreary curtain back away from the window. "Why didn't you say that in the first place? Why didn't you warn us?"

"What does it look like we're doing right now?" said Martin. "This whole thing was your plan, not ours Grandalf, you can't blame us!"

"Well, this is just what I wanted to hear," said Ringo. The dwarf's dark eyebrows curled as he glared at the lot of them. "If you would've left me in my cell, I probably would've been released this morning, but now I'm an accomplice to jail-breaking."

"Keep your bitterness to yourself," said Wondell. "Ungrateful dwarf. You should be on the ground kissing this hobbick's feet for releasing you."

Frobo shuffled his feet and crossed his arms behind his back, trying to fix his eyes anywhere except for on the dwarf. He had never felt comfortable while being thanked.

"Thank him for what?" said Ringo. "Getting me arrested again and locked up next to you!"

Frobo breathed a sigh of relief. He needn't worry about that awkward thank you.

"What are we going to do, Grandalf?" said Happy. "You've got to help us. Think of something quick!"

"I'm trying young hobbick," said the wizard. "But thinking is an arduous endeavor with these two bickering at each other."

Frobo wondered what the riders would do to them once

they were captured. They'd be taken back to Sauluman and imprisoned or killed. Only this time, Happy wouldn't be able to save them with his ring of invisibility! This time Grandalf would be inside the cell with them, but this wasn't Grandalf's first time to be imprisoned by Sauluman. He'd escaped before, but how? The wheels of Frobo's mind were spinning. To his left he spied a wooden ladder that climbed to a hatch in the roof. On the second rung of the ladder, a moth was fluttering. Suddenly, Frobo knew just what to do! The films had surely gotten something right.

"Everybody *quiet*," Frobo exclaimed. Silence stole over the place as all eyes turned to Frobo. "Grandalf look!" he said, pointing to the ladder and the moth.

"Good heavens Frobo," said the wizard. "I do hope you aren't wasting our precious time to point out a disgusting insect on the ladder to a roof hatch."

"But Grandalf," protested Frobo. "Can't you see what that is?"

"It's a moth that chews holes in people's clothing," said Grandalf, and with one fatal swat he smashed the moth with the palm of his hand, ending its fragile life.

"What's the matter with you?" shouted Frobo. "You were supposed to use that moth to call for help. To call for the *eagles!*"

"Right Frobo!" said Sham. "Good thinking. Just like you did in the films Grandalf, don't you remember?"

"What in the name of all that is good are you referring to?" Grandalf said. "I have never used a moth to call anything, much less the eagles of the peaks."

"Oh Grandalf," drawled Wondell, "but even I saw you send the message to them through the moth. In the films, my dear wizard, surely you remember..."

"I wasn't *in* the films," snapped the wizard. "And I can assure you that I don't remember because I haven't seen them."

Ringo gasped, "Haven't seen the films! What kind of wizard are you?"

"The best obviously," said Grandalf, puffing out his chest. "I am Grandalf, after all."

"Yeah, but you're not *the* Grandalf... haha, you're not Grandalf™, you're just the imposter bloke everyone is looking for, aren't you?" Ringo looked from Frobo to Happy to Sham to Martin, and finally even to Wondell in disbelief.

"I am *the* Grandalf," he said. "And I'm tired of those ridiculous letters after my name. Save your trademarks for synthetic fabrics and new flavors of pipeweed! Now, someone tell me about this business with the moth and the eagles."

Frobo hurriedly explained the scene where the film Grandalf uses the moth to summon the eagles to save him from entrapment at the top of Sauluman's tower. "If you didn't use the moth, can't you call them some other way?" Frobo said. "How did you call them when you were stuck with the dwarfs in the trees?"

"Oh, I didn't call them that time, we escaped by mere chance," said the wizard. "But your mind is sharp, young Frobo. Everyone needs to climb up on the roof. Ringo, Wondell, bar the doors before you meet us at the top. I am going to have a conversation with the wind itself!"

With that, Grandalf ascended the ladder faster than a squirrel climbs a tree. Frobo followed more cautiously and slowly, ascending rung by rung and desperately trying not to look down. With every rung on which his feet stepped, his stomach felt more and more queasy. None too soon, he reached the top, and the morning light beamed at him like a glowing fire from the open hatch above him. The top of the roof was no higher than half an Olifont's shoulder from the ground. Despite Frobo's inauspicious fear of heights, he had made it, and he collapsed onto the plastered roof as soon as he was off that wretched ladder.

It was only coincidence that Grandalf had just warned him, "Stay down Frobo. There's an entire army of sheeriffs down there! And the nine riders are with them!" Frobo stayed below the parapet wall of the roof, (which he would've barely been able to see over had he been standing at its edge) while Martin, Happy, Sham, Wondell and Ringo climbed the ladder, one by one. Frobo looked to the wizard. He was crouching below the parapet wall with pursed lips, gazing into the open sky. Frobo wasn't sure, but he thought he heard a sharp and barely audible whistle was pierce the morning silence.

"What do you think Mister Frobo?" asked Sham. "Do you really think the eagles will come save us like they did for our dear old grandads?"

Frobo's stomach turned at the thought of soaring into the sky in the clutches of an eagle's talons. He'd barely made it up the ladder without fainting. But before he could answer Sham, a deep melodic voice interrupted them from below, "Grandalf! Grandalf show yourself!" Frobo recognized the voice instantly as Sauluman's.

"What do you want, Sauluman?" shouted Grandalf from behind the parapet.

"What do I want?" asked Sauluman. "What do I want? You *know* what it is I want."

Frobo glanced towards Happy who was anxiously fidgeting for the ring in his front vest pocket, as if it might fly away from him at Sauluman's voice or presence.

"What I want..." Sauluman continued, "is for you to cease and desist in all impersonations of the real Grandalf™, a wizard who is the intellectual property of Middlearth Enterprises! And since you will do nothing of the sort, you leave me no choice but to arrest you and your gang of miscreants, and fine you for damages incurred to that prestigious company!"

"And what if we are unable or unwilling to pay that fine?" replied Grandalf. The wizard raised his eyebrow and glanced back at his companions, winking at them as if this was some sort of joke. A wry smile, the like of which had rarely been revealed upon the wizard's face since he'd been with the hobbicks spread across his face. Perhaps he was glad to be in conflict with a true foe instead of his allies.

"Then you shall be *executed*," shouted Sauluman. "Middlearth Enterprises will not tolerate the theft of its intellectual property!"

Grandalf rolled his eyes, and at the same time scanned the skies. "Now, as for the rest of you," Sauluman continued. "I may be able to find some *leniency* in the law for the aiding of this fugitive. Perhaps he has coerced you or kidnapped you or lied to you with tales of fame and fortune. Come down and turn yourselves in, and you will be given whatever mercy you deserve."

"And how much time will you give us to consider this offer?" shouted Grandalf to Sauluman below.

"Look down Grandalf, ahem, Grandalf impersonator... you are surrounded. There is no escape. How long do you think I can hold off these sheeriffs who are so eager to perform their duty?"

Grandalf approached the parapet and peered over the wall. Frobo and the others followed and looked over in turn. At least two hundred sheeriffs were below, some men, some hobbicks, as well as an irritated looking magistrate and nine tall, hooded men who stood behind Sauluman. Townspeople were gathering around now too, for rarely were so many sheeriffs seen all in one place.

"I cannot hold them back for much longer," said Sauluman. "If you will not come down, then we will come up, and if we cannot come up, then we will burn the magistrate's station to the ground!"

"We will?" asked the magistrate, his eyes widening in shock at what he had just heard. His long green coat had been pulled over a nightgown. Frobo even thought he spotted slippers on the man's feet instead of the long leather boots he'd worn the night before. Clearly, the magistrate had expected this event to be of little importance. He had come in a rush and up until it had been suggested that his station was to be burned down, he had probably been more concerned with the unfinished break-fast he'd left behind on his kitchen table.

"Of course, we will!" shouted Sauluman. The former white wizard's face turned red with passion, and a mad expression possessed it. He produced a large glass phial made of two chambers. One end the phial was empty, the other was filled with sand. "We will do whatever is necessary. Prepare the fire! You have until the sand reaches the other end of this phial, Grandalf. I can guarantee no more!" Sauluman flipped the phial over and the sand began to pour from the top chamber to the one below.

Grandalf and the others backed away from the parapet as the magistrate began his protest of Sauluman's intention to set his station on fire.

"Well, I don't think there's much of a decision is there, Mister Frobo?" said Sham. "I'm going to turn myself in."

"You would prove yourself a fool if you do," said Grandalf. "You expect to receive mercy from the same wizard who tried his best to turn the Chire into his own version of Morbor eleventy-one years ago? The moment you'd escaped from the fire he'd throw you right back in!"

"And what about me?" asked Ringo. "I didn't ask to get mixed up in this mess of yours and now I'm wanted for harboring a fugitive!"

"If you think you'll find mercy from that band of sheeriffs down there, go right ahead," said Grandalf. "But I've never seen a more jealous group of men for the women of their town. You're more a fugitive than I am."

"Then what's your plan to get us off this roof?" said Martin. "Where are the eagles you promised?"

"I promised you nothing of the sort, ungrateful hobbick. I do not command the eagles and I cannot make them come here to rescue us." But just as Grandalf had uttered these words, Frobo felt a great humming rush of wind zoom past his head. A flash of dark brown feathers shaded the sky above them for a moment and turned in the air. Frobo looked up and saw the flapping wings of the largest birds he'd ever seen descending in the sunlight amid a shrouded cloud behind the wizard's hat. "Lo!" shouted Grandalf. "They have come!"

Five brown eagles alighted atop the roof of the magistrate's station. Though they were massive compared to any birds he'd ever seen in the Chire, or throughout the entirety of his life, the eagles were slightly smaller than Frobo had always imagined the powerful birds, or at least, they were smaller than the ones he had seen rescue his grandfather in the films. But they were proud and majestic, and Frobo had no doubt they would be strong enough to carry them to safety. But there were only five eagles and there were seven companions atop this roof. Would two of them be left behind? Or would the eagles double up to rescue the hobbicks? Perhaps they did not realize that hobbicks could be as thick and heavy as full barrels of matured mead.

"Behold!" Grandalf exclaimed, extending his arm to the great bird, "This is Morondor! Grandson of the same eagle who rescued the grandfathers of Frobo and Sham from the peaks of the fiery mountain eleventy-one years ago. Pay him the respect he is due!"

Feeling a bit strange, as he had never bowed to any beast before, Frobo bowed at Grandalf's request. The others all did the same, save Sham, who puffed out his chest, flapped his arms up and down and began to caw like a crow.

The eagles suspiciously eyed Sham and the eagle Grandalf had referred to as Morondor began squawking and cawing at Grandalf. It spread out its wings and flapped them a few times, all the while, its deep sharp brown eyes blazing at Sham likes wells of fury.

"What in the name of the Chire are you doing, Sham?" asked Martin.

"I'm showing them respect," said Sham. "Showing them in their own way."

"You speak *Eaglish*?" asked Frobo.

"If he does, then he should apologize quickly," snapped Grandalf, as Morondor continued to squawk in his ear. "Because he just called Morondor's mother a silver turkey. Keep your mouth shut and your arms to your sides. I have no time for foolishness!"

Grandalf squawked back to Morondor, apparently apologizing to the bird, and they began to converse back and forth. "I wonder what they're saying..." said Happy.

"I can translate for you," said Wondell. "All of my people can at least understand the language. Now let's see... *'bawk, scrill, shreek, craw,'*" Wondell counted on his fingers as if he was adding in his head. "Grandalf just asked if Morondor and the eagles could rescue us from the roof."

Wondell continued to translate the strange conversation to Frobo and the others:

"Eagles grow tired of rescuing those who walk upon the ground and should be better at solving their own problems," Morondor said. "Why can't the walkers save themselves?"

"Look below," said Grandalf. "We are surrounded with no escape. We have no weapons and no way out. It's only a matter of minutes until they set us all ablaze!"

"What do you think we are? Your *deus ex machina* to call upon every time you've written yourself into a corner? A last resort when all other means have failed you?"

"What are you talking about? And when did you learn to speak *Latin*?"

"I know you Grandalf," Morondor replied. "I know you

better than my grandfather did. Instead of using us to help you destroy the ring eleventy-one years ago and be forced to share the spotlight, you hire a band of hobbicks to do the job for you, that way *you* can take all the credit. What's your quest now? Another ring that needs to be destroyed? We could've flown it directly to the mount of fire and destroyed it immediately. We could've been the heroes of the films. But no! Your selfish ambition made sure that never happened!"

"By the wind itself!" cried Grandalf. "That's the most ridiculous notion I've ever heard! Will you rescue us or not Morondor?"

"We will be your puppets no longer, Grandalf! Call me when you want to give me a real role in your quest."

With that, Morondor and his four accompanying eagles ascended into the air. Grandalf stood in disbelief. "And your mother is a silver turkey!" he shouted up at them. "Nay! A grey buzzard!"

"Better a grey buzzard than a stormcrow without wings!" shouted Morondor back to Grandalf, this time in perfect *English*.

"Mister Grandalf, sir," said Sham. "What are we going to do now?"

"I don't know what we're going to do! So, save your breath and my sanity and keep your questions to yourself," said Grandalf.

"They've almost got the fire ready, Mister Grandalf, and the sand is almost all down to the bottom of the phial," said Happy from the parapet's edge.

"Alright, think, think, think!" the wizard shouted to himself. "The eagles are gone... the eagles are gone.... What do you want me to do? What do you want me to do?" he shouted frantically in the opposite direction of the still rising sun. He then fell to his knees in agony. Grandalf was terrified. His plan with the eagles had failed. Now they needed a *miraculum ex machina* if they were going to get out of this mess.

As Grandalf continued to wail and moan, pacing from side to side, always gazing into the west, fear fell upon the others. The display made Frobo feel very uncomfortable. His last name wasn't Daggins if Sauluman's offer to turn themselves in wasn't sounding better and better by the second. The *stormcrow without wings*, as Morondor had called him, had no plan or method to save them.

"Grandalf," the voice of Sauluman called up from below. "Grandalf, this is your last chance. Come down from the roof or be consumed by the fire! This is your final warning."

"Now listen, Grandalf," said Wondell, placing his arm around the wizard's shoulder, and joining him in the nervous pace back and forth across the rooftop. "Maybe this time we should take him up on his offer. We don't have another choice!"

"Isn't that just like an elf?" said Ringo. "Fleeing at the first sign of danger. Hah! I say let them set the place ablaze!"

"This is hardly the *first sign of danger*," said Wondell. "But this is madness. If we stay up here, we'll be burned alive!"

"Well perhaps if you were made of tougher stuff than fine elfish wafers and sparkling wine, you'd be able to withstand it!" said Ringo, bursting into laughter at his own joke. He was however the only one of them who found the slightest amount of humor in it.

Grandalf fell to his knees and closed his eyes, holding his hands together and muttering to himself in gibberish. He removed his broad grey hat from his head. Frobo imagined him suddenly being spirited away, vanishing before them, leaving his boots, that disgusting dirty robe, and that broad rimmed, pointy hat as the only signs that he'd ever existed. He would then turn up somewhere else, perhaps a few miles outside the town, and then he'd have to find clothing. Then he'd assemble a new group of companions to accompany him on his quest to destroy the rings of power. And Frobo's one chance at achieving a life of greatness would die. Frobo had no idea *how* Grandalf would do this, but it somehow seemed like a viable possibility to him.

"They have made their decision!" shouted Sauluman's voice from below. Frobo's vision of treachery faded as the reality of their circumstance flooded back into his mind.

Then the voice of Sauluman shouted once more, "Release the fire!"

Frobo ran to the parapet edge and stood up on his tip toes, peeking over the edge. But all he could see was the roof of the next building across the main street. He'd come to a particularly tall section of the parapet wall. What confounded builder had done such a thing? However, he had no time to draft a formal complaint to Carrabud about the construction of his roof. For at that moment, a flurry of flaming arrows shot up from the ground and landed on the plaster on which they stood. Wondell dashed from arrow to arrow, gathering as many as he could and hurling them back to the ground. The rest of them tried to stamp out the small fires that were starting.

"Hah! Don't they know that fire burns upward?" asked Ringo. "It'll take ages for them to burn the place like this. Even I could've told them that. We haven't got a thing to worry about."

But the men had also set their fires from below. Frobo finally found a relatively small section of parapet wall that he could peek his entire head over. Two sheeriffs stood there outside one of the windows to the magistrate's station. One was pouring a large bucket of black liquid inside it, and once empty, the other tossed a flaming torch into it. An explosion of flame shot out of the window that blackened the faces of the sheeriffs and knocked them on their backs, but the greater damage was done to the station itself.

Frobo glanced back up to the sky. Could the eagles return?

He could see nothing but the growing smoke that billowed around the walls of the building on all sides. The crackling fire was growing, and it must've been great indeed below them. For some strange reason, the flames sounded to Frobo like a storm that was brewing off in the distance. Like rolling thunder or a stampeding herd. It grew louder and louder and louder. Frobo couldn't believe how loud it was for the roaring sound far outmatched the blaze. He glanced out to Sauluman and the sheeriffs who had all stopped shooting their flaming arrows and were staring down the road that led to the magistrate's station. Had he been on the ground as the sheeriffs were, Frobo would've felt the earth quaking beneath his feet.

The thunderous sound that Frobo had heard was now almost deafening. He had never in his wildest dreams thought that such a sound would precede burning to death. But then, from around a street corner, through the billowing black smoke, a herd of stampeding horses shot into Frobo's view. They were running straight down the road to the magistrate's station. If there were a hundred of them there were a thousand, and the sheeriffs that were quick enough abandoned the streets before being trampled by the stampede.

Leading the herd, sitting atop a great red horse, was a man Frobo recognized at once! "Look Grandalf, it's Roban Hoods!" Frobo said, bouncing like a child and pointing at the man on the red horse.

"He's stolen every horse in Breetown," said Grandalf. The wizard pulled the grey hat back over his head. "There's our *miraculum ex machina!*"

The flames were now licking up from around the parapet of the roof as the stampeding horses, driven by Roban Hoods alone, pressed through the road, forcing the sheeriffs, the magistrate and Sauluman away from the streets and into the surrounding buildings.

"Now is our chance," shouted Grandalf, though his voice

was barely audible through the thunderous herd. "The horses! Find a steed and ride to freedom!"

"I dare say I will not!" retorted Sham. "You said those poor animals are stolen property!"

"Save your morals for your dying penance, Sham," said Grandalf. "Which will be coming very quickly if you don't escape from this roof and this town immediately. In the meantime, spare us all the anguish of having to listen to them!"

There were no more objections to riding away on the stolen horses. Frobo, with the rest of the fugitives, waited at the parapet wall that stood before the sloped roof of the porch in the very front of the building, which by some strange fate had not yet caught fire. The horses were running like a roaring river only feet below.

"Wondell, help me get the hobbicks onto the horses!" said Grandalf. The wizard was beyond the parapet, crouching out on the overhang, looking very much like a cat that was about to pounce into a river. "Ringo, have you ever ridden before?"

"Of course, I've ridden a horse!" the dwarf shouted. "What do I look like to you, a..."

But the grumpy dwarf was cut off by the shouting of Grandalf, "Wondell, speak to the horses and get us four of them. Be swift!"

Frobo considered the wizard's plan. There were seven of them on the roof, and if they got four horses, the hobbicks could each ride with one of the bigger folk. Of course, Wondell would find them trusty steeds, as elfs had the mysterious ability to speak with horses and any other animal for that matter.

"Yes, yes, one, two, three..." the wizard numbered the horses as Wondell gathered them below the overhang of the porch roof.

"Come along, Wondell, gather the rest. Now, Happy, you will ride with me, Sham with Ringo, and Martin shall accompany Wondell..." Grandalf paused. It was difficult to hear the wizard through the great rushing rumble of the galloping horses, despite the fact that he was only feet away from them and was practically screaming at them. Frobo wasn't exactly sure he'd heard everything Grandalf had said, nor was he was quite sure deep down he'd be taken care of.

"That leaves you Frobo," Grandalf said. "You will ride alone. And we must leave now!"

"Ride alone?" Frobo said. The paralyzing fear that often overtook his good hobbick senses when he felt inept overwhelmed him. It rushed through his veins like a rare cold storm from the north in the summer.

"I'm sorry, Frobo," said Grandalf. "But Martin's too reckless, Happy's too valuable, and Sham is far too dimwitted! You're the only choice. Besides, you're the only hobbick with experience, from when you drove the wagon."

The horses continued to stream through the road, their hoofs clopping along on the cobble stones, but their numbers were thinning. Wondell had gathered the other three horses beneath the overhanging porch roof and was sitting atop his own. Across the road on the other side of the sea of horses, the sheeriffs, the Magistrate and Sauluman all gazed with shocked faces out of the windows of the buildings they'd taken shelter in. But not a one of them was foolish enough to try and stop the stampede.

"Come Martin," Wondell shouted. To Frobo's complete and utter shock, Martin hoisted himself over the parapet, ran down the sloped overhang porch roof and leapt without hesitation out into the stampede of horses! He had done it as easily as if he was a young tween skipping over a small stream. And by the luckiest of chances that Frobo could fathom, Martin's leap from the rooftop landed him squarely in the arms of Wondell.

It was Grandalf and Ringo's turns next to leap from the rooftop into their horses' saddles. While they didn't alight onto them as easily as Wondell and Martin, they each made the whole affair look far too easy. Grandalf crouched at the roof's edge and sprang with the lithe finesse of a pouncing Chire Cat onto the back of his white horse.

Ringo went next, and though he more resembled a leaping badger than a limber cat, he landed on the back of his horse, nonetheless. It was like the whole lot of them had been practicing this! Like they jumped from the roofs of burning magistrate's stations onto horses quite frequently and thereby acquired the necessary skills to do so in a pinch. And the fire that was burning the roof he stood on was growing hotter by the second.

"I don't know about this, Mister Frobo," said Sham. "Stealing horses is not the half of it. I'd sure prefer the good green earth beneath my own feet, instead of that big black four-legged stallion..."

"Come on you fool! Come on!" shouted Ringo. Sham then crept down upon the roof feet first, crawling like a turtle if it was dragging the back of its shell along the ground. Then, to Frobo's pure amazement, he hopped like a bullfrog from the edge of the overhang, landing squarely behind Ringo atop the saddleback. The two sped off behind Wondell and Martin. Happy followed Sham, easily gaining the saddle with Grandalf's long arms to help him. Now it was just Frobo. He stared into the eyes of the big yellow horse that was left for him to ride.

Frobo shuffled, stamping back and forth along the roof and straightened out his coat. Oh, how dreadful this all was! If only that wretched building beneath him wasn't about to burn to the ground! Then he'd be able to take hours up here trying to figure out a plan, how exactly he was going to ride that wretched yellow beast. If only he'd... well if only they'd... why didn't anyone realize that not two nights before he'd tried to get a team of horses to run faster by snapping his fingers? The insanity of this plan was... well, it was insane!

"Come Frobo!" shouted Grandalf below. "It's now or never."

Frobo leaned his waist over the parapet, and as he did so the roof that had just been below his feet collapsed in flames. Son of Ashelob! There was no more time for dilly dally, this was the moment, and by the most famous hobbick who ever lived, he had to make it count. The sloped porch was now all that stood apart from the wall of fire. The heat of the flames felt so hot he could barely stand. He expected to burst into flame himself at any moment, and if not for that, Frobo did not think he ever could have leapt from that roof.

But leap he did. As the flames consumed the magistrate's station, the last remnants of the stolen stampede sprinted through the streets and the first of the bravest sheeriffs popped their heads out of the doors where they'd taken shelter, Frobo jumped and landed, by luck or by miracle, on top of his horse.

Jubilee, elation, and adrenaline rushed through every fiber of his small body. He'd done it! He'd done the *impossible*. He'd jumped five feet from a roof and landed on a horse. And it was moving, the horse was in fact running away from the town. He hadn't even had to snap his fingers, err the reins this time.

"It must be a smart beast," he thought to himself, *"to take off all by itself like it did."* Frobo could see the Magistrate, the sheeriffs, and even Sauluman returning to the street, now trying desperately to put out the fire they'd started. "Take that, Sauluman, you bad old baldy!" he shouted back at the crusty old degenerate.

Sweet relicf flooded every part of him, and all he could do was close his eyes and laugh as the horse sped away from the town. Then in a rushing climax of clarity, Frobo fully realized the gravity of his situation. He was riding a horse. Him. Frobo Daggins of the Chire! He'd never so much as ridden atop a dog in his younger years, and now he was riding a full-sized horse. How was he doing it? What would people say about him? But upon further consideration, he noticed something, something about this horse that wasn't quite right. There was something funny about this horse, something he hadn't seen when looking at the horse from above. This horse that Wondell had chosen... had no head! And furthermore, it was running backwards!

He couldn't believe his luck. The horse's head and neck had completely fallen off! Of course, this would happen to him. The first horse he'd ever jumped on had lost his head, literally. Recklessly, he leaned over the front of the horse, just to make sure it wasn't running with its head down. The pungent smell of... well that was strange. It reminded him of *Foraging Felga's Famous Fertilizer*, that Sham purchased weekly for use in Frobo's garden.

But he'd seen what he needed, the head and neck of the horse were definitely gone, though the mane was still somehow intact.

"Frobo!"

Had someone just called his name? The galloping bumps of the horse were so loud and jarring, he could barely hear himself think, but he'd thought he could hear someone calling.

"Frobo!" the voice shouted again. He looked to his left to see Grandalf and Happy, riding on their horse not twenty feet away, with a host of other horses between them, all galloping at a great pace. Of course, Grandalf and Happy's horse still had its head. They were the lucky ones. Frobo could imagine how silly he looked, riding around on a horse with no head. He must look like a foolhardy hobbick indeed. But he hadn't made the horses head fall off, it'd done that all on its own!

"Frobo!" Happy shouted again, and then he said something Frobo couldn't understand. Frobo assumed it was something about the fact that he'd chosen a horse whose head had fallen off to escape from the town.

"I know, I know!" Frobo shouted, rolling his eyes in frustration, and throwing his hands in the air, only to quickly throw them back down again as he started to lose his balance. "His head fell off, I know!"

But Grandalf and Happy were still waving at him furiously.

Some people... why did everyone feel like they always had to point out the obvious? Was he blind? Of course, he knew the beast's head had fallen off. He was riding the wretched animal.

Grandalf maneuvered his horse nearer Frobo's. They were still screaming at him, and Grandalf was laughing out loud. What were they saying?

"Frobo, turn around, you're sitting on the horse backwards!"

Finally, he'd made it out. But that was utter lunacy. He wasn't sitting on the horse backwards; it was running backwards! Wasn't it? Frobo considered all the facts. Had he ever seen a horse run backwards before? Of course not. Had he ever seen a horse run without its head before? Why... quite no, but then again, he was a hobbick, and he had very little experience with beasts that stood taller than he did. Was it possible? Just to satisfy his curiosity and make sure he wasn't being *Dagginsed*, he stole a quick glance over his right shoulder. A flowing mane ran down the neck below two ears and the head of a grinning yellow horse glancing back at him.

He was riding the horse backwards. *He was riding the horse backwards*. The horse was going forwards, head intact, and he was sitting on it backwards... of course! How had he not realized? Backwards! He'd suspected something wasn't right about this whole thing. Something... something... A queasy dizziness churned his stomach. His vision faded, then everything turned blue, then black.

CHAPTER 8

THE THIEF IN THE NIGHT

WHEN FROBO AWOKE, NIGHT HAD FALLEN. FLAMES CRACKLED and licked up at the evening air from a fire that was burning next to him. He was lying in a dark wood, through the top of which peaked a starry sky. Voices pierced the night, loud and sonorous, but Frobo felt far too groggy to discern their words. A sharp twinge shot up from his lower back, his ribs cracked, and his head throbbed. How had he gotten here? He remembered the fire on the station roof, then his triumphant leap from the porch overhang. And wait a minute, there was more... had he ridden his horse... *alone!?* Had he, Frobo Daggins escaped from the dangerous wizard Sauluman, on a horse, quite alone, riding one for the first time in his life?

Well, even Grandalf would have to admit that was impressive. He might just be the grandson of the most famous hobbick who ever lived after all.

"Frobo?" said a panicked sounding voice from behind the fire. "Bless us all, he's alive!" The voice was, predictably Sham's.

"Of course, he's alive!" snapped Grandalf. "That was never in question as he never stopped breathing!"

But Sham, being Sham, obviously felt that it was his

personal duty (as Frobo's gardener) to treat the poor hobbick as if he was a dying elf fairy that had just flown in from across the sea, faint and near death from the stress of the journey, whom Sham and Sham alone had the power to revive. Frobo tried his best to lean against the back of a knapsack that had been placed behind him. Sham already had a bowl of stew ready at Frobo's mouth, anxious to nurse his patient back to health. The first spoonful was inside him before he could refuse, and the second was there before he'd swallowed the first.

"Come off it, Sham!" said Martin. "All you're going to do is drown the poor lad!"

"I suspect what's best for him is less nurturing and more falls from my horses. If he thinks he can steal one from me, he should at least be tough enough to ride." Frobo recognized the gruff voice. He'd heard it before. But he was still too groggy from the fall to discern the face of the hooded stranger speaking.

"I'll wager he's made of tougher stuff than you are!" spat Sham.

"Maybe he is…" said the rough voice. Frobo rubbed the sleep away from his eyes and shook himself, sitting a little further up against the knapsack and pushing away the next spoon of soup that Sham was trying to feed him so he could see clearly. They were gathered around a small fire that had been built on the edge of a forest tree line. Frobo could see a broad plain before him that was lit by the full moon. There the thousand horses were splayed across the field, some still grazing, many others lying down. Around the fire, Frobo's companions were sitting, and there also sat the stranger. His long, disheveled hair with flecks of blonde mixed with dark brown betrayed him. It was Roban Hoods.

The man was drinking from a small flask, and every sip soaked his beard with drips from the drink that had missed their mark. Roban wiped his beard with the sleeve of his dark garment. "Maybe he is, but don't forget who these horses belong to."

"Don't forget who these horses belong to?" laughed Wondell, who was leaning back against the same golden mare he'd ridden from the station. "Don't worry, I won't. This is my horse, Starbell, whom I've known since she was birthed."

"We will be taking the horses we need, Roban..." said Grandalf. "Whether you like it or not."

"Now hold on just a minute!" shouted Roban. "I stole those horses fair and square! It wasn't easy! And if I hadn't run them through the middle of that town, you all would be nothing but a pile of smoldering bones at the bottom of that Magistrate's Station!"

"Only we aren't a pile of smoldering bones," growled Ringo, rising from his haunches and standing up to the man from across the fire. "We will take the horses we like, whether we've known them since birth or not!"

"I'd like to see you try!" said Roban, springing up at the challenge and drawing a sword from the belt at his waist. Frobo was surprised. It seemed like a drastic and unnecessary escalation from the man.

Before Roban could strike, Grandalf sprang from his haunt and stood between the two, staff in hand. Ringo looked from behind Grandalf's cloak and jeered at Roban.

"Stay calm, ranger," said Grandalf. "We can help you, Roban. Stealing every horse in Breetown all by yourself was an impressive feat, but you can't drive a thousand horses to sell all by yourself. We'll help you for a small fee, four horses of our own."

Roban considered the offer. "What makes you think I'm selling?" he asked.

"Well, you're either selling," said Grandalf, "Or you stole these horses for your own private army. Either way, you're going to need our help. Any cunning man can start a stampede as you did. It takes a team of men to *stop* a stampede or to prevent another. You need us to help you."

"Alright, old man," said Roban. "You've got yourself a deal. Four horses for the assistance of your... team? What kind of group is this, anyways? Four hobbicks, an elf, a dwarf and a bearded old peacemaker. Hah! If I didn't know any better, I'd say this reminded me of the films. What's your real name, then? I'm sure it isn't Glandalf like you told me in the *Shetland* Pony."

"It isn't, and his name isn't Flobo Blaggins either," said Grandalf, pointing out Frobo. "But perhaps there is something to your recalling of these parasitical films that seem to have burrowed their way into the minds and hearts of all Middlearth since last I left it. For I am Grandalf. Yes, *the* Grandalf, and if you follow my name with those deathly letters, I will cast such a horrid spell upon you that Sauluman will want to trademark it! And the hobbicks before you are none other than the heirs of the ones whom the stories were written about. Frobo Daggins, grandson of the most famous hobbick who ever lived, Sham, grandson of the most famous hobbick's gardener, and Happy Brandybeer, grandson of their friend."

"I see," said Roban, eyeing them all with suspicion. His face reminded Frobo of how Happy had looked at him recently after he'd bluffed in a hand of cards. "And what about him?"

"That is Martin Shaken-Nottstird..." said Grandalf. "His ancestors were about as heroic as a field of mice."

"He couldn't be more right, sir," said Martin. "Pleased to make your acquaintance. I'm not related to anyone famous like these other chaps see. I'm just along for the adventure."

"And what of the descendant of the other hobbick who was the friend of their grandfathers? That Tooken fellow?"

Frobo, Sham, Happy and Martin all cleared their throats loudly and started stamping their feet against the dirt in the ground. They did it in such a sudden and coordinated fashion that a small dust cloud began to form around the fire.

After the proper amount of time had passed from the saying of the name, according the Chire reckoning, Happy responded, "That's a name that hasn't been mentioned in the Chire for quite some time sir, and it isn't proper for Chirefolk to speak of such things."

"It isn't proper for Chirefolk to speak of *what* things?" asked Roban.

"Things that haven't been mentioned for quite some time, obviously," explained Sham, annoyed at Roban's lack of understanding of the Chire culture.

"I was just..." began Roban.

"Moving on!" said Grandalf. "Believe me, you will be glad you did. Now tell us Roban, where are we taking these horses? Who are you selling them to?"

"What difference does it make?" said Roban, sitting back down. He settled himself back against his saddle where he'd been before the confrontation by Ringo.

"None, unless you are selling them to the enemies of the free peoples of Middlearth," replied Wondell.

"Enemies?" said Roban. "What enemies? The true enemy was defeated when this fellow's grandad did what he did, wasn't he? Wasn't evil defeated forever when that happened?"

"Absolutely," said Sham.

"Not!" continued Grandalf. Sham scratched his head and tried to consider the ramifications of that statement.

"Just because the true enemy was destroyed, does not mean that evil has been defeated and Middlearth cleansed! What a foolish thing to believe. There are still orks, trolls, monsters, men, elfs, dwarfs, and hobbicks that can be worse still than the evils that have already been conquered! Not to mention Sauluman."

"Sauluman?" said Roban. "I thought that old snake was dead?"

"He was, but he has returned," said Grandalf. "Now tell us who you are selling these horses to."

"But I really don't see how..." protested Roban.

"Cough it up, horse thief," said Ringo. "Out with it."

"Alright, alright!" said Roban. "I lost them in a card game in a bar in Karzaban."

"Gambling?" spouted Sham. "Well, well, well. If my old grandgaffer could hear this. He always spoke against it, yes he did, and now I can see it with my own eyes why he espoused against it so."

"Thank you for those enlightening platitudes, Sham," said Grandalf. Sham, oblivious to the sarcasm, tried his very hardest to look down his nose at Roban for the rest of the evening.

"Yes," continued Roban. "I was gambling. But in my defense, I'm the best card player this side of the Musty Mountains."

"But unfortunately, you weren't on *this* side of the Musty Mountains, were you Roban," continued Sham, chuckling to himself, again oblivious to the glares he was receiving from everyone else who wanted to hear the rest of the story. "No, you were just southeast of them weren't you! No, south by southeast to be exact. And you lost! You gambled away everything, didn't you, Roban! Because this fellow in Karzaban was just a better card player than you, wasn't he? If only you'd been wearing my shoes, growing up hearing my old grandgaffer's wisdom."

"Is he always like this?" asked Roban.

Frobo elbowed Sham, flinching as he did so at the sharp pain from his bruised ribs. "Enough with your grandgaffer for tonight," he said, grimacing and gritting his teeth. "Let him finish."

Sham looked very hurt by this, but as Frobo could do or say nothing wrong in his eyes, he shut his yapper and tried his best to listen.

"As I was saying," Roban continued. "I'm the best card

player this side of the Musty Mountains, and when I was playing this fellow, I knew I had him beat. I knew his tells, knew his game, knew his bets, I could see right through him. But the problem was, I drew a *King's Trademark*."

Each one of them gasped. To say that the King's Trademark was an improbable hand to acquire would have been a gross understatement. It wasn't improbable. It was legendary.

"As you know," Roban continued, "the *King's Trademark* is the greatest hand in Middlearth Poker. It's so rare that ninety-nine percent of players have never even heard of somebody getting one. There's only one hand that can beat it, but that hand can't beat anything else in the game."

"*Absolutely Nothing*," they all said in unison with awestruck hushed voices.

"Well naturally, you can imagine what I did," said Roban.

"What? Folded?" asked Sham.

"Yes Sham," said Roban. "I folded. I folded on a hand so legendary that it had probably never even been seen this side of the Musty Mountains."

Frobo was stunned, not noting the sarcastic tone in Roban's voice. His jaw dropped, but at least he didn't do what Sham did.

"Well, what did you do that for?" asked Sham. "No wonder you lost."

"I didn't fold, you idiot!" shouted Roban. "I'd have to be a fool to do that. I was just being sarcastic. There was no way he could beat me, see? The only thing that could beat me was an *Absolutely Nothing*, and there was no way anyone would wager against me with an *Absolutely Nothing*, because the only hand *Absolutely Nothing* could beat was the *King's Trademark*! It literally loses to every other hand in the game."

"So, what did he do?" asked Wondell.

"He raised," said Roban. They all gasped. "He raised, and I re-raised everything I had, and then I made a bet I couldn't pay. In addition to all of the chips I had on the table, I bet him a thousand horses. He'd been talking about how he needed horses the whole game, how he was in desperate need of hundreds of horses, and I thought that then he'd most certainly call the hand. Well, call it, he did. And before I could blink, he laid his cards on the table in front of me. He had the only thing that could beat me. The easiest cards to get in the game, but the ones everybody with half a shred of sense wanted to get rid of. He had *Absolutely Nothing*. 'There's only one hand you could have where I win,' he said. 'And I'm wagering that's what you've got. The *King's Trademark*.' I was mortified. I turned my cards over, desperately hoping I'd somehow made a mistake, that I'd read them wrong. But there was no mistaking it, the trademark was right there in front of me. I'd lost. All because some idiot had bet a thousand horses with *Absolutely Nothing!*"

"Pardon me for saying so, Mister Roban," said Sham. "But it seems to me that between the two of you, you might have been the idiot. He did beat you, in case you forgot."

Frobo cringed at Sham's rude remark.

"Thank you Sham. I'll try to remember that," said Roban.

"I'd *wager* he does remember it, Sham, seeing as he just told us he lost in his story," said Grandalf.

"So anyways, here I am," said Roban. "I guess I'll have to steal a few more horses now that I'm giving four of them to you, but the man told me to meet him with the horses in Brohan. That's where I'm headed."

"We can be in the plains of Brohan in two days or maybe three, if we ride hard," said Grandalf. "Of course, we may have to make a few stops along the road."

"As long as it isn't too far out of the way," said Roban. "I've got a deadline. I have to deliver these horses before the new moon rises."

"That's seven days from now," said Grandalf. "And don't worry, Slumbervell is only a few leagues out of the way. I believe the stop will be well worth our time."

"Slumbervell!" said Wondell in sudden alarm. Frobo had nearly forgotten the elf was there, the same way he often forgot that Happy was around. The two of them seemed to share a certain indefinable quality. Perhaps his alleged grandfather would have called that an *elfish air*.

"Grandalf, I'm not going to Slumbervell," Wondell said. "And that's that."

"Then go somewhere else..." sneered Ringo, "on foot."

Wondell ignored the dwarf as best he could. "What do you want to go *there* for anyways? Why not go anywhere else in Middlearth?"

"Because I am on a quest, Wondell," responded Grandalf. "A quest which I believe is the second most important quest of our time, and certainly the most important quest of this age, which just so happens to be a brand new one. And when one goes on a quest, one should never attempt to do so without three things."

"And what might they be?" asked Wondell.

"A full belly," Grandalf began.

"Amen to that!" cried Sham.

Grandalf continued, "Weapons and supplies for the journey, things we have little to none of right now."

"But we could get those anywhere," drawled Wondell. "Why do we have to go to *Slumbervell?*"

"And finally," continued Grandalf, as if he had not heard Wondell's interruption. "The third thing one should never under any circumstances begin one's quest without is..."

"A warm bed and a pint of ale," said Martin.

"No," said Grandalf.

"A kiss from mum and a glass of warm milk?" asked Happy with an air of utmost sincerity.

"Hah!" laughed Roban. "This is who you choose to accompany you on your *quest*, Grandalf? The most important quest of this young age?"

"Now that you've decided to let me finish my sentence, the

answer is neither a 'pint of beer' nor a 'kiss from mum.' It is *counsel*. And that is one thing the Lord of Slumbervell may be more prepared to give us than anyone else in Middlearth. We are going to Slumbervell to seek counsel, and that is final," snapped Grandalf. "And now, if you don't mind, I'd like a little peace and quiet from you all, because I am going to sleep."

Frobo found himself dozing off not long afterwards, as each of them found their place around the fire and began to drift into the sweet dreams of the night. But Frobo's sleep was troubled and anxious. Every time he felt himself drifting off, he saw a hand with furry paw-like fingers reaching out to him through the darkness. Behind it were glowing eyes. But then he would awaken and remember he was asleep under a large ash tree, at the edge of a forest glade outside of Breetown. "I've got to get some rest," Frobo scolded himself. "I'll be worthless tomorrow if I can't get some good hard sleep."

Just as he began to doze off again, he started! He'd seen something moving in the bushes behind the mat where Happy was snoring. But that was strange, and it was probably naught but a marauding mole or a rabbit. He would pay it no more attention. He was just too tired to stay up all night, keeping watch for them. Everyone else was asleep. Why couldn't he sleep like them? But he could, and he was at that very moment. And there he was, dreaming again, dreaming of the furry hand with the paw-like fingers reaching out from the bushes to Happy. The hand was reaching for Happy's trouser pocket... and that was strange, for what in Middlearth could that furry hand want with Happy's trouser pocket? Was that where he kept *it?* Was that where he kept Sauluman's ring?

Frobo shot up from his sleep. Of course, the *ring*. His heart was beating like a drum, and he looked across the fire to the bushes behind Happy... but nothing was there. However, Frobo was too anxious. Cautiously, he rose from his sack beneath the tree and crept as quietly as he could to the bush. What if someone was there? What if the creature with the furry hands was behind that bush, lurking in the shadows? He saw a stout looking stick on the ground. He picked it up, just in case he had to beat this creature over the head with it.

Step, step, step... he could only be so quiet with the leaves crunching beneath his feet, and his heart beat so violently that it was louder to him than the crunching of the leaves on the ground!

"By the Brandybeer!" he whispered in frustration, as he crunched a particularly loud cluster of leaves. But when finally he did reach the bush, it was quite devoid of anything at all. No glowing eyes, no furry paws, no mysterious creature trying to steal Happy's ring. *"Unless, it already had stolen it,"* a voice in Frobo's head rebutted.

Terror gripped him. Although he couldn't understand its complete significance, Frobo knew that ring was going to be an important part of what they had to do in their conflict against Sauluman. Just like his grandfather (or his supposed grandfather), had needed to destroy that *Insidious Ring* to defeat the great evil of his time, Frobo would need to destroy this ring to do the same. And he couldn't destroy it if someone else had it, could he? *"But you don't have it!"* he told himself. *"Happy has this ring! You don't! You're not even important in this story! You should just go back to sleep, or even better yet, you should go back home."* Frobo considered this voice, his own voice. Wasn't it true? He wasn't nearly as important as his supposed dear old Grandad and he never would be, because Happy had the ring and he didn't.

Then he remembered, if what he'd seen in his dream had actually happened, Happy might *not* have the ring, because that strange little creature with the furry paws might have stolen it from him. There was only one way to be sure, he'd have to search Happy's pockets while he was asleep to make sure he still had the ring. There was nothing else for him to do. He couldn't wake the others if he was wrong. He'd never hear the end of their jokes about how he'd dreamt he'd seen the furry clawed boogeyman if he woke them all and Happy still had the ring. He had to do this himself... by himself, for himself.

Now he crept, imagining he probably resembled a stalking ork, bending over Happy's sleeping body. *"I'll just check his trouser pocket,"* he told himself. *"Just to make sure it's there, and if it isn't, I'll wake him up."* With the skill of a seasoned pick pocket, and a rushing thrill pulsing through his veins with every heartbeat, he slipped his hand into the right pocket of Happy's trousers. It was empty. Frobo felt the left trouser pocket and found it like the other. He would have to go for the vest now. Of course, that was where it would be, unless the little bugger had actually stolen the thing! Gingerly, he felt the outside of the vest pocket and... there it was, he was almost certain of it. He could clearly feel its round protrusion through velvet lining of the pocket. Frobo breathed a sigh of relief. Now he could go back to sleep. He could rest now. And he wanted to. He wanted to sleep with all his heart, but something, something...

Something was keeping him there, crouched over Happy like a hunching ork. If only he could be given the chance to prove himself, to be as great as his grandad. If he was given that chance, to bear this ring, would anyone be able to doubt him as the heir of the greatest hobbick who ever lived? His lineage would no longer be in question. He wouldn't be a Sackville-Daggins, he'd be a real Daggins! And maybe even better! But he had to have the chance. And this ring was that chance. It was *his* chance.

Frobo reached for the vest pocket, and as he did, he remembered his dream. Now he was the creature with the furry hand, hiding behind the bushes, reaching for Happy's ring. *"What are you doing, you fool? You'll be a Sackville-Daggins for sure and worse if you take it away from him!"* He was disgusted with himself, ashamed, guilty, condemned, and yet he could not pull himself away. His head, his mind, and his heart were all screaming at him to not do this, to not reach for it...

"Don't do it!" he said aloud, unable to control himself in the struggle.

At that moment, he was thrown from over Happy's still sleeping body by a weathered white hand. "Fool of a hobbick!" rasped Grandalf from above him. "For that is what you have been tonight. You have been a fool, Frobo!"

"It's not what you think!" Frobo tried to explain between breaths in a hushed whisper. "I saw something. I saw something reaching for him, reaching for *it*, from the bushes! I had to make sure it was still there. I had to make sure it hadn't stolen the ring, and then..."

"And then, your true motivations were unmasked!" snapped the wizard. Grandalf was a fearful sight indeed to Frobo from this angle. His white hair hung down over his face like a broken spider's web, and his vicious black eyebrows cut across his fore-head to his crooked nose. In the moonlight and the dim embers of the fire, the dying flames reflected in the wizard's black eyes. Each one resembled the burning fire of the seeing stones from the films. The sight was terrible to behold.

"I didn't mean to," Frobo continued, "honest I didn't! I just wanted to make sure it was still there, and then... and then I felt like I couldn't stop myself, even though I wanted to."

"Mark my words, my young hobbick, had I not heard you say with my own ears, 'Don't do it,' I don't think I could've allowed you to continue on this quest. I *know* the temptations of the rings, believe me. And now you know them too. Do not be so foolishly entwined by it again. Give it no place in your mind. Believe me, you have been granted a much greater gift than your grandfather by *not* possessing one of the great rings. Now, can you go to sleep? Can you forget about it?"

"Yes, I can. I think it's past now, whatever it was," said Frobo.

"Good," said Grandalf, exhaling a sigh of relief. "This creature you thought you saw... you say it had furry fingers?"

"Oh, I don't know if it did or not, Grandalf," said Frobo. "I was probably just dreaming. But you know, it's funny, I thought I saw the same fingers grabbing me when I was drowning in the Brandybeer River. I was probably just seeing things then like I was tonight."

"Yes..." said Grandalf, looking him over suspiciously. "Yes, you probably were. Well now, back to bed my young hobbick. And don't worry about anyone else sneaking up on our camp, I'll keep watch for the rest of the night." The wizard pulled a long-barreled pipe from beneath his cloak. "I need to think."

The last thing Frobo saw when he shut his eyes was the steady fluctuating glow of Grandalf's burning pipe. The last thing he thought of before falling asleep was the image of the wizard's black eyes, glowing like the fire of the seeing stones. The sight of them would have been enough to keep him awake for hours when he was in his tweens. As old as he was now, he shut them out of his mind and considered himself fortunate to still be on their quest. After all, he had no other place to go, and no other friends to turn to. When he finally did fall asleep, Frobo had no more dreams of the furry handed creature.

CHAPTER 9

A UNIQUE ENCOUNTER

THE FOLLOWING MORNING, FROBO AWOKE TO THE BLESSED aroma of Sham's cooking. A few of the others had already begun to break down the camp. "Glad to see you awake, Mister Frobo," said Sham, pointing to some large eggs he was frying on a pan over the fire.

"Where'd you get those?" Frobo asked.

"Oh, wait till you hear the story, Mister Frobo," said Sham, "just you wait."

"What are those scratches on your face and neck?" said Frobo. Sham's broad grinning face and rosy cheeks were adorned that morning with bright red scratches and several welts. It looked like he'd run face first into a thicket of thorns. What's more, his usual shining golden hair was disheveled and the white shirt beneath his vest was tattered and shredded. Sham had always managed to keep himself looking smart and clean as Frobo's employee, despite the fact that he labored in the dirt of Frobo's garden for hours and hours every day. Frobo almost felt ashamed to see the hobbick presenting himself like this. Sham had better have a good excuse because this was downright unprofessional.

"I got those from the turkeys," Sham said, completely unaware that his employer had an issue with his appearance. "In the turkey's roost when I was trying to steal the eggs! I got up to get them before sunrise and was waiting for the proper moment to fry 'em up for first breakfast, see, when everyone woke up."

"You found a turkey's roost and stole their eggs this morning?" asked Frobo. Now that he was eager for the story, he would forgive Sham's appearance. "Sham, you're a marvel!"

"Oh, you don't have to say that sir," said Sham. "But I did go through quite the painful experience to acquire them, not that any of these other chaps care about that. Those ungrateful... well never mind. See, I was walking along the road this morning before sunrise trying to find some breakfast for you sir, when away to my left, off in the distance at the end of a far golden meadow, I spotted two great brown turkeys! And I said to myself as I sometimes do, *'Where there's birds, there's eggs, and my Mister Frobo does like his eggs when he's breakfasting!'* So straightaway, I sprinted across the golden meadow for the turkeys, because I didn't want them to get away. But they were further away than I thought, and I actually had to stop and catch my breath a few times before they spotted me and turned round to run."

Frobo tried to keep himself composed and remain attentive. Sham had a dreadful habit of sharing unnecessary details when he was recounting a story. Frobo's gratefulness for the frying eggs compelled him to listen patiently however long-winded the story became, without interruption.

"Thankfully, the turkey's roost wasn't far from the end of the field," Sham continued, turning over the eggs in the pan. "Because I was completely out of breath when I caught up to them. They'd built an enormous communal nest on the ground, where they all lived together, from sticks and tree branches and the golden grass of the field. The two turkeys whom I'd spotted were the first I had to wrestle my way through. They pecked and scratched and plucked with their beaks at me so much I feared I wouldn't make it, I did sir, and many times I thought about turning 'round and leaving them. And there was more than just them two! Once the other hens heard the commotion, they all swarmed me, sir. I've never been surrounded by so many feathers in my entire life, not even the time I cut open my mattress accidentally. They did not want me to steal their eggs, Mister Frobo, that I can assure you."

It was not overly difficult for Frobo to imagine the tussle, with the evidence of the scrap right before him scratched all over Sham's face and the tangled mess of the hobbick's hair. For some strange reason, it reminded Frobo of a badly kept garden.

"But the hens weren't really that bad. I just didn't realize that until I got to the gobbler." said Sham. "The biggest gobbler you ever saw. I tell you, Mister Frobo! He was taller than I was!"

"Alright Sham," interrupted Grandalf. "Enough with your cooking and tall tales. You best finish both quicker than you started them because we are soon departing."

"Like I said before," continued Sham, "they're ungrateful, the lot of them. Why are the big folk always so busy, Mister Frobo? They always have somewhere more important to go, and something else bigger to do, but us little folk, we know how to enjoy the simple pleasures of life, which is why I cooked us all breakfast."

Happy and Martin came bursting into the camp clearing from behind some bushes and took their places next to Sham. Frobo, wondering if they could tell, felt his face grow warm from the shame of his actions the previous night. He cleared his throat uncomfortably, looking over his shoulder to see if Grandalf was watching him.

But if the wizard was watching, it was only out of the corner of his eye. This was perhaps to spare Frobo shame; nevertheless, Frobo accepted this grace, whether given intentionally or not.

"Is the food ready yet?" said Martin. "I'm starved... I haven't eaten since yesterday!"

"Now hold on just a minute," said Sham, turning his precious fried turkey eggs once more. "I'm in the middle of a story Martin, and you're just going to have to wait for your breakfast, seeing as I am the one who got it for you in the first place!"

"Then why don't you finish your story so we can eat?" said Martin.

"Alright, alright, but don't rush me!" said Sham. "You know I don't like to be rushed when I've got a good story. So there I was, Mister Frobo, in the turkey's roost. I'd fought my way through the hens and I'd just gotten to the gobbler himself. I was face to face with the great bird, and he was the only thing between me and my prize, the eggs!"

"What happened next? Go on!" said Happy. "I didn't realize the turkeys were still there when you stole these Sham."

"Oh yes, they were, Mister Happy. They quite were... so as I was saying, I was face to face with the great bird, so close that I could see the gleam in his eyes, and if I didn't know better, I'd have thought he wanted to eat me about as bad as I wanted to eat those eggs. So all of a sudden, in the middle of our standoff, he stretches out his wings and starts flapping them back and forth like this, see." Sham swept his arms forwards and backwards in great, broad deliberate strokes and began to prance around the fire on the tip of his toes. "So, I didn't know what to do of course, seeing as how I've never been in a standoff with a turkey gobbler over his hen's eggs before."

"So, what'd you do?" asked Frobo.

"What else?" said Sham. "I started doing the same dance right back to him... to show him I wasn't afraid of him. So then, he did two great big flaps and shot up into the air in a flash all of a sudden, leaving the eggs exposed right in front of me!"

"So, you beat him? Well done, Sham, well done." said Martin.

"Not quite Mister Martin sir," said Sham. "Although I'll admit I thought the same thing at first. I dove for the eggs as soon as he left the roost. Great, big brown shells they had, and all I could think about was how juicy and delicious they were going to be. But then I heard a great humming sound above me..."

"A humming sound?" said Happy.

"Yeah, like '*hummmmm*,'" said Sham.

"What happened next? What was the humming?" said Frobo.

"The great gobbling gobbler was the humming," said Sham. "He crashed into the back of me like a flood hits a failing dam! Hit me hard he did, with his claws first and before you knew it, I couldn't see naught with all the feathers, dust, and debris from the nest flying every which way!"

"What about the eggs?" said Martin. "Had you already gotten them?"

"Oh no sir, not at all," said Sham. "I left the eggs and high tailed it out of there as quick as I could."

"Then where'd you get these?" asked Frobo.

"These?" said Sham. "I bought 'em from a roadside peddler I met on the trail back from the turkey roost. Only cost me five Chirelings for the lot of them."

Frobo rolled his eyes. "You mean these eggs aren't the ones that were in the turkey's roost?"

"What do you mean?" said Sham. "Of course, they aren't. I just told you I bought them from a street peddler for five Chirelings."

"But..." Frobo began.

Grandalf interrupted, "Alright hobbicks, you've had quite

long enough to eat your breakfast." He poured a bucket of water on Sham's fire and nearly flipped over his frying pan. Smoke billowed up like a fog. Sham just saved the hot frying pan, grasping the hot handle with his bare hand before Grandalf could tip it over. "It's time to move, my short friends."

"Oy!" shouted Sham from the burn as he set the pan on the ground. "What'd you have to go and do that for, Mister Grandalf? It's bad enough that we can't sit here and enjoy the eggs slow and proper like."

But Grandalf was not in the mood for discussion this morning, "Find your horse, Sham. Find your horse, or you can walk to Slumbervell."

Frobo reached down and grabbed one of the golden turkey eggs from the pan, shoving it into his mouth as quickly as possible. For all of Sham's densities and slow wits, there was one thing about him which no one could deny: his ability to make the finest food. His skills were nigh unmatched to Frobo's knowledge, and the delicious egg was yet another mark on his long list of culinary feats.

After Martin and Happy stooped to grab their eggs from the pan too, there remained one golden egg for the disheartened chef, who still felt they weren't giving nearly enough attention or time for the "most important meal of the day."

"Alright, alright!" said Sham. "Find Ringo and our horse first, and then I'll eat my breakfast on the road. That's what a good chef does, I tell you, he always thinks of others first."

Frobo found *his* horse, the big yellow mare, with head and all, conveniently tied to a tree. It shook his head when he approached as if it knew exactly what he'd been thinking the last time he rode it. "Alright then," said Frobo. "There's no need to bring that up again. It was an honest mistake; it could've happened to anyone." The horse whinnied as if in laughter at Frobo's misgivings. It was an incredibly calm beast, so calm that Frobo was able to support himself between the horse and a nook in the tree to mount it. He felt much more comfortable this time atop the animal. The ability to lean forward and not feel like you were going to fall straight off the back of the thing made all the difference in the world when it came to horse riding, not to mention how relieving it was to know he wasn't riding an animal that had been decapitated.

Frobo's horse circled around the campfire, seemingly capable of taking him where he needed to go without any direction. Sham had gathered up his things and Ringo was sitting on his horse before him. "Alright, Ringo, now let me get my breakfast and I'll mount."

Sham turned back to the frying pan he'd left on the ground just in time to see two squirrels scurrying away from it back into the trees. The frying pan was empty. "The little scoundrels!" Sham said rushing to the pan that the squirrels had licked clean. "Oh no no no! Now I'm going to be hungry for the rest of the day."

"Mount up, Sham," said Grandalf. "Mount up before you make a fool out of all of us!"

Reluctantly and begrudgingly, Sham mounted the horse with help from Ringo. They were on their way to Slumbervell.

Frobo had never traveled cross country on horse before. For that matter, he'd never traveled cross country at all. He was amazed by the creature's ability to cover long distances so easily and tirelessly. But what stood out to him most was how dreadfully tiring it was to ride atop it. All he had to do was sit, and yet it was the most exhausting sitting he'd ever done in his life. Up and down, back and forth, up and down, back and forth he went as the great animal trotted along across the terrain.

Grandalf rode at the front, leading the group, and behind him the great multitude of horses followed in a giant mass. Ringo and Sham were positioned on the right side of the herd, and Frobo followed just behind them. Happy and Wondell rode on the left side, and Roban took the rear, as he was the most motivated to make sure none of their horses strayed from the herd. Occasionally, when a horse would begin to veer from the herd, he would ride around and steer it back. Although he was far ahead, Frobo could see a long line of grey smoke rising out of Grandalf's pipe above his pointy hat. Just above his head, it was naught but a thin plume, but as it rose higher and higher in the air, it spread, growing wider and wider. If anyone (like the sheeriffs, the new black riders, or Sauluman) was close by they would have instantly been alerted to their location, but it also seemed to be acting as a signal for the horses to follow. Frobo thought that perhaps the herd was drawn to its scent like a charm. He sniffed the air as a wisp of the smoke floated past him. It had an odd and unexpected, sweet aroma, almost like honey baked ham.

Both Wondell and Ringo had separately suggested that the wizard put the pipe away, and Sham had shared his fair piece of advice in regards to the dangers of "smoking incessantly."

But each suggestion was rejected by the grumpy wizard, and he directed them all in turn to go back to their positions around the herd and "mind their own business."

Frobo couldn't help but wonder what was wrong with the old grey wizard. He was so much less cheerful than the depictions he'd seen of the joyful old grandfather-like character in the films. He honestly couldn't remember enough of his own grandfather's book to know what Grandalf was *supposed* to behave like. He just felt disappointed with the Grandalf he had, somewhat shortchanged. Maybe he even would have said he felt *Dagginsed* if it wasn't so self-derogatory.

Watching the "incessant" smoke billow up from the wizard gave him a hankering for his own pipe. He pulled it from his red waistcoat, placed it in his mouth, pinched some pipe weed from his pouch, and struck a match with his other hand on the rough end of his heel. Soon, he had a small fire burning the sweet embers of the Chire's finest leaf inside the bowl of his pipe.

"That old wizard might not be as cheerful as the one I remember in the films," Frobo remarked (though there were none within earshot to hear him but the horses). "But I reckon those films weren't entirely accurate in their portrayal of him either. I really should read that old book again."

A feeling of deep peace began to overtake Frobo as he smoked and spoke to himself atop his big yellow horse. Back in the Chire he never would have been able to do this. There was always someone listening, someone trying to make sure he lived up to his grandfather's good name. There were too many hobbicks in the green rolling hills of that land for him to impress. But out here, past the many forests and woods that surrounded the Chire and Breetown, there were no busybodies or orchestrators to try and mold him into societal adherence. Out here, he was free.

The terrain eased away from clusters of trees, tall hills, and sharp bluffs to good open country. Very few trees could be seen at all, and they only sprouted up with occasional infrequency. Far on a distant horizon, Frobo could see another forest that lay before a vast mountain range. For what was surely leagues and leagues between here and there (though Frobo was no great judge of distances), there was nothing but hard land and a few sharp cresting buttes. It was not at all the type of place to begin growing a garden. The pines were just sparse enough that Frobo didn't feel closed in or trapped by them, but dense enough between the hills and the buttes to make him feel like someone could've been following them without their knowledge.

"Look Frobo!" shouted Sham from in front of him. "Mister Grandalf is signaling something. He's seen something."

Frobo's vision had always been better than Sham's and indeed Sham was right. Grandalf was waving his right arm high above his head. The wizard let out a long, piercing whistle. Frobo looked beyond Grandalf, straining his eyes so that he could just make out what Grandalf might have seen. It was definitely *something*. Past the wizard at the bottom of a wide depression between two cresting hills, a brown discoloration distorted the golden grass. But Frobo couldn't quite discern what it was, despite his superior vision.

"Looks like a wagon that's lost its front wheel!" said Sham.

Frobo stuttered, flabbergasted that Sham had been able to spot... well obviously he could tell it was a wagon now, that was easy to see. And of course, Sham had spotted it first, he was a good twenty feet ahead of Frobo! Yes, yes, it was coming into his vision now very clearly. He could see the wagon, hitched to two horses, and there it was, the broken wheel that had fallen from it.

Ringo and Sham rode up behind Grandalf. Frobo's horse, for whom he still hadn't come up with a name, instinctively rode ahead with them. Roban, Wondell and Martin were close behind. When they arrived, the company waited for a moment at the top of the hill, looking down on the wagon in the depression. The thousand horses meandered on the plains behind, but didn't stray as they were still captivated by the smoke of Grandalf's pipe.

"What can you see Wondell?" asked Grandalf when they all had caught up to him.

"There's a man trying to put the wheel back on that wagon," said Wondell. "He has a sword, and his livery is that of the knights of Grondor."

"Grondor?" said Roban. "What would a Grondorian be doing so far from home? In a wagon nonetheless?"

"This is only a guess, but could he have been driving it?" asked Sham.

Grandalf, like the rest of them, was far too annoyed to respond to the remark. "If this man is a knight of Grondor, then he is a friend not a foe, and we should help him. Come, come, let us see what we can do for the man."

Grandalf spurred his horse ahead with Ringo and Sham

following, but Roban held his horse back. "I don't like this," he said. "We've got a job to do, and I don't have time to help every Grondorian beggar we meet along the road."

"Ahh, it seems to me that our horse thief doesn't wish to get arrested by the knight," said Wondell, grinning and winking at Frobo. "Don't worry, we're just helping him with his wagon. Then we'll be one our way in no time. I won't tell him you stole the horses!" Wondell rode ahead with Martin, leaving Frobo alone with Roban.

"Mark my words, Mister..." Roban paused, setting his jaw and looking at Frobo.

"Daggins," said Frobo.

"Right, Mister Daggins," he said. "Mark my words. This wagon is going to be more trouble than any of us could've ever dreamed. I've got a bad feeling. A really bad feeling. And I don't at all like the look of that so called Grondorian Knight." Roban sighed. "But such is the way of things. Let us go and find our fate."

Frobo did not share Roban's feelings about the knight and the wagon. He was excited that the monotony of the ride was about to be broken. If nothing else, this would give him an excuse to dismount from his horse and rest a while without appearing weak or tired. He'd never helped anyone with their wagon before and doubted he'd be useful, but in general he'd always found pleasure on those rare occasions when he'd been able to lend a hand to others. Probably, Roban and Ringo would do the heavy lifting, and if he was lucky, Frobo would be able to sit back and supervise. Frobo and Roban rode ahead, the last of the company to reach the wagon. As they approached, Frobo heard Grandalf greeting the man.

"Greetings Grondorian!" said Grandalf. "And may I ask with whom I have the pleasure of speaking on this fine day?"

The man wore the same black livery as all Grondorian knights. As he rose from the broken wheel of the wagon, he rested his hand on his sword hilt and surveyed the arrivals. He had broad protruding cheek bones and a clean-shaven pale face. His eyes were the same color as his livery, as black as night. His mouth was shut so tightly as he examined his new acquaintances, that Frobo could only guess the force of it was crushing the man's teeth. His thick jaws pulsed and bulged like they were under intense strain. The man's hair was thick and black like the feathers of a crow, but it was drenched with sweat from his labor with the wagon, and it dripped as it hung from his brow. He was a very broad-shouldered fellow, that much Frobo could see beneath his livery. He was truly a strong, muscular specimen. Frobo doubted there were many men in Grondor who could best him in a fight. "Greetings to you as well," said the knight. "Forgive me if I don't ask the name of the strange company that approaches and outnumbers me before I surrender my own."

"We come in peace, Grondorian," said Grandalf. "That I can assure you. But here we are. I am Grandalf... yes *the* Grandalf, and this is Happy Brandybeer, Ringo the Rugged Dwarf, Sham Gramgee, Wondell the Dashing, Martin Shaken-Nottstird, Frobo Daggins and finally, as I'm sure he will be known hereafter in legend, Roban the Gambling Horse Thief."

"Horse thief?" said the Grondorian, drawing his sword and eyeing Roban. "So, these coming up behind you are stolen? Know it now, I will tolerate no thieving of horses here! Not in the northern realm of Grondor that I'm sworn to protect."

"Oh brother," drawled Roban, as if the drawing of the knight's sword did not scare him in the slightest. "Save your piety for the presence of your king! This is what we get for trying to help this stupid sap of a knight who can't even fix his own wagon. Threats and insults..." Roban shook his head and sighed from atop his horse. Frobo was shocked at Roban's nonchalance. He himself had nearly jumped out of his saddle from fright when the man drew his sword! He certainly didn't want their new friend Roban to be arrested.

"Leave your sword in its sheath, friend," said Grandalf. "We come in peace. And though this man is a horse thief, we owe him a debt."

"Forgive me," said the knight with sword still drawn. "I did not know that Grandalf was ever in league with thieves. My king will be quite interested to learn of it."

"As I said before, we owe this man a debt," Grandalf said. "Coincidentally, his thievery has helped to stymie the plans and schemes of a great and unknown enemy to your king. And perhaps for that, he can be forgiven. Now, will you let us assist you? Or are you going to keep threatening to fight us, eight against one?"

The knight sheathed his sword and screwed up his face to try and look grim. It worked. Frobo was still terrified of the man and would not be turning his back on him any time soon. "I will let you assist me, though I like it not."

"Ungrateful," said Roban.

"And will you tell us your name, Knight of Grondor?" asked Grandalf.

"I am Uniborn the Great, Protector of the White City," said the knight.

"Uniborn the Great?" laughed Roban. "That's... well it's somewhat lame, isn't it? Who goes around referring to themselves as 'the Great?'"

"Stay your tongue, Roban. This is a man of honor," snapped Grandalf. "Tell us, Uniborn, what brings you so far from your homeland?"

Roban was still laughing from atop his horse, but it seemed to Frobo that the laughter was hardly genuine. It reminded him of the way Sham laughed sometimes when Frobo told a joke at Sham's expense.

Uniborn ignored it and answered Grandalf. "I am on a rescue and protection mission from my king."

"Protection of whom?" asked Grandalf.

"That is for me alone to know," said Uniborn.

They all turned to the wagon with the broken wheel. It was in fact a carriage, the type of which the wealthy or royal would ride in. Its windows were shut, and Frobo wondered why he had not thought to look inside before. Of course, someone was in there. Someone Uniborn was protecting!

"Oh, don't be such a drama queen, Uniborn," said Roban. "Get over yourself and tell us who it is."

"I will surely not!" shouted Uniborn. "I am on an urgent quest for my king. Are you going to help me with this wheel or simply distract me from my duties?"

"Come, let's give the man our help," said Grandalf, dismounting his horse. The rest of them, save Roban, did the same.

"First he's ungrateful, then he won't tell us who's in his carriage, and now he demands our help," said Roban, spitting on the ground. "I'm going to check on the horses."

Frobo and the others, directed by Uniborn, worked to reattach the dismantled wagon wheel. It had completely dislodged itself from the carriage in a muddy rut, and the long piece of wood that spun when the wagon rode, the one they kept calling the axle, was buried in the mud. Whoever was inside the carriage couldn't have been sitting at a comfortable angle. Frobo wondered that the wagon hadn't completely tipped over. Uniborn was growing increasingly frustrated.

After working for nearly an hour, they finally managed to uncover the axle, only to find it broken in two. This carriage was not going anywhere until it could be replaced. "Son of Ashelob!" shouted Uniborn. "Now what am I going to do?"

Roban had returned quite some time ago from 'checking on the horses' and had been offering tips and advice for them while they worked to uncover the axle. "You know Uniborn, the more I think about it, I really can't understand how you managed to do this. You were driving the wagon, you had to have seen the muddy rut right in front of you... what were you thinking?"

"You'll hold your tongue if you know what's good for you, horse thief!" said Uniborn.

"I mean, it was right in front of you," said Roban. "You'd have to be a complete idiot not to see it."

"Ignore him," said Grandalf. "And do not fret about the rest of your journey. You may come with us if you choose. We are headed to Slumbervell. You and your *accompaniment* can ride with us there, where you can acquire all the provisions you need for the rest of your journey."

"That is most kind of you, Grandalf," said Uniborn. He glanced once more at each one of them. It seemed like he was sizing them up, judging each of them for merit and whether or not they were worthy to discover who was being transported inside the carriage. "Allow me time to consult with my... *accompaniment*." Uniborn returned to the door of the carriage and knocked upon it three times. A small speaking slot, large enough for only a mouse to crawl through slid open and Uniborn began whispering with whomever was in the carriage.

Roban still sat atop his horse and the rest of them backed away to give Uniborn and the rider of the carriage some privacy.

"Who do you think is inside?" asked Wondell.

"Probably someone important," said Ringo. "Some Grondorian nobility or fair lady."

"Perhaps it is the king himself?" said Happy.

"No, no, it isn't the king," said Grandalf. "He would never be guarded by a single knight, not even one as noble as Uniborn. My guess is with Ringo. It is probably some lady of high status, or some nobility in the carriage. And Uniborn is her protector."

"You are right Grandalf," said Wondell. "A fair Grondorian lady of nobility is the only explanation."

"A *fair* Grondorian lady?" scoffed Roban. "Hah! I don't know who is in that wagon, but my guess is, she's hiding in there because she's too embarrassed to show herself. She probably has the teeth of an ork and the nose of a horse."

"Ho now!" said Ringo. "I have seen many beautiful Grondorian ladies in my day."

"Hah! Well if *you* think they're attractive then by all means," said Roban. "I tell you, I've seen my share of Grondorian women and I wish I could forget them all. But the royals are the worst. I'm telling you, I've got a bad feeling about this one. She's likely to be so ugly, she'll be a sight to behold. Nobody with any looks hides in a carriage like that."

The small sized speaking door on the carriage door closed and Uniborn turned to them. He stood like a servant squire, with his legs together and arms folded behind his back. Though he was still the same tall knight who'd threatened the arrest of Roban, he no longer seemed so menacing and threatening. "We have decided to accompany you to Slumbervell," Uniborn said.

"Who has decided?" said Grandalf.

"Here we go," muttered Roban. "Better hold on to something boys, before sickness sets in at the sight of her."

"May I present to you the flower of the gardens of Grondor, descendant of the most esteemed steward and former princess of Brohan, the Lady Ellamir." Uniborn opened the full door to the carriage and stood back, bowing in respect for the "Lady" that was about to descend the carriage steps.

Frobo found himself wincing and bracing for what would undoubtedly be one of the most unattractive persons he'd ever seen before, as the feet of the person Uniborn had introduced stepped into view. Uniborn reached out a hand to help her as Frobo saw the locks of golden hair, neither brown nor blonde, falling over the shoulders of the woman who stepped down from the carriage.

The sight of her figure stole the breath of every one of

them, as she gracefully looked up to meet their gaze. Then they all beheld once more the green eyes of the woman they knew as Ella. This was the same woman who'd caught Ringo's shirt in the Inn of the Prancing *Shetland* Pony. And yet, their brief familiarity with her did little to ease the shock that accompanied one who beheld her beauty.

Frobo felt himself blushing. Roban cleared his throat from atop his horse, clearly affected. Ringo was the first to speak, "Ella? Ah, we meet again! How enchanting it is to see you."

"Ringo? Ringo the *Rugged!*" she shouted. Nervous laughter bubbled out of her like a hot drink that was too full. "Well, if this isn't the strangest thing. Oh Uni, you didn't tell me Ringo the *Rugged* was here."

"Wait a minute, wait a minute... did she just call you 'Uni'?" Roban asked Uniborn, who was grimacing at the utterance of the name.

"The Lady Ellamir may call me whatever she wishes," said Uniborn, trying his best to appear resolute through Roban's laughter.

For some reason, Frobo assumed the Lady might be nervous or afraid to speak to Roban, after all she was a fair lady, and they were strangers to her. Roban was a gruff man and a horse thief at that. Perhaps her voice might tremble or quake as she spoke to him. But Frobo assumed wrongly, for when she spoke, she did nothing of the sort.

"And who might *you* be?" the Lady asked Roban, rolling her eyes and addressing him like he was a young hobbick eager to attract attention.

"Who am I?" said Roban, recovered from his laughter. "I am Roban Hoods, greatest card player this side of the Musty Mountains. But you're not a *Lady of Grondor*, you're that girl who was on stage with *him* in the Prancing *Shetland* Pony. A woman of nobility would never let herself be seen in that setting."

"You will show the Lady Ellamir the respect she is due!" shouted Uniborn.

"Oh, did you see me there?" asked Ella. "I guess I forgot to mention, I prefer Ella, but yes, my real name is Ellamir."

"A lady of Grondor watching the *Rugged Dwarfs*?" scoffed Roban. "Some *lady*..."

Uniborn growled in anger, furious at the connotations Roban was directing at Ella.

"And just what were *you* doing there?" asked Ella. "Seems like *you* might have a thing for the *Rugged Dwarfs* yourself."

Frobo felt himself laughing but tried to restrain himself. It would be impolite to laugh at Roban, someone he barely knew. But he was impressed with the Lady. She was quick witted, and far smarter than she looked.

"I was there for the beer," said Roban.

"Interesting. There are a dozen taverns with beer in Bree-town, yet you found yourself in the very one where the *Rugged Dwarfs* were performing," she said.

"Pay him no attention Lady Ellamir," interrupted Uniborn, stepping between the Lady and Roban. "He's a good for nothing horse thief. Someone of your status should not be troubled by the likes of him."

"Thanks *Uni*," jeered Roban.

"A scoundrel, is he?" said Ella, doing her best to look at Roban with scorn in her eyes. "How unfortunate. And who are the rest of them, Uniborn? Wait a moment, well you were all in the *Shetland* Pony, weren't you? What a small world it is," she laughed.

"All of us but Uni," said Roban.

Grandalf introduced himself first, "Lady Ella, I am Grandalf, yes that same trademarked individual who knew your grandparents and has returned." Grandalf introduced the rest of their company to the Lady, save Ringo whom she already knew.

"Yes Wondell!" she said. "You're that poor elf who can't find a wife because of the films, aren't you?"

"Well, he can hardly blame the films," interrupted Ringo. "What woman could be beautiful enough to marry him? I mean..." Ringo stopped himself, realizing what he'd said, "I mean what woman, save the beautiful Lady Ella herself," he corrected. "Although," he added quickly, "of course, I'm not suggesting such an arrangement, my lady!"

"And what type of arrangement would you suggest for the Lady?" asked Wondell. "One with yourself as the groom, no doubt!"

"The Lady Ellamir will not be disgraced by such suggestive talk!" snapped Uniborn. "You will show honor to one so high above you in Middlearth! Now, give us our horses so that we may begin our journey to Slumbervell."

"Hah," laughed Roban. "You really are an entitled chap, aren't you? But I'll give you the horses Uni, a couple of the red mares I stole from Breetown. I just hope they aren't too far below your *noble status* to be able to ride like the rest of us here." Roban whistled and instantly, two red horses galloped up to them from the herd.

"How did he do that?" Sham asked Frobo. "We only just stole the horses yesterday!"

"Beats me, Sham," said Frobo.

"Oh, and my apologies, madam," said Roban. "We're fresh out of saddles, so I hope you know how to ride bareback. Of course, you could just ride with me if you don't feel safe riding alone..."

"I ride bareback just fine, thank you," said Ella, glaring at Roban.

Uniborn had begun the quite awkward process of helping the Lady Ella quite onto her horse. Frobo felt himself blushing, but he and Sham were quickly enlisted by Grandalf to load the Lady's luggage from the carriage and onto the backs of the two horses that had been pulling it. It was a surprising amount of luggage for a Lady of her status (though what her status actually was, Frobo had no idea). He also had no idea how much luggage was to be expected for a Lady who had recently travelled cross country from Grondor to see the Rugged Dwarfs dancing in a tavern. But none of that was his concern. He only cared that he and Sham did a decent job getting it all on the backs of the horses, and they did. Once finished, he looked up at Grandalf with pride.

"Well, it took you long enough," said Grandalf. "But I guess it'll have to do."

"Son of Ashelob," said Roban, returning on horseback from another check of the herd and seeing the job Frobo and Sham had done. "She's got enough luggage for four princesses!"

"I never said I was a princess," said Ella, now firmly sitting atop her red mare.

"You may not have, but you sure do act like one," said Roban. "Let's ride! If we hurry, we might still be able to reach Slumbervell by nightfall."

Uniborn mounted his horse, and they set out. Frobo rode in the same place in line as before, as did the other members of the company. Uniborn and the Lady Ella rode up at the front of the herd with Grandalf. From where he was, Frobo could see Grandalf and Ella conversing back and forth. She rode side saddle of course, her green dress splayed across the red horse like a waterfall. Frobo occasionally would hear the sounds of laughter coming from the two of them, the wizard's old rumbling barks, followed by Ella's young melodious chirping. *"What a wonderful time they must be having,"* he thought to himself. But although he was far away from them, one thing he did know for certain. The whole time they rode up front, he didn't once hear the laughter of Uniborn the Knight.

CHAPTER 10

THE SONG IN THE DARK

HOWEVER FAR AWAY THIS SLUMBERVELL WAS, IT WAS A SIGHT further than Frobo had originally imagined. As the sun began to set overhead, it became abundantly obvious that they would not reach it before nightfall. They had just come upon the edge of the far blanket of trees at the end of the open terrain where they rode. Wondell had told Frobo that Slumbervell was somewhere in those trees, but how far they had to travel inside them to find it, Frobo did not know. He rode up beside Ringo and Sham.

"It doesn't look like we're going to make it to Slumbervell, does it?" he said.

"Nay it does not, my young hobbick," said Ringo. "But what the devil do you think that old wizard is doing up there, laughing like a lunatic. Perhaps you should go remind him that night is soon to fall upon us. The Lady Ella cannot ride into the night."

As if his horse had heard Ringo's suggestion as a command, it trotted Frobo ahead to the front of the herd with Grandalf, Ella, and Uniborn. Upon seeing the Lady Ella again up close, he couldn't help but be amazed by her captivating beauty and joy.

It was like she was a perfect foil in contrast to the sullen Uniborn. She looked as beautiful as the colorful spring with her tight waisted green dress, her bare white shoulders and her long golden hair, flowing in the wind like a flag at the shores of the sea. Uniborn on the other hand was as dull as the dreary grey winter. He looked uncomfortable in his dark knightly livery. The white crest of the tree across his breast was the only glimmer of hope in his whole bearing. His face was red, either with anger or from heat. His long black hair was still drenched with sweat and hung about his face like a damp shirt after a wash, drying on a line. Being near the Lady made Frobo feel light and springy himself, but it seemed to have the opposite effect on the knight.

"What do you want, hobbick?" Uniborn asked him, quite in character with Frobo's perception of him.

"Shame on you, Uni!" said Ella, "That's no way to talk to him. You're Frobo, aren't you?"

Frobo nodded, his mouth becoming dry at the lady's acknowledgment of him.

"See Uni," Ella continued. "This is the grandson of the most famous hobbick who ever lived! You need to learn to be more open; you can be so judgmental sometimes."

Uniborn muttered under his breath as Ella continued, "Now, what is it Frobo?"

"Yes, we were wondering..." Frobo began, "well Ringo was wondering if perhaps it was about time to break and make camp for the night. Unless we are very close to Slumbervell?"

"Ringo was wondering? Hah!" snapped Uniborn. "The dwarf you travelled so far to see? I'll wager he was."

"Yes, he was," said Frobo, annoyed by the uncouth manners of the knight. Was this really a man of nobility in Grondor? Frobo couldn't understand how Ella could tolerate him, and yet it seemed like they were old friends, at least for Ella's part.

"Perhaps he is right to suggest it," said Grandalf. "The sun is setting, and we are not nearly as far on the road to Slumbervell as I had hoped we would be. Let's make camp here and we can reach Slumbervell in the morning."

"Hold on Grandalf," said Uniborn. "Where do you suggest the Lady Ellamir sleep? She is a woman of royalty, and she cannot rest amongst your company and these horses like some hired hand."

"Oh Uni, relax," Ella said. "If we need to stop, we'll stop."

"I shall build you a shelter," said Uniborn. "I won't allow these ruffians and horse thieves to share your presence in the dark of the night."

The company had just ridden up on a grove of leafy beech trees. The trees were tall and broad, and shrouded a swift flowing stream that cut through the middle of the grassy field. Smelling the water, the horses galloped up to the stream, lining up on both sides of it to drink their fill. Uniborn dismounted his horse and let it join the herd to drink. Then he stalked off to begin the construction of Ella's 'shelter,' muttering curses under his breath as he went. Frobo wondered how someone could be so sullen and rigid.

Grandalf dismounted his horse and began to make camp, whistling for the others in signal that they were stopping for the night. Frobo dismounted his horse, nearly losing his balance several times in the process. Once he was firmly on the ground, he thought of the Lady. If he had trouble getting off his horse, how would she dismount? *"Help her, you idiot,"* he scolded himself for not thinking of it sooner. But before he could offer, Ella slid from the back of her horse with the grace and ease of a seasoned rider. Well, he'd lost that opportunity, but he had to think of something to do for her. She seemed so out of place in this wild country, like a bright iris growing in a tangle of brush and brambles. "Allow me to take your horse, my lady," he said.

"Take it?" she laughed, looking down at him, revealing the perfect white teeth in her open mouth. "Take it where?"

"Oh, I don't know," he laughed in turn. What a stupid thing to say. He could be so stupid sometimes. "I was just trying to help. I'll be on my way."

"Where are you going?" asked Ella. "Come and gather some firewood with me. A stroll with good company would do me well after sitting for an entire day. And I shouldn't go alone."

"You gather firewood, Lady?" he asked timidly.

"They wouldn't like that, would they?" she said sarcastically. "You can gather the wood, and I'll walk beside you. I haven't gotten to walk since Uni found me in Breetown and bought that carriage to take me back home. That Uni is something else, Frobo," said Ella.

The two of them set out to look for fallen branches and wood together while the others started setting up camp. Frobo would make sure they didn't stray too far or go out of sight, as he was quite sure doing so would cause Uniborn to grow angry with him. They walked together for a few minutes in silence, and Frobo occasionally stooped to pick up any dry branches he thought would be suitable for the fire. He was very nervous to speak to her, but eventually, the silence between them became too awkward for him to endure. The Lady Ella looked quite comfortable walking with him in the silence however, and she smiled at him when he looked up at her. Nevertheless, he felt he had to say *something*.

"I read about you in the Morning Muffin," said Frobo. "I mean, in the newspaper in my home country," he added, seeing the look of confusion on her face. "I read a headline about how you were missing from Grondor. So, you just ran away? You hadn't been kidnapped or anything like that?"

"Yes," she said. "I suppose you could say I ran away."

"Why?" asked Frobo. "You're practically a princess! You probably have... well you probably have an awful lot of things! Why would you want to leave?"

"You think possessions and title are the only things of

importance in life?" she asked sincerely. "How interesting. But I can't say that many do not share your point of view. I had my reasons for leaving, and I do not wish to share them now. I tried to explain that to Uniborn when he caught up to me, but it was no use. I told him I didn't want to go home yet, that I had a purpose for being gone, but he refused to listen. He thought I needed to be rescued and that was the only point of view he was willing to entertain. I do believe that if I hadn't agreed to return with him, he would have tied me up and brought me home in a sack."

"Who is he?" Frobo asked.

"He's a friend," Ella said, as they walked. "An old, old friend. We grew up together, Uni and I."

"You grew up together?" asked Frobo, now intrigued.

"Yes, we did," said Ella. "Our fathers were friends and were both very important men in Grondor, although seeing as my father was the son of a Brohanian Princess and the former Steward of Grondor, he was just slightly more important, though that never did get in the way of their friendship. So, we grew up together, quite the same age and with quite similar childhoods. And we were friends, we were always friends, although I was like the next best thing in Grondor to royalty, and Uniborn was a good man. Now he was becoming a very good man, mind you, but still he was not royalty, and neither was I for that matter.

"So, when Uni and I grew older, one day it felt like something had changed between us. There wasn't the same playful fun any more like there had been for so long. Something had changed. His playfulness and friendship towards me turned to grim stares and dark glances. I started to feel like he hated me altogether. Now that I'm older, I know that wasn't the case at all, but in fact that he loved me," Ella said.

Frobo could not believe the openness of the woman who walked next to him. Why was she telling him all of this?

"How do you know he loved you?" asked Frobo. "Did he tell you?"

"No, he didn't," Ella said. "He told my father when he asked for my hand in marriage."

Why had she chosen *him* to confide in? But of course, she thought he was the descendant of the most famous hobbick who'd ever lived. He had an important ancestor, just like she did. She didn't realize that he might be nothing more than a lowly Sackville-Daggins.

"What did your father say?" Frobo asked.

"What else could he say?" said Ella. "Of course, he told Uniborn he needn't ask his permission, that he was like the son he never had, and that he wouldn't refuse his proposal to me, but only to allow him to speak with me about it first. So, when my father came to me to speak about it, he was very surprised that I had no desire to marry Uniborn. For already, I had begun to see the changes coming over him in his feelings for me. I told my father I would not have him if he was the last man in Grondor, and there was quite the uproar when my father returned that news to Uniborn. Our families haven't been able to be friends since. All because of Uniborn's love for me."

"Dear me," said Frobo. "But pardon me for saying so, my lady, and I hope this isn't taken the wrong way, but I've seen the way Uniborn looks at you, and that isn't love."

The lady Ella turned sharply to him, looking down at him from her perfectly furrowed dark eyebrows. "What do you mean?" she said.

"Well, I don't mean it disrespectfully," said Frobo. "I don't mean it like he *shouldn't* love you, or *couldn't* love you, I just mean to say that... love is supposed to be looking out for the best for someone else. If he really loved you, wouldn't he have let you move on when he saw that you weren't interested? Wouldn't he be able to move on himself and be happy he hadn't ended up with someone who didn't love him back? But here he is... obviously unable to do so, and even though he's doing a noble thing in bringing you safely back, it doesn't seem like he's doing it for the right reasons." Frobo shut his mouth quickly. Now he was the one that was speaking far too freely.

"You think he's not bringing me back for *the right reasons?*" she said. "But you do think he *should* be bringing me back. Hah! Well Mister Frobo, if someone does something good for the wrong reasons, can it really be counted as a good deed at all?"

Frobo paused. It was a puzzling question indeed, and one he was not sure he could answer. But he felt a sense of unmerited duty and loyalty to the lady, for reasons he could not discern, and felt that not answering the question would be to do her a great disservice. So, he resolved to answer it, however foolish his answer might be, while asking forgiveness for what may have earlier caused offense. "I was simply trying to explain the difference between love and what I perceive to be this Uniborn's feelings for you. But it seems that I may have over-stepped the gracious welcome my lady has given me to speak."

Ella marvelled at him and smiled. Frobo felt relieved. "I must say, you impress me, Frobo. Do all of your people speak so eloquently? Surely that was a gift inherited from your grandfather. But in Uni's defense, I will say only this. When you really *love* someone, it can make it difficult to see these sorts of things clearly. It's not always so simple and straightforward as you would think. It gets very complicated, very easily."

"I see," said Frobo, whose own experience in romantic love was as virgin as his loins. Obviously from her speech, the lady had some acquaintance with the subject. Without thinking of what he was doing once again, he asked her bluntly, "Have you ever felt that way towards someone?" He immediately regretted this question, for the lady in an instant, turned such a flush shade of red, realizing she had revealed quite too much of herself to him. Frobo looked away, pretending he had not seen the lady's blush.

Ella cleared her throat, "Of course not. I am unmarried, unpursued, and as singular as the Lone Mountain. Why do you ask?" she said.

"Oh, just curiosity," said Frobo, kneeling to gather wood for the fire. He then desperately tried to avoid eye contact with Ella, wondering who it was in Middlearth that someone as beautiful as she could be in love with.

"Perhaps we should return to camp," said Ella, with a discomfort that would only be discernible to one who'd heard their conversation.

Frobo gathered as much firewood as his short arms could hold, and the two of them walked the short distance back to the camp being made by the others. They were at the very edge of the green wood out in the golden field. The herd of horses were tired from the long day's march, and grazed freely, but remained close to the camp. Behind them and beyond the trees, the tall mountain range loomed like a menacing fortress. The jagged grey peaks cut the blue sky like spears, swords and axes, a terrible sight to behold. Frobo imagined falling from the top of one of one of their tall peaks, tumbling for miles and miles to his death.

But he quickly shook the image from his mind. His feet were on the ground, far, far below the high mountains. For the time being, he was perfectly safe. Frobo approached the camp behind Ella, carrying his bounty of firewood, feeling a mixture of sheepish guilt at the questions he'd asked of her and pride at his service of wood gathering.

Uniborn, of course, was the first to see Ella. "What were you doing out there?" he said. "You shouldn't be walking alone."

"I wasn't alone," Ella corrected, "I was with him."

Uniborn had failed to see Frobo in the dim light of the evening and the shadows behind Ella, but he stepped forward with the firewood in his arms, as if he was quite the fellow for Lady Ella's protection duty.

"With him?" exclaimed Uniborn. "Why, you would've been as safe going with a field mouse! What did you want with her anyways, you little half sized..."

"You'll keep your mouth shut, if you know what's good for it, mister!" barked Sham. He rolled up his sleeves and stared down Uniborn like a mother bear if the man was a wolf threatening her cub. "Where I come from words like that can get a chap quite a bit more than he bargained for!"

Ella interrupted before anything else could be said. "Frobo only accompanied me as we gathered firewood, Uniborn. He was very *honorable*. I don't think *anyone* else here could've done it better."

That shut him up. The idea that a half-sized hobbick could walk with the Lady Ella in a more honorable manner than he could, probably made Uniborn absolutely furious inside. But on the outside, all it did was make him sneer and silently continue the construction of her 'shelter.'

"Come Frobo, bring me that firewood," said Roban. The man had already started a fire. Small flames licked up around the kindling that lay across them. "Set it down right there," he said. "Don't worry about that *Eunuch*-born fellow, he can't help it he was born jealous."

Frobo laughed, relieved that at least Roban wasn't envious of the time he'd spent with the Lady. "I'd be jealous too," said Roban, "if I was born a *eunuch*."

Grandalf chuckled too, but he was the only other one of the company within hearing. "It is a rather unfortunate name, isn't it," said the old wizard.

Uniborn glared at the three of them as they built their fire, indeed suspecting the laughter was at his expense. They continued to laugh so hard and were so exuberant that they didn't even notice the Lady Ella standing before them, quite awkwardly clearing her throat.

"Ahem," she said. They continued laughing, oblivious to her. "*Ahem!*" she exclaimed.

Roban was the first to note the lady. "May I help you?" he asked.

"You may," Ella replied. "It is customary in Grondor that a man of nobility offer a seat to a lady when she approaches."

Frobo stopped laughing immediately and leapt to his feet, a feeling of guilt rushing over him. Roban continued to sit comfortably at his place and tend the fire he was building. "Well *Lady*, this isn't *Grondor*, we aren't *men of nobility*, and besides the spot on my lap here, there aren't any seats to offer," said Roban.

Grandalf, who was in the middle of a drink from his water jug, snorted its contents out upon Roban's fire in laughter. He might have been able to maintain a gentlemanly decorum had he not already been coaxed into a laughing mood. Upon seeing the Lady's disgust, the old man tried to save face with a quick slap across the back of Roban's head, but the attempt was too late, and the damage to her perception of him was done.

"Well, I have never..." Ella began.

"Oooh!" Sham exclaimed, instantly rushing over to the fire and crouching on his knees. "Are you playing *Hobbick's Never*? I positively love this game! I'll start! Or wait, no, you were already starting, weren't you Miss Lady Ella? Never mind, you'll get your turn later, I'll start the game. Let me see, oh yes, I've been wanting to use this one... ahem. This hobbick's never been to Breetown. Now, if you've been to Breetown, you've got to stand up and say something you've never done before. Now, has anyone here ever been to Breetown?"

"But you've been to Breetown," said Frobo. "We all just came from there."

Sham himself looked as confused as they all felt, staring in the same stunned silence. All he could do was very slowly say the words, "Quite right, Mister Frobo," while looking up and to the left as if he was trying to remember something. He then stood to his feet and slowly backed away from the fire, shaking his head as if his ear was clogged with water.

"Lady Ella, fair and lovely, with locks to rival my own hair... please accept my humble gift of this handmade, holly chair." From behind him, Ringo the dwarf appeared, carrying a magnificent wooden rocking chair, with an intricate design on the back that had flowers carved into the wood. Frobo's jaw dropped. This would've taken hobbicks months to carve, and they never would've been able to do so this perfectly.

"Oh Ringo, you shouldn't have," Ella gushed, and clasped her hands together in shock. "How did you... did you *build* this for me?"

"For whom else could I have made such a chair?" the dwarf chuckled, grinning ear to ear.

Wondell shot up from where he was hunched over to inspect the chair. "This isn't holly!" said the elf, "It's Longleaf Murkwood. And there isn't any Murkwood within a hundred leagues of here."

Ella was still giggling hysterically at her gift. She sat down in the chair and rocked back and forth, smiling ear to ear. "Oh, it's wonderful Ringo, it's just wonderful. How did you do it? How did you make it?"

"Yes, tell us Ringo," said Wondell, crossing his arms and examining the dwarf intently. "Tell us how you designed, cut, planed, sanded, polished, and stained your Longleaf Murkwood chair in half an hour, without knowing the type of wood you were using."

"Well," laughed Ringo, "I must have been confused on the species, that's all. Just a beginner's mistake. A woodworking *prodigy's* mistake!"

"Oh, I don't care how he did it," said Ella, still rocking back and forth in her new chair like it was a swing. "I'm just glad I have somewhere to sit while we watch the fire."

Wondell glared at the dwarf with an almost deranged look

of anger on his face, but Ringo was content to laugh with Ella as she tried out her new chair. Frobo knelt to help Roban with the fire. "How do you think he did that?" Frobo asked. "Building that chair so quick and all." He looked over to Roban and placed another log into the fire.

"Built it?" laughed Roban. "That stout little bloke didn't build that chair. He bought it from the same travelling merchant Sham bought those turkey eggs from this morning. I watched him do it myself. Dwarfs are stone workers; they don't know the first thing about working with wood. That's an elf's craft."

"He bought it from the merchant!" exclaimed Sham so loudly that he was heard by Ella and Ringo. "Where is he? Is he close? Tell me quick, I'll go and buy us something to make for dinner."

"Oh! He's around the corner, young fool!" shouted Ringo, wincing as he looked up to see Ella's reaction.

Wondell on the other hand, looked thrilled and relieved. "I knew it! I knew he didn't build that chair himself, Lady Ella. I knew it."

"Oh, shut up, will you!" cried Ringo. "You know what my mum used to tell me? The only thing worse than a tattletale is a tattletale elf! And you my friend appear to be both!"

"Rather a tattletale than a lying dwarf without the faintest knowledge or skill in woodworking!" shouted Wondell.

"No one calls me a liar!" screamed Ringo.

Just as a fight was about to commence, Ella intervened.

"Boys, boys, boys! Now I know you two have had your differences in the past, but is fighting over my new chair really worthy of a row? Ringo, of course I am a little sad that you pretended to make this chair yourself, but..." she continued before Wondell's grin could widen too far, "Wondell, I am still grateful to have it! Ringo was the only one here thoughtful enough to procure a chair for me, even if he lied about the manner in which it was procured. For that Ringo, I am eternally grateful. And Wondell, to you I am also grateful, for desiring to reveal the truth to me." At this, the Lady Ella arose from her chair, curtsied as was the custom for stately Grondorian women, and then resumed her seat.

Both Wondell and Ringo seemed pacified for the moment. They no longer looked as if they were about to strangle each other, and instead sat like obedient pets often sit when they've just been given a treat from their master.

Roban did not seem as satisfied. He muttered something under his breath that was impossible to discern, but too loud to be missed by anyone who was sitting at the fire. Frobo could only make out that he'd said, *"Mahhnipyouhlatiffwhich..."*

"Did you want to add something Ranger?" asked Ella.

"Nothing you haven't heard before I'm sure," he replied, and then aside to Frobo but still under his breath, "manipulative witch! See how she strokes both their egos to get what she wants? This *Lady* is no dummy, at least I'll give her that."

"I'm sorry Ranger, I can't make out what you're saying," said Ella.

Just as Roban looked ready to announce to all of them what he'd said about Ella under his breath, Uniborn returned. "I'll tell you some other time, *Lady*," said Roban.

Frobo felt very uneasy sitting beside Roban with Uniborn there. He knew the man was suspicious of him, (that was clear enough by the scowls and glares Frobo endured from him every time their eyes met) and association with Roban would help that feeling little. Next to Frobo on his left were Happy and Martin, who were quite contented in their own conversation. They discussed the events of the day, smoked their pipes, and enjoyed their rest after a "hard day's work," even if that did only include riding on the backs of their horses.

Sham returned to sit at an empty place next to Happy and Martin. His arms struggled to hold the various foods and provisions he'd procured (with what money Frobo knew not) from the travelling merchant who was apparently stationed not very far away from them.

Frobo couldn't help but wonder at that merchant (whoever he was). It really was a silly thing for him to be doing, travelling so close to them for such a time. If Frobo ever decided to write this all down in a book someday, he was quite sure nobody in their right mind would believe any of this ridiculous business about the travelling merchant. He'd have to consider completely changing that plot point if it ever came down to it.

Immediately upon sitting, Sham began sorting through the carrots, onions, cabbage and fish that he'd purchased. He'd laid it all out across his knapsack, and began feverishly seasoning, crushing, and grinding as if their fates depended on it. Next to Sham was Ringo, whose focus was split between entertaining Ella, sneaking looks at his own flexing muscles and an extremely loud growling stomach as he watched Sham prepare their dinner. Ella rocked in her new chair, bubbling with the most charming laughter Frobo had ever heard. Uniborn stood behind the empty space between Ella and Wondell, who ultimately seemed more interested in maintaining the braids of his own hair than he was in the Lady.

On the other side of Wondell, and next to Roban, rounding out the circle sat Grandalf with his white beard and staff laid across his waist. Grandalf and Roban were quite engrossed in conversation.

Frobo felt his eyes drawn past Ella to Uniborn, who was still standing out of place behind her, outside the circle. Suddenly and without warning, he interrupted the pleasant conversation. "My Lady, it is time to retire to the lodging I have prepared for you," Uniborn said.

"But I don't want to," said Ella. "I want to stay here and enjoy myself, and the new chair Ringo made for me."

"Bought for you!" corrected Wondell.

"Yes, bought for me," said Ella.

"But, my Lady," said Uniborn. "This is not the type of place... a Lady like you shouldn't be... if your father..."

"Oh, hush Uni! I'm not going to bed now and you can't make me. I haven't even eaten anything yet, and..."

"I can bring your dinner to your shelter once it is prepared," said Uniborn.

"But... but..." said Ella.

"There'll be no more buts, my Lady, you're going to bed," said Uniborn, grabbing hold of Lady Ella's arm.

Frobo's heart fluttered. He didn't like this one bit, and glancing around the fire at the tense faces, he could tell he wasn't the only one.

"But I haven't even heard any songs yet!" said Ella, as she jerked her arm out of Uniborn's grip. Before he could reach for it again, he was stopped.

"Hold it, Uni," said Roban. Still reclined casually by the fire, Roban's voice was strong and authoritative.

Uniborn spun, reaching for his sword, as if Roban had sprung upon him from behind in attack. "This is no concern of yours, horse thief!"

Roban stood to his feet casually, as if Uniborn's threatening tone did not concern him in the least. "Leave your sword in its scabbard. Only a man with no honor would draw on one unarmed."

"You will not speak to me of honor!" said Uniborn. He still threatened Roban with the point of his sword, standing between him and Ella as if to shield her from view. "I will not be lectured by a horse thief in the ways of honor. Not I, a knight of Grondor."

"Then why not start acting like one?" Roban said. "You've been offered company and horses by my good friends here, and no matter how stringent your orders of protection for the Lady Ella are, they can't include robbing her of all joy along the way.

Now, your good lady mentioned just now that 'she hadn't heard any songs yet.' It just so happens, that I've personally heard Blondy and Stout over here sing before, and let me tell you something, they're pretty good. You'd be crazy to miss out on hearing them because of something like 'patrol duty' for our lovely lady here."

"We sing too!" shouted Martin and Happy in unison.

"An excellent plan," said Grandalf. "Sit down Uniborn, enjoy yourself for once in your life! There will be plenty of time for all to sleep later."

Uniborn growled but relented, taking his place on the ground next to Ella's chair. Ella tried to suppress squeals of excitement, and Frobo noticed her giving Roban a second glance. Perhaps she was trying to assign a motive for him stopping Uniborn from dragging her off to bed.

"Who goes first?" she asked, leaning into the circle on the edge of her new chair. "My vote is the two hobbicks, I've heard Wondell and Ringo before!" Wondell and Ringo both looked crestfallen. "I mean," Ella continued as an aside to them, "you wanna save the best for last, right?"

Martin and Happy, not hearing this last comment, burst up from their seats.

"*Happy* to oblige, madam!" said Martin.

"You're not Happy, you're Martin! I'm Happy!" said Happy to the laughter of all but Uniborn, who was still sneering, and Sham, who was too engrossed in the preparations of their meal to hear anything going on around him.

The two hobbicks huddled for a moment, conversing over a song to suit the present crowd, and emerged after a few moments. This was the song they sang. It was one that Frobo had never heard before, and one in which, as was custom among hobbicks, the singers alternated between verses, as the song was composed before the audience. Happy began and sang the first two verses, and was followed by Martin, who had to create a

rhyme that made sense in the same melody. The two had practiced this their whole lives, and as Frobo knew, were the best
spontaneous singers in all the Chire.

Houses have rooms, Witches have brooms,
And hobbicks have holes for their lodgings,
Ladies have furs, cats have their purrs,
And thieves have their ducks and their dodgings!
But if you searched all of this world far and wide,
You'd be short of one thing for sure,
You'd never find hobbicks well fed and satisfied,
Cause for hobbick hunger, there is no cure!
Fried chicken legs, butter with bread,
Pork sausage brine with potatoes,
Beer battered eggs, or just plain instead,
Burgers with fried green tomatoes!
Feed us all that and what do you have?
A hobbick whose well fed and full?
But if he's a hobbick then before he's through,
He'll simply demand that you bring out course two!
Ooooh oooh oooh!
Houses have doors, children have chores,
And mothers have babies to love and adore!
Dwarfs have their mines, elfs have all time,
And good Roban here is the king of horse crimes!
But try to feed hobbicks with elfen way bread,
And one thing you'll find out for sure,
We'll fry it up in biscuits and eat that instead,
A meal we find quite less demure!
Fried chicken legs, butter with bread,
Pork belly stuffed in potatoes,
Beer battered eggs, or just plain instead,
Burgers with fried green tomatoes!
Feed us all that and what do you think?

That by now we'd be quite satisfied?
No sir, three times a day, with good food and good drink,
Is just enough to make sure, we don't shrivel up and die!
Ooooh ooooh ooooh!
Hobbicks we are, and hobbicks we'll be!
And where you find hobbicks, be sure they're hungry!
So we don't starve, we eat lavishly,
Nothing's better than eating, save eating for free!
Fried chicken legs, butter with bread,
Pork belly stuffed in potatoes,
Beer battered eggs, or just plain instead,
Burgers with fried green tomatoes!
Feed us all that and what'll we say?
That we've eaten our fill and are through?
Don't bet on that! We'll eat till we're fat!
And order the entire menu!

Martin and Happy concluded their song, bowing before the campfire travelers to applause. Frobo was especially impressed. He'd heard Martin and Happy perform many times, but never had they sung a song that so encompassed the spirit of hobbicks. The Lady Ella was probably the most impressed, or at least she pretended to be. While the rest of the group remained seated, clapping and laughing, she shot up out of her chair at the song's conclusion, serenading the hobbicks with a standing ovation and shouting, "Encore! Encore!"

Frobo laughed heartily at the many bows from Martin and Happy, who were clearly intoxicated with the attention they were receiving. Uniborn urged Ella to resume her seat, but she did not listen, and whistled loudly for the two singers until she was quite ready to sit without instructions from anyone else to do so.

"Well done, you two rascals," laughed Grandalf, as the two hobbicks finally took their places at the campfire. "I'd begun to think you weren't good for anything except annoyance and headaches, but I suppose you're also good for disposing of leftovers!"

Frobo laughed at this along with the others. Sham was still furiously laboring over their dinner, as if he hadn't heard a single line of the melody.

"Who's next?" shouted Ella.

Ringo was the first to spring up from his perch. "I will serenade thee, my beautiful lady, just as I have done before." The dwarf did his best to then gaze into Ella's eyes, though Frobo did not think she noticed. She was much too busy giggling and squirming around in her seat to make eye contact.

Wondell sighed, rolling his eyes. Ringo then took a long bow and looked off into the distance. He was just about to begin his song when another voice interrupted him. To say that this voice was singing would have been an extreme insult to musicians all across Middlearth. It was not singing, but it was clearly attempting to, and it came from the dark beyond the light of the campfire. The rasping, lurching voice made Frobo cringe. He couldn't see the singer, and he did not have a good feeling about him.

> My mother showed a film to me, when I was but a babe,
> Covered in slime and mold I was, an evil little slave.
> Roaches for breakfast and rot for dinner, I watched the spinning reel,
> The story of the disgusting dwarf, and the beauty he tried to steal!
> If an elf maiden can love a dwarf, the way that I observed,
> Then orks like me might have a shot, for our appetites to be curbed...
> I told myself, I'd marry an elf, and by garn, I'm gonna do it!

"Did he just say, 'then orks like me?'" asked Happy.

"Yes, I'm quite sure he did," said Grandalf, rising to his feet. "Show yourself, stranger! Come into the light!"

From the darkness where the voice had been singing, Frobo

heard the sound of crunching leaves as the stranger stepped toward them. He then saw gleaming yellow eyes, like the eyes of a gigantic cat, shining in the firelight on the dark face of an ork that stood as tall as Grandalf above the ground.

Uniborn leapt from his seat and drew his sword. Wondell stood warily, and Ringo crouched in a defensive position. The films had been released long ago and it was now peacetime in Middlearth. The orks and other fell beasts were now leaderless and lived in caves up in the mountains, rarely, if ever showing themselves. But apparently, this ork had seen the films. Suddenly, Frobo remembered back in the Chire, the night they'd left. He'd seen the orks watching the films from the trees! But if they were in the Chire, then they obviously weren't living in the mountain caves. He could have sworn he'd seen those yellow eyes before too. A memory flashed in his mind. The last time he'd seen those yellow eyes... had been in the Prancing *Shetland* Pony. He remembered now. These were the same eyes that had been staring down through the upper window when Ringo tried to kiss Ella. This was a very strange ork indeed.

"Don't be alarmed, don't be alarmed!" the ork said. "I come in peace!" He now came fully into the fire light, spreading wide his long strong arms to show them that he bore no weapons. But the gesture had little effect in making Frobo feel heartened at his presence. The ork was tall, even as tall as Uniborn was, and he was dirty. Besides his boots, he wore nothing but a grey rag, tied about his loins. His bare chest was huge and bulky with pulsing muscles, a truly terrifying sight. Frobo felt that the ork could have crushed him with a single squeeze of his hand. Those sharp claws on the ends of his fingers would pierce his neck, or whatever other part of Frobo's body the ork held in his clutches. Now that the thing had come into the light, they could all see his pale ashen body, as cold as a stone.

Other than the orks he'd seen watching the films from

beyond the tree line on the far side of the party tree field, this was the first ork Frobo had ever beheld. And he'd only seen those orks for a fleeting moment, he hadn't had time to stop and study them. It was a very odd looking at the beast. He walked and even talked like a man, and the more Frobo studied him, the more man-like he seemed. Of course, this beast was a monster, something that should've had no familiar qualities whatsoever, a dreadful thing that he should've balked at the very sight of. But the more Frobo looked at him, the more he scrutinized and studied, Frobo couldn't get over his feeling of surprise that the ork looked like a man. It wasn't the slits for nostrils, or the catlike yellow eyes, or the greasy hair, or the sharp yellow fangs instead of teeth, or the deathly gray skin that made him look like a man. It wasn't any of those things. In fact, the more Frobo thought about those features, the less like a man the ork looked. What was he thinking? Of course, this creature wasn't anything like a man. It was a monster! Nevertheless, Frobo desperately wanted to trust the ork, if for no other reason than that he was terribly afraid, but something made him unable to do so. Why was that? Because he was prejudiced?

"What is your purpose here, ork?" asked Grandalf. "Your people were allowed to live up in the mountains and that is where you should be. Why are you here? So far away from your home?"

The ork cackled with a sinister devilish laughter. The sound cracked and split the open air like a flaming whip. "Do you not even wish to know my name so that you may welcome me to your fire? Allow me to introduce myself... I am Barzabag, leader of *The Free Orks*."

"And why are you here, Barzabag?" Grandalf asked.

"You mean to say, 'why are you here, Barzabag, Leader of *The Free Orks*.' Perhaps my song did not fully explain," the ork said. "Allow me to continue..."

Frobo braced himself, wincing before listening to another rendition of music sung by the wretched voice.

I told myself, I'd marry an elf, and by garn, I'm gonna do it!
By hook or by crook, by the hobbick's red book, I promised myself, I'd
do it!
In my dingy, filthy, maggot ridden cave, I've told others of my plan,
To marry the beautiful elf of my dreams, just like that little dwarf man,
I'll make her fall in love with me, she'll kiss my crusty lips
And then she'll sail away with me, on some rat infested ship!
'Beauty shall not be deprived from me', is the message that I've said!
And those that didn't agree with me, didn't get to the keep their heads!
Now is the time for Barzabag, to reach out and take his love,
If the dwarf can do it in the films, then I'm entitled... to an elf
maiden too!

Barzabag seemed to have forgotten the last line of his *song* in his eagerness to finish it, the only line that didn't remotely rhyme. He stood tall and proud after it, but unlike with Happy and Martin's song, there was no applause.

"I'm sorry Barzabag, but I'm afraid you're going to have to be a little more clear with your purpose," said Grandalf. "I was cringing through most of your song and couldn't make out all of the words."

"I've come to take my elf wife," said Barzabag, cackling again with that hideous laughter. Frobo turned to Sham and held his arms tight across his chest. He had a very uneasy feeling about this whole thing.

"You would die if you tried!" said Wondell. "Fortunately for you, there are none here!"

"What about her?" said Barzabag, pointing to Ella. "Let me have her!"

Ella put her hand over her chest and sat back in her rocking chair. Frobo feared that the poor Lady might faint at the very thought of the ork taking her away, but even though she gasped and held her breath, the Lady held a brave face and stood firm. Well, she *would* have stood firm, had she been standing in the first place. Instead, she merely continued to sit in her chair.

Uniborn and Ringo sprang in front of Ella, shielding her from Barzabag's view. The sword of Uniborn flashed in the fire-light, and Ringo retrieved a hewing axe at his belt. With one hand he grasped the handle, and with the other he patted the axe head like it was a hound being held at bay. The ork did not raise any weapon, but instead stood firm and tall. His yellow eyes gleamed and an evil smiled curled on his lips.

"Wait a minute, wait a minute, wait a minute," Roban finally rose from the ground. His skin shone red in the light of their fire and the tangled golden streaks in his dark brown hair glowed like they were melting in a fiery crucible. However, his face and features were calm and relaxed. He stood with an easy gait, leaning to one side with his thumbs tucked under his belt. "Barzabag, is it? I'm Roban. Do you prefer Barz or Bag for short?"

"Neither!" shouted the ork. "I am Barzabag! Leader of *The Free...*"

"Right, right, I heard it the first time... listen Barz," said Roban, striding over to the ork nonchalantly and placing an arm around his shoulder. "I hate to be the bearer of bad news here buddy, but I feel like I'd be doing you a disservice if I didn't tell you this."

"Tell me what?" said Barzabag.

"You see that girl over there?" said Roban gesturing to Ella in her chair. Uniborn gripped his pointing sword more tightly and Ringo rubbed the handle of his axe.

"Oh yeah, she's pretty!" said the ork. "She's my type. A really pretty elf that will fall in love with Barzabag."

"Well Barz, I'm going to tell you a little secret," said Roban. "She's not... actually an elf at all. She's just a regular woman."

"What?" said Barzabag. "But she's so... pretty!"

"Ha!" laughed Roban to the amazement of Barzabag, Frobo and all the others that were listening. "Her?" Roban gestured to Ella with a look of indescribable incredulity. "Barz, you must be joking. I mean look at her... she's about as beautiful as a baby troll!"

Ella's jaw dropped from shock. In all likelihood, such a thing had never before been suggested about her, and she endured it the only way she could: by crossing her legs and sneering with the most sour face she could conjure.

"You will watch your tongue, horse thief," growled Uniborn.

"You lie," shouted Barzabag, paying Uniborn no mind. "She is an elf, and she is pretty! She is a pretty elf!"

Roban simply shook his head, "Barz, Barz... I feel sorry for you mate, and I'm trying to help you. That... over there," he said pointing to Ella. "That *thing*..." he shuddered, "is no elf. She's not the girl for you. You need someone way prettier than her, and trust me, a girl like that won't be hard to find. They're practically a dime a dozen!"

Ella scoffed and leaned back in her seat, looking away in anger.

"This is your last warning, horse thief!" said Uniborn.

"But Barzy-boy," Roban continued, ignoring Uniborn. "If her looks don't scare you off, I can only give you this one last warning. She is completely and totally *crazy*, which wouldn't be that bad, but she also never shuts up!"

"Really?" asked Barzabag, with the first hint of doubt forming in his voice.

"Oh brother, let me tell you," said Roban. "Just imagine you come home after a long hard night of mole hunting and cursing at the light of the stars. Just as you plop up your feet and you're sitting down to drink a nice glass of rat blood, *she* comes in and starts yapping at you about your honey-do list."

"My honey-do list?" asked Barzabag, confused.

"Oh yeah," said Roban. "You don't know about those? Cause if you're thinking about finding someone to fall in love with you, especially a regular girl like her who's not that attractive, you'd better believe she's gonna have a honey-do list. Honey do the dishes... honey clean the blood off your teeth... honey you've got another tumor to cut off."

"It sounds like torture!" shouted Barzabag.

"Oh, just you wait Barzo... you think you've had it tough?" said Roban. "Think your life's been hard? Well just imagine living with *her* every day for the rest of your life!"

Although Frobo was almost certainly sure of what Roban was doing (saving poor Ella from being kidnapped by this hideous ork), not everyone in their party seemed to share his knowledge. Uniborn had finally heard enough insults at Ella's expense, and he turned his sword from Barzabag to Roban.

"You will take back what you have said about the Lady Ella," he demanded.

"No," said Roban, with a look at Uniborn that was trying to communicate without speaking. "No, I certainly will not. I am a man of the truth if nothing else. I'd never spell a falsehood, especially not to a good ork like Barzabag."

"Lower your sword Uniborn," said Grandalf, sensing the urgency of the situation, and comprehending Roban's intention.

"I will do no such thing," said Uniborn, pointing the sword at Roban's throat. "The Lady Ella is a noble woman," Uniborn began. Frobo noticed that Barzabag perked up his ears. "She is fairer than elf maidens, and more beautiful than lilies. Lovelier is she than a battle steed!"

"What?" growled Barzabag. "I knew it. I knew she was a pretty elf!"

"Hah," said Roban. "'Lovelier than a battle steed,' is she? That's not really saying that much Uni. But if *you* think she's pretty mate, then go right ahead and take her..."

"I will take her!" said Barzabag. "For I know your tricks!

This man said she is prettier than even elfs."

Ella shuddered and whimpered, holding tight to her legs that she had just tucked up onto her new chair, causing it to rock back so violently Frobo feared the thing might tip over.

"You will die before you touch her," said Uniborn, redirecting the point of his sword to Barzabag.

The same devilish laugh bellowed from Barzabag as before. "You think I am alone! You think one sword will stop me? I am Barzabag, watcher of the films, and leader of *The Free Orks!*" A chorus of horns reverberated from the hills and a thousand torches were lit in unison. They were completely surrounded, outmanned, and out-armed by Barzabag and his army of Free Orks.

"We will let you live," said Barzabag, "for as I said before we come in peace! But this elf maiden I will take for myself, and she will fall in love with me, just like the elf in the films fell in love with the disgusting dwarf!"

"I will die before you touch her!" shouted Uniborn.

"Don't be a fool Uniborn!" said Grandalf.

"And one more thing," continued Barzabag, "You have many horses, far too many for you. We will take them too... as a wedding gift."

"I will die before you touch them!" shouted Roban, suddenly seeming far less noble and heroic to Frobo.

"Well, isn't that noble of you?" said Ella, rolling her eyes. "Alright, boys let's get this over with," she said, rising suddenly from her chair as if she cared not what was about to befall her. Placing her finger and thumb in her mouth, she whistled and a horse quickly met her call. Without help, she mounted the steed as gracefully as a swan alights upon a tranquil lake. Frobo was shocked. Never in all his years had he imagined any woman, especially a Lady of nobility, could act this way. Not one minute earlier, she had looked as if she was about to break into a thousand pieces, and now, she was mounting a horse alone to ride away with the orks. And she was doing it *willingly!* It was incomprehensible.

"My lady," Barzabag said, "I look forward to the coming days, when I shall woo you to my side and you shall become my bride!"

"No," shouted Uniborn. "By the blood of my honor!" But as he charged Barzabag he was tackled by three orks and pinned to the ground. Barzabag mounted a different horse, who seemed to little like its new rider. But seeing the ork on one of his horses made Roban react in the same manner Barzabag had. He flung himself at Barzabag in a flash. Frobo thought he might succeed in pulling the ork off the horse, but Barzabag kicked down from atop it, his foot landing squarely on Roban's chest. The man fell back and was immediately restrained by teams of orks. Frobo and the rest of them looked on in horror. They could do nothing against the countless orks that surrounded them, watching with gleaming eyes as their companions mounted horse after horse until none were left.

"Farewell, my companions!" said Ella from atop her horse. "Do not mourn for me long, and do not look for me in the morning. Ringo, Wondell, I'm sorry I will miss your songs. Frobo, I looked forward to hearing yours also. Happy and Martin, your songs were delightful. Sham, I'm sorry I missed dinner. Grandalf..."

"Enough chatter!" interrupted Barzabag, grabbing the reins of Ella's horse. "We ride!"

"Don't interrupt me!" said Ella, slapping the hand of Barzabag's that had grabbed her reins.

He drew it back quickly. "Err, sorry my lady. Please forgive me. In time you will grow to love me."

"I do not forgive you!" she shouted. "Don't ever touch my horse's reins again and don't *ever* interrupt me again, do you understand?"

"Ahem, yes marm!" said the ork. Frobo couldn't believe his

ears. Was that fear he heard in Barzabag's quaking voice?

"Yes *marm*?" shouted Ella. "Don't ever call me that! Do I look like your mother? Do you really think I'm going to fall in love with someone who thinks I look like their mother?"

"No, of course not!" said Barzabag. "That was very foolish of me, my lady, very foolish!"

"Yes, it was," said Ella, now raising her voice. "It was very foolish of you, indeed."

A few of the orks shook their heads, looking on at the scene with a hopeless sense of dread.

"My Lady," said Barzabag, trying to recover himself, "you were speaking earlier, and I interrupted. Please continue."

"I can't continue now, I've lost my train of thought!" said Ella. "Let's go! Move out!"

"But, my Lady..." said Barzabag, "It is I that am the leader of..."

"I said move out!" shouted Ella.

Barzabag bowed his head, his pride having taken another blow, and gave the consenting order for his army to depart.

"Poor monster," said Roban. "I tried to warn him."

As Ella rode away with the orks on Roban's horses, the members of the company found themselves alone. Ella had been kidnapped. Ringo fell to his knees and began to sob. Uniborn cried out in rage, ripping his cloak. "I've lost her!" he cried out, falling to his knees. "I've lost her!"

"No one to blame but yourself," muttered Roban. "I almost had that dumb ork convinced to leave her with us."

"You almost did no such thing!" said Uniborn.

"Enough!" said Grandalf. "We cannot pursue the orks now, with them on horses and us on foot. We lack weapons and provisions, and they have an army. We must continue to Slumbervell as originally planned. There we will receive counsel and help, for there are more matters in Middlearth that demand our attention than these orks and the Lady Ella. I fear that our encounter tonight is only a sign of other things to come. Let us go now."

"We must go with speed and haste if we are to save the Lady Ella," said Uniborn.

"And the horses," added Roban.

"Save your words for the gallows, thief!" said Uniborn. "Perhaps you will meet your justice when Slumbervell we reach."

At last, when all parties had made their snide remarks and Sham had packed up their dinner, they began to run. Frobo kept pounding his short legs one in front of the other as fast as he could carry them. They ran by the light of the moon and the light of Grandalf's staff through brambles and creeks, into the heart of the dark forest. If it was minutes or hours or days, Frobo did not know. Although of course, it couldn't have been days, since their entire journey was in the darkness of the same night.

When they finally stopped, they stood in front of a large iron barred gate that blocked their road. Frobo wanted to collapse, and all but Wondell seemed to be on the brink of utter exhaustion from the run. It was still dark, but the moonlight shown through wrought iron letters in an arch over the top of the gate. Grandalf read the sign aloud, still standing up straight, but through heavy breathing, "*SLUMBERVELL, Literally the Last Place in Middlearth to Watch the Films.*"

"Those blasted films have caused more damage than I could ever have imagined," said Uniborn, keeling over and gasping for breath. "If this was the last place to view them, then I am glad we are here. Its inhabitants must have some strange power to be able to resist them for so long."

"Do not forget the merits of those films on account of what that beast said," said Ringo. His hands rested on his knees, as he tried to breath along with the rest of them. But still, he refused to let the films be defamed in front of him without speaking up in their defense. "Do not speak ill of them."

"Oh yes, of course you like them," said Wondell. "Look what they did for you. You're one of the most famous people in Middlearth because of them. But just look at the state of things now and think about what they inspired!"

"Enough," said Grandalf. "We are here now, and we are all on the same side. It is time we all started *acting* like it. Now Wondell, tell me... How do we get in here?"

"Someone just needs to yawn into the gate key to unlock it," said Wondell. "I would but I'm not... *yaawwwahh*... tired." Instantly they heard the sound of a *clink* as the lock of the gate turned, and the doors magically opened before them. Wondell yawned once more and said, "Welcome to Slumbervell." He then walked through the open gate as the others followed. The strange gate closed behind them, just as soon as they were each through it. As they walked along the dark road, Frobo saw that the gate was not the only magical part of Slumbervell. A mystical glowing light emanated all through the grounds on either side of the road. There were moderate sized trees, strange trees the likes of which Frobo had never seen before everywhere he looked. Each one had a kind of bowl shaped ring just above its roots that formed a circle. Inside the rim of the circle some benevolent being had conveniently placed pillows, mattresses, and blankets. It was one of the most bizarre sights Frobo had ever beheld.

As he considered the queer nature of it all, he was overcome by his severe exhaustion from their miles and miles of running. Just to his left, he saw that Roban was already curling up under the blankets inside one of the bowls. Grandalf did the same just beyond him. They were all, each one of them falling asleep. Frobo could resist the temptation no longer. The urge to sleep was now so strong. Without further fight, he collapsed into one of the bowls, still fully dressed, unable to resist the desire for sleep any longer.

CHAPTER 11

THE COUNSELF OF SLUMBERVELL

FROBO WAS AWAKENED THE FOLLOWING MORNING BY THE sound of a familiar humming snore, buzzing and thrumming from a tree not far away from his own. He did not know which of his companions it was that snored, but he did not care, for he had rested well during the night. Still, he felt that if he wanted to, he could've gone back to sleep and rested for hours more, even though he could see that the sun was already high above the tops of the tall green trees. There was something strange about this place indeed. Just thinking about the wasting day made him want to rise from the bowl of his tree and run as he had so the night before, but it also felt like the bowl was holding him down. He regretted sleeping in as long as he had but from where he lay, getting up seemed like a daunting task that would be accomplished none too easily.

But he was out of his wits if he thought he was going to snooze all day. He was a *Daggins*. He had to prove that to himself no matter what, and he wasn't going to do that lying down. Therefore, he steeled himself and arose from the bowl.

"There now," he thought, *"that wasn't so bad. What were you so tired for anyways? That little run wasn't all that bad and..."*

Suddenly the events of the night before came whirling back to his mind. The orks had *taken* Ella. He shuddered to think of what had befallen her. Frobo couldn't imagine that Barzabag would try to win Ella's affections for long, as the ork had insisted the night before. Eventually, the ork's patience would wane and he would take what he desired by force. That was one thought Frobo could not bear to imagine. They had to save the Lady before that happened. And perhaps they would get the tools they needed to do that here, wherever this place was. He yawned. Had he ever felt so groggy?

Frobo stumbled past the bowls of Sham, Happy, Martin and Ringo, who were all still fast asleep in their trees. He walked randomly in a general direction that he thought was opposite the gate they'd entered last night, though he could not see the gate in any direction.

Everywhere he looked, there were simply more and more of the strange trees with the sleeping bowls at their base. Someone had smartly planted them in organized neat rows, so that each one was about five feet apart in all directions. It was the strangest thing he'd ever seen. Not even the neatest most fastidious garden in all of the Chire would've been planted with such uniformity. Privately, he thought the planting rows were ridiculous, but he would never say that aloud to the owner of this strange land, Slumbervell, or whatever it was called. And when had the trees been planted? As tall as they were, it had to have been hundreds of years ago, but there were enough of them in this forest to sleep an entire army.

As he continued to wander aimlessly through the uniform rows of trees, he thought he heard the sound of voices, and following them, he came upon the courtyard of a large white house. He could not tell whether the grand pillars of the place were hewn of stone or cut from the same wood of the many trees around him, but the house was a sight to behold. He was facing a courtyard that lay between the two tall wings of the place, each one a perfect mirror image of the other. They rose out of the ground like the walls of the white tower of Grondor, a place Frobo had only seen in the films. Of course, they were much shorter than the tall white walls of that city, but Frobo knew that not. He could only see the beautiful white stone walls into which many windows had been carved so that the inhabitants of that great house could gaze out into the surrounding trees or into the garden courtyard. At the back of the courtyard between the wings of the house, large white columns rose from the ground supporting the roof. This was where the voices had been coming from.

Frobo looked across a bubbling spring of clear water that rose into a broad pond in the very center of the courtyard. It was flanked by exotic trees and (where Frobo stood) a cluster of lilacs and lilies. Peering through them, he could just see at the base of one of the large columns three people speaking to each other. He crept closer, trying to remain hidden behind the plants and making his way around the fascinating spring of crystal clear water. As he drew close, he saw that one of the speakers was Wondell. Next to him were two more elfs, a male and a female. Frobo's abilities of perception enlightened him that they were older than Wondell, though *how* he knew this was a mystery even to him.

"I just don't understand Wondell..." said the voice of the elder female elf, "I just don't understand why you're still single. I mean three hundred and seventy-six years is a long time to wait for a daughter in law!"

"What is his hurry?" responded the male elf. The two elder elfs seemed very strange to Frobo, far different from Wondell or from his imagination of what an elf should be. Though he couldn't exactly tell what it was about them that made him know they were old, he perceived that they were, from some deep innate instinct within him.

The female elf stood tall and thin. Her skin glowed like a

cream colored pearl without any wrinkle or flaw. Locks of hair hung upon her shoulders the color of pure white snow.

The male elf was also incredibly youthful for how old Frobo perceived that he was. His thick midsection bulged between the open flaps of his cloak. Seemingly, this elf had eaten far too much way bread throughout the course of his lifetime, and this quite shocked Frobo, having never seen nor imagined an over-weight elf before. His rosy red cheeks curled around the edges of his smiling lips when he spoke like bright apples hanging from a tree. Like his female companion he had white hair, but his was braided in the back and covered every part of his head except the very top. That part of the elf's head peaked up above his hair like a round bald egg. Despite all this, Frobo had no idea how he had perceived that the two elfs were very, very old, since it was impossible to tell an elf's age from looking at them.

The male elf with the rosy cheeks continued, "He doesn't want to get hitched up with the first elf girl he finds does he, and then be tied down for all eternity?"

"Oh, and is that what you are? Tied down for all eternity? With me!"

"Tied down?" said the elder male. He drew back and dropped his jaw, manufacturing the appearance of being appalled by what she had just said. "Of course not, sweetheart, how could I be 'tied down' with someone as beautiful and sweet and well-mannered as you?"

"Don't play those games with me, Yawndell!" snapped the older female elf. She rolled her eyes and stepped back. As he stretched out an arm to console her, she slapped it away. "You probably wish you were still swinging in solitude, just like your son here! You should have seen him the other night, Wondell. He was talking about the time he met the Lady Galadriyell again and how he thought he had a chance with her."

"What's the big deal?" Yawndell asked, shooting both of his hands out in interrogation. "I told you when the Lady

Galadriyell and I met, I saw a twinkle in her eye. If you'd seen a twinkle in the eye of Glorfindale, I wouldn't pester you about it!"

"Please, enough!" shouted Wondell. He then rubbed his forehead and closed his eyes.

The older female elf's countenance softened as she drew near to comfort her son. "Now, now, Wondell, now, now. I know life is hard for you. You're single, alone, totally solitary... with practically no prospects, and therefore no means of giving us grandelfs anytime soon."

"Oh, give it a rest Gloria, you're smothering him!" said Yawndell.

Without thinking, a stifled snorting chuckle burst out of Frobo as he stood at the far end of the courtyard. Yawndell heard him, and turning away from his son, the old elf spied Frobo watching them.

"Oy vey!" shouted Yawndell. "Come, my small guest, come! Shame on you, Wondell... you should've led your companion straight to the Hall of Feasts for breakfast!"

"But he was still a..." Wondell yawned, "sleep when I brought the others."

"Nonsense, nonsense!" said Yawndell. "No guest of mine should wander the grounds with an empty stomach. Pardon my son. I am your gracious host Yawndell... *aaahhyaww*, and welcome to Slumbervell, literally the last place in Middlearth to watch the films."

Frobo couldn't help but yawn himself before responding, "Thank you *yahhhww... aahhawwnnnn*dell. Sorry about that, I am still dreadfully groggy after last night."

"Oh, not to worry my lad, not to worry!" winked Yawndell, beaming down at Frobo with glowing blue eyes from above those bright red cheeks that were redder than any tomato Sham had ever grown in Frobo's garden. "That happens here all the time. You'll get used to it."

"Ahem," the Lady Gloria cleared her throat.

"Oh yes, of course, I nearly forgot, allow me to introduce you to the Lady of Slumbervell, *Literally the Last Place in Middlearth to Watch the Films*, my beautiful bride, Gloria." Yawndell bowed as a performer would after a play.

Frobo bowed respectfully after the customs of the Chire, as did the Lady Gloria, after the customs of Slumbervell.

"And who is it that we have the pleasure of speaking with?" asked Wondell.

"Oh right, sorry for not introducing myself sooner!" said Frobo. "My name is Frobo Daggins..."

He was cut off by the bellowing, bubbling laughter of Yawndell, "A good one my short little lad, a good one indeed! But the joke would've been better had you called yourself a *Mister Underthehill*, if you catch my meaning. See, my joke has more nuance than yours, because you know what *Underthehill* is don't you?"

Yawndell winked at Frobo and raised his eyebrows but continued before Frobo could respond. "Oh, come on, you know, it's what *he* referred himself as... you know, the most famous hobbick who ever lived? See the nuance? Ahh? Now tell me your real name chap, come now."

Frobo of course, had understood Yawndell's little joke. "Mister Underthehill, yes sir, yes, that is very nuanced. But my name actually is Frobo Daggins, and I am... at least rumored to be... the direct descendant of the most famous hobbick who ever lived. Although, I suppose I could never be sure unless I spoke with him directly, which is impossible, seeing as he is drownded."

Yawndell stood before him, looking Frobo up and down as if attempting to assess what he might be able to sell him for. "Is he telling the truth, Wondell?" he asked.

"I dare say he is," said Wondell. "I was just as surprised when Grandalf told me."

"*Ahhyahwnn*... Remarkable. Especially when you consider... Well, it's simply remarkable..." said Yawndell. "A pleasure to meet you, Frobo Daggins. Now, please join myself, my *ravishing* bride, and my celibate son for breakfast."

"I'm not celibate!" said Wondell. "I just haven't found the right elf yet because of those accursed films."

"What do you think of that, sweetheart?" asked Yawndell, ignoring his son. "I just said you were *ravishing*..."

Wondell groaned in the background.

"Trying to make up for the Galadriyell comment last night, I see..." observed Gloria. "Well, it won't work. I know who the *twinkle* in your eye is for." With that, she stormed away into the house.

"Gloria, please!" said Yawndell, following her. "Glo... *yahh-wwahhh*... oria please! You do have the twinkle of my eye! You do!"

Wondell yawned and Frobo stood awkwardly. "Shall we go to breakfast now?" said Wondell.

"Yes, certainly!" said Frobo, eager to fill his growling stomach and escape the awkward silence left in the wake of Wondell's arguing parents.

As they walked to the hall, Frobo had one question for Wondell. "Why is it Wondell, that Slumbervell was the last place in Middlearth to watch the films?"

"Hah! Isn't it obvious?" asked Wondell.

"Well, no..." said Frobo. "Is it because they dislike them?"

"Oh no, it's not that!" laughed Wondell. "Although, it's true that we care little for the films. No, the real reason is far more simple. It's that they're so *long!* Do you really see yourself being able to sit through something *that* long without falling asleep first, especially here? I guess my father's slogan should be, 'the last place in Middlearth to *finish* watching the films,' but you get the point. It took us years to finish them. I'm still not sure my parents have seen any of them all the way from start to finish."

"Yes... of course, *ahhhhawwwn*... that makes sense," said Frobo. "I've been tired ever since I got here. And I slept like a log last night!"

"Ahh yes, that is the ma*ahhhaa*gic of this place. Some elfs can manipulate earth and water, trees and stones, creating incomprehensible beauty and perfection. My father has a little of that same magic, except with sleep," said Wondell.

"Hence, the name Slumbervell," said Frobo as comprehension dawned on him.

"Yes," said Wondell. "The last place in Middlearth to watch the films, literally..."

Frobo followed the tall slender elf out of the courtyard and around the eastern wing of the magnificent house. They walked along a pathway of flat white stones that was flanked by bushes of various species, eventually leading to an opening in the house. Instead of doors at this entrance, leafy vines hung down and covered the entrance from above.

Frobo squinted to be sure his eyes did not deceive him but there was no mistaking it. The vines were in fact poison ivy.

"Mellon," said Wondell strangely, then reached out his hand to pull back the vines.

"Wait," said Frobo. "Do you know what kind of plants those are?"

"Oh yes," the elf smiled wryly. "That is why I said 'Mellon.' If I had not, I would have reached out and been stung with a horrible itching rash."

"Fascinating," said Frobo, as they brushed away the enchanted ivy and ducked beneath the entrance. Once inside, Frobo found the place was truly marvelous. The ceilings were higher than any others he had ever seen before. Every column, every pillar, and every wall were adorned with stones and inlaid with precious metals of the highest value. There was a window frame wrought out of gold, a column studded with emeralds and rubies. The effect was breathtaking, and Frobo was apparently only in the foyer. Above him, a brilliant light shone down from the ceiling, which Frobo then realized was made entirely of glass. The light was the sun itself, but because of some magical tint, the light had a bluish-green hue to it.

Frobo thought he could hear voices beyond at the far end of the foyer. There was another opening in a smooth white marble stone frame. Frobo ran through the door to find the so-called Hall of Feasts. There he discovered the rest of his friends already breakfasting away, looking well rested and refreshed. This room was far less ornate but was also far homier. High ceilings were supported by chestnut wood trusses that rose to the full height of the deck. Every piece of wood and trim in the large room flowed together from the top of that ceiling so that Frobo could not tell where the joints had been crafted by the builders. In fact, they came together so perfectly, that Frobo wondered if they had been crafted at all. Maybe the house had somehow been magically grown from the ground instead of built. Of course, he'd seen the depictions of the elfen homes in the films, but in real life, the actual structure stole his very breath. The room was the most simple and also the most beautiful one he had ever seen.

"Mister Frobo!" shouted Sham, flinging himself up from a plate of biscuits. "Mister Frobo, you're safe! You're here! I was worried sick about you when I woke up and you weren't there! Are you alright, Mister Frobo?"

"Yes Sham, I'm quite alright," sighed Frobo. "I was just up and about for a walk, and I found Wondell here. Nothing to panic or worry about. It's not like I have the... well, the *you know what* or anything like that."

Frobo stole a glance at Happy and couldn't help but feel a twinge of jealousy. If only he had that blasted ring. Then maybe, he could prove himself as something more than a Sackville-

Daggins once and for all. If he had that, he wouldn't even need to be the heir of the most famous hobbick who'd ever lived. He sighed and yawned all at once and a yawn from Sham followed.

At that moment, Frobo realized there was one member of their company missing. "Where's Uniborn?" asked Frobo.

But he did not have to wonder long where the tall man was, as tall double doors at the head of the hall were thrown open at once and Uniborn burst through them.

"Speak of the devil," said Roban.

"To arms!" Uniborn cried, leaping through the like he was sieging the walls of the Deep Helms. "To arms! To arms, each and every one of you. You have had your rest and you have had your food and now we can take provisions and weapons. Let us go and let us win back the hand of the Lady Ellamir. Who is with me? All who are not shall be held as cowards!"

"Do not be so, *yaaaaawwwghhh*, rash Uniborn," said Grandalf. "There is one thing which we have not yet received, which was one of our main purposes for coming here, and that is counsel. And I personally, *aaaayeaaggghh*, will not be leaving this place until I've had it."

"Did you hear that, Happy? That old buzzard won't be leaving until he's '*aaaayeaaggghh* had it,'" said Martin in a mock yawn.

A real yawn followed from Happy, and all the rest of them in turn. "I don't know about you all, but all this yawning is making me sleepy," said Happy. "I think I could use a nap after breakfast."

"Do you care nothing for the tribulations of the Lady Ellamir?" shouted Uniborn. "My *yeaawwwwhhaaahhh* Lady, the finest lady perhaps in all of Middlearth is kidnapped by orks and all you can do is sit here and *aaaayeaaggghhnn*, yawn!"

"For the record Uni, you did just yawn twice yourself," said Roban. "And also, for the record, you're not the only one whose got something special that was kidnapped by orks."

"Am I really to believe that you care for the Lady Ella also? Ha!" laughed Uniborn. "How pathetic. A wild ranger horse thief with affections for the fairest lady in Middlearth?"

"No, I was actually talking about my horses," said Roban. "I had a thousand of them, remember? Only difference is, those were actually mine, and you only wish you had the Lady Ella."

Uniborn's face coiled with rage like a viper about to strike. He marched into the Hall of Feasts like he was on a mission for the king himself. "You are a man of no nobility! And you are a *coward*. I will not abide the presence of such men!"

"Careful," said Roban. He rose from his seat at the table, matching Uniborn's intensity, but his face was expressionless and nonchalant, as Frobo had noticed it always was when a joke or quip was coming.

"*No nobility* is almost a double negative, which could make it seem like you were saying something positive about me. But see, I think Grandalf has a good point. We should wait here, even you should Uni, as much as I hate to abide your presence. Wait for counsel before you do something foolish."

Frobo thought he observed a slight crack in Roban's voice when he uttered this last sentence. The man's words were usually so clear and strong. Perhaps he wasn't simply a humorous self-serving thief, and there was more to him than he let on.

"There will be no more laughter at my expense, horse thief," cried Uniborn. His red face betrayed his humiliation and fury as he stormed towards the double doors. "I will not wait for cowards. I shall save the Lady Ellamir alone and win her affections once and for all!"

"You will prove yourself a fool if you go," shouted Grandalf. He rose from the table in turn like a snowy grey mountain rising from the depths of the earth. "You would try to take all the glory you can handle and when we arrived, there would be two prisoners to save from the clutches of the orks."

Uniborn was arrested by these words, and somehow despite his fury, he saw the truth of them. Even he, one of the most famous knights that Grondor had ever seen, could not rescue the Lady Ella from the orks alone. His outstretched sword fell from his hand and clanged against the stone floor of the hall. The man then fell to his knees and hung his head, letting his long sable locks fall before his face.

"There is no hope," he said, as pale despair colored his face with the pallor of death. "By the time we reach her, she will be lost."

Roban strode up to him and offered Uniborn his arm. "Hope," Roban said. "For I see the same despair in you that would take the heart of me! But still, I tell you to hope as I do. For my heart tells me yet that my horses can be saved!"

Uniborn slapped Roban's arm away and bristled in anger. "Enough about your horses," he said, picking up his sword and rising to his feet on his own. Clearly Uniborn didn't feel that Roban and himself were in similar plights. "I will wait until this company is ready to set out. And horse thief, when we arrive, I hope your *property* has been turned into lunch meat."

Without another word, and with a renewed look of fury on his face, Uniborn stormed out of the hall, leaving them to finish their breakfast. Frobo couldn't help but feel guilty as he watched the black cloak of Uniborn furling behind his stomping boots. He wanted to save the Lady too, but for different reasons than Uniborn. He would wait though, *yeaaaawwwwahhhhnn...* yes, he would wait until they'd had their counsel.

"What's he all on about again?" asked Sham, as Uniborn stormed out of the Hall of Feasts, slamming the two large doors behind him.

"Weren't you listening?" said Frobo.

"Oh no, I wasn't honestly. I rarely do," said Sham. "I was more focused on the biscuits I left at the table and couldn't stop thinking about them getting cold for that entire conversation. I dare say, I didn't hear a word of it." At this, Sham returned to his precious biscuits.

Wondell stared incredulously. "You hobbicks are something else entirely when it comes to food," he said.

"It's true, we certainly are," said Frobo, who felt famished himself after the run to Slumbervell the night before. "But Sham is different. I once saw him put five hobbicks to shame in an eating contest, with all of their plates counting together. Granted, he couldn't stand for days after it was over, but nonetheless."

"Quite remarkable," said Wondell.

Frobo and Wondell joined Sham and the others at the table of the hearty breakfast. They all ate their fill, Sham included, through many yawns. After the outburst of Uniborn, it seemed that a grim mood had fallen on the companions. Grandalf muttered and bumbled to himself at the end of table like a thunderous storm growing in the distance. Ringo scarcely uttered a word, but kept taking deep breaths between belabored bites of food. Sham anxiously asked for a second, and then a third helping of the fare, worried he might receive the same response his mother used to give him when he asked for supplemental helpings. But he found no limit to Yawndell's table, and Sham was adequately fed even by the standards of hobbicks. Roban joked and jested with the hobbicks, laughing and making light of their situation, although Frobo wondered if it was a cover for his true feelings. He kept babbling on about how he didn't know what he'd do if they couldn't recover his horses, which hardly seemed appropriate considering the more pressing issue of the Lady Ella.

After an hour or more, a large gong chimed from where a short elf had struck it behind them. The sound was followed by the appearance of the Lord and Lady of the house.

Yawndell then addressed them all, "Welcome friends, guests

of Slumbervell, literally the last place in Middlearth to watch the films, not because we don't like them, just because we have trouble... *aaaahyeaaawwnn*... staying awake here. Although it's true that we don't take much pleasure in the films. If I had to choose, I'd take the first three over the last three any day of the week. Come to think of it, I actually really enjoyed the first three when they first came out. But on a more intense study and a second glance, you really start to get a sense for all of the errors in them. The last three though were a plain and simple abomination!"

"Father, enough!" shouted Wondell in protest of his father's tangent. "Could you get to the point already?"

"Oh yes, right you are my son," laughed Yawndell. "Gloria constantly reminds me of my terrible habit of getting distracted, don't you dear?"

Gloria exhaled a slow anxious breath as she tried to retain her composure but she did not respond to Yawndell.

"It's a good thing I've got so many people to help keep me on task," Yawndell continued. "Sometimes Gloria tells me I babble for hours. Now, where was I? Oh yes, welcome. And that brings me to the reason you are here which is obviously more than just a weekend visit from a son to see his parents. Although, it wouldn't be bad of you to do that every once in a while, Wondell. Your mother and I miss you very much. Although of course, she'd like it if maybe next time you brought a nice elf girl home with you... but there I go again, going off on another rabbit trail! Now, your good leader Grandalf tells me that you are here for counsel. And that is good. For I am not only the Lord of Slumbervell, but I am also a *Counselfor*."

Martin spit out the biscuit he was chewing, "A what?"

"A *Counselfor*," said Wondell, sighing and shaking his head. "My father coined the term years ago. It's a combination of the words; counselor, and elf. Elfs are usually very reluctant to give counsel, but my father is different. He is perhaps the only elf in

Middlearth eager to give it. I've never known if that means he is very wise or very foolish."

"And I've never cared!" laughed Yawndell.

"Whether he is wise or foolish is no concern of ours now," said Grandalf. "Either he is a wise fool, or a foolish sage. Regardless, he will give us counsel, provisions, and weapons, the three things we desperately need. Yawndell, let us begin this council. The morning sun grows high!"

"Let us begin the *Counself*," Yawndell corrected. "Come with me, my guests." He led them out of the breakfast hall back into the courtyard in which Frobo had first come upon Wondell, Yawndell, and Gloria earlier that morning. However, Frobo was amazed to find that now, in addition to the well-manicured garden and the clear bubbling spring of the pond, eleven trees of the same kind in which they'd slept the night before had sprang up in the courtyard. They formed a perfect circle with the bowl or bed of each facing the circle's center. Frobo could have sworn that the trees had not been there previously. He would have remembered if there were any trees in the garden. This time, the pillows of the bowl were propped up so that one could sit in the bowls instead of just lying in them.

"How did these get here?" Frobo asked Wondell. "Isn't this the same courtyard I met you in only an hour ago? But now there's a circle of those sleeping trees in it."

"It is one and the same," said Wondell. "But that is the magic of this place, the reason it was literally the last place in Middlearth to watch the films. There is nowhere in Slumbervell where one cannot rest."

"Truly... *yeeaaawww*mazing," said Frobo.

"Take your seats at the *Counself of Slumbervell*," said Yawndell. "Gloria, you know I hate to be indelicate but... *scram*."

Gloria rolled her eyes and glided from the courtyard with the bearing of a swan. Each of the remaining members of the company took their seat in the sleeping trees in turn: Grandalf,

Roban, Ringo, Wondell, Happy, Martin, Frobo, and Uniborn. Sham was left standing last of all with Yawndell.

"Sit my young hobbick, sit! Relax! Recline!" Yawndell insisted.

Finally, Sham relented and sat, leaning back in his tree. "Pardon me, Mister Yawndell sir," Sham said. "But there are only nine of us by my count, then there's you and that makes ten. Who is the last tree meant for?"

"Your count is accurate, but that is not for you to know. Not yet," said Yawndell. "But all shall soon be revealed to you!" Yawndell was like an eager storyteller, immensely excited that his audience had never heard the conclusion of the tale he was spinning. Frobo and his companions were simply unwitting listeners, unable to know who the final tree was meant for until the proper time.

"What is this, Yawndell?" said Grandalf. "Why this concealment? Do not hide anything from me. Who is the final tree meant for?"

"In good time, my old friend," chuckled Yawndell, as if he thoroughly enjoyed the knowledge he alone possessed over Grandalf. "In good time! Don't put the cart before the horse. Now, you are here, you are comfortable, let our *counself* begin!"

Grandalf then began to recount their entire journey to Yawndell, through many yawns and dozings-off by each of them in turn. Grandalf told the tale in full, everything from his own departure from Middlearth eleven-one years ago, to the filmmaker's request that the rings be given him, to the drowning of Frobo's grandfather, whose fate had come upon him in the same tragic fashion as his parents had. Grandalf's story of the meeting of the four hobbicks in Daggend was told, although the story became much more difficult to get through at this point, as *one of them* kept asking if he was in fact the same 'Sham' Grandalf was referring to in the story. Sometimes that hobbick did baffle Frobo.

With great disdain, Grandalf told of how Martin turned him into a wax statue, their temporary capture and escape from the clutches of Sauluman, and the discovery of the next apparent ring of power that was made by Sauluman in mockery of that *Insidious Ring* that had come into the possession of Happy, after it was found by his ancestor in the flotsham and jetsham of Isengrad eleventy-one years ago. It was the first time that Wondell, Ringo, and Roban had heard these details of the incredible story, and although Yawndell should have known the least about the tale, an onlooker at the Counsell might have thought him the listener least surprised.

Grandalf then recounted the events that occurred in Bree-town, the company meeting Wondell and the performance of Ringo and the Rugged Dwarfs, the chance meeting of Ella at the Prancing *Shetland* Pony, the rescue of Wondell and Ringo from the Breetown jail, and the escape from the jail rooftop without the help of the stuck-up credit seeking eagles. The story of the coincidental help from Roban the horse thief ("greatest horse thief in Middlearth" as he had begun to call himself) was also told by Grandalf, as well as the meeting with the Lady Ella for the second time and Uniborn the Knight, her esquire. Their quest, Grandalf said, until the events of the night before, had been to destroy the new ring of power and all of the other remaining rings of power to prevent Sauluman from regaining control of Middlearth, and to prevent the filmmaker from using their powers of creativity to produce more films, now that he had no more original stories to corrupt and ruin. Now, they had an ancillary mission. They could not leave the Lady Ellamir in the clutches of the orks with Barzabag their leader. Not to mention the fact that if the orks had seen the films, as Barzabag had, these kidnap-pings could become more and more frequent. Barzabag could lead a revolution of orks against the free peoples of Middlearth. It appeared that the hard fought for time of peace with the orks for the last eleventy-one years could be coming to an end.

"Which brings us here to you Yawndell, the Counselfor, as you have so dubbed yourself," said Grandalf. "For counsel is exactly what we need. The peoples of Middlearth are scattered, separated, divided, and most of all enraptured with these films and trademarks. Sauluman seemingly has control of the nine rings, and will gain control of the remaining rings, wherever they are, if we do not destroy the new ring of power. That is the only way to prevent the filmmaker from influencing the minds of the peoples of Middlearth with new films.

"But destroying these rings alone may not be enough, especially if the current films continue to act as a poisonous seed in the minds of the orks and the rest of the watchers. Look how they influenced the army of orks we just told you of. I fear that is only the beginning of the madness they will unleash upon Middlearth. We come to you, the Counself, for counsel, provisions and weapons for the fight ahead of us."

A long silence proceeded at the conclusion of Grandalf's story until at last, the Counselfor spoke.

"Before the Counselfor gives his counsel, he will hear from another. He will hear from one whom one might expect him to desire to hear from least of all..." Yawndell said with an air of mystery.

"Father, how many times do I have to tell you," Wondell began, "no one can understand you when you start referring to yourself in the third elf."

"Speak plainly, Yawndell," said Grandalf. "We don't have the entire fourth age to sit here and solve your riddles of spell-binding diction."

"I shall now introduce you to the final member of this Counself," said Yawndell. "For whom the last tree has been prepared. I present to you, once and for all, *him!*"

Frobo heard creaking hinges turn as the doors to the courtyard opened. Then into the green grass of the lawn strode someone that was instantly recognized by all: the infamous filmmaker himself. He was broad shouldered and heavy with long dark unkempt hair, a thin beard and a wardrobe that could only be described as a complete and utter anachronism. They all, including Grandalf, sat in their trees in utter silence and shock.

At last, Wondell cried, "It's the scoundrel himself! Seize him!"

However, not one member of the couself rose from their tree. For they were all of them restrained. As each of the members of the company attempted to leap upon the film-maker, branches of the magical sleeping trees closed around them, locking their bodies in the beds. Vines and branches entwined Frobo's arms and legs, holding him firmly in place in the bowl of the tree.

"Son of Ashelob, Yawndell!" shouted Grandalf. "What is the meaning of this?"

"He is a traitor!" shouted Uniborn through the constricting branches of his tree. "In league with the filmmaker himself!"

"Father, what are you doing? Let us go," said Wondell. He wrenched an arm out from beneath several shooting tendrils, but more instantly enveloped it, binding him to the spot.

"In good time, in good *aaarrryyeaaawwghhh* time!" said Yawndell.

"How can you *yeaaaaawwhhhhawwwn* at a time like this?" said Grandalf. "Our enemy has just appeared and is in our grasp!"

"He is not your enemy," corrected Yawndell. "But let me say no more, and let you listen to his tale before you continue your judgement. He has made his mistakes, as I am sure you know and will hear, but let this man speak his peace before another word is said."

The companions fell silent as the filmmaker stood before

them, hands folded behind his back and hanging his head. "Thank you, Yawndell," he began. "Hello again Grandalf, and greetings to the rest of you. It is with a heavy heart that I stand before you. Above all, I am overcome with feelings of regret for what I have done. You all know me as your enemy, the filmmaker, whose films have caused an almost irreversible domino effect in Middlearth that could result in a complete societal and monarchical collapse of the free world. But please, before you assume me no better than one of the orks of my films..."

"The filmmaker!" Sham suddenly exclaimed. "Mister Frobo, be careful. It's the filmmaker. It's him!" The hobbick then began to writhe in the bowl of his tree, thrashing about in a vain but useless attempt to escape its branches.

"Yes Sham," said Grandalf. "Welcome back to the world of the awake. The filmmaker has been standing in front of us for the last five minutes, and he was talking before you interrupted."

"But I was dreaming," said Sham, with the conviction of one who knows what he has to say is of the utmost importance. "I was dreaming that we were all sitting here, wrapped up in our little trees, drinking the biggest, most golden pints of beer you've ever seen before. Oh, how good that beer was. If you don't mind Mister Elf sir, you can bring mine out now, I shan't wait a moment longer for it. But then, I dreamt that the film-maker had come, and we all had to listen to him tell a long, drawn-out convoluted story of lies. So, I cried out as loud as I could, 'The filmmaker! Mister Frobo, be careful it's the film-maker. It's him!' I thought it best to warn Mister Frobo, since I am his gardener, and he seems to need the most caring for, if you understand me."

Grandalf could barely contain himself, but before he could speak, Martin said, "Sham, the filmmaker *is* here. He's standing right there."

The hobbick froze. "Right where, Mister Martin?" he said with a quaking voice and wide eyes.

"He's standing between you and me right now," snapped Grandalf.

"So, if I look over to Grandalf," Sham began as his eyes slowly turned across the lawn to Grandalf's tree, "Grondorian Gargoyles!" he exclaimed. "It's him. Slap me Mister Frobo, I'm still asleep."

"Yes, it is I," said the filmmaker, laughing at Sham. "And if you don't mind, I would like to continue telling you my side of the story."

"Yes of course sir," said Sham. "I'd never interrupt the films or their maker on purpose."

Finally, the filmmaker continued. "It was eleventy-one years ago. I was an aspiring young filmmaker, and I was fascinated by the handwritten account of the story of the most famous hobbick who ever lived. Of course, undertaking the making of films to tell that story was not a thought that I had dared to entertain.

"I was penniless, visionless, and not nearly creative enough on my own for such an undertaking. Of course, the entire story was written right there in front of me in undisputable absolute perfection, but I knew that I would have to make revisions and throw in my own flavor if I was to become a *really* famous film-maker. But I had no funding, no vision, and most of all no ambition to accomplish what the job required. So, I simply peddled my way through my own little miserable existence, thinking of the changes I would have made, had I been the writer of the story of the most famous hobbick who ever lived."

"I don't think anyone can blame you," said Sham. "For some of the *changes* you're referring to, that is, Mister Filmmaker sir. I think, in his infinite wisdom, the most famous, *yeeearrrgggh-hawwn*, hobbick of all time, may have been a bit caught up in his own social status. You can see through the dark undertone of his story that he was a bit of a classist, if you will. You can see that, quite clearly, in his depiction of his errr... his gardener."

Frobo could hardly believe his ears. Sham was slandering Frobo's grandfather for his treatment of his own ancestor to the filmmaker under the guise of an unbiased third party! He'd never heard something more ridiculous!

"Yes!" the filmmaker responded quickly. "I quite agree, my young hobbick. When you first started speaking, I confess, I thought you as witless as a bullfrog, but I was clearly mistaken. The depiction of the gardener of the most famous hobbick who ever lived was clearly one of the most important things for me to change."

"Personally, I always saw the gardener as a bit of an *unsung hero* of the story and the films," said Sham. "Who's to say he wasn't just as important as any of the Dagginses were?"

"Exactly," said the filmmaker. "I can tell you've really studied this issue. And what might your name be, my young hobbick?"

"He's only the grandson of the very gardener he's talking about," said Frobo. "So, he's obviously unbiased."

"Bless my stars," said the filmmaker, clasping his hands over his mouth. He looked at Sham as if he'd just met an elfen princess. "I had no idea. Sham Gramgee the Third. It's an honor to meet you sir!"

As if he had never received a compliment, Sham blushed and swelled with pride. To Frobo, it seemed that Sham's head was suddenly so large and red, that it might even explode. But Frobo was incensed. Since when was it an honor for anyone to meet Sham, when he himself, the heir to the most famous hobbick who ever lived, was also right there. He was about to introduce *himself* when the filmmaker continued.

"Of course, there were other problems with my desire to make my own film version of those events. Not only did I lack the money needed to finance such a project, but the story was obviously not my own. It did in fact belong to the most famous hobbick who ever lived.

"My dream, as small as it was, was simply that, with no way of being achieved. Someone else, someone with money, cunning, power and foresight would have to make these films. If I ever even attempted to make one, I knew I would've been sued blind for every penny I ever made by the hobbicks and the Daggins estate. Not to mention all the other peoples of Middlearth who'd want their piece of the pie when the films arrived, and they were mentioned."

"You say you lacked foresight," interrupted Grandalf, "but I see it in abundance."

"Unfortunately for all of us, I was *quite* lacking in it," the filmmaker continued. "But what I did have, even though I had no means to make the films I desired to, was a camera, film and a reel. I made several short films on my own in that time."

"You don't say," said Sham. "I had no idea there were other films. Were they any good, these films of yours?"

"Yes, quite good, if I do say so myself," said the filmmaker. "Yawndell here has seen them, and he can attest to their quality."

Yawndell gave an affirming nod as the filmmaker looked in his direction but shook his head in vigorous warning when the filmmaker turned away. In fact, he made such a ghastly face at them that Frobo thought Yawndell might even be sick. It was as if the elf was about to wretch at the very thought of those other films that had been made.

"So, there I was, living my life, wishing desperately for the ability to make the films of the story of the most famous hobbick who ever lived, but with absolutely no means of doing so. Until one day, when I had almost completely given up my ambition, I was approached by a man in dirty grey rags and a piece of paper in his hand. 'I have what you've been looking for, young filmmaker. In my hand, I have the filmmaking rights to the story of the greatest hobbick who ever lived, and I have the trademark rights to every character and being who appears in that story. And you, my young, inexperienced filmmaker, you will be the one to make my films. There is only one condition,' he told me. 'You must give me the complete final say on the story and you must give me complete power in every decision on which we disagree.' Considering I had no other means of making these films, and this unnamed man was going to finance the entire project, I readily accepted his offer.

"Only after I had done this, did I realize who he really was... Sauluman™. He'd purchased the filmmaking rights from the hobbick's own son, Froyo Daggins, a person I'd never known even existed, and whose true identity has since come into great debate. Whether or not he truly was a Daggins, we may never know. You may believe that Sauluman™'s life ended when it is shown to end in the films, when he fell from atop his tower in Isengrad onto the spike of one of his giant wheels. Of course, that detail only made it into the extended editions of the films, but that is irrelevant. If you have read the story of the most famous hobbick who ever lived, you know this is not the case. Sauluman™ returns to the Chire and ends up making quite the racket before he is defeated by the most famous hobbick who ever lived and his three companions. Then Sauluman™ is killed by his accomplice, Grema Snakelips. This was one of the changes that Sauluman™ insisted I make to the films from the original story.

"He wanted as few people as possible to remember the way he died, because he desperately didn't want anyone thinking he'd ever been back to the Chire. It was years later when I finally got the truth out of him. He'd been searching for the thing that had kept him alive even after death. A ring he had made, fashioned for himself after that *Insidious Ring*, and made in mockery of it, in case the one was not recovered, or it was destroyed. Then, he would be able to control the remaining rings of power with his own ring. But he lost it, and he believed that one of the three companions of the most famous hobbick who ever lived had recovered it."

"Pardon me for interrupting, Mister Filmmaker, but this is an incredible backstory," said Sham. "Did you ever think of making a film about all of this? Sort of a *Who's Who* documentary behind the making of the films? I can see something like that generating some serious interest amongst fans of the films."

"Oh yes, believe me, I have. But Sauluman™ would never allow it. His secrecy is one of his greatest weapons. If people knew that one of the greatest villains of the third age was still at large... but I digress. Search as Sauluman™ did, he never found the thing after he returned from the dead. But now he had a new plan for ruling the world, and that was through the films themselves. He did something to them, or I should say, he did something to the original film before we made all the copies. And that film, that original film, he keeps hidden safe in his tower at the headquarters of Middlearth Enterprises. Into that film he poured his power, his will, his malice, and his overwhelming desire to rule and dominate all Middlearth. It is a curse, a scourge, a plague. All who watch it fall under his spell and are under his control and influence. They will do his will without knowing it! I warn you to forget everything you know about them and rid your mind of them! For as long as you can remember them, you too can be influenced for his evil purposes, which I can assure you, are to make him the new ruler of Middlearth. I tell you all of this at my own great personal risk. For Sauluman™ told me that if I revealed any of what I knew of his plan, to be assured that my death and violent end would soon come. But after all the years have passed, and I have watched and sat idly by as nearly all Middlearth fell under his spell, I knew that I could keep silent no longer. I had no idea who I should tell, and so I went to the one place in Middlearth that had been influenced less by the films than any other. Slumbervell, *literally, the last place in Middlearth to watch the films*."

"Hah," shouted Yawndell. "I'm still not sure I've made it through all of them!"

"And a good thing too from the sounds of things," said Grandalf. "I had a feeling these films and trademarks were nothing but ork mischief! If we don't act soon, all of Middlearth will be lost. But now the question of all. There are far too many films to destroy to cleanse all of their influence from the world. How can we convince people to stop watching them and destroy their copies?"

"I've got an idea," said Martin. "What if we made our own film? Retelling the story with our own flair and countering the propaganda of *the* films. Just think, we'd be rich if our films were better than yours."

"In your attempt to distract people from the films, you would only draw more attention to them," said Grandalf. "Another film would simply lead people back to the originals. And if Sauluman got wind of our aims, he might find a way to corrupt our version too. If Sauluman could control Middlearth with these films as well as he is, whose to stop someone else from doing the same thing to ours?"

"The solution is more simple than you think, but it may also be impossible," said the filmmaker. "As I said before, Sauluman poured his power of persuasion into the original film, from which all other copies were made. In order to preserve his power from copy to copy, he had to magically link each of them so that his influencing propaganda would pervade them all. One could individually search all of Middlearth for every copy, but if the original is destroyed, the original that I myself made, my very own corrupting work of art, then the rest will perish along with it."

"Destroy the one film and destroy the power of Sauluman over Middlearth forever," said Grandalf.

"It's like the mission in the films themselves," Sham mused, grasping his chin like a sage. "Only instead of destroying that *Insidious Ring*, the film itself must be destroyed. How ironic."

"It's not like the mission in the films, it's like the mission in the *story* that the films portray!" corrected Grandalf. "And haven't you been listening? Rid your mind of the films or you will be under the control of the enemy."

Up until that point, the members of the company had been sitting back in their tree bowls, constrained by the branches, twigs, and limbs that held them in place. But Grandalf, inspired with fresh frustration at Sham's lack of understanding, spoke to his tree in a slow commanding voice, *"release your prisoner, old man bowl. Release me now or become a pole."*

As if he had turned a mechanical knot, the many branches of the tree pulled away from Grandalf in a flash. The wizard stood to his feet, towering over the other members of the company who now twisted in their arresting bowls, attempting to free themselves from the grip of the branches that held them. Yawndell looked disappointed that his spell had been so easily broken by the wizard. Sham spoke to his tree with the same words, but the branches of his tree did not recoil, move or even slightly stir.

Grandalf stood tall in the middle of the circle of trees like stone pillar. Towering over the filmmaker as much as the rest of them, he turned to the sturdy round unkempt individual whom they'd all seen as a villain only moments before.

"But I do have one more question for you, filmmaker. Why did you ask me for the elfen rings of power when we met on the ship? It appears the power over Middlearth is no longer in the rings at all, but in the films themselves."

"Hold on a moment," Sham said. Frobo shook his head. That

confounded Hobbick just didn't know when to shut up and stop trying to be the center of attention. His blue eyes sparkled with fervor and his mouth opened wide as each word gushed out of it. "I've just thought of something! Mister Grandalf here keeps saying the films can be corrupted by Sauluman... so we don't make a film, instead we hire someone to write a story. What if someone wrote a story about all of this? A story about what's happening right now, with us as the main characters. That's even more ironic than thinking about how similar our mission is to the films..."

"Are you finished?" said Grandalf.

"Can you imagine..." Sham mused, clearly not finished, "actually having to read this part of story? All of us, sitting in a Counself, listening to the filmmaker tell us about his wretched life." His eyes darted to each listener as he continued. Even he could read the blank stares and discern how dreadfully uninteresting this idea was. "Well, I suppose maybe the idea needs some work. I could always skip over this part; it might be rather boring to read after further consideration."

"I'd rather save my imagination for things of consequence," said Grandalf. "Now please continue, Filmmaker."

"Alas, I knew then what it was that I must do in betraying Sauluman and attempting to destroy the very films that I had made. They were the most incredible thing I had ever created, very precious to me. I attempted to obtain the rings of power from you because I thought I might be able to recreate the films if they were ever destroyed. The creative capability of the rings was the only chance I'd ever have to make something that was their equal on my own."

"You would have been a fool to do so," said Grandalf. "Haven't you seen for yourself how they can be corrupted and controlled by one with the power of Sauluman? Creating more films can only bring further ruin and destruction upon this Middlearth. You must not make more films."

The filmmaker hung his head. "That I now know," he said, before beginning to weep.

"Good," said Grandalf. At last, it is clear what we must do. We must destroy the rings of power and the one film in the tower of Middlearth Enterprises. If the rings are not destroyed, especially the one ruling ring that is possessed by you, Happy, then Sauluman's life will continue, and his ability to make and corrupt more films will endure with it. If the film is not destroyed, then his influence and power over Middlearth will continue to wreak havoc across it until he is the sole and solitary ruler of Middlearth and all its people are under his sway."

"But how many of the rings of power are left?" said Yawndell. "Does anyone know? And how can one destroy them?" he asked.

"They can be damaged more easily than one might think," snapped Grandalf. "That we have discovered thanks to young master Martin here. Yawndell, you mentioned the number of the magical rings. The nine we know of, for we must assume that they are now worn by the new Black Riders who pursued us from the Chire. The three are safe. I was given charge of them all, to return to Middlearth and destroy any way I might when I parted with Galadriyell and Felrond. The seven are lost or destroyed, although we must assume that at least a few were left to the Dark Lord in his dark tower. We do not know if any survived until this day, or if they were all consumed by dragon's fire. That we may never know. But we must destroy the rings we do know of. The elfen rings, the rings given to men, and the new ruling ring possessed by Happy."

"That will be no easy task," said Yawndell. "The nine are under the direct command of Sauluman."

"Their bearers are fierce fighters," said Grandalf. The pale color of face turned ashen grey as if the old man's spirit had departed and all that was left before them was a corpse. "But they are not immortal, nor are they neither living nor dead.

They are men who are alive. And they must be killed for us to succeed in our quest. The rest of the rings, we must assume are already in our possession."

"But why not destroy the rings that you have now? It seems that the ones you have are the most powerful rings of all," said Uniborn.

"Because they are the best weapons we have against the enemy," said Grandalf. "We need their power to obtain the other rings and accomplish our quest."

"*Yeeeaaaaarrhhhwwwwnnn...* now this is just a question Mister Grandalf, so there's no need to go and get cross with me," said Sham. "But doesn't that seem like a conflict of interests? How do we know you and Mister Happy won't be corrupted by their power? They never used the rings of power against the enemy in the films."

"*Never used the rings of power against the enemy!* Hah! You reveal yourself an uneducated, witless..." Grandalf was cut off.

"Well, he's not wrong Mister Grandalf," said the filmmaker. "I tried to make my characters purer with their use of the rings of power in the films than they were in the story. Seemed more proper to me. Sham here is just noting the film's difference and (one might say) superiority."

"How wonderful for you both," mocked Grandalf. "But regardless, we will use the rings of power on *this* quest, not because it is more or less pure to do so, but because we must to have a chance of defeating our enemy."

"You forget only one thing," said Ringo, "and that is our other mission. We must rescue the Lady Ella from the clutches of the orks."

"And we must also rescue my horses," added Roban.

"Yes, you are quite right," said Grandalf.

"Do not forget what the filmmaker said, Grandalf," said Yawndell, "that nearly all Middlearth has come under the dominion of Sauluman because of the films. If your mission becomes known to those who have fallen under his spell, who knows what armies and forces may begin to try and stop you."

"That is why I also think it would be wise to send emissaries to Grondor," said Grandalf. "The king must be warned that Sauluman has corrupted the films and that his subjects could be compromised. It will be a bitter pill for him to swallow, but swallow it he must."

"Well pardon me for asking, but with all of these goings on, I think it's fair of me to ask where my assignment is going to be, and to put in my request to accompany and assist good Mister Frobo here, as my old grandgaffer assisted the most famous hobbick who ever lived," said Sham. "One might argue of course that my role in these events that are yet to play out, will be that of the unsung hero of our quest, although Gramgees aren't the type to seek credit for their actions. 'Boasting isn't proper', my old maffer used to say, 'and just because you're a Gramgee doesn't mean you can't *act* proper.' Oh, my old Maffer, she really was a wonderful hobbick."

"Hah," laughed Uniborn. "This one must be joking!" Somehow the man then wrestled his arm from beneath a branch and pulled his sword from his side. Turning in his tree, he held the sword to the main trunk, "release me now, or I shall hew you in one fell cut!"

Instantly, the branches released him and Uniborn stood to his feet, eager to be out of the bowl.

"Yawndell, enough of this," said Grandalf. "Tell the trees to let them go."

Yawndell rolled his eyes, annoyed at the request, then flicked his wrist. The trees complied in a moment and released the rest of the company. The hobbicks and Ringo leapt from their bowls in a flash, but Roban and Wondell remained in theirs, apparently unconcerned with the possibility of being locked in them again. Sham fell to his knees and erupted into a fit of coughing, as if gasping for breath.

Uniborn pointed to Sham, "Look at him. These little folk don't actually think they'll be joining us on our quest, do they Grandalf? Don't you remember how much trouble they caused in the films? Besides, what could they do against an ork like Barzabag, as weak and small as they are?"

Frobo's ambition was squelched for a moment as he was reminded of his utter helplessness in combat situations. What if Uniborn was right? He hung his head, but then wondered if he would feel differently if he really was a Daggins.

"Perhaps you have forgotten that if not for their ancestors," said Grandalf, "the Dark Lord's dominion over Middlearth would've been absolute eleventy-one years ago. But there are other acts of valor from their ancestors that the films ignored. The choice to accompany us on this quest, wherever it may lead, is their own."

The eyes of the Counself turned upon the hobbicks: Grandalf's appraising gaze, Uniborn's doubting glare, Ringo's roving watch, Yawndell's groggy stare, and the filmmaker's ashamed eyes at each of them. Roban was the only one who seemed to have an encouraging look to the hobbicks to join them, unconcerned with their physical weakness and lack of skill in combat. Uniborn on the other hand, looked at them with absolute disgust, as if they were unwanted baggage that he was going to have to lug across Middlearth until he reached his destination.

"The way I see it," began Martin, "is that this quest can bring either death, or fame and fortune the likes of which to attract the finest hobbick lass this world has ever seen. But it's not as if we can turn back now, the four of us are practically fugitives in the Chire. We don't have a choice."

Frobo gulped as the uneasiness of that reality began to sink in. He was a fugitive. He was wanted by evil, powerful men who were much stronger and bigger than he was. But Son of

Ashelob, he was a Daggins for Pete's sake (at least he wanted to be a Daggins, no matter who Pete was).

"The *new* ring was given to me by my grandfather," said Happy. "Just as the uncle of the most famous hobbick who ever lived passed on his. Although I'm not a Daggins, it's only right for me to follow in their footsteps. I will continue to take the *new* ring until we destroy it, Grandalf. I only hope I will not go alone."

Frobo couldn't stop the twinge of jealousy that curled into his chest as Happy spoke. It was so easy for him; he'd been given a ring of power. He truly didn't have a choice. If this story was ever told like his dear old granddad's was, would Daggins even be the last name of the most famous hobbick who ever lived anymore? Or would a *Brandybeer* take over that mantle? It just wasn't *right*. Frobo knew he should be the one destroying that ring.

"Just as my grandgaffer, the unsung hero of the films served the ringbearer, so will I," said Sham.

"You're going to serve the ringbearer, or you're going to serve Mister Daggins?" asked Roban.

"Err, well this is awkward, isn't it," said Sham. "The way 'ringbearer' just slipped out like it did. It's just that Happy seems so much more *important* now for some reason. Like he's where the action is going to be in this story, you know? Sorry Mister Frobo really, I am. I know I'm your gardener and everything but on a quest like this, even I have to think beyond herbs and potatoes, which believe me is no easy task."

The feeling that was brewing inside Frobo was what he assumed the fiery mountain must feel right before it exploded with flames. He wanted to erupt at Sham, to chastise him in front of the entire Counself, to destroy his employee with a fierce storm of hurtful words, but as he almost always managed to do, he restrained the great fire of his anger and sat back. At least Sham had made his position clear. Now that he had no more use for Frobo, now that he didn't need Frobo to pay a salary and put his precious food on the table, he was abandoning him for good. Well Sham would get his, Frobo knew that much at least. Sham would get his when Frobo was the ringbearer because Happy couldn't handle the burden. Sham would get his when Happy begged Frobo to take the ring from him because of the terrors of the journey. Sham would get his when...

"Frobo?" said Grandalf. "And what is your decision? If I didn't know better, I'd say you looked like a ghost from the past when Sham was speaking."

Any fear he had felt had dissipated after Sham's scathing disrespect for him. His doubt was gone. He would go. He would go and he would become the Daggins he'd always wanted to be. "I will go," he said, glaring at Sham as vilely as he knew how to. "I will go and play my part in the quest, whatever it is, with or without my gardener's assistance."

"Excellent!" said Yawndell, springing up from the bowl of his tree. "You will all be going! That is good, because truthfully, I was not looking forward to the prospect of extended house guests, especially ones that dine as voluptuously as you four do. And will you be accompanying them as well, filmmaker? I'm sure you're quite ready to be out in the world again, out of this dreary place."

"Not at all," said the filmmaker. "Your hospitality is unmatched, Counselfor. I'd have to be a fool to want to leave this place! Besides, I am still musing about my mistakes, attempting to find a truly repentant heart within me for all I have done. I cannot leave now. I am simply not ready. Of course, I am sure you understand."

Yawndell rolled his eyes after the filmmaker bowed his head, "Unfortunately I do. My house is always welcome to those who seek rest, even to you, filmmaker. But you're quite sure you're not ready to leave?"

"Quite sure, Yawndell," the filmmaker said, with as somber a voice as he could muster. "Yes, I'm quite sure."

"Then, the companions of your fellowship are settled," said Yawndell. "Grandalf, Uniborn, Wondell, Ringo, Roban, Happy, Martin, Sham, and Frobo. Nine members, each bound to fate and to each other, on what might just become the second most famous quest of all time."

"Second most famous quest of all time... with those accolades they might make a film about us yet," said Sham grinning at Frobo and rubbing his hands together.

Frobo shook his head in private frustration. Hadn't Sham been paying attention to anything they'd said? They were supposed to forget about the films! But Sham was clearly obsessed with the power and glory he might receive from a film's portrayal of him. He didn't care about saving Middlearth, he only cared about being a film star. Frobo didn't need any of that. All he wanted was to take his rightful place in the lineage of his ancestors and prove once and for all that he was in fact the heir of the most famous hobbick who ever lived. How could he do that without doing something incredible and amazing like destroying a ring of power? But they'd see. Eventually they'd all see and understand that he was not a Sackville-Daggins, but was in fact Frobo Daggins, grandson of the most famous hobbick who ever lived.

CHAPTER 12

AN HONEST FOOL

AFTER THE CONCLUSION OF THE COUNSELF, THEY SPENT THE rest of the day gathering the necessary weapons and provisions for their quest. Here at last, Frobo was given a sword, if it could be called one. The only problem was that it was much too, well he wasn't sure what it was about it, but it didn't feel right. He would've given anything to have his grandfather's old sword, *The Stinger*. Of course, the most famous hobbick who ever lived had left that sword to his gardener Sham, who had then passed it on to his descendants. But Frobo's father Froyo had taken it back from them when making his claim that he was the son of the most famous hobbick who ever lived, and Sham's father had not refused to surrender it. Frobo's father Froyo had surely left it somewhere in Daggend before he disappeared that strange night so long ago, but Frobo had never found the thing after his father's disappearance. If he only had it now, it would at least help make up for him not being the bearer of the new ring of power, and maybe someone would start treating him with a little respect.

Instead, he had an ugly looking sword given him by Wondell with ornamental leaves on its handle that probably wasn't even sharp. He ran his finger across the blade and, "Ouch!" he exclaimed. A drop of blood ran down his hand. The blade had sliced his finger.

"I guess that sword does still have some life in it," said Wondell. "It was my own when I was a young elfling. It was well chosen. And it appears to have also chosen you."

"Chosen me?" said Frobo. "What do you mean?"

"See those crafted leaves ornamenting the handle?" said Wondell. "My father magically imbibed this sword so that if any enemy ever took it, their hand would instantly swell and become infected as with a rash of poison ivy."

Frobo dropped the sword immediately, grasping his hand to the laughter of Wondell.

"Don't worry!" Wondell said, "If the sword thought you were an enemy, your hand would be red like a flame and itching so badly you wouldn't be able to stand. But it has chosen you. You have nothing to fear. The name of your grandfather's sword was *The Stinger*, yes? Well, this sword's name is *Itch*."

Frobo picked up *Itch* more cautiously this time and examined it. It was no *Stinger*, but at least there was something special and important about it. He would take it with the knowledge that if it was ever stolen from him, the thief might not be able to hold on for long.

Frobo placed *Itch* in its sheath, which he strapped to his belt. He felt so awkward with it slapping his leg every time he took a step. But he was going on a quest now, and he'd have to get used to it. He didn't know how this quest was going to end, and he could barely remember all of the details they'd discussed at the Counself yesterday, but he was ready for it to start. And according to Grandalf, to the relief of Uniborn, it was starting today.

Frobo gathered with his eight companions outside the house of Slumbervell. They stood behind the courtyard and to Frobo's amazement, when looking out at the vast array of sleeping trees, he saw that they were no longer in well-arranged rows. Frobo rubbed his eyes, squinting in disbelief. They were growing so haphazardly now that they might have been any random Chire grove. Slumbervell was a very strange place indeed.

Yawndell, Gloria, and the filmmaker were there to see them off. Horses had been saddled for each of the companions as even the four hobbicks would ride their own (though Frobo doubted Sham had the faintest idea of how to ride his). Grandalf then spoke up, "Yawndell, it is time to begin our, *yeaaawwwwrrr,* quest. You have been a most gracious host and an adequate Counselfor."

"Thank you, Grandalf thank you," said Yawndell. "And now I will say a parting word of wisdom to each of you."

Uniborn groaned, but Yawndell continued as if he hadn't heard it.

"First of all, to my son, Wondell... my first born, my only child..." he began.

"Why would you need to state that he's your first born if he's your only child?" said Gloria, "He is your only child, so *first born* goes without saying."

"Ahem, quite right, my angel," said Yawndell, without turning to look at his wife. "Now please, let me finish. Wondell, some believe that all eternity is too long to spend with one person. Are they right or wrong? Who knows? I am not the one to say. But my single son (pun intended), who might've been the heir of queen Galadriyell if things had played out differently, I pray thee find the truest love that thy heart seekest. And perhaps, if I may suggest a pairing, this Lady Ellamir could be a fine selection, if you wish to release yourself in time from the bonds of immortal matrimony."

"Grandalf," Yawndell continued, "May you lead this fellow-ship of the new ring with less unnecessary drama than you led the last one... what I'm trying to say is, could you try not to die this time?"

Grandalf rolled his eyes and said, "Are you finished yet, Yawndell?"

"Oh no, Grandalf," said Yawndell. "I'm just getting started. Now to the four hobbicks, may your bellies be full of the finest provender in Middlearth, and may you make your ancestors... supposed or real, proud."

Frobo gritted his teeth at the jab that was clearly intended for him.

Yawndell continued, "To the brash man in a hurry and to the horse thief... do your best to stay away from young elf maidens if this all ends up working out and they get over their little dwarf fetishes. The West knows my son needs a chance at one, and he'll need the best shot he can get without having to compete with both of you.

"And finally, to Ringo the Dwarf. May you find an occupation that is worthy of your stature and befitting of a good gentledwarf like yourself. And may you find the wherewithal to accept forgiveness for taking advantage of and pulling on the innocent heartstrings of elf maidens all over Middlearth."

The dwarf growled and gritted his teeth, just as tired of Yawndell's speech as the rest of them.

"You shall be called," Yawndell proclaimed, "*theeeaahh-wwwggggghh*... the Fellowship of the Films. May you find fame, fortune, adventure, love, conquest, and above all, the true meaning of life upon your journey. Go in peace!"

With the speech finally over, and the companions feeling insulted each in their own respect, the Fellowship of the Films departed from Slumbervell. With their bellies full, and their swords girt to their sides, each one of them noted a discernable sensation of alertness come upon them the moment they passed beneath the arch of the gates.

Frobo soon became accustomed again to riding atop a horse.

He had in fact far more practice than Sham or either of the other hobbicks, seeing as he had been forced to ride alone before any of them. However, he doubted a film would ever make note of such a detail if one was ever made about their present quest. Those films had missed quite a bit, and they'd been especially generous to Sham's grandfather. Now that he thought about it, he also supposed they had missed most of the details about at least half of his family, the Sackville-Daggins side. They were nothing but a fleeting aside of the films, only to be recognized by a true reader of the story of the most famous hobbick who ever lived.

To Frobo, the following days on horseback passed slowly. The Fellowship of the Films rode in pursuit of their bounty and the hours drifted by him like a light breeze in a meadow, slowly traversing every blade of grass. His thighs grew sore from the saddle and his hands became weary from grasping his horse's reins. The sleeping trees and babbling brooks of the gardens of Slumbervell vanished soon after they left the gates. Since then, they'd been entrenched in a monotonous forest of dark green trees, riding on a dreary, winding road that was leading them to a place Frobo knew not where. These trees were of such a height and of such a leaf, that one could not see more than ten feet in any direction. Only the road could act as a guide and provide a sense of direction, and it wound and snaked through the forest in a such a fashion that Frobo assumed they would never be out of these woods.

Finally, after three monotonous days, the terrain began to assume more drastic shapes. Frobo and the others welcomed the change. That day (the third day), a steep mountain rose high in their road, and the company began to climb it. Roban assured them that he'd intercepted the ork's tracks after leaving Slumbervell, even though four days had passed since they'd been made. They were close now, and the fear of what they might find at the mountain's top chilled Frobo's heart.

Indeed, looking through the tops of the tall trees, he could see the cold grey peaks were close, standing tall and high and blocking out nearly half of the blue sky. Of course, the only mountain ranges he'd ever seen before had been in the films, so he had nothing to compare these to. They were quite cheerful when compared to the darkness and death of the mountains of Morbor.

The further they went, the easier it became for Frobo to tell that the orks had come this way. They had cut through the wilderness like a great grinding wheel, gashing everything in their path on the journey back to their mountain home. They were not much for subtlety. Frobo shuddered to think of what they could do to the poor Chire and its helpless beer gargling citizens. They had hacked every tree and broken every branch and blade of grass they had touched. By the end of the day, the fellowship had followed their trail to the very edge of the tree line. Now they were separated from those dreadful creatures by only a mountainous climb, or at least, so they thought.

"We make camp here for the night," said Grandalf. "Tomorrow, we make our ascent."

"Let us go tonight," said Uniborn. "I will slay them all myself if need requires it. But I will sit on my hands and tarry no longer."

"We cannot go up tonight," said Grandalf, glaring at the impatient man. "We would never reach the top of the mountain if we did. At night, the orks of the mountain hunt by the light of the moon, although that light they despise. They would see us and slay us long before we slew them. But in the day, they hide in the shadows of their caves beneath the earth in the belly of the mountain. That is when we will make our climb. Pray we find the entrance to their haunt before nightfall."

"The way these orks hack and grind a path, finding their

mountain caves should not be too difficult a task," said Ringo, patting the handle of a sturdy axe he'd procured from the armory of Slumbervell.

"Do not speak too soon, Dwarf," said Wondell, dismounting from his horse in a single gentle gliding movement. He made it look as easy as water flowing down a stream. For Frobo however, it was a laborious process of awkward positioning and terrible fear that he would suddenly fall and be trampled by the great beast. Wondell continued, "these orks may not appear to be so, but they are cunning. Far more cunning than many a dwarf that I have known. Though perhaps not more cunning than you, who can pull the wool over the eyes of many who are wise."

"And what is that supposed to mean?" growled Ringo, wielding his new axe and glaring at Wondell with deadly eyes.

"I know why it is that you accompany us on this quest. Do you assume that I do not see the lust in your heart for the Lady Ellamir, and for all of the fairest elf maidens left in this Middlearth?" shouted Wondell. He stepped toward Ringo in a threatening way, eyes red with anger as they had been the night Frobo had first met him in the Prancing *Shetland* Pony. "For I have seen your heart and know that it seeks only its own fulfillment."

"Would you have the Lady Ellamir for yourself then?" said Ringo, shouting at the top of his lungs. "Is that what this is about? You, Wondell, the finest looking male elf left in all of Middlearth, are jealous of a dwarf? Hah! I never thought I'd have the pleasure!"

"Do not speak so of the Lady Ellamir," warned Uniborn. "She will be saved for none but the finest in all of Grondor!"

Wondell continued as if he hadn't heard Uniborn, "I'd sooner be jealous of an ork like Barzabag than a flea ridden, chest shaving, beer bellied, dwarf gypsy like you."

"Enough!" Grandalf interrupted before they could continue.

"Be silent, each and every one of you. For if you do not keep your voices down, you will alert every ork within a mile to our position. We cannot fight amongst ourselves. Our enemy must be from without, not from within! Put aside your petty differences until our task is done."

Through much muttering under their collective breath, Ringo and Wondell each proceeded to make their camp on the base of the mountainside. The others did the same. When the camp was made, they all gathered around the small fire as they had done only four nights ago. Sham volunteered to cook them all a nice big dinner and was busying himself with the preparations. Seemingly, the only difference between this fire-lit fellowship and their last was the lack of the Lady Ella's presence. No evening stroll with Frobo would occur, no surprising chair would be produced for her, and no joyful song would be sung by Happy and Martin.

A grim mood befell the Fellowship of the Films. The taste and warmth of Sham's stew should have heartened even the most depressed traveler. But there was neither a smile nor hint of joy to be found in the face of nary a one of them. Grandalf began to speak of the coming day. Despite his eager desire for the glory and fame that a day like the coming one could bring Frobo (being part of a noble quest to save a damsel in distress), the reality of their aims was starting to hit him like a wet blanket, squelching the fire in his chest to be as great as his supposed or actual grandfather. Barzabag and his army of free orks were very big orks indeed, and Frobo was, after all, nothing but a small, unimportant hobbick, whose ancestors quite possibly might never have done anything of any significance at all.

"Tomorrow, we ascend the mountain and find the halls of the orks. We must have a plan of action," Grandalf began.

"We do have a plan," said Uniborn. The man's eyes were glazed over as he stared into the burning fire. "We storm their caves and rescue the Lady Ellamir. No ork can stand in my way."

"Maybe one ork cannot, but a thousand orks might be able to," said Grandalf. "Uniborn, Wondell and I might possibly be the only members of our fellowship with any substantial experience in combat."

"The Rugged Dwarfs were not just an acting and dancing troupe, Master Grandalf," said Ringo. "I can fell an ork with an axe as well as a tree. I was brought up to not be so trusting as to the peace we struck with the orks as the rest of Middlearth."

"And what of the horse thief?" said Uniborn. "Does he have any talents besides his ability to chatter his tongue?"

"None that would interest you, Uni," said Roban. "Of course, I did single handedly steal a thousand horses from a fully populated town in broad daylight, and I am the finest card player this side of the Musty Mountains. If you consider those things, in addition to being your superior in practically every way as talents, then yes, I'd say I have a few."

"So, we have four fighters, a gambling horse thief," said Grandalf, "and four burglars."

"Four burglars?" said Sham. "Pardon me for saying so, Mister Grandalf, but we aren't burglars. We're hobbicks, and proud of it."

"You're burglars," said Grandalf. "Just as the uncle of the most famous hobbick who ever lived was a burglar when I met him, so are you, until you find another skill by which to distinguish yourselves other than singing, eating food and being extraordinarily more annoying than your ancestors were."

Sham sat back aghast and offended. "Can you believe he would say that while he slurps down the stew I made him? I'll have you know that I'm quite offended, Mister Grandalf sir."

"Oh, enough Sham. I meant it as a compliment!" snapped Grandalf. "Now, to the plan. We cannot hope to rescue the Lady Ella with brute force, no matter how skilled the four of us may be with our weapons. We will be in foreign territory, in darkness and in the very place these orks call home. It would be a hopeless mission."

"Only a fool's hope, Mister Grandalf," said Sham. "That's what my old grandgaffer used to say, and that's all he needed when he was completing his quest in the films, saving the life of most famous hobbick who ever lived."

"Your old grandgaffer never said that, I did!" shouted Grandalf. "But you will certainly be a fool if you try to rescue the Lady Ella with brute force. That would be a fruitless endeavor, one in which we all forfeit our lives."

"Then how will we rescue her?" asked Roban, before adding quickly, "I mean, how will we rescue the horses?"

"It's a curious little puzzle," said Grandalf. "But fortunately for us, one that a little *magic* can help us work out. We must become *invisible*."

From a pouch beneath his cloak, Grandalf produced two golden rings. Both were adorned with a stone, one was blue, and the other green. They shone bright and fierce in the firelight. Frobo beheld them in awe. "Behold the other two elfen rings of power," said Grandalf. "The third is, of course, upon my finger, but these two were entrusted to me by Galadriyell and Felrond, before they left Middlearth forever. I was entrusted to destroy them, and to never let another touch them save myself. But I am old, and I am tired, and the West knows I should have been allowed to leave just like them, so I am breaking the rules a bit in the name of haste. If you've got a problem with that, then you can speak up now, but I dare say you should be ready to suffer the consequences if you do, Sham."

The fellowship sat in uneasy silence around the wizard, unsure of what he might be capable of doing if one of them did in fact disagree with his methods. They all looked at Sham, who seemed to have gotten the hint that this was not the time or the place for objections. He dipped his spoon into his bowl of stew and slurped a large mouthful. It was probably the only way he could keep himself from speaking.

Privately, Frobo was very uncomfortable with what he thought Grandalf was about to do. He had always been raised to believe, perhaps through a misinterpretation of the films, that the rings of power were inherently evil. And it sounded like Grandalf was about to pass them out like presents at a birthday party. On the other hand, he couldn't help but feel as if one of these rings of power might have been just the thing he needed to silence his critics once and for all.

"Good," Grandalf said, looking about the fire at each face. "Then if there are no objections, I will proceed: I propose that we use these rings, along with Happy's, to become invisible, sneak into the caves of the orks, and rescue the Lady Ella. Happy will be the key, as his ring is the most powerful and still grants true invisibility. He will take us in, two by two and find a hiding place, then return the rings to the outside for the next two to follow."

"Wait a moment," said Martin, "we have four rings of power, not three. "Happy's, the two you hold in your hand Grandalf, and the other one that is on your finger. Why not use all of them?"

A twinge of anger curled upon Grandalf's face, but before he could respond, Wondell said, "I have a question also, Grandalf. As these rings were made by elfs, and they are the *elfen* rings of power, I think it's only right that after we finish this little mission, that I should be able to keep one."

"None of us are *keeping* them," said Ringo. The dwarf stood to his feet and his large oval-like green eyes beamed across the fire at Wondell. He pointed his stout but well-manicured finger at the elf as he said, "Haven't you been paying attention? Our mission is to destroy the rings of power!"

"Grandalf," Happy began. The hobbick opened his mouth between bites of his nails as he always did when worried about something. "Didn't you say earlier that even though that *Insidious Ring* has been destroyed, these rings could still corrupt? Are you sure it's the best idea to start passing them out like candy?"

"Oh right," said Frobo. "So you and Grandalf get to hold a ring of power, but no one else can?"

"The only corrupting power left in these rings comes from their bearers or from their companions, not from the rings themselves!" said Grandalf. A fire blazed in his eyes as he interrupted the flurry of speech and opinion that had broken out. "Perhaps it is time we all grow up and realize we are doing this for a greater purpose than our own personal benefit!"

Frobo knew that Grandalf was right. This was a good plan, whether Happy liked it or not. He would gladly share a ring of power if it could help them save the Lady Ella, but he would not hope to keep one for himself. After all, their mission was to destroy the things. If he could help them do that, even in a small way, he would be able to gain enough fame and glory to last a lifetime.

Grandalf explained the rest of his plan to them in turn. The only truly risky part was how visible they would each be in the concealing power of the rings. There was only one way to know for sure, and that was to test them. When they tried them on, Uniborn and Roban appeared only as shadows or whisps of wind, barely visible to the naked eye. Frobo could only see a dim glow of their eyes in the firelight and dark masses moving as they walked. The moment they removed the elfen rings from their fingers, they snapped back into full view.

Wondell enjoyed wearing the elfen ring with the blue stone, but for some reason he could become invisible more easily without it by a secret art he had learned from his father. Grandalf had no problem becoming invisible with his ring.

The hobbicks all boasted that they would be able to easily conceal themselves without magic rings. When they put them on, even Wondell said that he could barely see them. None but the most cunning ork eye in Middlearth would be able to discern their movements.

Ringo proved the most difficult to conceal, as his dwarf nature seemed to resist the power of the rings the most. But by a strange coincidence, the moment he held the elfen ring in his hand, he noticed five gold coins hidden in the dust beneath his feet.

Frobo's heart shuddered at that the thought of what they were to do the next day. To tell the truth, it scared him out of his good hobbick senses. He was more terrified of what they were planning than he'd ever been in his short uneventful life. Perhaps it was even more frightening than the fact that he might never live up to his supposed grandfather's good name. As he lay there that night, desperately tossing and turning, he dreamt of the orks and other terrors they might meet. Orks saw much better than normal folk could at night. They'd be caught and captured; he was quite sure of it! Was any amount of fame and notoriety worth what they might endure at the hands of the orks? At the hands of Barzabag? He shuddered as yellow eyes spotted him in a cave and a roaring mouth of sharp teeth cried out in the darkness. The rings hadn't concealed them and they'd been caught! The sharp claws drug him before a throng of orks and there was Barzabag, holding a bludgeon before them, laughing as the films played in the background! They were doomed! Doomed!

Frobo awoke to a racing heart and a clear starlit sky above him. In the distance somewhere atop the mountain, he heard the howls of orks or wolfs; he knew not which. They were on their evening hunt. Grandalf had been right to not ascend the mountain yet. Frobo just hoped the orks would stay up there where they belonged, the same place where he was going to be tomorrow. Was he mad? Had he gone completely crazy in his quest for greatness? He, Frobo Daggins, was about to willingly take on a thousand orks to help rescue a Lady. "Yes, I'm quite sure I have gone mad," he said to himself. "And as far as I am concerned, Happy and Sham can keep their magic rings and reputations, I don't know what I've been thinking! I've got to get back to the Chire, is what I've got to do. Have a nice warm glass of milk and get my senses back. I'll have to hire a new gardener, and then..."

As he ran through the to-do list in his mind, Frobo had subconsciously risen from his mat and began rolling it up to stow away. The rest of the fellowship was fast asleep and Frobo hadn't even taken the time to glance at the camp, but as he knelt and rolled up his sack, out of the corner of his eye, he saw a shaggy brown dog stooping over Happy. It was just standing there, perfectly still. Frobo wondered what it was doing, but he didn't have time to think about it, he was leaving to go back to the...

"Shaggy brown dog?" he thought to himself. *"But that's strange. We don't have a shaggy brown dog. Must just be a lost stray."* But it looked awfully big for a stray. When Frobo finally looked up from rolling his mat, he saw a dark brown creature crouched on all four limbs, with long shaggy fur, and deep brown eyes that stared at Frobo.

What was this creature? It was certainly not a dog as he'd first thought. It was longer and taller than a dog. Besides that, it had no tail. But it was certainly dog-like. Frobo could see claws at the end of its paws, or were they fingers? It was a very strange creature indeed. They continued to stare into each other's eyes, and each one of them seemed frozen in place. Frobo was utterly confused at the sight of the thing. He didn't know if he should cry out for help or run for his life. The odd thing of it was, although he'd never seen nor heard of anything like the creature that stood before him, there was something familiar about it. And that was almost as strange as the creature itself was.

Then in a sudden flash, the creature bounded away like a

frightened squirrel into the bushes. As soon as it was gone, Frobo realized where he'd seen that furry claw before. It was the same claw he'd spotted reaching out from the bushes outside Breetown to take the ring of power from Happy. *"Holy goblets of beer,"* he thought to himself. Frobo quickly unrolled his bed mat and laid it back on the ground in his place. He couldn't leave now. There were obviously enemies out there! Enemies who were trying to steal their rings of power! But what if... what if that creature had already stolen Happy's ring of power? What if he'd stolen it just now?

Frobo shuddered at the thought of it. They'd have no chance of rescuing the Lady Ella without Happy's ring. He tried to quiet his thoughts as he pulled the thin blanket up over his mouth and curled his legs up to his chest as he always did when trying to fall asleep. Hopefully that foul dog-like creature hadn't taken Happy's ring. But if it had, he supposed they did still have Grandalf's rings. And maybe, if Happy's ring was gone, they'd finally stop treating him differently than they treated Frobo. Maybe he'd finally start getting the respect he deserved. Yes, at least they still had Grandalf's rings. Hope was not lost yet.

Frobo fretted himself with worry the rest of the night, falling in and out of sleep with restless thoughts. Every time he awoke again, he rolled over, looking for the shaggy dog-like creature crouched over Happy. But no shaggy dog-like creature was seen.

When morning came, Frobo awoke to the dim yellow haze of light that flooded their campsite. Sham crouched over the rekindled fire, making breakfast, humming a song to himself. Frobo went to sit by Roban who was drinking a mug of hot coffee, no longer worried for the orks to spot their fire now that the sun was coming up. Frobo sat and eyed Happy as the Hobbick arose from his mat. His right hand reached into his trouser pocket and came up empty, and then the action was mirrored on his left side. Then the hobbick felt with both hands for his vest pockets. With those apparently empty of what he was seeking, he began to search the ground beneath his bedroll. Frobo shifted uneasily, pretending not to see what was happening. His stomach lurched with the guilt that was starting to envelope him. What a fool he'd been! That dog creature had stolen Happy's ring! He should've woken them all up immediately, as soon as he'd seen the thing. But still, there was something in him that was slightly pleased the thing was finally gone. It seemed a certain justice had finally taken place.

"It's gone," Happy cried in shock, so loudly that each member of the fellowship awoke. The whites of his eyes beamed at all of them beneath his shining red hair. Utter panic riddled the face that normally bore Happy's customary smile. With all the rosy hue drained from his cheeks and only the pallor normally brought on by the loss of life remaining, he repeated his cry. "It's gone! Someone's taken it!"

Frobo looked to the surrounding trees, hoping that no orks could hear Happy's madness.

"What the deuce are you talking about? Who has taken what?" said Grandalf.

"My ring!" Happy cried. "Someone's taken my ring! It's gone!"

Frobo wondered if they were all watching him. He felt incredibly self-conscious, sitting at the fire, trying his best to appear surprised and nonchalant all at the same time. But Frobo was completely unprepared for what came after that.

"My rings are gone too!" Grandalf said. The wizard's face grew as white as his beard in shock as he felt the empty pockets of his cloak.

Every member of the fellowship, Happy included, fell silent. Frobo's face grew flush with red embarrassment. He looked up and saw to his utter horror that Grandalf's piercing, fiery gaze was directed solely at him.

"Do you have anything you wish to say, Frobo?" asked

Grandalf, who was clearly trying to restrain the anger in his voice. "I warned you before about the temptations of the rings. I gave you a second chance that night outside Breetown, when I caught you pawing over Happy as your lust for his ring consumed you. But now you have gone too far!"

"What's he talking about, Frobo?" said Happy. His face was indescribable. Had Frobo stabbed him in the back with a knife, and Happy turned round to see his murderer, a greater look of pain and betrayal might not have been fixed upon on him.

"You tried to take my ring?" he asked.

"Now wait just one moment!" said Frobo, trying desperately to explain himself.

"Yes, he tried before," said Grandalf. "But now I fear he has gone and done the thing. Frobo, I will give you one more chance to come clean and stop this madness before we take the rings back."

"Wait! Wait! I can explain," he said. "And I can explain what happened that night outside Breetown too if you'll let me. I saw the same thing that night that I saw last night. Happy, that night outside Breetown, I couldn't sleep. I woke up and saw a clawed furry hand reaching out from behind some bushes towards you. I think it knew that I was awake though, because it ran off. Then, I went to check and make sure that it hadn't taken the ring from you, and that's when Grandalf saw me... and yes, for a moment that night, I was thinking of taking the ring from you, only to look at, mind you, I just wanted to hold it for a time. But I didn't take it, alright! Well, last night I couldn't sleep, and I got up to walk around. Lo and behold, out of the corner of my eye, I see the strangest looking dog-like creature I've ever beheld, with long shaggy dark brown fur. It crouched over Happy on all four of his legs like this!"

Frobo crouched down on all fours and began to bear-crawl over to Happy, trying to imitate the dog-like creature as best he could. His face took the form of a tooth revealing snarl, and his eyes narrowed into fearsome slits. As he crawled on all fours, a deep guttural growl started to purr from within him. Without realizing it, he had almost transformed in the fellowship's eyes into a loathsome creature. If not for his clothes and his dark brown locks, they might have thought he was Grollum himself.

Frobo still hadn't seen the horrified looks at his impression on his companions faces. And oblivious to the distasteful display, he leapt at Happy like a cat. "Lie down, lie down, Happy," Frobo urged. "Let me show them exactly what the creature did."

Through pangs of unease, Happy obliged him, and Frobo knelt over his body just as the dog-like creature had. "Then, it looked up, and it just stared at me, and I stared right back at it, for it seemed oddly familiar to me. Then that's when I realized, it was the same creature that had stuck its claws out of the bushes to try at Mister Happy outside Breetown. But as soon as I realized where I'd seen it before, it bounded away into the night without a trace."

"So, you saw this creature crouched over the ringbearer, and you didn't think to warn any of us?" said Grandalf.

"I'm sorry, truly I am. I just didn't think to. I was dreadfully afraid," said Frobo. He wrung his hands in agony at this lame excuse. "But I had no idea he'd taken the rings. And I thought if he had, maybe he'd only taken Happy's ring. I never dreamed he'd take all of them."

"And you thought to yourself," began Happy, "with Happy's ring gone, that perhaps we'd be on an even playing field, didn't you, Frobo? Then there wouldn't be a hobbick who was more important than you, right?"

"That's not true," said Frobo, kicking himself for revealing too much of his true thoughts. "I told you, I was afraid. I didn't know what the creature was doing!"

Grandalf eyed him inquisitively. "You are a fool, Frobo. But you are an honest fool in that I know you didn't take the rings.

However, your ambition may have cost the Lady Ella and the rest of us our lives. It is time for you to leave it by the wayside. It is time for all of us to do that. If you have done nothing else on this quest so far Frobo, you have proven one thing to all of us. You have proven that you are a Sackville-Daggins through and through. No grandson of the most famous hobbick who ever lived would do what you did last night."

Frustration at the injustice of this accusation gripped Frobo. Didn't they hear what he had said? He hadn't taken any of the rings! That stupid dog-like creature had taken them. And now they were all looking at him as if he was worse than Sauluman himself. Once more, his power of restraint kept his tongue at bay. He so wanted to lash out at them, to defend himself, to break down crying with sadness from the injustice of it all. But he couldn't. They were all watching him with such disgust. All he could do was keep to himself, brooding with inward rage, hating their false belief that *he* was somehow responsible for what had happened last night.

"Rings or no rings," said Uniborn, flexing his chiseled jaws like he was posing for a painting of himself, "the Lady Ella is up there somewhere in that mountain, and I am going to save her."

"If he can save that woman without those rings, then I'd say I can save my horses without them," said Roban. "Count me in." He plucked a few blades of grass and held them up to his borrowed Slumbervellian horse. The horse ate gladly from his hand and snorted with joy.

"Of course, we're still going to rescue the Lady, no matter how much this Sackville-Daggins does to stop us," said Grandalf. "Frobo, I will only say this, if you do still intend to accompany us, leave your ambition once and for all behind you!"

Frobo grumbled to himself as they packed up their camp to begin the long climb up the mountainside. He was not a Sackville-Daggins, no matter what anybody said. Stupid stinking good for nothing... How dare they insult him as they had. How dare they insinuate what they'd insinuated. How dare they glared at him as they were glaring that very instant. He was the heir of the most famous hobbick who'd ever lived! Happy couldn't say that. Grandalf couldn't say that. How strange would that have been if he could? But that was irrelevant. The point was that NONE of them could say that, and that was why they were all trying to discredit his lineage. They were jealous, plain and simple. He'd keep his mouth shut about it though, for now at least. And they'd see. When he saved every one of them and they all saw his true heroics, then they'd see. And then, they'd be crawling back on their hands and knees to beg for his forgiveness.

When the camp had been fully dismantled, and each member of the fellowship had eaten their fill of Sham's delicious breakfast stew, they mounted their horses.

"I will do my best, with the little magic I have left, to conceal all of us when we reach the entrance to the mountain," said Grandalf. "It won't be as effective as the rings would have been, but since they're gone," he shot another dagger of a look at Frobo, "we'll have to do our best without them."

"Oh Grandalf," pined Sham, "It's a fine gesture, you, offering to *try* and conceal us... but I doubt you could make any of us invisible, concealed, or look differently than we truly are at all without your magic ring. Surely you only say this to ease poor Frobo's feelings of shame for completely flummoxing our quest. Do you even have any real power at all without it? Without your ring? I assume your true nature is more of a traveling magician, a conjurer and talisman seller."

"Do you, Sham?" asked Grandalf. "Is that so? I can hardly say that surprises me considering the level of intellect you demonstrate to us on a daily basis. Even I couldn't conceal that."

Sham stuttered to himself but was far too busy trying to interpret the meaning of Grandalf's remark to respond to it.

Grandalf continued, "if you ever find yourself in need of a traveling magician, I do hope you hire me, because as your grandfather rightly feared, I am quite proficient in turning people into toads."

Frobo then beheld Sham (still sitting atop his horse) suddenly transform into the shape and texture of a plump dark green swamp toad. The fascinating transformation left the toad as large as Sham, and the creature still wore his clothing. The entire company bellowed with laughter as Sham shook in terror atop the horse, ribeting protests against the unsightly change to his body. With the wink of an eye, Grandalf removed the transfiguration from Sham, who was in a mid-air fall from his horse with his hands clutching his throat and coughing as he turned back into himself. Had the poor hobbick been trying to choke the toad to death?

"I can change the look of any of you that I wish," said Grandalf. "That is how we will breach the mountain. If we cannot go invisibly, we will use disguise. Had you read Frobo's supposed grandfather's uncle's translations of the history of Middlearth, this would've come as little surprise to you."

Sham was still coughing and sputtering and rolling around on the grass of the mountainside like a depraved lunatic.

"Oh, cut it out, Sham," said Martin. "He changed you back already, you can stop acting like the film version of Grollum."

"Did he really?" shouted Sham, springing up from the ground. "Oh, thank you sir! Thank you Grandalf, bless my stars you are a powerful wizard sir. That's what I've always said and believed."

"Give it a rest, and let's be on our way," said Grandalf. "The task ahead of us will most likely be the most dangerous any of you has ever undertaken... save Uniborn maybe. Do not think these disguises will make us immune to danger. Orks see in many ways, and we will smell different than we look. We must still attempt to avoid our enemies at all costs. Come. We ride! We must reach the entrance to the Orkhold by nightfall. I will use the magic only if I must, to conceal us on the way. I just hope you take to your illusions more favorably than Sham did."

Frobo grinned from atop his horse. Someone other than him was the center of Grandalf's disgruntlement. There was still something to be happy about.

The company then began the day's ride up the mountainside, with Roban leading the way, as he was the self-proclaimed "best tracker among them." Personally, Frobo didn't understand why tracking a thousand horses running all together was that difficult. But Roban seemed to truly cherish the title, and Frobo didn't need to make any more enemies than he perceived he already had.

"The trail may be easy to follow now, my friends," Roban said, riding through the clear-cut path of broken branches and trampled grass. "Perhaps even Uniborn could follow it. But higher up, on the barren rock when there is no more trampled grass, and the hoofprints no longer delve into the ground, then you will be glad to have me."

A few miles later, exactly as Roban had predicted, the soil and grass gave way to hard gray unadorned stone. "Now you shall truly see a tracker at work," said Roban.

"What's that?" said Martin, pointing ahead. Frobo's eyes followed Martin's hand to an incredibly large mural that had been erected on the mountainside. A huge ork was painted upon it with a striking resemblance to one from the first film. His mouth was open in a howl and Frobo could see his sharp gleaming yellow teeth, with long red tongue sticking out between them. Letters had been scrawled upon the mural reading, "Isthay Ayway Ootay Ilmsfay, Amefay, andway Ethay Eefray Orksway Mtay! Ecretsay Entranceway Wotay Ilesmay Upway andway Irstfay Oulderbay onway Ethay Ightray! On'tday

Evenway Inkthay Aboutway Omingcay Ithoutway Ethay Asswordpay!"

"It reads in the common tongue," Grandalf said, "This Way to Films, Fame, and The Free Orks™! Secret Entrance Two Miles Up and First Boulder on the Right! Don't Even Think About Coming Without the Password!"

"Do you think you'll still be able to lead us there, *tracker*?" asked Uniborn.

"It appears that we are closer than we thought..." said Grandalf. "So, the Free Orks are recruiting, and all we need now is this *password*."

"There it is again," shouted Sham, shaking his head. "It's uncanny!"

"There what is again?" asked Ringo.

"Don't you all remember?" said Sham. "In the films... when they're trying to go under the mountain for their quest. They get to the side of the mountain, and they can't get in without the password. Do you remember Grandalf, do you remember?"

"Of course, I remember you dimwitted numbskull," shouted the wizard. "I was there in person eleventy-one years ago. The films were only a portrayal of our actions. A portrayal that was a grossly inaccurate portrayal of that particular occasion!"

"Well, I'm sure the orks have seen that part of the film is all I'm saying," said Sham. "And that's why I'm sure the password will be the same this time. What was the fruit you named Grandalf? Apple? Orange?"

"I do not have the time or patience to recount the events of my life to you, Sham. Now all of you, when we reach the cave entrance, you will let me do the talking. This is not the time for any sort of 'Flobo Blaggins' mischief!"

The wizard turned a sharp eye in Frobo's direction, who took offense at the remark. He still thought 'Flobo Blaggins' had been a much better undercover name than 'Glandalf.'

"Now I will place your disguises upon each of you," said

Grandalf. "Please wear them with more dignity than Sham did. And remember, these are only illusions. Your best disguise is still to stay hidden and out of sight. We don't know what it will be like once we're in the Orkhold, but stay together, stay calm, and whatever you do, try to act natural! Our quest is to save the life of the Lady Ella."

"And my horses," added Roban.

"Yes," said Grandalf, eyeing Roban curiously, then the wizard began to wave and point his staff at each of them in turn. Slowly, before Frobo's eyes, they were transformed into the likenesses of orks. The gradual process was as hideous as the end result. Frobo's turn was coming up. As Grandalf pointed his staff at him, he first saw the very tips of his fingers turn black, like they were covered in the soot of his fireplace. His well-trimmed nails that he bit frequently to keep from growing too long turned into sharp yellow claws. The bright red vest he wore seemed to burn up before his very eyes into a disgusting grey tunic pulled across his body. Over the tunic was a rusty chain connected to a clasp around his neck. His breath suddenly tasted foul, and he shuddered to think of what he would have seen had he gazed in a mirror. His only comfort was that he couldn't see his own hideous face.

"Your disguises are now complete," said Grandalf, "But remember that they are only shadowy illusions. Stay as far away from the orks as you can. Stay together. And whatever you do, don't speak! Your voices will give you away worse than your scent will. Our aim is to remain completely unseen. The disguises are only a backup plan."

"Apple, orange, grape, strawberry, confound me which fruit was it, Mister Frobo?" said Sham.

"Sham, I have no idea what you're talking about," snapped Frobo.

"Quiet, you two!" rasped Grandalf.

Sham continued, now whispering... "Don't you remember,

Mister Frobo? The elfish word for friend! That's the one that got them into the cave in the films."

"But this isn't the same cave, Sham... why would it have the same password?" Frobo whispered. Of course, he remembered the stupid film reference, but making Sham try and rack his brain for the word was far more rewarding. Couldn't they all see how much of a dunce Sham was?

"Kiwi, grapefruit, banana, pineapple, ahh, bless my potatoes, I can't remember!" Sham pined.

Sham continued to mumble and recite different fruits to himself while they rode up the mountain in full disguise. The only unbelievable thing about the image of nine orks riding up the mountainside on horseback was the oddity that they were doing so in broad daylight. Their only hope was that no roving eyes were watching them from the mountain.

After another hour of climbing in the direction the mural had led them, Grandalf announced, "We're here."

Looking up, Frobo saw the entrance to the Orkhold as plain as the day itself. Set into the mountainside, a statue jutted out of the stone. It stood there, as still as any statue, and faced them with a motioning hand, as if it was directing some invisible army. Behind the statue, a stone door was clearly hewn in the mountainside, next to another sign with text in the same strange language of the sign they'd read before, reiterating this door was the mountain's entrance, and they needed to state the password.

"Would you look at that?" said the voice of Wondell from a tall, slender ork. "Is it just me, or is that statue of the filmmaker himself?"

"By Middlearth!" exclaimed Grandalf. "I never would've recognized it, but it's a spitting image of him. These orks, or whoever constructed this door, must be quite taken with his work. We must be on our utmost guard."

"But Grandalf," said Sham, "how will we get in? By the film-maker himself, I can't remember the password!"

"Fortunately, Sham, I do remember it. And I also remember which ork you are because you haven't shut your mouth since I disguised you. But since I am about to utter the password that opens this door, I will state for the final time, be silent!"

At last, the dense hobbick seemed to get the message, and he did shut his mouth. The ork version of Grandalf stood before them and faced the door, but for some reason his posture assumed a certain dramatic flair. He took a firm stance with his feet as if he was about to have to withstand an extreme gust of wind, though they hadn't felt the faintest gale for miles. He then outstretched both of his arms like they were eagles wings. Just as he was about to exclaim the password in what was sure to cause the triumphant opening of the stone door, he was interrupted, to the surprise of not one member of their company, by Sham.

"Mellon!" cried Sham. "Mellon! Mellon! Mellon!"

Grandalf groaned in frustration and threw up his hands. "Ridiculous hobbick, I wanted to say it this time! Don't you ever know when to keep your mouth shut? I wanted to say it this time!"

The wizard's ork face seethed with anger, and as he continued to verbally berate Sham, Frobo noticed that the door remained closed.

"Excuse me, Mister Grandalf," said Martin, "But I don't believe that was the password. The door still hasn't opened."

"What?" said Grandalf.

"The door hasn't opened sir... 'Mellon' wasn't the password."

"It... wasn't?" Grandalf began, "I mean, of course it wasn't. Why would they make the password the same as the one that was in the films? Wouldn't that be a little obvious? Next time, keep your mouth shut and leave the passwords to the wizards, Sham."

"Right sir," said Sham. "Of course, I will sir, and trust me, I really am trying to, I just keep on letting it open. Stupid good for nothing Gramgee..." he scolded himself. "Now look what you've gone and done! We'll never get through that door now, will we? All because you had to open your big mouth. And they told you not to open it enough times, but you just couldn't listen, could you?"

Frobo had to shut his ears along with Happy and Martin at the uncomfortable conversation. Grandalf however, was truly finished listening to Sham. Taking a kerchief from his knapsack, the wizard strode over to Sham and tied it over his mouth. "The kerchief is a reminder to you, young Hobbick. Don't speak! If you remove the kerchief, I'll have to find some other way, some *magical* way, to keep your mouth closed. I hope I make myself clear." The ork illusion of Sham struggled and squirmed and flailed his arms out like a turtle that had been rolled over on its shell.

"Now that we have that problem settled," said Grandalf.

"You should've done that ages ago," said Ringo. "At last, I can hear myself think without that bludger-brained mischance interjecting all of his hobbified wisdom."

"Don't lump us in with him," said Happy. "The poor bloke may have the sense of a log, but it's a good-hearted log that means well for the most part."

"Enough about Sham," said Martin. "I still have the creeps from when he was talking to himself earlier. Now that he really has shut it, aren't you going to get us into the mountain, Grandalf?"

"Yes," Grandalf said. He brushed a long white strand of hair from his eyes that had fallen over them during the fit of madness when Sham had said the incorrect password before he could. The hair was a nice touch for his disguise, for if he spoke to any of the orks in the mountain, they'd surely note the age in his voice.

"Yes, that password... it was right on the tip of my tongue, it was, before that hobbick opened his yapper. Of course, I wasn't going to say, 'Mellon.' That would have been far too obvious."

"And what exactly, were you going to say?" asked Uniborn. The ork disguise somehow could not suppress the bearing of the Grondorian knight. Frobo could only shake his head and marvel at the man. He had never thought an ork could look so noble and knightly.

They all waited in anticipation. For it seemed that the wizard was about to make a great proclamation. One so great and magical that perhaps the entire mountain would collapse beneath their feet. Grandalf spread his arms wide again like he was trying to grasp the very air. His eyes blazed with fierce intensity. Then he cried out at the top of his tongue, "Ellonmay!"

When nothing at all happened, he sighed before beginning to utter a lengthy phrase that sounded to Frobo very much like absolute nonsense, "Ademarktray, Andalfgay, Egolaslay, Andyway Erkisay, Iddlearthmay Enterprisesway Mtay! Imligay! Odofray Agginsbay!"

"What in Middlearth is he saying?" Frobo asked Roban.

"Sounds like a new language," said Roban. "Though admittedly it is a strange sounding one... certainly one that I have never heard spoken before. But then again, he is getting quite old... perhaps he's cracking."

"Ilbobay Agginsbay!" The Grandalf ork continued to utter the nonsensical language at the door and statue for all of an hour before hurling his staff onto the ground and collapsing onto the hard stone in a heap.

Their hope for entering this door seemed as foolish as the hopes that the very similar fellowship had had of entering the door to the haunted mines, eleventy-one years ago. Then the way into the mountain had been a riddle, but what the answer was this time, Grandalf seemed unable to decipher.

Frobo stared at the likeness of the filmmaker that had been etched out of the stone, standing tall in directorial posture. He looked as if he was pointing to someone, perhaps motioning to an actor to stand in a certain position for a shot, or perhaps reminding one of the orks of their lines for the next scene. A thought occurred to him... the password in the films had been a riddle, but perhaps this time the clue to this riddle was standing right before them.

"Grandalf," said Frobo, jumping over to the wizard as if he was a spring rabbit. "How do you say the filmmaker's name in the strange language you've been speaking?"

"Eterpay Acksonjay," Grandalf muttered.

Without a moment's warning, the stone door swung into the mountainside.

"So that was the asswordpay," said Roban.

The light of midday flooded the apparently empty chamber that the doors swung into. From the dark hall the pungent odor of ork's excrement arrested the fellowship so that they almost lost their wits and turned round on the spot. Their borrowed horses needed no encouragement to leave and return to their home in Slumbervell. Frobo had never seen horses run as fast as theirs sped away down the mountainside after each companion had retrieved the small amount of supplies they were allowed to carry into the cave by Grandalf.

"Now," Grandalf whispered, "I will remove the handkerchief from Sham's mouth... but let it not be taken as a sign to speak and converse. Remain as silent as possible throughout our journey below the mountain. You know our mission."

"For the glory of rescuing the Lady Ellamir," said the voice of Uniborn.

"And for the..." Roban began.

"Horses, yes we know already..." interrupted Martin as his short ork illusion rolled his eyes.

"We enter the mountain... now," said Grandalf, and without another word, he untied the gag from Sham's mouth.

From the hobbick issued a nasty guttural *grawl*. Strangely, it sounded to Frobo like he was coughing up of rotten fish bones.

"That'll do just fine if you must make a noise," Grandalf muttered. "You sound just like a proper ork, Sham."

Tears flooded the hobbicks transfigured face in a dramatic flood of emotions. "I can speak again! I can speak again!" he whispered in complete restrained jubilee.

CHAPTER 13

THE PATHETIC ILLITERATE

THE TALL VISAGE OF THE ORK THAT SHROUDED ITSELF AROUND Grandalf's body stalked into the darkness of the mountain. The other members of the fellowship followed. Not a moment after Roban passed over the threshold, the stone doors clanged shut behind him. He was the last one in, and the light of the open doors vanished. They fellowship was enveloped in complete darkness. Frobo waited in the silence, listening to their every breath as they stood in the black. He couldn't help but think this was about the time that Grandalf should reveal some secret hidden light like he did in the films. Perhaps the wizard was thinking the same thing, but before any such light could be revealed, Frobo heard footsteps. He guessed by the clear sound of each one, that they were not fifty paces away, and walking towards them, but he had no way of confirming this notion.

Chills of fear crept down Frobo's spine. The steps that approached them were soft and light, but prodding and swift, and Frobo imagined that it must be a dark creature indeed that made them. As they came closer and closer, Frobo thought he could hear not two feet stepping, but three! And the third trailed the other two, or led them, in sound entirely different than the others. The third foot of the loathsome creature clanged upon the stone, while its other two feet padded lightly upon it. Perhaps its third foot had been shod as a horse's hoof. Though Frobo had never shod a horse himself, he had heard that men sometimes shod their horses. Imagining this creature, this thing that walked towards them with a third shod foot terrified him. And to think, they had only been in this dreadful mountain for thirty seconds. Now the three footed creature was not ten paces away, and Frobo expected to hear the harsh broken gnashing voice of the tortured mutilated monster at any moment.

The voice he did hear was not what he expected, "Oowhay oesgay erethay?" it said. Each syllable of the voice echoed off the dark stone walls like a resounding gong. The voice was that of an old man, perhaps the same age as Grandalf, however old he was. The language was the same unintelligible jargon that Grandalf had spoken the password in.

"Orkway's oowhay ishway otay ecomebay embermays ofway eethay eefray orkways mtay!" rasped Grandalf from next to Frobo in the most orkish voice he could muster.

The sound of a striking match preceded a small flame that shone in front of the creature. Frobo's eyes followed the flame as it lit a torch the creature was holding and illuminated the chamber, the creature, and the fellowship of the films. The creature that stood before them was not a *creature* at all. It was...

"Radagrass the Tan™?" exclaimed Sham. The members of the fellowship each groaned in unison, for when he spoke, Sham sounded very much like a hobbick, and very little like an ork.

"Yes, of course I am Radagrass!" the old man said, "But who are you? No ork has ever been smart enough to decipher our password. They always have to wait outside until nightfall when we open the gates. If I couldn't see you with my own eyes, I'd say you were men or elfs or something even worse, trying to get in here. And even though you have the look of orks, at least one of you has the sound of something else! Something finer and softer."

Sham blessedly did not respond to this, but Roban spoke up in a gruff orkish voice, "We didn't decipher the password... it was given to us by my nephew."

"By your nephew?" asked Radagrass. The old wizard of legend raised an eyebrow and looked inquisitively at Roban. "I didn't know orks had nephews."

Frobo winced and bit his lip. Roban had just given them away with a mistake so stupid Sham might have made it. But he didn't quaver or become silent, instead the ghoulish face leaned in close to Radagrass and grinned. "Oh yes," he snarled, "my nephew told me. Us orks, we have nephews. But it just so happens that my *nephew* is also my half-brother, and my cousin."

Radagrass turned up his nose in disgust and shuddered.

"Ork incest!" laughed Roban. "It really can get confusing sometimes, can't it boys?" Roban started bellowing harsh disgusting laughter at this quip, which Frobo did not find amusing in the slightest. But all of the others of the fellowship laughed or at least feigned laughter to keep up the appearances of orks.

Radagrass muttered to himself in apparent disgust. "Well, if you do want to join up, I suppose we'd better get you sorted out. Follow me."

They had no choice but to follow Radagrass and the light of his torch. Frobo's mind was racing. This wasn't what Grandalf had planned for them. Perhaps one or two of them should slip away and hide in the shadows until Radagrass was gone. Grandalf spoke up before any such plan could be enacted.

"And what are you doing with the Free Orks, Radagrass? I thought you were fighting for the other side... I woulda stuck my blade in you if I'd seen you anywhere else besides here."

"A fair question, my ork, a fair question," said Radagrass. "I was indeed on the 'other side' until the films were being made. Of course, I'm sure you've seen them, but since you're orks, you'd have absolutely no way of knowing that before the films, there were also books written about the same story."

"Really?" said Sham, "you don't say!" He elbowed Frobo, grinned and winked to indicate his delight that he was playing the part of the ork. The fellowship all held their breath dreading that this would begin some conversation between Sham and Radagrass to reveal their true identities. But Radagrass simply continued. Sham had sounded enough like an ork that time.

"I know that you all can't read, but it will suffice to say that the depiction of myself in the books left much to be desired. I was made out to be no more than a fool, I was. But when Sauluman™ and the filmmaker started making the second round of films, I approached them with a proposition. After the films were released, I'd help them do their dirty business by watching over their ork armies or whatever else they needed me to do. I just asked that they'd give me a more favorable and important role in the films so I could show the audience and Middlearth my true self. And that's exactly what they did... bless them! Bless the both of them. Now, I watch this gate and keep tabs on their growing ork army... and in the meantime, I watch the films every night in the big room with the orks, projected on the cave wall. It's a wonderful life, being able to see yourself in the films."

Without another word, the Grandalf ork's own staff appeared in a flash of movement from beneath his ragged clothing. He stretched it out towards Radagrass, who seemed to sense its power and extended the end of his staff towards Grandalf. In an instant, two separate blinding flashes of light, one white and one brown filled the dark hallway. The fellowship's disguises melted away as Grandalf's power was funneled instantly towards the light of his staff. The two lights converged, clashing against each other like two shooting stars smashing together in the night sky.

A sound like lighting peeled through the cave as the two lights battled in mid-air. Each wizard seemed to be struggling to keep hold of his staff. "I should have known it was you Grandalf," shouted Radagrass. "Orks don't know how to read pig latin!"

"And I should have known that you would prove yourself an even greater fool than the portrayal of you in the old hobbick's books," said Grandalf. The two wizards stood in the struggle of light. So strong was the grip on his staff, that it seemed the bones of Grandalf's knuckles would break through the skin of his fingers at any point. But he did not let go, and the two lights dazzled the eyes of the onlooking members of the fellowship.

"Old Grandalf, with your clever tongue," replied Radagrass as he continued to struggle to hold his staff. "Your once white robes are looking grey of late. For you are old and you are weak. Now I will cast you down just like the *Witching* did, when he broke your staff!"

But at this, Grandalf laughed and threw back his head as his white hair flowed from the power that was coming through him and out of his staff. "Your precious *Witching* never broke my staff, you pathetic illiterate!"

As Radagrass tried in vain to comprehend what this could mean, the light from his staff faded and became completely enveloped by white fire. Radagrass was then thrown back against a rock wall and lay still, unconscious, but perhaps still alive. A trickle of blood dripped down from his nose onto his brown robes. Grandalf approached the unconscious wizard, as the rest of the fellowship stood in awe of him. While their companion the wizard had stood high and proud as a strong man during the fight, he quickly hunched over and seemed considerably shorter. He hobbled toward Radagrass as a feeble beggar might have.

"That was amazing!" exclaimed Sham. "I've never seen a wizard's fight before, sir. And I thought for sure when he said he would cast you down like the *Witching*, that you were nothing more than a goner. I'm still not sure how you got out of that one. You didn't look quite as powerful in the films as that *Witching* fellow."

"Didn't I?" asked Grandalf. A wry smile formed around his lips as he spoke to the hobbick. "How intriguing. Then I am glad our enemies share your ignorance, Sham. It seems that no matter how many times we tell you to rid your mind of the films that you'll be unable to. But perhaps their fallacies can be our greatest weapon against the enemy. Come. We must hide ourselves. Someone will surely have heard this fight."

"But what of our disguises?" asked Wondell, seeing his true self and the others.

"My power is spent for the time being," said Grandalf. "Perhaps, if I still had my ring," he glanced at Frobo, "then things would be different. But alas, we must go on for now in only the secrecy of the shadows."

Frobo not only felt the pain of Grandalf's jab, but the weight of the others despising looks. Of course, they all blamed him as if he himself had stolen the rings. They'd all become so prejudiced and judgmental, and Frobo didn't understand why.

Before continuing their descent into the mountain, Ringo and Uniborn bound the hands of Radagrass and gagged his mouth. Sham pined that it was the greatest waste of a kerchief he'd ever witnessed, but he was overruled. When he was tied, they hid him in a dark crevice of the cave between two black pillars of jagged stone. Frobo didn't want to think about how far into the mountain the crevice went, or what creatures might have been lurking inside of it. It wasn't like they could take Radagrass with them, and neither could they leave him out in the open for any roving ork to find. And so, they laid him in the crevice. Frobo just hoped the poor wizard wouldn't have to lay there for all eternity.

Grandalf then led them through a tunnel of stone by the faintest light his staff could produce, and the company followed, with weapons drawn, in silent dread of what they would find the further into the mountain they crept. Frobo felt the cool handle of *Itch* in his hands and wondered if the sword would have any merit were they forced to fight the orks. He imagined tens of thousands of orks rushing for them in this dark wet cave, all at once. Would he feel as helpless as he had felt on the wagon when he tried to *snap the reins?* Or would the slow awakening courage of his ancestors overtake him, allowing him to fight for the Lady Ella with honor? The Lady Ella... now there was a comforting thing to lift one's spirits when imaging the things that might lurk inside dark black crevices beneath mountains. She had been down here for days now, and Frobo was probably the best hope she had. *"Well, you'd best start acting like it then, Frobo,"* he said to himself.

The dark tunnel reeked of foul odors. Ork filth, or the filth of some larger more dreadful creature littered the place. The smooth stone they walked on was wet and covered in a slippery moss. The tunnel, which was the only visible pathway to them, climbed high above their heads so that the fellowship had to crawl on all fours to traverse it. It then fell further and further into slippery slimy darkness. With every step, Frobo marveled that not a single one of them had yet fallen. When at last they reached the bottom of the steep descent, the corridor seemed to funnel out into a broader network of caves. It was nothing fancy as it had not been crafted by the dwarfs, as the haunted mines of the films had been. No, Frobo surmised that this network had only been hewn into the stone by rushing water over many years. He did not know where it had all gone, but the stone was smooth and polished as only water could make it, like the round rocks of a Chire creek.

Grandalf led them through one of the passages out onto what seemed to be a sort of broad flat platform, behind which was a vast flat stone wall. Though they couldn't entirely see it, for the light of Grandalf's staff was still only barely a glow, it felt to Frobo like they were now in a very large open chamber. Their boots echoed with every step and the airflow had completely changed. There was even a faint wind here, but still there was no light save the light of Grandalf's staff.

But stranger than that was what they found at their feet. All sorts of odd trinkets were splayed across the platform: swords, scepters, bows, arrows, scimitars, helms, breastplates, a light paste that looked like paint, and several crude likenesses of horses that had been hewn from wood. Frobo walked over to one of the swords and picked it up. Although it had been painted to appear like a real sword, it was made entirely of wood.

"What in Middlearth could all of this be?" asked Wondell, who held the flimsy likeness of a war helmet in his hands. "These are like the playthings of children..."

Frobo gazed out across the vast chamber away from the huge stone wall behind them. Grandalf too was curious to see what lay beyond the platform, and he walked to its edge with Frobo. The soft glow of his staff seemed to ignite, kindling a greater fire within the thing that wielded a bright blaze of light. They then saw that once past the end of the flat platform where they stood, the cave rose in levels away from them like broad stairs that spanned a distance so great it could have been a furlong. Every few feet another level jutted up from the rock, like smoothly hewn stairs. But the breadth and width of this chamber of the cave was incalculable. Frobo would not have thought a chamber so massive could exist beneath a mountain. It was enormous. An entire army could have sat on the stone levels that rose every few feet in steps across the vast span of the chamber.

"Grandalf," said Martin, stunned at the sight, "where are we?"

"On a stage," said Roban. "We're on the stage of a massive ork theater."

"It's not just a theater," said Grandalf. "Look at that."

Grandalf's forefinger was outstretched to a shiny dark box that was suspended before them and out above the stone seats of the theater. A small pin sized red light like the eye of a bird was shining on it.

"What is that?" asked Uniborn.

"That," said Grandalf, "is something I've only ever seen once before. It was on the ship of the filmmaker. It's a high definition, three-dimensional camera. And we're not just standing on the stage of a theater... we're standing on the set of a film studio. Run!"

But before they could exit the same way that they entered, a stone trap door fell from atop the tunnel where they'd entered the platform, blocking their escape. The fellowship stood on the stage, with no apparent way out of the studio. Frobo gripped *Itch* with every ounce of strength he had. The *Three-Dimensional Camera*, or whatever Grandalf had called it, was moving closer to them.

Wondell's hands flashed with whiplike speed to Frobo's right, stringing and letting loose an arrow at the suspended camera. The black glass window broke as the arrow struck it, shattering into a thousand pieces, and the red light of the camera died. Wondell's arrow had killed the thing. The pole that held the camera up shuddered as the box was injured and slowly the camera was let down in front of them. Ringo strode out, bellowed with a bear-like roar and swung his axe at the thing, obliterating and decapitating it from the long pole that held it.

Then, from beyond the steps of the vast theater, they heard the sound of marching steps, and at their utmost end, from the highest steps in the back of the theater a ring of bright red light appeared. It began like a barely visible sunrise, but it grew brighter and brighter with the ever-growing sound of marching steps and ork howls.

"They are coming!" said Grandalf.

"Doesn't that mean we should be somewhere else?" said Sham, who was quaking and trembling next to Frobo like a coward. Frobo was also afraid of course, but he had no intention of revealing it in the way Sham was. "Like in the films when you said, 'they are coming,' but then you said 'run!' right afterwards, Mister Grandalf!"

"And where exactly do you propose that we should run?" cried Grandalf. "We are surrounded! And for the last time Sham, this is real life, not the films!"

"Onway eethay ontrarycay!" boomed a growling voice that was somehow being magically amplified throughout the theater. Each member of the fellowship froze. The sound of marching ceased.

"Who are you?" shouted Wondell into the empty theater. "Show yourself!"

"And speak in a language we can all understand," cried Uniborn.

Cackling laughter echoed through the theater from the magically amplified voice. Frobo wondered at the sound. Could it have been amplified the same way the sound of the films was? Through the giant booming speakers next to the projector screen? Despite his confusion at the amplification of the laughter, he clearly recognized it, just as they all did.

"Hello Barzabag," said Grandalf through gritted teeth.

The gargling guttural projected voice of Barzabag spoke back to them. Frobo couldn't see Barzabag, but upon hearing his voice, recollected the image of the hulking ork. In his mind's eye, he pictured his shining fangs, beaming yellow eyes, and grey bare chest. He even thought he could feel the foul breath of his voice when the ork spoke. "Good day, my old acquaintances who delight to speak in falsehoods. And old man, unfortunately, I must tell you that you are incorrect in your statement that you are in real life, and not the films!" The cackling laughter of thousands of orks echoed through the theater from the ring of light beyond.

"Is that so?" said Grandalf.

"Yes, that is so," replied Barzabag. "For the all-seeing suspended black box before you is indeed a *Three-Dimensional Camera*. And as we speak, this very instant, it is filming you. That's right Grandalf, you, yourself are being filmed. And you will be in a film. Not some carbon copy hollywood actor dressed up with a painted face to look like you, but you yourself, Grandalf™! And I, Barzabag, the one who trapped you and captured you on this film, will profit greatly from it." Cackles of laughter erupted from the host of orks that were just out of sight, somewhere beyond the outermost stone rings that overlooked the stage.

"We have seen this box you speak of... but I must apologize," Grandalf pined. "We had no idea it was a *Three-Dimensional Camera* when we destroyed it. You'll have to forgive us, I am so old and out of touch, I had no idea what the thing was, and neither did any of my companions. First, we shot the thing with an arrow, and then we smashed it to bits with an axe. Unless you have another one of those cameras, I don't think you'll be filming anything at all."

Nothing but silence could be heard throughout the theater for several awkward moments as Barzabag tried to comprehend what had happened. "You did... what?" the voice through the loudspeakers screamed.

"We destroyed the camera," repeated Grandalf.

"But that was the only one we had!" cried Barzabag from the speakers. His voice reminded Frobo of a whining hobbick lad whose father had just told him it was time for bed.

"You can't blame us!" replied Grandalf. "Not only did we not give consent to be filmed, but we also don't even know what a *Three-Dimensional Camera* is."

A loud screeching cry followed by the sounds of crashing and breaking came from the speakers.

Uniborn stood with his sword drawn near the front of the stage, listening to the exchange between Grandalf and Barzabag. At the sound of Barzabag breaking things and screaming through the speakers at the loss of his camera, he decided to speak up. "Listen to me, you monster scum" he began, "I have not come here to be filmed or to converse with you in the ridiculous language of Pig Latin. I have come for one thing, and one thing alone. The hand of the Lady Ellamir!"

"Wait, no Uniborn. Don't say that," said Roban, coming up from behind Uniborn and grabbing him.

"Away from me, second class thief! I can speak for myself!" said Uniborn shoving Roban back. "I am Uniborn, Knight of Grondor! The hand of the Lady Ellamir is something I will not leave here without, ork."

The voice of Barzabag sounded confused through the speaker. "You just want... her hand?" he said.

"Yes," exclaimed Uniborn. "I state my intention here and now before all. I will take the hand of the Lady Ellamir in marriage. And none shall prevent me, least of all a second-rate horse thief like you, Roban, and least of all a power hungry ork like yourself, Barzabag! Now tell me once and for all, has she been sullied? Has my future bride been kept pure? If you allow me to take her hand in marriage, we will all of us leave in peace."

"Uniborn listen," said Roban. "He thinks you mean..."

"Silence vagabond!" cried Uniborn. His commanding voice boomed and echoed across the stone stadium of seats. "If I must tell you again, it will be your head!"

Roban crossed his arms and sighed in frustration, rolling his eyes. Frobo wondered what he was so concerned about. Did Roban want the Lady's hand in marriage for himself? Or did Roban understand something about this situation that the rest of them were missing.

"You are trapped and outnumbered and have destroyed my personal property!" growled Barzabag. "For that, there must be payment! But you, brash speaking Uniborn, Knight of Grondor, I have heard of you before. There is no doubt you would not escape from this place with your life if I chose to prevent you, but you would take many Free Ork lives with you. I will let you go with the hand of the Lady Ellamir, though I do not wish to part with it. Tell me, which of her hands you would take with you in marriage? Tell me, and I will let you be on your way."

"Which hand do I want..." mused Uniborn aloud. "What in Middlearth is he talking about?"

"Bring the Lady Ellamir to me!" they overheard Barzabag say through the loudspeaker.

"Don't you realize what he's going to do!" said Roban. "He's going to..."

"For the last time!" cried Uniborn. "Would you be quiet? I'm trying to think. Now why in Middlearth would that monster ask me *which* hand I want... it doesn't matter to me which hand I take as long as it's *her* hand..."

"Uniborn, he's going to cut off one of her hands," said Roban, striding back to Uniborn's side. "That idiot just wants you to choose, left or right!"

"What!" cried Uniborn. "No, he isn't, you foul-minded criminal!"

Then they heard the voice of Ella through the speaker. "Get your hands off of me! What is this about Barz?"

Each member of the fellowship listened with hushed lips and trembling hearts, for the Lady Ellamir was precious in kind to all of them. At the sound of her soft voice, even when heard through the speaker, they were all in some way arrested, as if a calming spell had been placed upon the whole company.

The voice of Barzabag quickly broke that spell. "Do you know who has come to visit us today, my future bride?"

Frobo shuddered at those words in Barzabag's voice.

"Do I look like a mind reader, Barz?" she replied.

"Humor me," Barzabag chuckled. "Guess..."

"Oh Barz, come on! You know I don't like it when you make me guess."

Frobo found himself glancing to Roban as the two of them made eye contact, eyes squinting in confusion. Had they just heard Ella flirting with an *ork?* Frobo shook his head as hard as he could and looked from fellowship member to fellowship member. Each of them had the same dead eyed stare into space as they listened to the conversation in pure stupefaction.

"Guess! Please!" whined Barzabag. "Do it for me just this once, *Ellalellalella!*"

"Barz, I told you not to call me that anymore," she protested playfully. Had Frobo heard her giggle after that last statement? He was starting to feel nauseous, and he was sure that the rest of them felt the same.

"Okay, okay," the ork replied. The words sounded so strange when spoken in the harsh, grinding tone of his voice. "Just guess for me, please. I really want you to guess who it is that has come to visit us today!"

Ella sighed in frustration and said, "Okay! Okay. Just stop breathing so heavily! I can't stand it when you do that. Alright, who came to visit us today... who came to visit us today... ummm, the person you've been waiting for ever since I got here... Sauluman?"

"No!" shouted Barzabag so loudly that Frobo flinched and thought the loudspeaker might explode. The hobbicks had broken several of their speakers back in the Chire by having the noise too loud during the black rider screeching scenes.

"Geez, Barz," scolded Ella. "Would you calm down? I'm standing right in front of you, I can hear you, you don't have to scream!"

"Sorry," the ork apologized. "I'm so terribly sorry, my sweet blood cake!"

A sound like the crack of a whip peeled through the speaker. "I told you not to call me that anymore! That's disgusting! Do I look like I want to be called your 'sweet blood cake' for the next forty years? Believe me when I tell you Barzabag, the next time I hear you call me that, I'll slap you even harder."

Martin whispered from behind Frobo, "they seem to have a very interesting relationship..."

"I'm sorry!" Barzabag's voice yelled through the speaker again. "I just... I just forgot, that's all!"

Frobo heard the sound of other orks laughing softly in the background, but this was quickly interrupted by Barzabag. "Perhaps you all will think it's still funny when I stick this blade in you and feed you to the wolves."

The laughter ceased quite abruptly.

"Oh Barzy," Ella continued. "I just don't know about us sometimes! I mean, you're a strong, powerful, dominating, *virile* ork..." Frobo couldn't help but notice an especially sour look on the faces of Ringo, Wondell, Uniborn, and Roban as she said this. "And well, I'm just a woman. Don't you think we just might be too incompatible?"

"Oh no! No, no, not at all, my sweet bloo..." Barzabag paused just in time.

"You're sweet what?" snapped Ella. "Finish the sentence."

"My sweet... blunderer, was what I was going to say."

"Your sweet blunderer? What in the world is that supposed to mean?" Ella asked.

"Never mind, forget I ever said it," Barzabag said in an overeager voice. "Just guess again! Who do you think came to visit us?"

"Ugghh," Ella groaned. "Okay! I know it can't be your mom because you killed her in a fight over a rat two years ago... it can't be Sauluman because I already guessed him... your brother is deformed and living chained up in the bottom of a well, so that rules him out. Hmm... the filmmaker?"

"Wrong again!" shouted Barzabag just as loudly as before.

There was nothing but silence from the speaker for a moment. Then Ella at last responded. "Barzabag," she said, in a calm soothing voice. "I thought I told you to stop screaming at me?"

"Oh yes, that's right you did, my lovely flower," Barzabag drawled. "And I'm so, so sorry. Just please, guess for me once more!"

"No," she said. "I'm finished with your little guessing game and getting shouted at every time I'm wrong. Tell me who's here, or I'm leaving."

"Alright, fine," shouted Barzabag, now angry in his own fashion. "I was trying to play a little game and have a little fun, but if you're going to act like that, I'll tell you! Here, in the cave, on the stage of the theater, and with us today at this very moment are the gang of miscreants I rescued you from."

"Rescued her!" shouted Uniborn. "You petulant lying monster, how dare you!" but both Barzabag and Ella seemed unable to hear him and continued to converse with each other.

"Sorry Barz, who are you talking about?" asked Ella. "I can't remember very much of my life before I met you... just bits and pieces here and there, although a there is a very vague memory of an annoying horse thief with bad breath."

Roban rolled his eyes and shrugged his shoulders.

This sparked laughter from all of the orks behind the speakers. Frobo imagined Barzabag grinning ear to ear. "You never told me you thought he had bad breath," the ork said.

"Well, not as bad as yours of course, Barz," said Ella to the abrupt end of his laughter. "Just that he had bad breath for a man."

"Of course," said Barzabag, "But on to the point. One of these men, whom I rescued you from, has offered to leave us if he is allowed to take one of your hands with him. Of course, they are all trespassing, and the rest of them will be brought to horrible and wretched deaths. I have agreed to give him one of your hands in exchange for his departure, and now he only needs tell us which hand he desires. Let's see what he has to say..."

"Ella, Ella!" shouted Uniborn. "Can you hear me? It is I! It is Uniborn! Are you alright?"

"Am I supposed to know who this is?" Ella asked in reply to Uniborn. She could hear them now.

"Of course, you are! It is I! And I have come for your hand in marriage!" shouted Uniborn. "Come away with me Ella and let us leave this ork dungeon!"

"Listen to me, whoever you are," said Ella. "I don't know you, or know what you're doing here, but I'm not letting you take either of my hands with you."

"*Take either of my hands...*" Uniborn muttered, upon whom comprehension was perhaps finally dawning, looking down at his own hands and holding them up to his face with the gleaming eyes of one who has just had an epiphany.

"Unfortunately," said Barzabag through the speaker, "that is not your decision. I will cut off one of your hands myself and give it to this man if it will make him leave. He is far too valiant of a warrior for us to risk fighting him. Now tell me Uniborn, which hand should I cut off for you? You have until the count of three, or I'm cutting off both of her hands to make sure you leave!"

A sharp high-pitched scream pierced their ears through the speaker. "She has fainted..." said Barzabag. "All the better, it will make it easier to cut without movement. One!"

"It might be time for you to explain you don't want her hand cut off!" shouted Ringo to Uniborn.

"Two!" the voice of Barzabag shouted through the speaker.

"Do something Uniborn!" shouted Wondell.

But Uniborn seemed suddenly mute under this pressure and unable to comprehend that the Lady Ella's hand was about to be hewn free by the sharp scimitar of Barzabag. Frobo thought she would likely bleed to death before she awoke from her fainting spell. Just as Frobo started to hear the number "Three!" and a rending slicing sound stream through the speaker, the voice of a member of the company, but not Uniborn's, interrupted the countdown.

"Wait!" A suave yet rugged voice cut through the eager cackling of orks through the speaker that were eager to see blood. It was Roban who had spoken.

"Who is that?" said Barzabag. "Which hand do you want me to cut off?"

"Believe me Barzabag. Cutting off one of those hands to get rid of Uniborn the Magnificent is the *last* thing you want to do," Roban said.

A silent pause proceeded, before the ork spoke again. "And why is that?" Barzabag said through the speaker.

"Barzabag, Barzabag..." drawled Roban. "You know something? You surprise me. You're a smart ork. You know that one hand of the woman you love isn't worth losing fifty good soldiers over. Because obviously, you'd have to be flat out dumb to not know how capable of a fighter that Uniborn the Grondorian Knight is. But I thought you were smarter than that... to let him just walk away like that when you could've had... well, I don't know if I should tell you now."

"Tell me what? Get on with it, I haven't got all day!" shouted Barzabag. His words were quick, and he sounded extremely annoyed.

"Oh Barzo," laughed Roban. "As smart as you are, I'm sure

you thought of it already. I mean, come on look where we are right now. Think about what you were trying to do earlier. With all of that in mind, I just don't understand why you would let Uniborn walk out the door. You are one confounding ork, do you know that?"

"Well of course," said Barzabag, although Frobo perceived a certain lack of surety in the ork's voice. "I would never let him walk out the door... and why wouldn't I let him walk out the door?"

"Barzy, Barzy, Barzy," laughed Roban. "You're a funny guy. I like you. I really do. But answer me only this. Where am I standing right now?"

"In my dark cave of madness and terror!" Barzabag shouted to the laughter of the other orks.

"Close, but really think about it. Where are we all standing right now?" Roban repeated.

"Umm..." Barzabag began, sounding very unsure of himself. "On... In.... *Raawwwrrr*, I don't know, just tell me already, you stupid riddling man! Tell me or I'll eat the Lady Ella!" he threatened.

"No, you will not!" Ella shouted, apparently awake again. "How dare you threaten me!" she said.

"Of course, I won't actually do that, my sweet blood cake!" they heard Barzabag whisper through the speaker. "But they don't know that, just play along with me..." but he was interrupted by the same slap that had come before when calling her his 'sweet blood cake.'

"I told you not to call me that anymore! It's disgusting!" she screamed.

"Barzabag, it seems that you have a lot to deal with at the moment," said Roban. "I'd hate to interrupt your lover's quarrel with my riddles and questions, so we'll leave you both here in peace. See you next time, and thanks for having us, really. It was fun to catch up, I do wish we could have stayed longer."

"No!" shouted Barzabag. His voice exploded through the speaker. Frobo winced at the sound. He *really* didn't want the speaker to blow and lose their only method of communication with Barzabag and Ella. "Tell me please! Tell me why I shouldn't let the knight leave!" The ork's voice was desperate in his pleas with Roban for the answer.

"I'm disappointed in you Barzy," said Roban. "But I suppose your ignorance can be forgiven. Barz, you do not want Uniborn to leave this cave! Because if you do... if you let Uniborn walk out that door, you will be letting one of the finest thespians in all of Middlearth slip right through your fingers!"

"Finest thespian," repeated Barzabag. "Finest thespian? What does that mean, 'finest thespian?' Someone tell me what that means!"

"It's a fancy word for an actor, Barz," said Ella through the speaker. "You know, like what the people in the films are doing. They're actors."

"I know they're actors," shouted Barzabag. "I know what an actor is."

"Of course, you do," said Roban. "And of course, that's why you wouldn't want to let one as accomplished as Uniborn just walk out your front door."

"And why is that?" said Barzabag.

"Because where we're standing right now Barz, isn't just in your cave, and isn't just a film studio, it's a stage! A stage at the front of a theater. Obviously, your Free Orks have gotten tired of watching themselves be killed and defeated over and over in the same six films again and again and again, which is why you've started making your own films! But now that your only camera has been destroyed, what are you going to do? Go back to watching the films you've already seen a thousand times?

"Or do you want to watch something completely new and completely unscripted that you've never seen before? Barzabag, imagine a completely live action, high quality, premier, larger than life play with men, hobbicks, orks, an elf, a dwarf and even an old wizard! Barzabag, we are prepared to give you the finest show in all of Middlearth. It'll be completely original, and it'll be completely yours."

"Finest show in Middlearth?" echoed Barzabag.

Uniborn stepped towards Roban and grabbed his arm. "What are you doing?" muttered Uniborn. The voice in his whisper was tense and anxious, but his face proved he was in fact mortally terrified. "You know I'm not an actor! Are you crazy?"

"Shhhhhhhhut... it," whispered Roban. "For once in your lives everyone, keep your mouths *shut*." He glanced into the eyes of every single one of his companions on the stage but held his gaze on Sham the longest. Once he was satisfied, he continued in his loud oratorical voice, "Of course it will be the finest show in all of Middlearth, Barzabag! Think of who is standing on your stage right now. First, there's the valiant Uniborn, whose fighting skills you knew of, but whose legendary acting prowess far outweighs his skill in battle. Then, as you said yourself, there's Grandalf, not an impersonator, but the real trademarked wizard himself! Next, there's four bonafide hobbicks, one of whom is the alleged descendant of the most famous hobbick who ever lived..."

"Really?" said Barzabag through the speaker. "Descendant of the most famous hobbick who ever lived?"

"The one and only!" shouted Roban. "And I haven't even gotten to the best part. Also in your show, will be the most handsome elf in Middlearth. I'm sure you've heard of Wondell the Golden-Haired. And then, after all that, the most desirable stage performer in the whole world! Ringo, *the* Rugged Dwarf."

"At your service!" Ringo said.

"That all sounds good enough," said Barzabag, "but I get worried with all of these famous names here amongst you. This show, this performance you intend to put on, how will it work...

I mean, who is coming up with the... what's the word I'm trying to think of?"

"Plot?" Ella asked.

"Yes, the plot!" Barzabag screamed. "Who will be coming up with the plot? Thank you, darling blood cake."

"Barzo, of course we'll give you complete and total editorial rights," said Roban. "But you still haven't realized the best part about all of this yet."

"Yes, I have!" shouted Barzabag.

"Good, so you know that with the names and notoriety that will be on this stage, you'll be able to attract many more orks to your theater, and you'll be able to charge admission for your new show?" said Roban.

"Admission?" said Barzabag. "What are you admitting? Speak plainly to me, you silver tongued horse thief."

"It means that the orks will have to pay you to get into the show!" explained Ella through the speaker. "So, you'll be rich. You can make a lot of money."

"Of course, I will be!" Barzabag screamed. "I'll be rich and powerful! The most powerful ork in all of Middlearth!"

"Your power and fame will know no bounds," said Roban. "But the orks won't be the only ones you'll be able to charge admission."

Whispers were barely heard through the loudspeaker. The group of orks were trying to discern the meaning of this. Frobo was personally amazed at Roban's abilities when it came to spinning this yarn. He had no idea of the end game, or if there even was one. Right now, he was trying to overcome the thought of acting on stage in front of a multitude of orks. It sounded absolutely terrifying to him.

"Ahh, you speak in too many riddles, horse thief," said Barzabag. "Who will I be able to charge admission to?"

"Just think of the names that you'll be able to advertise with," said Roban. "Wondell, the most handsome elf in all of

Middlearth; Uniborn, the gallivanting and noble knight; Ringo the Rugged Dwarf; not to mention myself, the finest gambler west of the Musty Mountains... Barzabag, isn't it obvious? There will be more beautiful women flocking to your show than orks! Soon there will be enough for every one of your soldiers to each have their own to fall in love with them! All you have to do is let us start performing and get the word out. This show will become something women all over Middlearth travel far and wide to see."

Nothing was heard through the speaker for a few moments. Then Barzabag screamed loudly, "The show starts tonight!" Raucous applause and roaring screams poured in through the speaker. Apparently, the entirety of the multitude of the Free Orks had heard the decision also, because the voices of those with the marching footsteps from beyond the rim of the theater could also be heard screaming with yells of triumph and joy.

"My future bride and I will be watching the show tonight, along with my host of orks, and their future wives, who also wish to see my new show!" cried Barzabag.

CHAPTER 14

WRITING THE PLOT

THE ORKS POURED INTO THE ROWS OF BENCH SEATS BEFORE
the stage like ants swarming the carcass of a dead animal, each
with an eager excitement to see a real live show. Roban bowed
before them like a hero from the edge of the stage. Frobo
wondered how they were ever going to get out of this mess
they'd gotten themselves into.

"It's four hours until nightfall," shouted Barzabag. "You have
until then to prepare for my show."

The members of the Fellowship of the Films were then
ushered off stage by a few burly orks. Strangely enough, they
were allowed to keep their weapons at the request of Roban,
who persuaded Barzabag to let them retain them on the
grounds of realism when the show began.

"We'd be crazy to try and fight our way out of your cave,"
Roban said, "but you'd also be crazy to deprive yourself and
your audience of the type of show we can put on with real
weapons."

Frobo still couldn't see exactly what Roban's angle was in all
of this. As far as he could tell they were in a dreadful plight now
that Grandalf's disguises had faded. He also hadn't forgotten

Radagrass, the illiterate wizard. What would happen to Roban's idea if Radagrass came back and told Barzabag this was all some big trick?

The ork guards led the fellowship through an arched passage in the stone wall behind the stage. Torches lit this tunnel as well as the many pathways that shot off to their right and left. They were led straight ahead, and the tunnel broadened and widened as they came upon a wooden structure with a swinging door. It appeared that the orks had made this 'room' inside their massive cave system. It had four walls but no roof, as one would have been entirely pointless. The ork unlocked the door and led them inside where they found mirrors on the walls, buckets of face paint, and partitions for them to change clothes behind. This must have been where the orks got into costume before making their own films. The face paint was for the orks to be able to appear like men in their films. Frobo shuddered at the thought of it.

When at last they were alone in the dressing room, Grandalf was the first to speak, "Do you have anything you wish to say to us, Roban?"

"Anything I wish to say?" repeated Roban, with a look of confusion. "Oh, yes naturally. You're welcome, for saving all of your lives of course."

"You're welcome," Grandalf chuckled, repeating the phrase. He spoke slowly as if he was having to carefully choose his words. "I might have thought as much; however, I was not planning on saying thank you."

Roban drew back and furrowed his dark brows in surprise. "Forgive me, Mister 'too tired to cast any more spells,'" said Roban. "But I did what I had to do to keep the Lady's hands from being cut off."

"And since when do you care about the hands of the Lady Ellamir?" demanded Uniborn. "Her hand was to be given to me! In marriage, imbecile!"

"I've never been in a live stage performance in my entire life," snapped Grandalf, throwing down his hands and stamping his foot on the stone floor. "I have stage fright, you idiot!" The wizard seemed to rise to a greater height than he could usually reach, as he sometimes did when angry. The effect was often used to intimidate those around him, but it completely failed to do so this time, as it was mingled with the strange confession.

"How dare you try and keep me from having the hands of the Lady Ellamir in marriage!" shouted Uniborn. Uniborn pointed his long forefinger in Roban's face as he spoke. Apparently, he was outraged that Roban had managed to find a way to save Ella's hands. Then as if a part of him broke, the tall Grondorian sprung forward, rushing at Roban until he stood but a foot from the man. "I should challenge you to a duel right now, thieving vagabond." Uniborn's black eyes burned with anger as he stared down at Roban, his face a riddled web of rage. In contrast, Roban looked exactly how Frobo would expect a gambler to. The man was cool, calm, and collected in the face of imminent danger. Roban's face was unreadable.

"Listen, Roban," said Wondell. The elf's voice cracked as he spoke, and he pushed Uniborn aside in order to gain Roban's full attention. "I know I have a beautiful face and everything, but I've never acted either. I'm not sure I can do this, not in front of a thousand orks at least."

"Count us in all the way, mate," said Martin, referring to himself and Happy as the two of them nodded eagerly. "We love acting. Live for it."

"Hold on, hold on, everyone wait a moment," said Sham. "Just who exactly are we all supposed to be playing in this production, that's what I'd like to know."

The murmuring protests of each one of them rose to a dull roar. Quite quizzically, Frobo noticed Roban take a seat on the hard stone floor, pull a deck of cards from his pocket, and begin to lay them out in front of him. What the devil was the man doing? How could he play a *game* in a time like this?

Slowly, each member of the fellowship noticed what Roban was doing and at last their rumblings ceased, save Uniborn who spoke up and said, "what is this hogwash?"

"This is a card game," said Roban, looking up at Uniborn. "I decided to entertain myself until you all were ready to listen. Now please, if you're ready, I'll explain. First, consider our situation. How many orks are out there right now, Sham?"

Sham, eager for the challenging question, began counting on his fingers with focused concentration. After several lengthy moments, and resetting his count twice, he proudly said, "Seventy at least, by my estimation."

"There, you heard it yourselves," said Roban. "Seventy at least, and he isn't wrong. Although the number is probably closer to ten thousand."

"I always thought I was good at math..." Sham said aside in a chuckle to Frobo.

"I don't care who is here with us," Roban continued, "but we aren't fighting our way through ten thousand orks, especially not with a wizard who's tired of casting spells."

"Then why don't you clue us all in on what your little plan is?" said Grandalf.

"And explain exactly what your concerns were with the hand of Lady Ellamir!" shouted Uniborn.

"As I was just saying," Roban continued. He seemed to feign annoyance that he had to explain himself. However, Frobo surmised that he was not disappointed to be the center of attention. The way the man communicated was by giving his audience small crumbles of information, just enough to keep them interested, but never enough to where he gave his true intentions away. It was a clever technique but could be extremely wearisome for the listener. "We aren't going to fight our way out of here on our own. Our disguises are lost, and we're caught in the clutches of what might just be the biggest film lover in all of Middlearth."

"Barzabag?" mocked Ringo. "He's no film lover. That ork has no appreciation for art!"

"You just don't get it, do you?" said Roban, shaking his head at all of them with airs of condescension. "He told us himself he grew up watching them, and he was so influenced by them, he decided to take a mate from the race of men for himself. Don't you see? He doesn't want to be an ork. He wants to be like us. We're practically heroes to him. He'd do anything to get to see us performing live on his own stage. His lust for real live heroes is our ticket out of here. Didn't you see how he let us keep our weapons? He probably worships us when he watches the films. That's how we're getting out of here."

"But I can't act, Roban," said Grandalf, grasping at Roban's sleeve like a pleading beggar. "I've never been on a stage in my life!"

"Neither can I," said Uniborn.

"Look around you!" said Roban. "Think about who this show is for. Do you really think these orks are going to know that you two idiots haven't performed on stage before?"

"It's a fair point," said Ringo.

"They all seem pretty dense to me sir, thick in the head if you take my meaning," said Sham.

"Exactly," said Roban. "And coming from you Sham, that's saying something. As for my concern with Lady's hand, Uniborn, do you really think I was going to let you get the blood from that hand all over whichever of my horses they let you ride off with? Not to mention the fact that I'd never let you ride away with one of my horses in the first place."

"Fair enough," Uniborn said, thinking hard to try and see if Roban's roundabout logic worked out in his head. "But how will we rescue the Lady Ella?"

"I'm still working that one out," Roban said. "But I think

the key will be getting her to be in the show with us. I imagine her up in the big box in the center of the theater with Barzabag for the first act. I just need to coax him into letting her come down and join us in the show."

"You *imagine her* now, do you Roban?" asked Ringo, his upper lip curling into a snarl as he glared at the man.

"Oh please, you know what I mean," said Roban.

Frobo wasn't quite sure he did.

"The key to this whole thing is to get the Lady Ella in the show with us," Roban said.

"And that's when we make our escape?" asked Grandalf.

"Exactly," said Roban.

"Now hold on just one moment," said Uniborn. The man pushed himself away from the stone wall he had been leaning against and stood before Roban. "The Lady Ellamir, part of a show, put on stage in front of thousands of orks to be gawked at and careened about like a... like a... like a piece of meat? I don't think I can allow that."

"Fine," said Roban. "Instead of putting her through the struggles of acting and performing before a crowd of orks, let her stay here, married to Barzabag, mothering their half-bred children and baking blood cakes for the rest of her life."

"Alright, horse thief," said Uniborn, unable to come up with another retort. "We'll do it your way." But though he resigned to follow Roban's plan, his eyes burned with wrath and hatred.

At that moment they heard a loud banging sound on the door of their dressing room. A gruff voice then shouted, "Boss man here to see you! Look sharp!"

"Well, it was kind of them to give us a warning," said Roban, rolling his eyes. "We could have been coming up with an escape plan in here."

The door swung open to reveal the huge hulking figure of Barzabag. The ork strode into the room with a proud bearing and swagger, accompanied by other large orks. Each of the orks had the same dark grey skin, though Barzabag was the palest of them all. They were a frightful sight, as they all towered over the fellowship. Their arms were strong, and their bodies were cut and chiseled like hewn stone. Barzabag still wore naught but his dirty loin cloth and long black knee-high boots that were tightly bound around his legs. His long black hair was dripped with sweat, and when he smiled, they saw his sharp catlike yellow teeth. But still, there was something about him that made him seem like a man to Frobo. Perhaps it was the fact that he wasn't trying to slaughter them like a ruthless barbarian.

Barzabag's brooding eyes scanned the room, looking from the left to the right, then back to the left. He sized up his new actors like they were one of his packs of wolves. "You look wonderful," he shouted at last. "You will be the finest actors in the finest play east of the Musty Mountains. All Middlearth will come to see my performance, and eventually, once we get another three-dimensional camera from the filmmaker, I will use your talents to create the greatest films ever made. I will be the filmmaker this time. I, myself, Barzabag the filmmaker will file for new trademarks! And you, the finest actors in all Middlearth, will help me do it."

"A truly riveting plan," remarked Roban. "Is that why you've come? To share it with us?"

"No," said Barzabag. "I have come to introduce the Lady Ella to you. For you see, after all of the *trauma* that she's been through, it just so happens that she no longer remembers any of you. And I promised her that I would allow her to meet the cast of my new production." An evil grin brimmed in Barzabag's mouth, bearing his yellow fangs to each of them.

"Doesn't remember us..." said Uniborn. "What have you done with her, you monster?" Uniborn reached for his sword but was instantly rushed by three of Barzabag's guards. They pinned the tall man to the wall before he could draw his weapon.

Barzabag laughed, ignoring the question. Frobo was growing very tired of that laugh. "What I have done to her is none of your concern, you feeble maggot! Now, I present to you, the bride to be of the most powerful ork in all of Middlearth, the first ever woman bride of an ork, the mother of my future children, the queen of my future empire, the..."

Roban yawned loudly from across the room, interrupting the diatribe and Barzabag's train of thought. He leaned against the wall with crossed arms and looked as if he was about to try and catch a quick nap.

Barzabag continued, despite visible disappointment at Roban's apparent lack of interest.

"Without further ado, I present to you, the Lady Ella," the ork said. He motioned towards the orks at his rearguard to usher her into the room.

Then the door swung open once more, and she entered. To merely say she *walked* into the room would've been an utter disgrace to her. For one as beautiful as the Lady Ella did not merely walk. Frobo could only note that she flowed into the room like the wind flows through the trees of a tranquil garden. He was mesmerized. Although, he wasn't the only one. She wore a shimmering silver dress that fell past her ankles and trailed behind her. A pale glow almost seemed to emanate from it. Though her beauty was that of a maiden queen she wore no crown atop her long, golden locks. Still, Frobo couldn't help but feel like she deserved one. He had no idea how something so beautiful could exist in such a wretched place, surrounded by such wretched creatures. Upon her bosom rested a shining necklace with a large white gemstone. Her steps made no sound, but the scent of her perfume flowed into the room like a rushing river, intoxicating each of them with sweet desire. None who beheld her were unaffected.

"My future bride," shouted Barzabag, whose voice broke the serenity of the moment. Frobo felt sick thinking of the unimaginably gorgeous woman who stood before him as the bride of the monster who was introducing her. A jealous spark struck inside of him. He had to stop this.

"Ella! Ella!" cried Uniborn. The man struggled and flailed as the ork guards restrained him, desperate to gain the attention of the Lady. "Come to me Ella. It is I! It is Uniborn! Come to me and let us leave this place together. I know you remember me! I know you remember the life we've shared together! Granted, we've never been lovers or romantically involved, but that hasn't been because I haven't tried. Run away with me Ella. Let us leave this place of darkness now and forevermore."

Frobo felt moved by the desperation in Uniborn's speech. The man's face was riddled in agony as he spoke, and though Frobo knew a fair piece in regards to their relational history, he half expected Ella to relent at his impassioned plea. The look of doubt on Barzabag's face indicated he was thinking similarly.

"Lying fiend," her clear firm commanding voice cut through the anticipation of her response. "How dare you speak to me that way. I've never met you in my entire life, and I won't be going anywhere with you. You really have gathered an amazing troupe of actors, Barz. That one almost fooled me."

The orks laughed long and loud, cackling, gargling, choking and howling at Ella's response. Uniborn fell to the ground in despair, landing on his hands and knees. He choked, gasping for breath in shock at Ella's words. Frobo's thoughts spun like a top. So, it was true. Ella, the most beautiful woman he'd ever seen before had been brainwashed by the trauma of her kidnapping. Would this make rescuing her all the more difficult?

"And who are the rest of you?" Ella asked, as her eyes scanned the dressing room for each member of the company. Whether it was from their collective awe at her beauty, or shock and fear at the horrible things that had befallen her by the orks, the members of the company were unable to speak.

Only Roban proved otherwise. He approached Ella and dropped to a knee in respect.

"My lady," Roban began. "My name is Roban, and I am known as the finest card player west of the Musty Mountains." Then without warning, Roban swiftly took the Lady's hand in his own and kissed it.

Ella seemed to almost enjoy her hand being kissed for a fleeting moment, but then she withdrew it, and slapped Roban across the face with it. Barzabag roared with a flash of anger at this, looking as if he would execute Roban for the sly attempt. "Step aside, Bloodcake," he shouted at Ella. "I'll handle this."

"You will surely not," she shouted in reply in a voice fiercer than his. "He has insulted me, and I will be the one to punish him." Barzabag stood still, with a conflicted look in his face, before relenting.

"How will you punish him?" growled Barzabag, as he glared down at the still kneeling Roban.

"I haven't decided yet," said Ella. "Just as I haven't yet decided how I will punish you for calling me 'Bloodcake' again."

Barzabag chuckled with the other orks in the room, before seeing the look on the Lady's face and turning his grin to a somber frown.

"But I can assure you this," continued Ella, as the members of the company and the ork guard looked on in fear, "I can assure you all of this: if any of you ever kisses my hand or any part of me again, you'll pay for it with your very life."

As the orks, including Barzabag shuddered behind Frobo in fear, Frobo thought he spied the left eyelid of Ella flutter in the slightest, quickest wink he'd ever seen. If it had been a wink, it had been one that only he had been capable of seeing, but its significance could have been completely inconsequential. Ella could have simply been batting a stray gnat away with her eyelashes, but perhaps she'd been trying to send him a message. What if this was all some sort of rouse, meant to fool the orks into thinking they'd brainwashed her? What if she actually did remember them?

It was a hopeful thought, for Frobo was sure that rescuing a Lady who remembered you and wanted to be rescued would be far easier than rescuing a Lady who wanted to marry an ork that you, the stranger, were stealing her away from. By Frobo's estimation, quite a bit was resting on that alleged wink, that could have merely been the twitch of an eyelid.

"So, have you decided on a punishment for this worthless slime?" asked Barzabag.

"From the looks of the wretch, it seems that he enjoyed being slapped far too much," said Ella, as she stared into the eyes of the kneeling Roban. "My threat will serve as a warning. If he tries something like that again, you can slit his throat, Barzabag." Without another word, she exited the chamber on swift moving feet, with the train of her silver dress billowing behind her. The dressing room was a dull and dreary place again once she'd departed, but the lingering scent of her perfume eased the disappointment of her swift departure.

Barzabag swaggered over to the still kneeling Roban. Somehow the ork appeared far fiercer and menacing without her in the room. He drew back his own arm and let it fly at Roban's head in what was to be a crashing blow of force, but Roban caught the blow with the swiftest reaction Frobo had ever seen. And what's more, he held the arm of Barzabag in place! Frobo had no idea (until then) how strong the man was.

Ork spears pointed at Roban in an instant. Barzabag looked at the hand holding his with terror and rage. Before he could react, Roban said, "Now, now Barz, you wouldn't want to hurt the face of one of the new actors in your show, would you? That wouldn't be very good for business."

Barzabag scowled and wrenched his hand from Roban's grasp. "No," the ork growled, "that wouldn't be very good for business at all."

"I agree," said Roban.

"So do I!" Barzabag shouted back in anger. "The show starts in ten minutes and I'm going to my box to watch with my future bride. I hope you're ready to give us a rousing performance." Without another word the ork stormed out of the dressing room, with his personal guard in tow.

Frobo anxiously awaited the start of the play behind a massive red curtain that had been hung to cover the stage. He was terrified of what was about to happen. Growing up, he had never been the theatrical type, and therefore he had no idea of what to expect. He could hear the anxious jeers and babbling voices of the throng of orks on the other side of the curtain. They sounded excited to behold the spectacle of whatever this play was going to bring them. Did they realize just how unprepared each of these 'actors' were? What would they do if Frobo forgot his lines? But what was he *thinking?* They didn't have any lines! This whole play was a complete sham! All they had was a few directions from Roban to "play to the orks vanity," and if they didn't know what to do, to try and play the part of themselves. "If you can't think of someone to play," Roban had said, "then just play yourself. The orks probably won't know the difference."

But with all of that being said, Frobo was in the opening scene. He was supposed to play the part of himself, or perhaps a version of his alleged grandfather, the most famous hobbick who ever lived, along with Happy and Martin when Grandalf came to visit them in the Chire and take them on the start of their quest. But he had no idea what he was supposed to do! However, there was no more time to ponder or plan, because at that very moment the curtain drew back, and the beaming lights shone on him, illuminating the scene to the onlooking orks.

Frobo sat in a dingy armchair and next to him stood a small empty bookshelf. A short wooden table was in front of him that was supposed to be a writing desk. The rest of the stage was totally barren of any decoration.

Playing the part of his alleged grandfather, he tried to appear as if he was back home in his old hobbick hole, safe and sound with no fear or worries of the world outside of the Chire. The voice of Roban, who was currently playing the part of the narrator, amplified through the theater out over the throng of orks. As he spoke, Frobo glanced out to see a most horrifying vision. He'd never imagined there were that many orks in all of Middlearth. He was instantly reminded of a scene from the films when an ork army presented itself to Sauluman before heading out to war.

There were thousands upon thousands of them in this audience. Their eager grinning faces were suspended in a trance of anticipation. Many of them were greedily stuffing the Chire's own popping corn into their mouths as fast as they could. Frobo remembered the orks he'd seen sitting just beyond the trees at the projector in the Chire, so long ago. In the very midst of the throng of Orks, in their own private box, Frobo spotted the Lady Ella, sitting with Barzabag, and he thought that perhaps he could even see her hand resting in his.

A jealous fire burned within him, but he steeled his nerves. *"Don't lose face!"* he told himself, sitting in his armchair. He had to act as if everything was normal. This was their best chance at rescuing the Lady. As he came back to himself, Frobo listened to Roban's narration.

"Scene One! Act One! The grandson of the most famous hobbick who ever lived sits in his cozy hobbick hole in the Chire, as hobbicks are often accustomed to doing. Their simple, dull lives are full of food and fluff, and they spend most of their time making complete imbeciles out of themselves."

Roban paused after this line, probably expecting laughter

from the orks, but instead their confused faces murmured to each other throughout the throng. Frobo saw one of them near the front row stand up. "Tell us what that word 'imbecile' means," the ork shouted. A chorus of cheering and approval roared out from the rest of the crowd. "We don't know what big words mean," he continued.

"Yeah," a different ork jeered. His skin was a dark marbled red and a single braid of hair fell from the crown of his head. He spat on those near him as he spoke and Frobo noted that the fellow was missing close to half of his teeth. He stood up in from his spot on the stone bench to address Roban. "Spare your *pig latin* for the secret door. Speak in a language we can all understand."

"He's trying to trick us!" another ork yelled.

The crowd quickly descended into chaos. They were never going to get through their play if the orks behaved this way. They were about to be out of control. Roban was trying to explain the meaning of the word when a louder voice boomed through the speakers.

"Silence!" Barzabag shouted from the box. "If you cannot control yourselves, then I will make you all leave, and I will watch the show alone. Do I make myself clear?"

In amazing unison, the orks all shouted in reply, "Yes, commander Barzabag!"

Barzabag continued, "I have asked my future bride, the amazing, beautiful woman who is so far out of all of your leagues, that I laugh to myself when I think about any of you imagining yourself with her... I have asked her to tell me what this word means, that has caused you idiots to interrupt my show."

"You mean, you didn't know what it meant neither?" shouted one of the orks from the crowd to raucous unanimous laughter.

"Who said that?" shouted Barzabag. "Who was it? Tell me

now!" But the laughter continued and the ork was not exposed by his companions.

"Silence!" shouted Barzabag to the instant reply, once again in perfect unison of, "Yes, commander Barzabag."

Barzabag stood up in his box. Snarling in anger and contempt at his army he paced back and forth inside its waist high stone walls. He still wore nothing but his loin cloth as he paced back and forth. His tall intimidating figure loomed above his now hushed soldiers. He continued, "I meant to say, I asked the Lady to confirm to me that I already knew the words meaning," he said. "And she did confirm it. The word 'imbecile' could also be used to describe *you* all. It means stupid or idiotic. Let me use it in a sentence you can understand: 'Barzabag's army of orks interrupted his show because they were imbeciles!' Now tell me, what are all of you?"

The orks shouted back in complete unison, "Imbeciles, commander Barzabag!"

"Exactly," Barzabag said, "Now shut up and watch my show."

The orks all took to their seats again and Roban continued his narration. "The lives of hobbicks are simple and dull, and most of the time to the outside world, it would seem that all they do is sit around making imbeciles out of each other," Roban paused again and this time his line received the raucous laughter from the crowd of orks he'd been expecting.

"But on this fortuitous day eleventy-one years ago," Roban continued. "And forgive me if you don't know the meaning of 'fortuitous,' this hobbick's imbecilic life was about to change."

"Knock, knock, knock, knock, knock..." Happy mimicked the sound of a loud knocking door while Martin pounded his fist against the air. They were standing at an imaginary door to Daggend. Of course, the entire scene was imaginary, save Frobo's armchair, improvised writing desk and bookcase. They had not been able to locate a free-standing door in the cave, so

they were going to have to act their hearts out for any of this to be believable.

"Hmm, I wonder who that could be?" said Frobo, glancing across his invisible hobbick hole to his invisible door. He mimed setting a newspaper down and glanced in the direction of the knocking, desperately trying to appear as if he had no idea who was at the other side. Martin and Happy knocked again.

"Alright, I'm coming!" Frobo shouted to the laughter of the orks in the crowd. He rose from his chair and started walking to the door.

When he reached the imaginary door, Frobo, whose confidence was catching up to him at the orks affirming laughter, mimed pressing his ear against the thing and said, "Who is it?"

"Goons of Middlearth Enterprises, open up. We have a warrant to search the premises for jewels, valuables, gold, treasure and *rings*," shouted Happy through the invisible door.

Frobo's heart pounded in alarm. That had not been what they'd discussed. *"Stupid Happy!"* He was trying to catch him off guard in front of all these orks so he could be the star of the show when Frobo didn't know what to say. Well, he'd show Happy once and for all.

"Goons of Middlearth Enterprises have no jurisdiction in Daggend," Frobo shouted back through the door. "You can take your warrant and stuff it where the sun doesn't shine, if you take my meaning."

Roaring laughter broke out from the orks at this.

But Happy and Martin weren't going to give up that easy, "You have five seconds until we knock down this door. And if we have to do that, we won't just be searching the place, we'll be taking you down to the Lockholes tonight. This is your last chance."

"I doubt the two of you could break down the door to a dollhouse from the sounds of you," Frobo replied in his most nonchalant tone, which resulted in more laughter and applause from the orks. "But go ahead and do your worst," he continued. "I'm rich enough to be able to afford a new door if you break this one."

"There goes that Daggins, bragging about his money again," said Happy. "Be it on your head, you rich snob."

Frobo couldn't help but wonder if there was a bit of realism in Happy's last comment. He'd always suspected they'd been jealous of his wealth. Of course, his line about his money had only been for the audience. They didn't have to get offended by it.

The countdown until Happy and Martin would try to tear down his imaginary door began. They were so stupid. In their eagerness to make a big show of breaking the door, they didn't realize that Frobo had never locked it, just like when he was home in the Chire. The dumb Hobbicks could've opened the imaginary door right up by simply pulling the latch.

"Five! Four! Three! Two! Last chance! This is it Daggins, after this, there's no turning back!"

"No, this is your last chance to turn back," Frobo yelled in defiance.

"One!" Happy and Martin reared back five paces, and as the Orks held their breath in anticipation, the hobbicks charged full speed ahead at Frobo's imaginary door.

The dumb blokes were actually going to break the thing. Frobo panicked momentarily, as he could see the two hobbicks would be headed straight for him, after they broke through his door. He side-stepped out of the way just in time as Martin and Happy tumbled through it like a couple of rolling boulders that had just been shot from a catapult.

Frobo stood at alert, with outstretched hands facing the two intruders, who sprang out of their somersaulting rolls to their feet.

"Alright, Daggins!" said Martin. "Enough jibber jabber. Tell us where the *ring* is or suffer the consequences."

What were they doing? This was a complete deviation from their plan! It was obvious that they were still obsessed with the ring, and they were doing this because they blamed him for its loss. But if they felt that way, they should have come and told him to his face. What was he supposed to do? He could feel the orks looking intently at them, and he could hear the popcorn crunching between their sharp rotting teeth. He had no choice but to act.

"You'll never find it. Never!" he cried.

"Where do you think it is, goon?" Happy said.

"I think he has it in his *pocketses,* goon," said Martin.

"Well, I think you are the shortest two goons I've ever seen," said Frobo to the laughter of the crowd. Then without thinking, Frobo instinctively reached for his right vest pocket, where he might have kept something as valuable as a ring, if he'd ever been fortunate enough to have one. Upon touching the outside of it, to his utter shock and horror, his hand felt a round cylindrical hollow object through the fabric of the vest. His eyes opened wide, and he froze in terror. He thought he felt his hear stop beating. He had just felt a *ring* in his pocket.

Happy reacted to the terror in his face, assuming that Frobo was acting. "Look at that, goon," he said. "It's right where we said it'd be. Now all we must do is take it from him and bring it to Saulman™ so we can trademark it, like we've trademarked everything else in Middlearth."

At this, Happy and Martin rushed at Frobo, who readied himself for what he was sure to be the fight of his life. If they discovered he had the *ring*, Frobo would be finished. What if the orks saw it? The show would certainly be over. But how in Middlearth did he have the ring? Perhaps the ring in his pocket wasn't Happy's ring, the new ring of power. There was a chance that was the case, but there was something inside him, a deep inner knowledge that told Frobo differently. In his heart of hearts, he knew that the ring in his pocket was somehow the new ring of power. But he had no idea how it had got there. Frobo ducked and rolled between the two charging hobbicks just in time.

Of course, he knew Happy and Martin would be 'film fighting' him, since this was how hobbicks fought when they were actually angry with each other. And if he didn't 'film fight' them back who knows how they might react? *"Fight them just hard enough,"* he told himself. *"Just hard enough to keep them at bay, but not hard enough to make them think I'm not acting."*

Frobo ran on nimble feet to his chair, the one part of the hobbick hole that was real and not imaginary, placing it between himself and Happy and Martin. The orks were already cheering for the coming brawl.

Happy and Martin approached slowly from his left and right, and at the last moment, dove at him from either side of the chair. But Frobo was too quick. He flipped himself over the back of the chair and landed on the cushion in a sitting position to the great delight of the onlooking orks. Behind him, Happy and Martin crashed into each other, and fell back in a theatrical exaggerated fashion. The orks erupted in applause.

Frobo stood to his feet and bowed before the crowd, 'breaking the fourth wall' as he'd heard the phrase described. As he stood back up with hands stretched wide however, he was knocked off his feet by one of the two hobbicks. They'd recovered quickly!

He could hear the orks booing as he was driven into the stage. Those stupid idiots might have broken his arm if hobbicks weren't made of the toughest stuff of the earth. Instead, Frobo spun around to see Happy crouched over him and begin landing fake blows upon his face. Frobo reacted to the blows as any good actor might and feigned their devastating effects. Then, Happy stood up and spread out his hands to the booing crowd as Frobo lay still upon the stage. At least the orks were on his side.

Happy then returned to Frobo's splayed out body after not receiving the cheer he'd expected. Then he dramatically reached his hand into the air and slowly brought it down towards Frobo's pocket. He was just about to take hold of what only Frobo knew could be the very ring of power, when Frobo caught Happy's arm in his own hand, taking a tight grasp on the hobbick's short forearm. Happy looked down at Frobo making eye contact, with a shocked look upon his face. Frobo then wrenched Happy's arm backward, and Happy obliged him, feigning that Frobo had flung him into a dive over his body. Then Frobo leapt to his feet, just in time to see Martin diving for him at the edge of the stage. Frobo dodged, and momentarily grasping Martin's breaches, hurled Martin offstage into the crowd of onlooking Orks.

Frobo had never heard cheers like the ones he was hearing now. This theatrical performance had turned into a wrestling match, but he would be the better for it, if he could keep Martin and Happy and the rest of them from realizing he had the ring! Martin was trying to emerge from the crowd, but he had landed in the lap of a huge ork that had been holding the largest bowl of the popping corn Frobo had ever seen. The corn had flown in a thousand directions when Martin hit it, and Martin was desperately trying to escape the ork as his companions restrained him.

Frobo however, had other problems to deal with. Happy had seen the extra help Frobo had given Martin assisting him over the side of the stage and had a look in his eye that Frobo thought might be more real than acting. He waited as the hobbick approached him and then, without warning, Happy drew his sword from his sheath!

This received quite the reaction. The crowd of orks gasped in unison.

Happy then cried out, "Enemies of Middlearth Enterprises beware. If you won't give up the ring quietly, then we'll take it from you when you're dead."

Neither Frobo nor Happy had ever film fought with swords before, but surely Happy wasn't planning to draw blood. Frobo drew *Itch* from its sheath. "To the death!" he cried, and the sword 'film fight' began.

It was a truly wild affair that Frobo then found himself caught up in. He had never swung a sword before, save a few times in Slumbervell through the empty air. But as the "fight" began, he thought he was developing a bit of a knack for it! The trick was not to try and hit Happy with this sword, but to strike the blade of Happy's sword itself.

He swung across, and so did Happy, their swords clanging between them. He swung down, and Happy parried the blow. Sparks flew from the metal. He moved forward, and Happy retreated, as the cowardly hobbick should have. The sword blows continued as Frobo marveled at himself. He'd never realized he was an expert swordsman. He was a prodigy. Swinging the sword was the revelation he'd been seeking his whole life.

Happy retreated from him again and again all across the stage as the crowd bellowed and cheered. Frobo thrusted a firm strike at Happy that the hobbick blocked just in time, before he returned a quick counter jab right at Frobo's chest. But Frobo blocked that blow with a swift parry and swung his sword in a full body spin back-handed blow that Happy repelled at the last moment. Of course, this was all for show. He and Happy both knew that, but swinging the sword gave Frobo such a rushing thrill that he felt like it could have been real. He could be a sword wielding hero who fought off orks by the thousands all alone, rescuing fair maidens from terrible monsters and freeing entire peoples by himself.

As he continued the film fighting assault on Happy, Frobo thought he heard the cheering change to cries of warning. "No!

No! Look out!" the orks cried from their seats. Were they cheering for Happy now? Was he the villain in the eyes of the poor witless creatures? He had started to see three to four swings ahead of the sword fight, wizard of the sword as he was, and he had just perceived how he would disarm Happy and win the fight. It would require a slight nick of the Hobbick's hand, but could Frobo be blamed for that? Was it his fault that he was an expert swordsman prodigy? Was it his fault that Happy had challenged him to fake sword fighting in their play? Was it his fault Happy had gone off script in their impromptu play in the first place? No. None of that was his fault, and therefore he couldn't be blamed for the cut he was about to make on Happy's hand. *"It's just a 'film fight,'"* he told himself. *"Happy won't mind; he'll realize it was all for the show."* But perhaps, in the rush of emotion Frobo was feeling, it was becoming slightly more than just a 'film fight.'

The orks were still crying out in warning. How could they see what he was about to do? A moment of doubt betrayed him, and his eye turned, for only the slightest of moments out upon the crowd. Then he saw, just in the nick of time, the sword of Martin, held high in the air and swinging down upon him with the speed of sprinting horse.

Frobo dove forward barely avoiding the blow of the crazed Hobbick. Had Martin lost his marbles? Was he insane? Did he not realize that none of this was real? The stupid hobbick would've cut Frobo's head off if he hadn't seen him! But Frobo had bigger problems than just hurt feelings. Now the fight was back to two against one. Happy and Martin stepped towards him with outstretched swords. It was all Frobo could do to fend off their oncoming blows as he parried with the skill of a fighter well beyond his years. Or at least, that was how it felt to him as he blocked the strikes of the two Hobbicks. Were they swinging for the play or for his life? It was growing increasingly difficult for him to parry the varied swings and jabs that Martin and Happy were throwing at him. Their swords were a barrage of iron, and Frobo no longer was even thinking of what he was doing. He had become one with *Itch,* as if the sword was an extension of his arm, and yet acted independently of his thought to parry the oncoming enemy.

But his mind was still racing. As Happy approached from his right, and Martin from his left, Frobo backed up to the very edge of the stage, facing away from the crowd. Once, he almost tumbled over the side and his heel stood on nothing but air, but his balance, or some other external force upheld him on the stage's edge. *Parry left low, parry right high, parry left middle, quick jab right,* but Happy blocked that blow, and Frobo brought his sword back round just in time to block another swing at his neck from Martin. He couldn't continue like this for much longer. It would soon be the end of him. Perhaps they didn't realize that blocking their swings was all he could do. No, he was no longer film sword fighting, he was fighting for his very life up on that stage. Fear slowly overcame him, and it felt as if the stage was mud into which he was sinking until it came all the way up from his feet to his waist, to his trembling swinging arms, then to his neck...

Suddenly, a sweeping strike from Martin knocked his sword out of his hand. Martin and Happy pointed their swords at Frobo's neck. He had failed.

"Kill me quickly," he said. "Let me die as the King of Brohan did upon the Pallenor Fields in the third film."

"We don't want to kill you," said Martin. His teeth gleamed inside his mouth as a smile broke across his face. "We just want your *ring.*"

Frobo looked sharply over to Martin as he said this. He thought he saw a lustful greenish glow in his eye, a burning, craving desire for power. Did this ring have the same power of corruption as that *Insidious Ring* it had been made in mockery of? But it didn't matter. He could not let Martin and Happy take the ring from him. It would be far too dangerous to reveal it here in front of the ten thousand orks.

As Martin held his sword out at Frobo, Happy reached for first his right pants pocket, then his left. Both were empty. Then the hobbick's hand went for Frobo's vest pocket. He touched it from the outside and Frobo knew it felt the ring. Happy's eyes flashed at Frobo for one glaring second. Then simultaneously, both their hands reached for Frobo's vest pocket with a force that could have ripped down the strongest of hobbick doors. The ring was flung high up into the air and a gasp was heard through the crowd. The ring was suspended for a moment as all eyes turned to it. Frobo was thrown back by Happy, landing hard on the stone floor just in front of the stage, but not in the crowd. As he lay on his back, he looked up in shock to see the ring falling from the air above him. He then reached out a trembling forefinger upon which fell the ring. Frobo became invisible.

If not for the boos, howls, and complete eruption of anger from the crowd at his disappearance, Martin and Happy might have been able to follow the sound of Frobo's thudding footsteps as he ran back across the stage. What had just happened? Hadn't his grandfather, the most famous hobbick who ever lived, done something similar almost eleventy-one years ago? Hadn't a different ring fallen upon his finger when he was performing in front of a crowd?

Frobo ran behind the stage, and past the onlooking faces of the members of the fellowship. He saw Grandalf throw his staff in frustration. Roban cringed and closed his fists, trying to restrain his anger. Their eyes all had the same shocked look of horror. Of course, they thought he had betrayed them. But he hadn't. He would have to explain that, somehow. He had no idea how he'd come to possess the ring! He didn't, did he? Did he? That stupid looking furry creature had stolen the rings, not him. Grandalf had said he wasn't lying! But as he ran past

Uniborn, he clearly heard the man uttering the phrase, "That little lying thief!"

Frobo kept running. There wasn't time to think of how this had happened. Surely the play had stopped and now there was a search commencing for him, the new ringbearer. Frobo ran the exact same way they'd come in. He slipped the past the ork guard that was waiting back-stage, then past the dressing room, and then ran all the way up the long stair through the narrow passage where they'd tied up Radagrass and hidden him in the dark crevice. He was soon staring at the large opening chamber where they'd entered. The stone door was shut just as they'd left it after entering, and Frobo tried pushing it open. It was a hopeless endeavor. What had that password been that Grandalf had uttered in the strange language? Frobo stood there, with the phrase on the tip of his tongue, trying to remember, but could think of naught to say.

"Stupid son of a Sackville-Daggins!" he scolded himself. But the harder he thought the farther the phrase went from his mind. He then heard the foul voices of the orks and saw the light of their torches. As their torches lit up the room, he felt exposed and naked, but the ring was still working its magic, for their roving eyes slipped over him like water over a rock. He left the chamber the same way he'd come but with softer footsteps, and returned to the only place he could go, the stage and the theater.

The play had not started back up yet, and his friends were nowhere to be seen as they had probably all been taken back to the dressing room. Orks were roaming every which way with torches and searching eyes. He had to be careful not to bump into them. Where could he hide? Where could he wait out this little problem that they would least expect? Looking out across the stage over to the private box, he saw the lovely silver clad figure of the Lady Ellamir. If none of the others understood him, at least she would. But would she? This was the same person whom he'd just seen moments earlier holding the hand of Barzabag, and who claimed to have no recollection of any of them. But he might have seen her wink at him. There was just the slightest chance all of that had been an act in some elaborate scheme.

Either way, Frobo reckoned that private box where only Ella and Barzabag sat, was the best chance he had at remaining hidden. Slowly, he made his way out into the bench rows of the theater. The orks were all up now in a massive sweeping searching for him. If they had simply remained seated and perfectly still, he never would've reached the box.

Frobo stepped gingerly on the long stone row, making his way to the box in the most direct way possible. An ork approached him from the front, and he hopped down to the level below him. But another ork with long striding legs was climbing the huge stone rows like they were stairs. It was headed straight for him. Frobo scampered ahead just in time. He continued to duck, dodge, and struggle his way across the enormous stadium of stone row seats until at last he reached the box. In the very center of the stadium of long stair-like rows, its walls jutted straight up from the ground. From where he stood, with the stage to his right and the side wall of the box before him, the top rim of the wall was at least twice as tall as he was. He tried to walk around to the entrance, but two ugly looking orks guarded it. Frobo walked all the way around the stone walls of the box, trying to find some sort of handhold or groove by which he could climb it. But this was to no avail. The stone walls of the box were sheer. He needed some sort of boost. A ladder or a rope of some sort would have helped but...

Two orks were headed in his direction, arguing with each other.

"I'll wager my left thumb there's something magical going on in that disappearance," one of them growled.

"Of course, there's something magical going on, maggot," the other said. "A golden ring fell on the hobbick's finger!"

Frobo stepped up to the stone level above where the two orks argued. He was so close that their foul odors made him cringe. The filthy creatures needed a bath, no they needed a lifetime of baths. The two orks turned their backs to him and faced the stage. The ork on the left stood only a foot away from the box.

"Would you just look at it, Moldbreath?" the ork closest to the box said to his companion. "That wonderful stage, this amazing play, all of its ours."

Then, lowering his voice, his companion (Moldbreath) said, "not to mention, that seductive creature up in the box. She's just beyond this wall, and she can be ours if we play our cards right."

The two orks bellowed in laughter in front of him. Suddenly, an idea struck Frobo. If he could stand on the back of one of these orks, he'd be able to reach the top of the wall with ease. It was his only chance, and it was standing right in front of him. As the two orks laughed, facing the stage, Frobo leapt from the upper level where he stood onto the back of the largest ork like a cat. He almost knocked the thing over, and the ork spun round to attack his companion for the perceived shove. It was just the opportunity Frobo needed. As the ork turned to its companion, it turned its back to the box, and Frobo leapt again from the back of the ork to the high wall, his fingers barely grasping the edge. If not for the commotion of the two orks below that were now fighting, someone surely would've heard his struggle to climb the wall.

He crested the wall and lay upon the top, balancing as a fat Chire squirrel does in a tree branch. Ella was alone in the box. She sat in a wooden chair that faced the stage next to another empty one (Barzabag's). Looking in his direction, but obviously unable to see him, were her piercing green eyes. Oh, how they did pierce him. His heart fluttered from the sheer beauty before him. But still, he didn't see her as Barzabag the ork did, something for him to possess. She was simply too high, and he was far too lowly for such childish dreams. She rose from her perch and approached the wall... had she heard his ascension?

He shimmied with the quickness of a cat to the next wall (the one facing the stage) as her hands touched the place on the stone where he'd just been lying a moment before. Could she feel his warmth upon it?

If she could, she gave no indication of it. She returned to her seat, continuing to look about in curiosity, but in complete ignorance of Frobo's presence. Ever so slowly, Frobo shimmied off the edge of the wall and into the box. He then crept over to her seat. The orks guarding the box were facing outwards as their job was to keep anyone but Barzabag from entering.

As softly as he could speak, he breathed her name, "Ella," he whispered.

She jumped so suddenly he thought she was going to fly right out of her chair! But somehow, by luck, fate or some other external force, she restrained herself from screaming. Hearing her jump, the guards opened the wooden door to look in for a moment.

"What are you looking at?" she snapped. "Mind your own business and focus on your job. Or I'll tell Barzabag, and you'll both be castrated for looking at me!"

The guards promptly turned their heads and closed the door, resuming their duties.

Ella made no further indication that she'd heard Frobo's voice. She sat upright and prim in her chair, maintaining a perfectly blank stare out of the box in the direction of the stage. She maintained this position for so long that Frobo began to grow worried that perhaps his voice had also somehow become invisible, which of course was ridiculous, since all voices were already invisible. But finally, without moving her eyes, or making the slightest indication that she was speaking at all, she whispered in reply, "Is that you, Frobo?"

Bless her! She did remember him! "Yes, it's me," he whispered.

"I don't understand," she said. "What are you all doing here? And why do you have a ring of power?"

"What do you mean?" Frobo asked. "We're here to rescue you of course, my lady. Did you really think we would abandon you to Barzabag and his Army of Free Orks?"

"Rescue me..." she sighed and broke her straight-backed posture, slumping in her chair as if the words were a death sentence, and therefore needed no longer keep up any pretenses. "That's what I need," she pined, speaking a little too loudly for Frobo's comfort. "Nine males traipsing across Middlearth to rescue me from ten thousand orks. And each one of them trying to take the glory of that deed for himself. Bless me dear Frobo, but I'm afraid I've had enough of that. Where do you arrogant men get your gumption? What makes you think I even need to be rescued in the first place?"

If nothing else, Frobo was insulted by her lack of gratitude. Was credit and petty glory all she could think of at a time like this? Didn't she realize that every single last one of them had risked their lives for her?

"What makes me think you even need to be rescued?" mocked Frobo. He crossed his arms and strode out in front of her in the box. He then tried his very hardest to fix his sternest, most guilt-ridden gaze upon her, the type that Sham's mother used to give the two of them when they'd been caught stealing biscuits from her cupboards. He stood there for a moment, thinking it might actually work, until he remembered that of course he was *invisible*. She looked right through him, her green eyes darting about and looking up and around her head where he'd last spoken.

"Oh, confound it Ella, I'm up here," he said at last in frustration. "What makes me think you even need to be rescued? Oh, I don't know. Perhaps the fact that you're soon to be the wife of the most fearsome and terrible ork that Middlearth has seen in eleventy-one years! That you're doomed to sit here and waste away, bearing his brood of orklings while you suffer for the rest of your life, as your beauty fades, your voice trembles and all of the fair things of the world fall away."

A breathtaking smile formed on her plump red lips. "Oh Frobo," she said. "You're all so silly." Frobo nearly fainted from shock at the sound of his name coming from the midst of that smile, from that woman. She did have quite an effect on him. But... hold on, she was still speaking.

"I am not the one in captivity," she said to him. "You are... or at least they are. I can escape whenever I please. Although, I'm not sure I want to. Being a queen does have its privileges."

"Don't want to escape?" gasped Frobo. "My Lady, I implore you! I protest! I... I... I demand you let us rescue you."

"You *demand?*" she asked, laughing at his gumption. "You, a hobbick of questionable lineage *demand* me, Lady of Grondor, future Queen of the Free Orks to *let* you rescue me?"

Frobo noted the firm tone of the Lady's voice. What in Middlearth was wrong with her? She remembered him, but Barzabag clearly still had too much influence over her. He had to get through to her to *save* her. "My lady, I know this might be hard for you to hear, but you have been brainwashed by Barzabag and these orks. You're not yourself. You *need* to trust me."

Ella rolled her eyes and touched her forehead as if it was aching. What kind of reaction was that? Couldn't she see he was trying to save her? And there she was, sitting on her throne, blowing off his efforts completely. "Even though I'm invisible, I can still see you. You could at least show a little appreciation for the fact that I'm risking my life over here."

Instantly her countenance changed. She sat up, ready and alert like any lady ought to when she was about to be rescued.

There was also more desperation in her voice when she replied to him, "Oh Frobo, thank you so much for coming and risking everything for me. The brainwashing... it comes and goes... you'd never believe what they... what they did."

The quiver in her voice and the look of sorrow on her face confirmed Frobo's suspicions all too easily. Had any other person whimpered and pined to him like that, he might have thought he saw a façade of sarcasm. But not Ella. She was far too attractive and desirous to toy with him in that way, and he refused to let his perception of her be sullied with such realism.

This was Frobo's worst fear realized. The monsters had somehow corrupted the most beautiful thing he'd ever encountered. Well, he would kill every last one of them, starting with Barzabag.

"What did they do?" he growled, fighting the consuming anger with every ounce of strength he had to speak to her.

"Oh, I can't tell you. I wouldn't dare speak of such things," she pined to him. "Just tell me how you're going to get me out of here! How, oh how will you rescue me, Frobo?" She was so perfect, and so beautiful, with her golden hair and her green eyes that Frobo would've done anything for Ella at that moment. Had she commanded him to leap from a cliff he would have obeyed. He was hers. He was her knight in shining armor. And he would defend her honor, even if it was the last thing he did.

"I'm going to kill Barzabag," he growled with such finality that Ella shuddered. "I'm going to kill him the moment I see him."

"No, you can't," she protested. "If you do, the other orks will find you and kill you. Then who will be left to rescue me; a poor, helpless, brainwashed woman?"

It took all the strength Frobo possessed to promise the Lady that he wouldn't kill Barzabag the moment he saw him. When he finally did, the rage that had overcome him seemed to fade.

"So, tell me," she whispered to him in her intoxicating voice, "how are you all going to rescue me? What's your plan?"

"I... I..." Frobo considered the question. "I have no idea," he confessed. "I think Roban has a plan, but he didn't share it with us. I just know it involved you taking part in the play at some point."

Ella jumped in her seat at this. "Take part in the play?" she exclaimed in a hushed voice. She groaned and shook her head back and forth, crossing her arms and taking quick short breaths. Then, steeling herself, she grasped the arms of her chair and leaned back again. "So, Roban has a plan," she said, rolling her eyes. "Of course, he does. What do you mean, take part in the play? Like as an actor?"

"Yes, that was his plan," said Frobo.

"A ridiculous notion," she said, quickly cutting him off. She then stood up from her chair, pacing inside the wall of the box in frustration. "Can you imagine it?" she asked, still keeping her voice low enough for the orks outside the door to not hear. "Me careening and strutting myself about in front of ten thousand lusty orks like a piece of meat! How dare he suggest it."

"That's so funny!" Frobo said. "That was almost the exact reaction Uniborn had when Roban told him the plan!"

"Was it?" she said. Frobo could almost see the wheels turning in her mind behind those lush green eyes. "In that case I..."

But she was cut off. Frobo heard the heavy footfall of stomping boots outside. Ella looked towards the door. "Out of my way!" The voice was Barzabag's and it was right outside.

Ella leapt into her chair and Frobo slunk into the back corner of the box as Barzabag charged through the door. The ork was fuming with anger and looked like he was about to explode. Had Frobo really been delusional enough to threaten killing this gigantic hulking creature only moments before?

He'd been out of his mind! Better to stay hidden and keep that ring on. "Don't make a sound," he told himself.

"Welcome back Barz," Ella said. "Did you find the..."

"No, I didn't!" he shouted, interrupting her. He then stomped over to the wooden chair next to Ella's and sat down with such fury and force that it shattered beneath him. "My throne!" the great ork cried as he fell back onto the stone floor of his box. Like a squirming turtle that had just been laid upon its back, he flailed with outstretched arms, trying to regain his countenance.

Frobo almost betrayed himself with laughter but covered his mouth with his hand just in time. Barzabag leapt up from the floor and erupted again in frustration. A new "throne" was brought out for him so quickly that Frobo wondered if this wasn't a somewhat frequent occurrence. Barzabag sat down again, more gently this time at the encouragement of Ella.

"So, you didn't find him? But where could he be, Barzabag?" she asked.

"I don't know where the sodding hobbick is," shouted Barzabag, fire blazing in his yellow eyes. "Just like I don't know how he disappeared! Either that ring that fell on his finger is magical, or that brooding wizard had something to do with it. The rest of them have been searched for magic rings and none of them have any. For now, we've locked them in that blasted dressing room. If another one of them disappears, I'll know it was the wizard!"

"But if the wizard could make them disappear, wouldn't he make them all disappear at once?" Ella asked. "And why would he choose the hobbick to become invisible?"

"Do not try to understand," he said, glaring at her. "That isn't your purpose in life!"

"And just what is that supposed to mean?" Ella protested. Her eyes opened wide in shock as she fixed them upon Barzabag. A fury brooded inside of them that Barzabag perceived, realizing what he'd done. Though the ork was strong, tall, and terrifying to behold, Ella somehow prevented Barzabag from having any power over her whatsoever. He could have crushed most men with a fraction of his strength, but all that power and machismo crumbled in her presence. Her beauty was so arresting, that he was no stronger than a child around her. Frobo wondered if perhaps she knew this. Could she possibly be using her looks to control the massive, fearsome ork? He could scarcely imagine one so perfect and pure as she was using beauty to manipulate those around her in that way. No, he wouldn't allow his perfect image of her to be sullied with that thought.

Regardless of the reason she did so, Ella continued to berate him. "You had better watch your tongue if you still want me to marry you, Barzabag! I don't care if everyone else here does everything you ask! I just won't do it if you keep treating me like that! I am not stupid!"

"Oh no, no, my sweet bloodcake, I swear I didn't mean it!" Barzabag said, before Ella's sweeping slap struck him on the cheek.

"I told you never to call me 'bloodcake' again!" she said. "How many more times must I tell you?"

What a pair the two of them made. Frobo sat there and listened to their quarrels imagining a lifetime of these repetitive arguments. Barzabag's cheeks were surely starting to get raw. Although you'd never think so to look at her, Ella seemed to pack quite the punch. Frobo took solace only in the fact that this was all an act by Ella. At least, he thought it was. He just didn't understand why she'd gone along with it so easily in the first place. Why had she been so willing to ride away with the ork?

Frobo sat up in the box with Ella and Barzabag for what seemed like hours, listening to the two of them argue and discuss everything from baby names to the extents of the realm of Barzabag's future kingdom. Barzabag sent word that the play would recommence as no one had been able to find Frobo and searching for him was obviously useless. The orks resumed their seats throughout the broad theater. The show was about to begin again. "Now, let's see them pull this show off," Frobo thought to himself. "Let's see how well they do, now that their only *real* actor isn't up there anymore." Of course, Frobo was referring to himself with these endearing terms.

As the roar of the crowd quieted, Frobo looked out over the edge of the box. Roban was strutting out to the edge of the stage. Ella shifted in her seat, and Frobo thought she might have even held her breath for a brief moment. Frobo turned back to the stage as Roban addressed the crowd. "I do apologize, my good orks, for that unfortunate disturbance earlier."

Boos echoed throughout the crowd.

"While I cannot guarantee that something similar won't happen again..." he was interrupted by louder boos, "I can assure you that if it does, it will be part of the play. Seeing as the actor playing himself, the grandson of the most famous hobbick who ever lived, has excused himself from the performance, his role will be reprised by the grandson of the actual real-life gardener of the same. Lady and gentleorks, playing the part of Frobo Daggins from hence forth, I give you, the one and only, Sham Gramgee the Third!"

Sham waltzed out onto the stage with the same dumb look that always adorned his face. For some ridiculous reason, he was receiving a roar of approval from the orks, and from Barzabag. Frobo wanted to cry out in anger. *"But just wait,"* he told himself. *"Wait until they see him make a fool of himself on stage, just like he always does."*

"I always loved watching his grandfather in the films," Barzabag told Ella, as she snuggled up next to him. "He was sort of an unsung hero of the story. I never understood why the Dagginses got all the notoriety."

Ella nodded in silent agreement.

Frobo burned with fire inside. *"Of course, you don't understand!"* he imagined himself screaming at the ork buffoon. *"You don't understand because you've never read the books! You don't even know how to read you 'pathetic illiterate!'"* he told himself, echoing the words of Grandalf right before he had defeated Radagrass. Frobo imagined himself removing the ring from his finger and challenging Barzabag in hand-to-hand combat for his trespass. How dare that moronic, illiterate, idiotic, imbecilic ork say such a thing. Everyone who'd ever *read* his grandfather's story knew just how stupid Sham's grandfather really was. And Sham himself was no different. Frobo could've written his own book about all the things the filmmaker got wrong. The injustice of it infuriated him.

Sham waved to the crowd as he was accompanied off stage by Roban. Frobo seethed with anger.

Then Roban's narration from somewhere backstage began: "After escaping the goons of Middlearth Enterprises, the grandson of the most famous hobbick who ever lived finds himself in a wooded forest just outside of his beloved home in the Chire. But he must be careful! He is still a fugitive and is being hunted by goons and perhaps other creatures worse than them…"

The crowd of orks murmured in anticipation.

Frobo saw in the very corner of the stage the boot of Sham peek out from behind the red curtain. The hobbick then crept in a catlike prowl out onto the stage, shuffling from imaginary tree to imaginary tree, and peering behind make believe corners as if he was afraid of being followed. The orks were really enjoying this ridiculous performance, pointing, laughing, and rejoicing in what their simple minds found to be hilarious. Frobo took little joy in watching Sham. He had a more critical eye than these hopeless buffoons did.

As Sham crept through the imaginary forest like a blind

wolf might have, the footfalls of another being were heard from behind the curtain. Someone, someone far more interesting than Sham, was coming. Frobo wondered how they were amplifying the sound of the steps. It sounded like a giant was going to come out from behind that curtain. Just as the curtain parted, Grandalf, Wondell, and Roban appeared. Sham leapt away from the imaginary road off into some bushes.

"Do you think we'll find him, Grandalf?" asked Roban.

"Ahem..." Grandalf stuttered as all eyes turned to the wizard. He peered out over the crowd and seemed almost to shrink. "I..." he began. "I believe..." he continued.

"Yes, you believe?" repeated Roban.

"I believe..." said Grandalf, bouncing up and down on his toes from nervousness. "I believe that we will... find him." He looked across the crowd again conspicuously. Frobo covered his face in embarrassment. The wizard was a terrible actor!

"And just what makes you so confident?" asked Wondell. "Even my elfen eyes couldn't spot a hobbick if he was deliberately trying to conceal himself."

"I... I... I!" the wizard's voice grew louder with each repetition of the word. "I... just have a feeling." he finally said.

"I hope you're right," said Roban. "I just hope the poor lad understands we're here to rescue him. The filmmaker knows there are worse things than the goons of Middlearth Enterprises looking for him right now."

As the three of them began to search, Sham's character, acting encouraged by the news that these strangers were seeking to help him, jumped out of the imaginary bush as quickly as he'd jumped into it. "It's me!" he cried. "The grandson of the most famous hobbick who ever lived!"

"Son of Ashelob!" shouted Grandalf. The wizard seemed legitimately frightened.

"Is it really you, Frobo?" asked Wondell.

"Yes, it is I!" said Sham triumphantly. "I guarantee it!" The real Frobo groaned in disgust from his perch on the wall of the box. Sham's lines were awful.

"Good," said Roban. "We are here because we heard you were in trouble, and we wish for you to accompany us on a perilous quest of the utmost importance."

"A quest?" repeated Sham.

"Yes," said Roban, "a perilous quest of the utmost importance."

"But," said Sham. "Surely, you don't want *me* to join you on this perilous quest of the utmost importance."

Finally, Sham was starting to see what everyone else saw in him. *"You're absolutely right, they don't want you to join them!"* thought Frobo. *"They probably wish they had me!"*

Sham continued, "After all, I'm not my grandfather, the most famous hobbick who ever lived. Come to think of it, he probably isn't even my grandfather at all."

Frobo's anger was rekindled. He'd forgotten for the moment that Sham was playing him. Sham surely wouldn't dare talk about Frobo's lineage... not here. Not in front of a crowd of orks and the Lady Ella. *He wouldn't dare.*

But Sham dared indeed.

"What do you mean, he 'probably isn't your grandfather?'" asked Roban. "I've never heard such nonsense."

"Allow me to sing you a song my good man," Sham said. And then his song began.

I'm not the Daggins that you think I am,
I didn't grow up like a prized show lamb,
I didn't grow up here, in the Chire,
I'm not the hobbick that you think I am.
Most people think that I'm a Daggins bonafide,
But my true nature is quite frankly classified!
I wouldn't tell you even, if I had to,

No sir, I'd simply rather lie.

But since you've asked me to go with you on a quest,
Just like my grandad, now you put me to the test,
Then dear old Grandalf I, need to tell you,
I'm not the Daggins that you think I am.

Because, I'm just a Daggins from Sackville
That's where the hobbicks get their backfill.
Yaah! I'm just a Daggins from Sackville,
The place us hobbicks get our backfill!
I'm not a hobbick from Hobbickton,
Anymore than I'm a Daggins from Daggend!
I'm just a Daggins from Sackville,
That's where the hobbicks, get their backfill!

As the song picked up, Sham seemed to gain confidence in his musical abilities. The crowd of orks had risen from their seats and were now clapping along to the rhythm of the melody and even joining in on the chorus. They'd picked it up quite easily to Frobo's utter horror. The reaction from the orks was even more positive than it had been when he'd been film fighting Happy and Martin.

Sham, his own gardener, was stealing Frobo's show, while playing Frobo. The injustice of it infuriated him. And the worst part of it all was that Sham's goal seemed to be to humiliate him. And now, the once stage frightened Grandalf was coming out to the center of the stage to join Sham. Was he going to sing with him? This would be good. Grandalf's stage fright would certainly disrupt the song and Sham's rhythm. The wizard began to sing in his old deep voice.

Even if, you're not the Daggins I want you to be,
Perhaps, you'll still come with me on my journey,

Unless you're, truly no more than a Sackville dog,
In which case, you would be no Daggins at all!

Frobo, you're just a Daggins from Sackville,
That's where the hobbicks get their backfill!
You're just a Daggins from Sackville,
The place the hobbicks get their backfill!
You're not a hobbick from Hobbickton,
Anymore, than I'm a Daggins from Daggend
You're just a Daggins from Sackville,
That's where the hobbicks get their backfill!

Frobo was seething with anger now, and for one of the few times in his entire life, he felt as if his feelings might be hurt. Was singing the cure for Grandalf's stage fright? When had they written this ridiculous song anyways? It was like Sham had been rehearsing it for months! And now Sham was continuing his horrible song. Frobo wanted to crawl away somewhere he wouldn't be able to hear it anymore. But there he was, trapped in the box with Ella and Barzabag, with nowhere to go until the wretched show's conclusion.

Dear old Grandalf, you are exactly right,
I'm no more Daggins than orks endure light!
My father Froyo sold, all our stories,
Characters, likenesses and names...

Sometimes I can't help think he had no right,
Because, he's not the heir to their owner!
He's not the heir to the hobbick who,
Is known, as the most famous to ever live.
He's not a hobbick from Hobbickton,
Anymore, than I'm a Daggins from Daggend!
You know, he's just a Daggins from Sackville,

The place the hobbicks get their backfill!
He's not a hobbick from Hobbickton,
Anymore! Than I'm a Daggins from Daggend!
You know, he's just a Daggins from Sackville,
The place the hobbicks get their backfill!

At last, it seemed that the song would end. Grandalf, Wondell, and Roban all joined Sham on the final crescendo, along with the crowd of orks. Frobo had never felt smaller as Sham took a long bow before the crowd of onlooking orks. The standing ovation lasted five full minutes. Frobo had never seen anything like it. Any hopes or fleeting thoughts Frobo had entertained of rejoining his companions if they ever escaped this dreadful place had died in his heart with Sham's song. It was now so obvious what they all thought of him. He was nothing more than a *"Daggins from Sackville,"* and the only reason any of them had ever befriended him was to somehow profit from his good name. They obviously all believed he'd *stolen* the ring, the blind fools! He'd tried to tell them. He'd tried to reason with them. He hadn't stolen the ring; the strange furry dog-like creature had!

Of course, it had been that strange furry dog-like creature's fault. It had stolen the ring, then run away from him, so that Frobo was blamed, and then... *somehow returned the ring to him?* How on earth would he explain that to the Fellowship of the Films if they were ever reunited. How on earth could he explain it to himself? Why would that strange looking creature steal the ring from Happy, only to give it to him, to Frobo, the supposed heir of the most famous hobbick who ever lived? This was the first time Frobo had really stopped and thought about the implications of the deed since he'd discovered the new ring of power was in his possession. Perhaps the dog-like creature was a good samaritan. Could it just be that the thing was some long lost creature with no understanding of the rings and their power or significance? Perhaps returning things was simply an instinctual act for the dog, as dogs were often accustomed to doing, but that didn't explain why the ring would be brought back to Frobo instead of Happy.

None of it made a mouse's nibble's worth of sense to Frobo. If he couldn't explain it to himself, how on earth would he ever be able to explain it to them, or to anyone else? It was the problem for which there could really only be one answer to someone who hadn't seen the dog-like creature. And for that reason, he would be forced to continue this quest alone, unless...

A new thought occurred to him. What if he could use his power of invisibility to save them? What if he could rescue them all, including the Lady Ella? Of course, she was the only one of them who deserved to be rescued, but even so. Wouldn't rescuing them with the help of a ring of power be the most *Daggins-like* thing he could possibly do? Isn't that exactly what his dear old, supposed grandfather, the most famous hobbick who ever lived would've done?

The ovation at last died down and the actors (Frobo's former friends) bowed their final time before the next scene. Frobo shook his invisible head in the box and gritted his teeth. Even if he somehow managed to rescue each and every one of them, he still doubted they'd forgive him for what they *assumed* he'd done. But forgive him or not, they'd be forced to admit that his lineage was *Daggins* through and through. His resolve was firm. He would do the unthinkable. He, Frobo Daggins, would rescue Ella and the members of the Fellowship of the Films. But *how* he would do it was a thought that had not yet entered his mind.

CHAPTER 15

THEIR FINAL ACT

WHEN AT LAST THE ORKS RELENTED IN THEIR APPLAUSE, THE play continued. Sham walked behind Grandalf, Roban, and Wondell all around the stage as the four of them mimed their way across rugged terrain and thick brambles. Frobo's jealousy of Sham's leading role grew with every step and every line that the Hobbick recited.

"If we see any ork's, you'll protect me won't you, Mister Grandalf? I'm not nearly the fighter my gardener is. Oh, how I do wish he was here with me right now. He always was such a valiant hobbick, not that he'd ever tell you about it! He's more of an unsung hero, if you take my meaning."

"Perhaps we should turn around and get him, this gardener of yours," said Roban. "He seems like quite the hobbick to have in a pinch."

"Oh no," said Sham. "I don't think he'll ever leave my gardens again, not since the tongue-lashing I gave him a month ago for a minor mismanagement issue. Of course, I can make every mistake in Middlearth™, but if one of my employees takes a single misstep, it's major trouble in Daggend. Sham is just where he should be, tending my garden to atone for the one mistake he ever made in his life."

"Sounds somewhat harsh, don't you think?" chimed in Grandalf. "Jumping down the throat of your gardener for making a simple mistake? What did the poor chap do anyways?"

"Forgot to water my daisies one morning," said Sham.

Frobo was completely flabbergasted at this entire sequence. He'd never so much as raised his voice at Sham, much less done anything like what Sham was suggesting. Where did he get the nerve to go lying about him and slandering him in front of ten thousand orks? Not to mention in front of the Lady Ella. The nerve of Sham. He was becoming quite simply detestable.

"Seems a bit harsh, wouldn't you say?" asked Grandalf.

"Absolutely not," shouted Sham in his best impression of Frobo. "The Dagginses have expected nothing short of excellence from their gardeners for generations, and if they can expect it, why can't the Sackville-Dagginses expect the same? It's your prejudice against my good family name that makes you think we don't deserve the same treatment!"

Frobo laughed to himself for his silly thought earlier. He had wanted to save the fellowship, and he would. He would save every one of them, except Sham. Sham, he would leave to his own devices, crying and wallowing in this disgusting orkhold, to perform before their throng forevermore, perhaps to never see the light of day again.

"It seems a bit harsh to me too," said Wondell. "After all, didn't you just say that he was something of an unsung hero?"

"Oh yes, I did, didn't I?" said Sham. Now the stupid hobbick was caught in his own little fabrication. He'd been trying to make himself look good and Frobo bad, and now he'd made himself look like a complete fool. Frobo would relish watching Sham try and wriggle his way out of this.

But before Sham could speak again, a loud piercing howl shot over the crowd of orks. At first Frobo and the orks believed that this was the sound of a real wolf, and many of them even looked about nervously, just as fearful as Frobo of a stray wolf in their den.

"Is that a wolf's howl I hear?" asked Roban. Striding out to the center of the stage, he peered out into the crowd, looking for the imaginary wolf.

"It was nothing but one," said Wondell. "It appears that the orks and their hounds have caught up to us! Ready yourself, Frobo. We are about to have a fight on our hands!"

Sham glanced anxiously out across the crowd of orks from one side to the next, looking from where the attackers would come. He drew his short, stubby, insufficient looking sword and held it at the ready. Wondell strung an arrow in his bow and pointed it out wildly into the crowd. Orks bellowed and gasped when the arrow was directed their way, leaping across each other's laps in their seats to dodge the arrows latest direction. Barzabag stood to his feet and roared, clearly swept up in the performance and not yet understanding that this was all done for dramatic effect. Roban and Grandalf drew their swords and stood in front of Sham, holding them at the ready. The orks in the crowd shrieked and bellowed, exchanging glances in panic. Several drew their own swords, ready to attack the actors on the stage if need be. They were probably wondering if they were expected to strike and attack for the play to go on. But they needed do no such thing.

From behind the curtain, four dark looking hunched over creatures appeared in a flash and an instant. Each one of them bore a sword. The tallest of the group instantly engaged in a skirmish with Roban. The stoutest began swinging an axe wildly about and looked as if his intention was to decapitate Wondell. The other two, who were smaller and looked strangely familiar to Frobo, went straight for Sham, completely avoiding Grandalf.

The fight was on, and the swords of the actors struck and

clanged all throughout the stage. Frobo struggled to keep his eyes on all that was going on. He first noticed that the fight between the particularly stout ork and Wondell was the fiercest. From where he was sitting, it didn't appear to be acting at all, and Frobo was legitimately worried the ork might be trying to kill Wondell. But there was something about the charging, quick fighting style of the stout ork. Frobo had seen it before. The smaller orks that attacked Sham seemed less like they were trying to kill him. Instead, he could easily see that they were doing nothing more than film fighting. Sham wasn't holding up against two swords nearly as well as Frobo had before when he was fighting Happy and Martin.

Wait a moment, that *was* Happy and Martin! They were simply wearing ork armor, and their faces were painted black. But it was them, he was quite sure of it! The stout ork's fighting style against Wondell had of course reminded him of Ringo. He'd seen this fight before, at the inn of the Prancing *Shetland* Pony. That also explained Ringo's tenacity. Clearly, the dwarf hadn't settled his grudge with Wondell, as the elf seemed totally overwhelmed. Grandalf tried to assist Wondell in parrying the dwarf's axe.

And that meant that the last ork was Uniborn in disguise, the valiant knight with such renowned fighting abilities that Barzabag had considered letting him leave the orkhold. Watching Uniborn fight Roban center stage, it was easy to see why. Uniborn was a master of the sword. The man was a greater natural talent even than Frobo himself. From the naked eye, it appeared that Roban was initially overwhelmed by Uniborn's flurry of masterful thrusts and swings, and the horse thief was pushed out to the brink of the stage's edge.

Uniborn's sword flashed with such quickness that Frobo could barely see it. Every thrust, jab, or sweep was a brilliant sequence of swordplay that Frobo imagined the tall man had been practicing his entire life. His long iron sword swung from the right, was blocked, and then swung from the left a moment later. When Roban parried on that side too, Uniborn thrust his sword directly at Roban's chest. Roban jumped backwards, barely avoiding the thrust and swung his sword down on top of Uniborn's, deflecting the blow. But Uniborn was unrelenting. Leveraging Roban's deflection of his thrust, he spun in a swift rapid movement, sweeping his sword across his body at Roban's neck. Roban ducked just in the nick of time to the gasps of the crowd (including the Lady Ella).

The audience was clearly enthralled by the show, and Frobo was no different. The first "death," was that of no one but Sham himself, and if Frobo hadn't been invisible, he would've had great difficulty hiding his pleasure. Happy and Martin had cornered the inferior swordsman Sham, and Martin knocked Sham's sword out of his hand.

For one moment Sham stood before the two of them, unarmed and looking like a frightened child. Then he screamed aloud, "Spare my life! I'm just a Sackville-Daggins, I'm not even supposed to be here!"

But the ork that Happy was playing did not accommodate him. In a flashing moment, he ran his sword through Sham's heart. Frobo jumped for joy and beat the air with his fist! Blessedly, he was unheard by Barzabag, as the roars from the orks in the crowd overwhelmed the sound of it. However, when Sham fell to his side, he could see that Happy's sword was of course only held between Sham's arm and his chest. And that was fine. Frobo hadn't actually wanted Sham to die.

With Sham taken care of and lying on the ground, Happy and Martin moved to help Ringo take on Wondell and Grandalf. The fight was now three against two. It seemed strange to Frobo, but it was almost as if Grandalf and Wondell gave up. The wizard dropped his staff as soon as Happy's sword struck it, and Wondell's sword fell from his hand without being touched at all! Were they throwing the fight and losing intentionally?

They were executed in a similar fashion to Sham, with the hobbicks doing the dirty work. Once Wondell fell, Frobo noticed Ringo use him as he might use a footstep when stepping over the elf to help Uniborn. It was now four against one, as Roban was the last survivor of the four companions.

The fight escalated to its greatest intensity yet, as Roban was surrounded by the four of them, his sword playing like a tempest in the flurry of their onslaught. But he was outnumbered, and his back was turned from Uniborn for just a moment longer than he could afford. In that moment, the sword of Uniborn began its crushing decent down onto the head of Roban. Frobo's heart skipped a beat. This was it. And Frobo wasn't positive Uniborn wasn't about to permanently rid the world of the horse thief he so loathed.

"STOP!" The voice of Barzabag thundered next to Frobo as Uniborn's sword fell and Roban collapsed.

"STOP! STOP! STOP! STOP! STOP!" the ork cried.

All eyes turned to the box where Frobo stood invisible with Barzabag and Ella. Why on earth had Barzabag stopped the play?

Roban stood up from the stage, (so he was still alive) and looked up to the box, "What's wrong Barz?" he asked. "You don't like the show?"

"You're ruining it!" screamed the ork. "As soon as you die, the show will be completely over! Then what are we supposed to watch? They were about to kill you! What were you thinking, putting on a performance like that?"

"But we've all seen the good side win in the films over and over," said Roban. "Haven't you all gotten tired of that by now? I thought you all would be happy to see the orks triumph in *your* play."

"But the orks aren't *supposed* to win!" Barzabag protested, leaping once again out of his chair.

Frobo was amazed. Barzabag, the leader of the army of the Free Orks didn't even want to see his own race triumph in a dramatization. He'd been that conditioned by the films. The orks all stared up at the box in dismay. As the troubled murmurs began to resound throughout the crowd, Barzabag realized what he had just said.

"I mean... I meant to say," Barzabag interjected, "the orks aren't supposed to win that quickly!" This received roars of approval throughout the theater.

"Of course, of course," said Roban, holding two fingers up to his right temple as if he'd just had an epiphany. "You want to build suspense! I should've thought of that. It's your play Barzabag, you can have it however you like it. Come on boys, back to your places, we're starting over."

"My play..." Barzabag mused. *"My play..."* The ork curled his lips and ran his fingers through a few of the meager strands of hair that were strung to the long ponytail at the back of his head. He was contemplating some matter he deemed to be of the utmost importance.

"Yes," Roban called back, breaking the silence that had filled the large stadium while the ork leader stroked his hair. "It is your play."

Barzabag strode to the front facing wall of his box and grasped the stone walls just as this epiphany of thought seemed to have grasped his mind. Raising his voice in dramatic crescendos with every word he cried, "You mean the play that I'm not even an actor in?"

The orks all collectively gasped for breath at the revelatory words.

"My apologies, your greatness," said Roban, bowing from the stage in a superfluous gesture. "I had no idea you possessed such abilities."

"Yes, I am an actor," said Barzabag standing tall in his box. "In fact, there are many of us orks that can act, you know, it's not just men and elfs and dwarfs and hobbicks!"

The orks echoed this sentiment. "We want to be in the play too!" they cried. "Let us play ourselves! Give us a role in the play!"

"You will no longer dress yourselves up as orks in my play," proclaimed Barzabag. "From now on, orks will play orks, men will play men, and hobbicks will play hobbicks! I myself will play the role of the main ork protagonist hero: Barzabag, leader of the army of the Free Orks!"

"You would do me the honor of performing on stage with us?" asked Roban. "The Lady Ella will surely enjoy watching you, her future husband, entirely alone from her box. Perhaps one of the young hobbick lads, could play her being rescued by you from us! Or maybe Wondell? He is, after all, probably more beautiful than even she is..."

Curious murmurs broke out among the oaks at this. Wondell rolled his eyes and stepped forward, seemingly about to speak up in protest but fell silent, resigning to accept the compliment (if it could be called one).

Barzabag however, did not simply ignore the remark. Pointing at Roban and baring his yellow fangs he shouted, "How dare you insult my future bride, especially in front of her! It would be one thing if you'd done so behind her back, but..." he paused for a moment, contemplating something. "Wait a minute, you really think that elf down there is more beautiful than her?" asked Barzabag. "Let me see him again. Come to the front of the stage, Elf."

Ella's jaw dropped and her eyebrows bristled in rage. "Excuse me?" she protested.

Barzabag didn't even turn around to address her. "Wait a moment, woman," he said, shooshing her away. "I want to see something!" His eyes were fixed upon Wondell.

The elf then sighed, shrugged his shoulders and walked to the center of the stage before them all. His cheeks burned red with humiliation at being called more beautiful than Ella.

Ella rolled her eyes as Barzabag and the rest of the orks in the audience studied Wondell. Some of them even had the nerve to look back up into the box, comparing his appearance to the lady's.

"Do you see what I mean?" said Roban. He grasped Wondell's shoulders and smiled, presenting him like he was a calf ready to be sold at auction. "After makeup and costume get their hands on him, you won't be able to tell them apart. I'll get them moving now. Come on Wondell, let's get you ready for the ball." Roban and Wondell began to walk off stage.

"Wait," shouted Barzabag. A hush fell over the crowd. Roban paused and looked back up into the box. Frobo thought he saw a wry smile begin to form on his face, but he suppressed it, waiting for Barzabag to speak.

"For my Lady Ella, Bloodcake of the Free Orks, there shall be and can be no substitute," Barzabag proclaimed. "She shall play herself in my play, and I shall rescue her. My army shall see my valor like never before! In theatrical form!"

And then, to the dismay and surprise of everyone in the orkhold, Barzabag leapt up onto the stone wall of his box, and broke out into song. Pacing back and forth on the wall he sang with the strongest displays of emotion he could muster.

Can't you just see me on that stage?
The greatest ork of the Fourth Age!
Can't you just see me standing there?
A breath of shining new fresh air!
I've dreamt of acting my whole life,
Ever since I broke free from my egg.
I have recited lines of script,
Growing great and tall in my disgusting crypt.

At last, my time has finally come,
To act and sing and finally beat my drum!
Can't you just see my on that stage?
The greatest ork of the fourth age!
And when she sees me there,
Perhaps she will not care,
That I am an ork!

I've heard it said that love is true,
But was it made for orks, like me and you?
The greatest question of our time,
The greatest poetry to ever rhyme.
If an elf can love a dwarf,
Then can a woman love an ork?
If an elf can love a dwarf,
Then what the heck! Why not an ork?

The greatest riddle and a shame!
Pondered by men and elfs and orks the same!
If an elf can love a dwarf,
Then can a woman love an ork?
If an elf can love a dwarf,
Then what the heck! Why not an ork?
Cause when she sees me there,
She might not even care,
That I am an ork!

"As you wish, Lord Barzabag," said Roban. Frobo immediately saw the smile crack upon his lips. This was what Roban had wanted to happen all along. "My good orks," Roban announced in a loud, theatrical voice, "any of you who wish to take part in the play should come and see myself and Ringo at the dressing room. The rest of you, prepare to enjoy the show.

We will be back in no time to continue the second act with your own Lord Barzabag and his very own Lady Bloodcake!"

The orks erupted with glee. Save the Lady Ella, who seemed as if she didn't know how to feel about the progression of events, there was not one being in the crowd who wasn't desperately excited for the second act of the play to begin. Somehow, Roban had gotten exactly what he wanted: Ella in the play. If only Frobo knew what he was planning next!

Barzabag leapt down from the wall and took hold of the lady's arm to lead her away. But she ripped it from his grip and briskly stepped in front of him.

"Thank you for volunteering your precious *'bloodcake'* to act in front of... in front of everyone!" she snapped at him.

"What's the matter with you?" said Barzabag. "I thought it was every girl's dream to be rescued by a knight in shining armor. Now we get to reenact when I did that for you, but more heroically this time, and in front of my whole army!"

"Maybe next time you can just get Wondell to play my part for you," she replied. "If you have to look that long to be able to tell which of us is more beautiful."

Frobo couldn't believe his ears. Why on earth did she care if *Barzabag* thought she was pretty? Why did *his* opinion matter at all?

Once again, she ripped her arm from his grasp and then scurried away, leaving Barzabag at a loss for words in front of his smirking guards. Frobo's heart shuddered with worry as she fled from the box. What was she doing? She couldn't be safe out there with Barzabag's ork army roaming freely about.

"What are you smiling about?" Barzabag snapped at the two guards who'd been staring in at him from the door. "After her! You have protection detail!" The orks shuffled away after Ella, and Barzabag stormed off in another direction. Perhaps he was going to brood over the complexities of the female that was to be the future mother of his orklings. Frobo followed in the same direction as Ella and the guards.

The box where Ella and Barzabag watched the play was at the very back of the theater of stone, and behind it, where he had seen the rim of fire and heard the marching footsteps of Barzabag's army was a large concourse where the orks all lived. It was nothing more than a huge cave, with small holes all around the rim of it and up the sides of the walls where the orks slept. It looked like a giant beehive. Some of the orks climbed the walls to their sleeping holes, others walked through the cave conversing with each other.

Ella and the guards walked through the concourse to a tower of stone in the middle of the huge cave. The tower jutted out from the ground like a huge spike and rose to a height of forty feet. But after Ella went inside, the door locked and the same two orks stood guard outside it. He could only assume that Ella lived inside, and he wondered about her quarters. She seemed well fed and cared for, obviously she had food and clothing, and seemed to be somewhat in a right state of mind, but he couldn't stand the thought of her being alone with all these orks about! He just didn't trust the dreadful creatures.

But seeing as Barzabag had stormed off in the completely opposite direction, he could safely assume that Ella was alone, preparing herself for her role in the play. At least he had assured himself that she was relatively safe for the time being. Now, he needed to try and find out exactly what Roban's plan was. He had to save all of them, not just the Lady Ella.

As quickly as he dared, Frobo made his way back to the dressing room. Orks roamed about every which way, and the going was very difficult. To the great pain of his ears, very many of them were still singing different lines of Sham's new song.

"I'm just a Daggins from Sackville! The place the hobbicks get their backfill!" sang one large ork that Frobo invisibly sneered at.

"I'm not the heir to the hobbick who... is known as the most famous to ever live," bellowed another shorter ork with a bent back who squatted when he walked.

It was the same all throughout the concourse as Frobo made his way, completely invisible, back to the dressing room. When he arrived, he saw a very long line of more than a hundred orks outside the door, standing single file, awaiting their turn to rehearse for a role in the play. What madness! These dull creatures wouldn't be able to act any more than he was the heir of... Frobo stopped himself mid thought. But he *was* the heir of the most famous hobbick who ever lived. He had to be. Stupid, useless Sham had gotten into his head, his own gardener for crying out loud. Frobo cracked an invisible smile. He needed to remember who he was, doubters, songs or naught, and get a grip. He had a fellowship and a lady to rescue.

Frobo walked to the front of the line until he was mere feet from Roban, who sat at a table interviewing an ork.

"What's your name?" said Roban, ready to write the answer on the scrap of parchment before him.

"Sharklice!" the ork responded.

"Sharklice," repeated Roban as he scribed the ork's name onto the parchment. "What a striking image. Have you ever acted professionally, Sharklice?" asked Roban.

"What does this mean, 'professionally'?" the ork asked him, immensely confused.

The other orks within hearing all bellowed in laughter.

"It means as a job," said Roban. "Have you ever been paid for acting? Have you ever made money from it?"

"What do I look like to you?" Sharklice replied. "A maggot farmer? Orks don't make money except by stealing it! And even if we did, what would we use it for?"

"Maybe, to buy something nice for the special ork lady in your life?" suggested Roban.

"I don't want to marry an ork!" Sharklice shouted. "I'm

going to marry an elf like the Lady Ella! That's why I'm signing up for this, to be seen and recognized for my talent and good looks!"

"Right, of course you are, Sharklice. And I wish yourself and that lucky lady a happy honeymoon," said Roban. "Your name is on the list. You'll be playing Ork Number Seventeen in the play. You can get your script from Ringo the Dwarf in the next line."

As Frobo continued to listen and wait, he overheard the same conversation again and again. No, the orks had never acted, neither professionally nor as amateurs, and they were signing up to act because they wished to find and marry an elf princess. It was like the stupid creatures thought that ten thousand beautiful elf women were going to march through the doors of their dark cave in the next half hour to watch them act. Or perhaps they knew better, but simply fancied that they'd stand out to the Lady Ella, and she would turn her affections from Barzabag to one of them. *"This will be the end of the ork race,"* thought Frobo. *"If every ork holds out for a woman as beautiful as Ella, there'll be none of them left!"*

That would be the case, unless the orks acted in violation of their treaty, and began to take the women of Middlearth as their wives by force. Frobo shuddered at the thought. And yet, here was Roban, stroking the ego of every one of them by inviting and encouraging them to take part in his play. What the devil did that man have up his sleeve? Whatever it was, Frobo needed to find out so he could help.

When the final role of Ork Number Seventy-Seven was assigned, the remaining orks were sadly dismissed back to the show. Ringo had distributed all of the "scripts" (that had been written by Happy and Martin) and told the orks that their stipulation to act in the play was that they must be able to read. Of course, the orks had all claimed to possess this ability so as not to be rejected for their roles. And this was good, for there was naught but a page of scribbled lines of gibberish more unclear than the language of pig latin written on them.

Roban then told the orks that the play would soon be starting and to study their scripts and memorize their lines. Ringo and Roban then left, and slammed the door to the dressing room shut, just before Frobo could enter it. How he desperately needed to speak to them! Or at least to hear what they were saying. By his pipeweed, if he didn't find out their escape plan, he wouldn't be able to rescue any of them.

But Frobo didn't have to wait long. The greedy eyes of the orks around him all turned and faced the same direction. Their eyes sought the oncoming splendor of the Lady Ella, arrayed this time, in a dazzling black dress, shining and shimmering in any light that hit it. It was the same cut as the dress she'd worn the first time Frobo saw her, fitted at her waist with no sleeves and a golden belt. Her rosy cheeks adorned her face and above her eyelids, she wore a dark shadowy makeup the likes of which Frobo had never seen before. She was dressed as if to slay all with her beauty, and the only thing that could tarnish the visage of her was that which walked beside her, arm in arm: Barzabag.

For the first time since Frobo had met the ork, he was wearing more than his loin cloth and long boots. Never before had Frobo seen an ork dressed so splendidly. Across his shoulders was draped a long red robe with white fur trimmings. Beneath it was a coat of shining mail, black pants (to match his Lady's dress), and leather boots were upon his feet. He wore a long, curved sword on his waist and a crown of gold rested on his head. There he was, Ella's "knight in shining armor." The sight of him made Frobo's blood boil. The pair walked straight past him and paused at the entrance to the dressing room.

Barzabag's ork guards then banged three times on the door and yelled, "King Barzabag and the Lady Ella here to see you." Then they flung open the door. Ella took Barzabag's arm, and the pair strolled into the room. This time, Frobo just managed to slip inside before the guards shut the door behind him.

Frobo tiptoed behind them as he crept inside, trying to coordinate his footfalls with theirs. The room fell silent at their entry. Each of the companions of the fellowship were awestruck by the Lady Ella. There was little other reaction one could have to her enrapturing beauty.

The two of them stood in the center of the room, arm in arm, surrounded by the members of the fellowship. Barzabag's evil eyes gleamed with satisfaction as he looked around him, watching the reverent gazes of the fellowship quickly turn to jealous glares. The Lady Ella dazzled them. She beamed and smiled, her tanned skin glowing like bronze in her black dress. Frobo stepped to the right of the door, finding a spot to stand next to a wooden crate full of old stage props next to the front wall of the room. Everyone's eyes locked on Ella and Barzabag. Everyone, save the wizard. Frobo couldn't help but see Grandalf's eyes roving about as he tried to situate himself next to the wooden crate. He backed up against the wall, facing Ella and Barzabag. Then, just as he was about settled, he nudged the crate with his left foot like a clumsy oaf. Grandalf fixed his eyes upon the exact spot where Frobo stood at the barely audible sound of the crate. The wizard couldn't see him (at least Frobo didn't think he could), but Frobo couldn't help but feel like the wizard's burning eyes were piercing his very heart.

Roban turned around, glancing at the crate for a moment, and then spoke up. "I trust you both received your scripts," he said, turning back to face Ella and Barzbag. "I had them sent to you by an ork runner." Frobo silently sighed in relief. The moment passed. He was unnoticed.

"Yes! Yes!" shouted Barzabag. "We received the script, but..."

He was cut off, "Good... and you didn't have any trouble *reading* it, did you?" asked Roban.

"Of course, I didn't. I read just fine!" said Barzabag.

"Excellent, my good ork. And you, my lady?" said Roban.

"But the script must be chang—*ouch!*" he cried. Frobo looked down. The Lady Ella had just slammed her heel down on Barzabag's foot. She lifted it, and Barzabag crumpled to the ground, reaching for the injured appendage and looking up at her like she was his punishing mother. "I think you broke it!" he cried. "What in the name of Morbor was that for?"

"I hope I did break it. Because maybe that will finally teach you to stop interrupting me," she replied. "How many times do I have to tell you not to do that? Roban, I mean, *that man* just asked me a question, if *I* had received *my* script, and I was about to answer him. I'd prefer a knight in shining armor who doesn't interrupt me constantly and treats me like a human being, not just a walking sculpture."

Barzabag growled through gritted teeth before saying, "I'm so sorry, my *dear*. Go ahead and respond to the man announcing to all of us that you received your precious script... *aarrgghh!*"

She stomped with the sharp heel of her shoe upon the same foot again. "I will not tolerate sarcasm, Barz! Not even from you. Do you understand me? Now to answer your question. Yes, I did in fact receive my script," she said.

"Excellent," said Roban. "Do you have any commentary on it? Was it suitable to you?"

There was something odd about the way Roban had asked that question. He paused before the words 'commentary' and 'suitable,' pursing his lips and furrowing his brow. Why would he ask the Lady Ella for commentary on her script? He'd seen the ork's scripts. They were nothing but gibberish of course, because none of the orks could read, but she... well the Lady Ella could read just perfectly.

Perhaps Roban had transcribed a message with the escape plan to the Lady inside the script! But how had he known she hadn't completely lost her marbles? Well, he was a card player, a gambler. He must've decided the bet was a good one.

"The script was..." the Lady paused, looking Roban squarely in the eyes for an awkwardly long moment. "It was exceedingly to my liking."

Had that been a secret communication between the two of them? By the Films themselves, did Frobo wish he had a copy of that script, but he had no idea where it was.

"There is one thing, however," she said.

"Yes, my lady?" asked Roban.

"The hobbick who disappeared earlier when he slipped on the magic ring," Ella said. Frobo was listening. Perhaps this would be a clue.

"Yes, what about him?" said Barzabag.

"I think we should add in a few lines where he returns to the play from invisibility, as if he is still here," she said. "He should be the final one you save me from, Barzabag."

What was she doing? Was she giving him away? Or maybe, she wasn't. Maybe she was trying to let Roban and the others know that he was still there! That he hadn't left.

"How ridiculous! He is obviously gone by now, what would the little fiend stay for anyways?" Barzabag asked. "Besides, we wouldn't be able to make him appear out of thin air when we wanted to reveal him to the crowd, now would we?"

"I think it's a splendid idea," Roban said, stepping forward. His eyes grew wide with imagination, and he motioned with his hand as he spoke. "An invisible character! Absolutely brilliant Lady Ella. I'll get started on working it into the play straight-away. And now, everyone else, we should go ahead and get back to the stage. It's high time for us to take our places for the final act. Barzabag, of course, you are up first with Ork Thirteen, as you know from reading your script. I'll see you under the bright lights."

Once again, the play was about to begin. Frobo slipped out

of the dressing room in between Happy and Martin just before Grandalf reached the crate. Frobo saw the surly old wizard inspecting it as he stepped out over the threshold. He then made his way slowly and invisibly behind the others to the backstage area.

All of the actors stood behind the giant curtains. The members of the fellowship huddled together stage left, and the seventy-seven orks were on the far right of the stage. The Lady Ella stood with Barzabag and the two guards who accompanied them in the center. What could she have intended for him to glean by saying that he was supposed to take part in the play? Had it been a secret message to let the others known that he was still present, or had she known he was in the room with them, listening? Had Roban also known? Had they been trying to tell him something? Oh, how he desperately wanted to take off his ring and reveal himself to all of them! He wanted to find out the plan, to tell them he was still there. But alas, there was no time, and he couldn't risk being seen!

The energy in the gigantic cave was palpable. Frobo peaked out from behind the stage's red curtain. Every seat was full, save the two in the special box reserved for Ella and Barzabag.

Barzabag then strode behind the outermost curtain in full knight's costume with one of his special guards. The other stayed next to Ella behind the second curtain, the backdrop for this act of the play. The outer curtain was drawn up. The crowd erupted in a roaring cheer at the sight of him in his knightly garb. Barzabag's play had begun.

"Gorshart, you know you have always been my most trusted advisor," Barzabag began, addressing his guard as the two of them strolled about the stage.

"Yes, my lord Barzabag," said the guard. Frobo wondered if his name truly was Gorshart. Orks always did seem to have the most unfortunate names.

"You will address me as King Barzabag!" shouted Barzabag.

"I have conquered all of Middlearth™ and the surrounding seas! No army can withstand me and no kingdom but mine is remaining! You shall address me as your king or you shall be beheaded! Do you understand?"

Gorshart looked entirely taken aback. This had clearly not been part of the "script." But the ork seemed to be quick of mind and reacted by kneeling before the "king."

"Yes, my king," he said. "Forgive me. You have conquered the whole world. I shouldn't dare address you as 'lord.'"

"Very good," said Barzabag. "Although I will expect more grovelling from my subject the next time I demand an apology."

"Certainly, my king," said Gorshart, now clearly annoyed.

"Excellent," said Barzabag. "Gorshart, my most trusted advisor, now that I have conquered all of the kingdoms of Middlearth™, and all of the surrounding seas, and have exacted my reign to devastating effects of the surrounding regions, and have cut down the trees of every forest, and have polluted every river and lake with the filth of my armies, and have starred in my own adaptations of the films, now that I have done all of that, my trusted advisor Gorshart, what else is there left for me to do?"

"An excellent question, my *king*," said Gorshart with specific emphasis on the last word. "Since it seems you have done all that this world has to offer, perhaps you should simply lay down and die."

"An excellent suggest..." Barzabag began, until what had been said registered with the ork. It seemed that Gorshart could also stray from the script. "What do you mean, I should 'lay down and die?' How dare you suggest such a thing! I demand you grovel before me in repentance!"

Barzabag then went so far in his threat as to draw his long scimitar from its sheath and hold it to Gorshart's throat. The ork fell to Barzabag's feet and began to *grovel* for his life. "Spare me! Spare my life, my king! I didn't mean it! Even me, your most trusted advisor, can make the occasional mistake from time to time!"

Barzabag looked over him for a long while, considering the fate of his servant. At last, he said, "I will spare your life... only if you tell me what it is that I should do with mine. Tell me now, or it will be your head!" Barzabag then kicked Gorshart, rolling him over on his back. He stepped on his chest and held his sword to the ork's throat.

Gorshart then whispered with a gargling voice up from the stage, "You have done more than any ork before you, but one thing you have not done that you must still do to be the most famous ork to ever live!"

"And what is that?" Barzabag asked with his sword point sticking into Gorshart's throat.

"Find! True! Love!" Gorshart spluttered as Barzabag removed the blade from his throat. Gorshart remained on the ground, spluttering and choking with both hands grasping his bleeding neck as Barzabag began to pace across the stage. Frobo couldn't believe his eyes. Had Barzabag meant to kill the poor ork, or was this all a tragic accident?

"True love?" Barzabag echoed the words as if he'd never heard them before. "True love? For an ork? Can there even be such a thing?"

"It's extremely unusual, my king!" Gorshart croaked out the words in a gargling voice from the ground. The ork writhed and twisted in pain as blood poured from his throat. More and more of it flowed out, streaming across the stage in a broad pool.

"But relationships between orks are purely physical," said Barzabag. "They are only for reproduction, and I have already sown my seed into many female orks throughout the earth, who have borne me many ork sons and daughters. I can assure you I have no 'love' for any of them."

The orks howled in approval at this remark. The scoundrels

seemed to take pride in the fact that they were loveless creatures. Frobo imagined they always would be.

"Love for another ork? No. This is impossible," croaked
Gorshart. "But I wasn't talking about love for an ork. I was
talking about love..." Gorshart sounded like he was choking on
his own blood. The ork couldn't finish his own sentence. Barzabag's cut was going to kill him!

"Yes, you were talking about love... you were talking about
love! Love for what, you idiot, finish your sentence!" shouted
Barzabag, now kneeling over Gorshart.

"I was talking about love... for a woman. A real woman.
Think of the dwarf in the films! If an elf can love a disgusting,
wretched little dwarf like him, then why not a tall, strong, handsome, powerful king like you?" And with that final word,
Gorshart drew his last breath, dying upon the stage. Barzabag
had *killed* his most trusted advisor. Frobo saw Ella shake her
head in disbelief. The rest of the fellowship stood with blank
expressions and dropped jaws. The orks in the crowd had a
different reaction. There was not a dry eye in the midst of the
entire throng of them, for their emotions were swept away
entirely with the dramatic death.

"Gorshart! Gorshart!" cried Barzabag, still kneeling over the
dead ork's body. "I won't forget you, Gorshart! I won't forget
your last words! What you told me, acting on this very stage,
before you died! You died as a necessary sacrifice, for only in
one's final breath does one speak true, and you Gorshart, have
spoken the truth. Find love in another ork, I never could, but in
a woman, nay, not just any woman, in a queen of immaculate
beauty, I could find pleasures and love forevermore!"

And then, without warning, and with the body of Gorshart
still spilling blood upon the stage, Barzabag broke out into yet
another song.

His death was the sacrifice that saved me from not knowing,

That love could also be for me, not men and elfs only!
I don't think that I'll ever forget his last wise words,
And after his body rots, we'll feed what's left to the birds!
But now I must go and find the love that fate has betrothed,
To me and my lucky bride, most lovely the worlds ever known!
Yes she, I will go and find, and save from the hands of men,
I'll rescue her and she'll be mine, and marry her here in my den!
We'll feast upon the blood of all the men that I have to kill,
In order to rescue her from the self-serving chains of their will!
And once we're together, we'll be the greatest pair!
And then for forever, she'll breed with me in my lair!
Yes once we're together, she'll fall in love with me!
And then for forever, she'll bear my little orklings!
His death was the sacrifice that saved me from not knowing,
That love could also be for me, not men and elfs only!
I don't think that I'll ever forget his last wise words,
And after his body rots, we'll feed what's left to the birds!
But now I must go and find the love that fate has betrothed,
To me and my lucky bride, most lovely the worlds ever known!
Yes once we're together, she'll fall in love with me!
And then for forever, she'll bear my little orklings!

To Frobo's great relief, Barzabag's song ended. Of course, the crowd of orks erupted with the loudest cheers and the longest standing ovation yet. The poor fools loved it. If only they knew that Ella wasn't going to fall in love with any of them! Perhaps for the first time, Frobo realized how much those wretched films had turned Middlearth upside down. After taking his final bows before the adoring crowd, Barzabag exited stage right. The body of Gorshart still lay upon the stage. The poor ork really was dead. Roban motioned to Happy, Martin and Sham for the three stagehands to clean up the mess. Sham performed the mop-up duty of the blood, while Happy and Martin dragged the body off stage. Instead of being appalled by Gorshart's death, the orks laughed loud and hard, pointing at his dead body as if this was the greatest comedy of the play yet. But of course, Frobo shouldn't have been surprised, as such activity was commonplace amongst orks.

Once the stage had been scrubbed cleaned by Sham's diligence, the play could once again commence. The next scene started with Ella and Grandalf. She entered from the center of the stage and Grandalf entered on the left. The orks held their breath and there was not one eye in all the crowd that was turned away from her.

"Oh father," Ella began. "Oh father, I'm so tired."

"Yes, my daughter," Grandalf replied, clearing his throat. "And what is tiring you these days?" The lines came far more freely out of his mouth now, as if much of his initial stage fright had worn off after the last performance.

"I've been looking everywhere, everywhere I tell you for true love," she said. She spoke like a naïve innocent young girl, and gliding across the stage, she stood up high on her toes each time she said 'everywhere.'

"I just..." she continued, paused, then collapsed into a huddle of sadness on the stage. "I don't think I'll ever find it. I've given up hope. All of the elfs are too weak, and the men are too ugly."

Raucous laughter.

"Perhaps a dwarf would be more to your liking?" Grandalf suggested.

"Too short," she said, dismissing him. "I just can't put my finger on what I'm looking for... in the male whose children I'll bear. It's a certain indefinable quality that just doesn't seem to exist in this Middlearth. I suppose I will be alone for all of my days. If only there was someone out there for me."

Grandalf shrugged his shoulders and sighed. "Yes, it's true," he said. "Masculinity is a quality that has become very hard to find in elfs, dwarfs and men."

"Masculinity," she echoed the word, musing on it and cocking her head as if she was in deep thought. "Masculinity!" she repeated the word, louder and firmer. She rose from her pitiful huddle and faced Grandalf, smiling for joy with a newfound hope and zest for life. "But that's just it, Father," she cried. "That's just what I've been looking for!" Then she broke out into song.

Masculinity! That sweet, solid, strong divinity!
Masculinity! To reject it would be insanity!
Masculine! Masculine!
Someone give me a male that's masculine!
Oh when I find one, I'll dive right in,
What I'd give to find a man that's masculine!
Oh, I've searched for all my life,
For a man who could call me wife!
But when it comes down to brass tacks,
They're all about as strong as a sculpture of wax!
Masculinity! That seductive intoxibility!
Masculinity! It makes me lose all my civility!
Masculine! Masculine!
Somebody find me a male that's masculine!
Someone to put all my hopes and dreams in!
And that someone is going to be masculine!

As if she had just called for him by using the word 'masculine,' Wondell sauntered out onto the stage to join her. He smiled from ear to ear and bowed his arms, strutting in the burliest manner he could muster. Ella turned at his approach and placed her hands on her hips. She looked him up and down, then shook her head in disappointment.

Would you just look at this elf right here?
The poor sap can't even grow a beard!

How could I ever settle down,
With him and build a nest...
The only thing he could beat me in, is a beauty contest!

Wondell hung his head as the orks howled in laughter. Roban then ran out onto the stage to meet him and put his arm around the poor elf's shoulder, patting him on the back as he walked backstage. It seemed that Roban was going to exit with him, but then Ella pointed him out to the orks as she began the next stanza of her song.

Or Father, would you have me marry a man?
A portly beer addicted fellow named Roban...
I'd rather throw up in my soup,
Than see his face and hear his jests,
He couldn't even beat me in a beer drinking contest!

Roban sighed, bearing the embarrassment as well as he could. But it was clear that he was not accustomed to being made fun of. The orks slapped their knees and choked themselves laughing in the crowd. Popping corn flew out of their mouths as they spit it in every direction from pure joy at the lines she sung. Frobo thought she might be finished but he should have known better. Grandalf held his hand up to his temple, as if remembering the other eligible race she hadn't sung about yet in her song. He held his hand up in the air and strode backstage to retrieve Ringo. He dragged the dwarf to the front of the stage, presenting him to Ella like he was the perfect picture of masculinity. Ella rolled her eyes and dragged the back of her hand across her forehead. She wasn't finished with her song yet.

And lastly please don't suggest a dwarf,
For rejecting them I feel no remorse!

On our date, he'll seem real funny,
until he forgets his money...
Even though he tries his best,
His head's barely level with my breasts!

Ooooh! Faaather... please!
I need a male, whose masculine and strong!
Father please!
Find me a male, who doesn't just write songs!
I need a male, who isn't just an ordinary guy,
I need a male whose masculine, but still knows how to cry!
But perhaps, I'll never find, the true love of my life,
Maybe perhaps, I'll never find, the male to call me wife...

Masculinity! That sweet, solid, strong divinity!
Masculinity! To reject it would be insanity!
Masculine! Masculine!
Someone give me a male that's masculine!
Oh when I find one, I'll dive right in,
What I'd give to find a man that's masculine!

It had been the greatest performance that Frobo had ever seen. He'd had no idea that Ella's voice was so rich and powerful. The meaning in her lyrics and the melody of the song astounded him. And near the end, he almost shed a tear when she'd sung about being alone and never finding the true love of her life. But one detail in particular had stood out to him. Ella had mentioned the three races in her song in whom she couldn't find a shred of masculinity. She had left out one race in particular. A race whose people might be known for the shorter stature, but were a strong and sturdy folk, hardy and wise and as masculine as any woman could ever want. And he wasn't talking about the race of orks.

The ovation Ella received far surpassed the rest. The orks

simply would not stop clapping and cheering for her. Shouts of "sing it again!" echoed throughout the vast theater. If they'd have known the word "encore," they'd have shouted that instead. Of course, this was all mixed in with orks flexing muscles and posing in false hopes that one of them might stand out. It was absolutely ridiculous. At last, Barzabag grew so tired of it, that he strutted out to the center of the stage and screamed for quiet. He raised his hands and shouted as loud as he could at the mob of orks, but he received only an onslaught of boos and jeers. The orks were cheering for their queen, and their demonstration of true masculinity would not be suppressed.

Roban, Wondell, and Ringo had all entered and exited the stage during their brief cameos in Ella's song. But as Ella stood on stage, taking her bows before the salivating orks, and Barzabag was booed off it, something happened far above Frobo and the rest of the onlookers. All of the stage curtains used in the play hung from a high wooden catwalk that was erected in the back of the stage and reached out towards each wing of the theater like broad wooden arms. There, the orks could walk and hang the curtains for their plays and films. And high up on that platform, Frobo thought he saw something creeping and crawling around. He squinted and looked as hard as he could at the dimly lit area. What the devil was that creature, crawling around on four legs like a dog... *like a dog?*

Frobo shook himself, trying to think clearly. What was a dog doing up on that high platform? He looked up again and squinted, but this time he clearly saw exactly what was up on that catwalk. It was the same brown furry four-legged creature who'd stolen the rings.

Suddenly, the thing scurried away from the edge of the platform and out of Frobo's sight. His eyes drifted down the side of the catwalk to a ladder hanging from it. Frobo strained his eyes. Someone was climbing that ladder. Now the figure reached the high platform that was above the far-left side of the stage. He blinked, desperately trying to see who it was. He saw long dark brown hair flecked with blonde streaks, a dark weather-beaten cloak, brown boots and if he was right, a circle of rope hanging from the right side of his belt. Yes, it was unmistakable. Roban was up on that platform.

In his arms, he held another long rope. It was a golden rope, the rope that was used for pulling back the stage curtains. One end of this rope was tied to the very center of the high platform, and Roban stood at the high end on the left side. What was he doing up there? Frobo watched as the man tied the rope around his waist, and then without a moment's hesitation, he jumped! He leapt from the top of the platform and swung in a perfect pendulum down to the bowing Ella, sweeping her off her feet in mid bow, and carrying her up to the other end of the platform on the opposite side.

The orks in the audience growled in fury and rage, for in that one grand swing, Roban stole away their prize. Roban and Ella balanced themselves on the other end of the high platform, then Roban ran back towards the rear end of the platform, dragging Ella with him to keep her close. The orks screamed and pointed up at the two of them. Roban had awakened the fury of the ork army, and they were a jealous, bloodthirsty lot. Roban dragged Ella to the very back of the platform and knelt down, unwinding another rope that was looped around the wheel of large pulley system. Once the rope was free, Roban released it. It fell to the stage in a massive heap and with it fell the massive curtain that had been the stage's backdrop.

Behind the curtain, Frobo saw that a scaffolding system was erected in front of the sheer stone wall that allowed the orks to ascend to the top level where they hung their curtains. Perhaps they used the scaffolding system for mining or some other purpose. Nevertheless, it had been right above him the entire time, and Frobo had never seen it. The scaffolds traversed back and forth, climbing up the rock wall, each one like a long precipitous ramp. Now high above him, Frobo could see that every member of the fellowship was standing along the various levels of the scaffolding system. Was this their plan for rescuing Ella? If so, Frobo was desperately out of position. He needed to climb. He needed to get up there, and quickly. Frobo ran to the right side of the stage where the ladder was as quickly as he could, and began to climb, trying to keep one eye on the fellowship.

He half expected them to escape through some secret door or passageway, but they did no such thing.

Instead, from atop the scaffolding, Ella began to shout. "Release me! Unhand me, you unmasculine buffoon! I will not be kidnapped and stolen away by a weak ruffian like yourself!"

Did she not realize that they were about to rescue her? What was she thinking? He had to get up there, and quickly, to talk some sense into her.

"I will not release you!" shouted Roban. "I have been searching throughout all of Middlearth for a woman, and at last I've found one. Maybe you aren't the prettiest or the smartest or the most enjoyable to be around, but you are a woman. And therefore, I will kidnap you."

"Not on my watch you won't, you slimy coward of a man," shouted Barzabag from far below.

"And who are you, that you think you can stop me from fulfilling my desire?" shouted Roban.

"The most *masculine* ork, there has ever been, King Barzabag! I'll save you, my future queen," he shouted. "I'll save you from that dreadful, disgusting, loathsome man if it's the last thing I do."

The orks that had been enlisted for the play then began to climb the winding precipitous pathway of the scaffold up to the very top where Roban and the other members of the fellowship were holding Ella. Barzabag did not follow them, but instead, began climbing the very same ladder that Frobo was currently halfway up. By the filmmaker, if that wasn't just his luck.

Frobo climbed the ladder as fast as his little legs could carry him and reached the top only moments before the long legged Barzabag behind him. The high platform was so thin that there was nowhere he could go to stay in front of the huge ork. He inched his way closer and closer to the action and fighting, trying to maintain a safe distance away from Barzabag as the ork prowled like a hungry cat behind him.

Below them, the fight had begun. Uniborn and Ringo were the first line of defense on the switchback scaffolding. They were fighting valiantly, but something seemed off about the strokes of Uniborn's sword, and Ringo's axe. It was like they were... film fighting. But of course! This was still part of the play. It had all been planned. And that explained why the orks in the crowd still hadn't charged the stage from their seats and were cheering on the action. What a fool he'd been! How could he not have seen that before? And now his stupidity had put him right in between Barzabag and the play's main act!

Fortunately for Frobo, Barzabag was also watching the fight on the first switchback platform. His yellow fangs were gleaming through his broad smile. He was... or so he thought, about to win his bride, if not for the secret rescue mission that was planned. If only Frobo knew what that was.

Frobo looked down again as he continued to make his way before Barzabag along the precipitous platform. Ringo and Uniborn were still holding off the orks. They had "film-killed" a few of them and the orks were still charging up the switchback, slowly gaining ground.

Then, all of a sudden, without any warning, Ringo did the unthinkable. He did the unimaginable. He did the most foolish thing he possibly could've done whilst performing in a play in front of ten thousand ferocious orks. In the blink of an eye, the dwarf swung his axe, and beheaded the ork he was fighting. There was no mistaking it for a simple "film-death."

The head of the ork clanged down the scaffolding, bouncing and crashing to the stone stage in a loud thud. Blood flowed from the empty place at the top of the ork's body and spewed onto Uniborn, Ringo, and the other orks that were nearby. Uniborn's shocked face betrayed that the beheading swing of the axe had not been a part of the script. Ringo dropped his axe as if he hadn't been trying to kill the ork at all. It had been an accident. For a moment, all was quiet, before the civility of the drama broke.

The orks, emboldened with a new fury, charged Ringo and Uniborn as the two of them tried to hold the ravenous beasts at bay, but to no avail. Uniborn, they threw over the scaffolding, and Ringo, they ran their own scabbards through. Frobo was sure they were not film fighting. The smile on Barzabag's face was now gone, and the ork wore only a grim expression as he continued to make his way, faster now, toward Ella and the last stand of the fellowship. The charging orks were not to be stopped. Frobo couldn't believe this. It had to be a dream! It couldn't be real! He watched as friend after friend was thrown to the side of the scaffolding or slaughtered by the hoard of orks. First Wondell's bow was broken, and he himself was slashed with the sword of an ork, his own blood staining his golden hair. Then Happy and Martin took on the charging creatures. If only he could save them! But they were too far away. Bless his friends! The two were run through with swords before his very eyes.

Frobo staggered on the high platform, gazing down at the horrible scene, and clutching the railing like his life depended on it. He was overwhelmed by emotions. Rage, fear, and grief at the loss of his friends flooded his heart in a hopeless torrent. Though he knew there was little chance of succeeding, he would attempt to avenge their deaths with his sword.

Grandalf was the next line of defense between Ella and the orks. The old wizard brandished his staff like a spinning baton, dashing in the heads of the attacking orks, but eventually, they were too many for the old wizard, and he was also slain. The orks cut him down from his legs and he fell. The fury of their blows was terrible to behold. Once they finished with him, they threw his body over the side of the scaffold, and Frobo watched as his old dirty cloak, now stained with blood, descended in a dead heap. Never, would he have imagined that Grandalf the Great would fall in such a manner. Sham was of little consequence to the orks after all they'd defeated before him, and the poor chap, for whom Frobo now realized he did still feel a shred of affection, was thrown to the side of the platform with dashing blows from the orks. Now it was only Roban and himself between Ella, Barzabag, and a host of orks. If he had anything to say about it, they would be able to hold out for quite some time.

Frobo now reached the back platform where Ella and Roban were standing. With his sword drawn, Roban faced the oncoming orks, and Ella stood behind him. The poor woman looked frightened beyond her wits. Just as the circling monsters were about to charge, Barzabag shouted, "Wait!"

The orks stopped, obedient to their king.

"I will kill this despicable traitor and rescue the Lady Ella for myself," he said. "Then we will marry this very night. And she will bear the fruit of my loins! And the sons she bears me will be the scourge of the earth."

Frobo expected to hear some witty quip from Roban, pointing out something the ork hadn't yet considered, but none came. Instead, the good man whose plan had gone so horribly awry, held his sword in anticipation as Barzabag approached him. Frobo stepped forward, timid and trembling in his boots to try and intervene as best as he could. Roban held his sword up and for the first time, Frobo saw fear in the man's eyes. Barzabag roared in anger and struck at Roban's outstretched sword. In a single fearsome blow, Barzabag knocked Roban's sword clean out of his hand, and it clanged against the wooden scaffold as it fell. Then Barzabag struck Roban down, slaying the man as he cowered before him. Frobo's heart froze. Roban had been his last hope at saving Ella. And now this... He had never seen anything so terrible.

Frobo took a deep breath, fighting back tears at the staggering scene he had just beheld. But there was no time for mourning. Not yet. He was now the only one left. There was a chance, Frobo thought, one chance, to save the Lady Ella from a wretched life with this wretched creature. He could stab the ork in the back with *Itch* that very moment.

Frobo stalked up behind him and reached for his sword. Barzabag stood over the body of Roban, looking down at the fallen man. And then Barzabag laughed. He laughed like a dreadful, thundering storm, bellowing like peels of rumbling lighting, striking all too near for comfort. Frobo drew his sword from its sheath and held it aloft, high in the air, ready to strike the ork down in revenge. The throng of orks echoed Barzabag's laughter. Frobo stood there, as the rushing air from their harsh laughter hit him like a strong wind, nearly knocking him to the side. But he gained his balance, standing firm in the wind. Holding his sword in the air, hatred filled his heart. But something held him back from striking the monster. He looked past the beast to Ella. There she stood, beautiful and radiant in the darkness of the din. As her hair blew in the wind of the laughing orks, she fought back a cringe for the laughing Barzabag.

Suddenly, Frobo's heart quickened with resolve. He would kill Barzabag. But he couldn't murder the ork in that furtive, cold-blooded method, invisible and in secret. If he was going to defend the Lady Ella in honor and glory, then he would do so, but only when the ork could see him.

"And now, I will have you, my bride, once and for all," shouted Barzabag, more to the crowd than to Ella herself.

"Not if I have anything to say about it!" shouted Frobo in the loudest voice he could muster.

Barzabag stopped, along with the cheering orks, turning to look for who had spoken but seeing no one. Fear gripped him. "Who said that?" Barzabag quailed. "Who is it? What are you, some ghost from the past, come to torment me?"

"Not a ghost!" Frobo shouted once more to gasps from the crowd. "It is I!" he said, removing the ring from his finger and revealing himself to the astonishment of all. He placed the ring in his pocket and held *Itch* with both hands, pointing it at the ork. Roban couldn't have written a more dramatic ending to his play if he'd tried to.

But seeing Frobo did not have the effect on Barzabag that Frobo had hoped for. As Barzabag looked into Frobo's eyes, he began to laugh and cackle with glee. Perhaps Barzabag had forgotten that Frobo was the prodigious swordsman of the first act. Frobo however, had not.

"You will not touch her!" he shouted from the top of his lungs. And then Frobo charged the hulking beast.

Barzabag was still smiling when Frobo's sword met his own, but as the two exchanged blows, his smile faded. They balanced on the topmost level of the scaffold like squirrels on a thin outer branch of a tree. Frobo swung *Itch* with the fury of a warrior legend, and his sword was an onslaught to Barzabag. Frobo struck and struck, swinging his sword with all the might and fury he could muster. One swing from Frobo almost struck the beast, but the monster dodged just in time. He stumbled backwards to avoid it, and Frobo noticed that with one step more, the ork would've fallen over the scaffold's edge.

After the initial onslaught though, Barzabag recovered. His long sweeping arms were too much for small Frobo to handle, and Frobo was thrown on the defensive against him. It wasn't long before Frobo realized that he was hopelessly outmatched. He parried a blow from the right, then one from the left, stepping back at every advance from the huge ork. Then Barzabag held his sword up high and struck down with what seemed to be all the strength he possessed. Frobo held up *Itch* with both hands to fend away the blow, but the blow was too strong for him. Barzabag's sword crashed down above him, and Frobo fell to his back, bouncing on the wooden scaffold as his sword fell from his hands.

Before Frobo could recover from shock at what had just happened, Barzabag leaned over him, reached into his pocket and took up the new ring of power! Frobo tried desperately to keep the ork from doing so, but he was pinned and held down by a strong arm, much stronger than his own. The ork held the ring up like a prized trinket, eyes gleaming from the silver circle, and then he put it in a pouch at his waist.

In his right arm, Barzabag still held his own sword, but with his left hand, he picked up *Itch* and stood over Frobo once more, this time to slay the defeated hobbick where he lay. His yellow eyes gleamed with evil rage, and he bore his massive fangs at Frobo, who lay below him, utterly terrified. The orks in the crowd chanted his name as he stood there, holding both swords, "Barzabag! Barzabag!"

Then something happened that Frobo did not expect. As Barzabag stood above him, raising both swords high to strike Frobo, a spasm of pain shot across the ork's face. He cringed like a great agony had just befell him, and then cried out in anguish. Instantly, he dropped *Itch,* along with his own sword, and crumpled his left hand, holding it tight to his chest. Before *Itch* could fall to the ground, Frobo caught it at the hilt, and slashed upward wildly at Barzabag who now crouched above him. *Itch* cut at the Ork's elbow, cleanly removing the right forearm of the great beast from him, as the blood and the forearm itself fell on Frobo's face. *Itch* was a formidable sword, and it had done the magical work promised by Wondell.

Barzabag fell back, writhing in pain, for he had one hand that itched with fire, and his other had been cut off at his elbow. The other orks then rushed at Frobo, holding their swords out at him in a threatening way, but not attacking.

Barzabag rose from where he had fell, no longer caring about Frobo, but holding his bleeding elbow close to him, and began walking toward Ella. The orks with drawn swords now stood between Frobo and Ella. Frobo was beyond angry, but their swords were too many. He sheathed *Itch* and held up his hands in surrender. He had failed.

Barzabag staggered across the platform as blood flowed from his hewn off right arm, but at last he reached Ella. It was the moment every ork in attendance had been waiting for. She stood before him in her shimmering black dress, the most perfect picture of beauty that Frobo had ever beheld, and Frobo's heart failed him. There was no hope. She would be Barzabag's.

But from far below, at the very foot of the stage, a voice cried out, "Wait!"

"What now?" growled Barzabag, looking down at whoever had interrupted his moment. It was... Radagrass! The old wizard had broken free of the ropes.

"Wait, Barzabag! The intruders! Two men, an elf, a dwarf..." he began.

"Yes, yes, I know all about it, Radagrass," interrupted Barzabag. His face was a flurry of pain and anger and he pointed with his stump down at the bodies on the stage and the lower levels of the scaffold. "There are your intruders," he said, pointing with his stump down at the dead bodies of the fellowship on the stage and the lower levels of the scaffold. His itching left hand was still crumpled tight against his chest. "We found them and now we have killed them all! Or at least most of them. They were acting in our play. You're only five or six hours behind, you old dunce!"

"But who is that up there with you?" Radagrass asked.

"This is the Lady Ella, my future bride, whom I will kiss at this very moment and wed this very night!" Barzabag shouted defiantly. With his left arm, he reached for Ella's waist and pulled her close to him in a firm embrace. Frobo burned with anger and almost lost himself. Ella looked appalled. She neither spoke nor cried out, but her face was wholly wretched with sadness.

"Wait! No!" Radagrass shouted from below. "The woman was with them!"

Frobo wondered what the wizard's last words could mean as Radagrass raised his staff and struck the ground. A golden light shot from the butt of the staff all through the theater. Barzabag pulled Ella to him and kissed her as passionately as he dared to. However, as the golden light from the Radagrass's staff reached the top of the platform where Barzabag and Ella stood, it revealed, just in the nick of time, and just as they kissed, that he was not kissing Ella at all, but was instead kissing one of the seventy-seven orks that had volunteered to act in the play.

Son of Ashelob! Frobo looked down. Across the levels of scaffolding below him, he saw that the slain bodies of Ringo and Uniborn were in fact only orks dressed like them. He checked them all: Grandalf, Happy, Martin, Roban, and Ella! They were all orks that Grandalf had magically disguised, the same way he'd disguised the fellowship when they entered the mountain. That brilliant old wizard! But where were they now? And who was that stirring over where the ork dressed as Sham had been tossed?

But it appeared that the ork dressed as Sham, was in fact Sham himself. Had the dull Hobbick not gotten the message that they were supposed to be escaping? How someone that dense had ever come up with the song, *Just a Daggins from*

Sackville was beyond him. Frobo then glanced out at the crowd to see what the works were reacting too. Grandalf himself stood in the midst of a ring of orks. The old wizard was dressed in ork rags, staff in hand, and shaking his head.

Barzabag's fury consumed him. He shoved the ork he had just kissed so hard that he fell from the top level of the scaffold. The body made a crunching sound as the ork died, falling on the hard stone stage. Barzabag pointed his itching hand at Frobo, Grandalf, and Sham. "Take them to the dungeons and lock them inside," he screamed. "And someone find out where the rest of them have gone."

"They escaped!" said Radagrass from far below. "That's what I was trying to tell you! The rest of them escaped with the Lady Ella just before I could stop them. I was tied up and I'd just awoken, but I didn't get free until just now."

"Then let us go to the horses," shouted Barzabag. "Each one of you, get a horse now!"

"They took those too!" said Radagrass. "Heard them riding off myself, thundering away like a stampede. The show was so loud then though, you all must've missed it!"

Roban, that conniving fiend of a man! If he wasn't the greatest horse thief in all of Middlearth, Frobo didn't know who was. Grandalf had disguised the orks to look like the members of the fellowship and they'd given them the slip when the orks were fighting on the scaffolding. Only Sham had somehow gotten confused by it all and left there. It was a miracle he hadn't been killed in the play. But still, what had happened to Ella? Was she alright? Had she come to her senses? Frobo supposed that wasn't what was really important. What mattered most was the fact that she wasn't still in this cave, and that his friends were alive. They were alive! And Frobo was overjoyed by that. The escape plan had worked, almost perfectly. But for himself, Sham, and Grandalf, escape from the orkhold would not be so easy.

TO BE CONTINUED...

BUT FOR NOW

THE END

At this juncture, the end of Middlearth Trademarked, the reader may find themselves with thoughts of anger or frustration at the author for interrupting such a magnificent, captivating story. You want to know what happens next, and you certainly don't want to have to wait for another book to be published to get the answers to all of your questions. "They never did that in the films," you might be telling yourself. "They never ended the story on a cliffhanger like that." Ahh yes, and you'd be right. They never did do that in the films. But if you'd ever actually read the story of the most famous hobbick who ever lived, perhaps your perspective of those films would be different. And perhaps you'd know that you were wrong to expect this book to end any differently than it did. For now, I must leave you to your own devices, and must I continue my work on the sequel and perhaps, epic conclusion to this story: Middlearth Trademarked Again.

ABOUT THE AUTHOR

Ben Cash is a relatively unknown author who works on his books whenever he isn't playing fantasy football and has some spare time. He desperately hopes this book isn't in violation of any intellectual property, trademark, or copyright laws and hopes that everyone sees it for what it is, an author's humble attempt at satire and parody.